Alvooooon:

Know you'll
find some familiar
names in here to
keep you celebrate
that dirty, old 65th Birthday.

As always,
Roger

ALSO BY JAMES KIRKWOOD

NOVELS

There Must Be a Pony
Good Times/Bad Times
P.S. Your Cat Is Dead
Some Kind of Hero
Hit Me with a Rainbow

NONFICTION

American Grotesque

PLAYS

There Must Be a Pony
U.T.B.U. (Unhealthy to Be Unpleasant)
P.S. Your Cat Is Dead
Legends!
Stagestuck (coauthor)

MUSICALS

A Chorus Line (coauthor)

DIARY OF A MAD PLAYWRIGHT

JAMES KIRKWOOD

E. P. DUTTON NEW YORK

Published in the United States by E. P. Dutton,
a division of Penguin Books USA Inc.,
2 Park Avenue, New York, N.Y. 10016.

Published simultaneously in Canada
by Fitzhenry and Whiteside, Limited, Toronto.

Library of Congress Cataloging-in-Publication Data

Kirkwood, James, 1930–
Diary of a mad playwright / James Kirkwood. — 1st ed.
p.   cm.
ISBN 0-525-24761-0
1. Kirkwood, James, 1930– Diaries.   2. Kirkwood, James, 1930– Legends!
3. Dramatists, American—20th century—Diaries.   I. Title.
PS3561.I72Z464 1989
818'.5403—dc19
[B]   88-27089
CIP

Designed by REM Studio

1 3 5 7 9 10 8 6 4 2

First Edition

To everyone who has ever written a play, and especially to anyone who might be thinking about writing one.

My thanks go to my editor, Carole DeSanti, and her assistant, Mary Wagstaff; to my agent, Jed Mattes; to John Fisher and Stella Kramer for their help; and to Carolyn (Kecky) Kirshenbaum and Arthur Beckenstein for everything.

CONTENTS

FOREWORD   xv

CAST LIST   xix

INTRODUCTION   xxiii

PREPRODUCTION   1

What to Do with the Baby?   3
Mike Nichols   7
Elvis Presley Rears His Head   9
The Presley/*Legends!* Game   12
Middle Mess   15
Chasing Peter Pan   17

Meeting Peter Pan   22
The Summer of My Discontent   29
Closing In on Mary   41
Well, We Did   44
Hello, Dolly!   50
Hurdles   54
One Tiny Little Hiccup   57
Other Problems, Etc.   60
How Carol Channing Became Carol Channing   64
Casting   71
Countdown   76

ACT I

                                                81

Legends!/N.Y. to L.A.   83
Off and Running   85
Off and Stumbling   88
Life Upstages Art   97
Mary Christmas   117
The Final Push   122
Dallas, Here We Come   137
The Dread Turk Arrives   146
Curtain Up   152

ACT II

                                                163

Opening Night   165
Post-Opening Oddities   170
More Oddities   178
Preopening Bumps, Thumps, and Grinds in L.A.   183
The Los Angeles Open   197
Los Angeles Opening Fallout   204
Work, Fear, and Loathing in New York   213
Work, Fear, and Loathing in L.A.   217
Getting Out of L.A. the Hard Way   225
Approaching the Frisco Quake   232
San Francisco   236
Muddles and Middles   244
A Miracle in Phoenix   247
The Week That Was   249

ACT III

251

Back in the Red Again   253
It Happened in Boston   258
Tomorrow Came   262
Fallout   269
Final Mistakes   277
Careful . . . !   288
Ping-Pong   299
The Palm Beach Story   317

EPILOGUE

331

FOREWORD

Like most people who will read this book, I was eager to get the "dirt" on two of the Broadway theatre's most enduring stars, especially as dished out by a fellow playwright, and extra especially one so devilishly witty as James Kirkwood.

After all, his play *Legends!* was already something of a legend itself. This was the play that had committed the unpardonable sin of Not Coming In. Not Coming In means that a play has decided not to open in New York City and thus face the critics and audiences of the city that still considers itself the pinnacle of theatrical aspiration and certainly the most discriminating. "Good" plays Come In. "Bad" plays don't. Plays with stars the likes of Mary Martin and Carol Channing that don't Come In fill the gossip columns for months with the latest intrigues and mishaps. I doubt if there was a person even remotely interested in the American theatre who didn't know that Mary Martin was having trouble learning her lines or that the Dallas and Los Angeles critics were less than enthusiastic about the play she was appearing in. Gossip about *Legends!* was everywhere and, as gossip goes, it was pretty heady stuff.

But isn't gossip meant to titillate the reader? Make him feel superior to the poor souls it skewers? Heaven forbid we should identify with the people we gossip about. In the first place, they're not really "people" with feelings and needs and aspirations of their own. They're clowns slipping on banana peels of their own devising for our amusement. We can laugh at them without embarrassment because there is no empathy between them and us. It would be as if James Kirkwood, Carol Channing, Mary Martin, and a cast of hundreds had deliberately decided to put on a play so that we could have a good clucking of the tongues and shaking of the heads at their expense. Good gossip doesn't ask us to care for the people it's about. Caring means that their story is somehow about us.

By that definition, *Diary of a Mad Playwright* is not good gossip.

What it is is a heartbreakingly accurate account of what it is like to work in the commercial American, Broadway-oriented theatre in the last decades of the twentieth century. In that sense, it is as important a document as Moss Hart's *Act One*, which told the truth about getting A Play On in the Broadway between the wars, one of its Golden Eras, which the 1980s, except for Big Musicals, have not been.

But *Diary of a Mad Playwright is not a lecture* on what ails the American Theatre either. Besides, there would be no point to writing that book. *Everyone* seems to know what ails the American Theatre. We seem to be a nation of experts on that one particular subject. (Why none of these experts is *doing* anything about it is the book we're waiting for.)

If and when that book is written, it will no doubt have a High Moral Tone and cause even more clucking and wagging and shaking than this one. But will it, I wonder, capture so neatly the personalities of the very people who bring a play to life? Its actors, director, producers, and playwright? Theatre is a collaborative effort and its true story cannot be told without acknowledging that. The collaboration that was *Legends!* was a difficult one but there was unanimity of purpose: to make it a success. Even though there was only that one goal, for *Legends!* there were perhaps too many different road maps on how to get there.

James Kirkwood is a passionate writer. If his tenacity in nursing his play from first draft to casting to opening night in Texas to the closing night in Palm Beach a year later seems obsessive, I recognize it as the authentic voice and behavior of a playwright who shares full responsibility for his creation. With that responsibility comes elation and despair, wild laughter and deep tears. I'm tempted to say there's nothing like it but there is something like it: your own life lived at full risk.

A playwright is omnipotent when he writes his play. He has his characters speak and act exactly as he pleases. He can even tell them when to sit down and shut up. But when his script is given to actors and directors, the omnipotence can easily turn to impotence. It usually does. Mary Martin and Carol Channing, like any other actors, have their own voices, minds, and behavior. Unlike any other actors, they are two authentic stage stars. Without their likes our theatre would be diminished and even more perishable. No one, even playwrights, especially playwrights, tells Mary Martin and Carol Channing to sit down and shut up. Instead, James Kirkwood tells us what he thinks of their endeavors to bring his characters to life. It is a profoundly respectful, sometimes hilarious, often painful, always human account of two legends at work and very much off their pedestals.

I am too young to have seen Mary Martin in *South Pacific* but I almost feel I have. I grew up on the original cast album and have listened raptly as more fortunate theatregoers have tried to describe the rapture of that performance to me. I am old enough and fortunate enough to have seen Carol Channing in *Hello, Dolly!* but I am not about to say that her performance as Dolly Levi is any more vivid in my imagination or real to me than Mary Martin's Nellie Forbush as described by parents, friends, and theatre writers. Since theatre cannot be preserved, its tradition is very much an oral one and this *Diary* is significant contribution to it. Maybe you didn't see *Legends!* After reading this you will have a stronger impression of it than many people who did.

There are fools in these pages. There are princes, too. When they behave badly, your heart will sink; when they behave well, you will be glad. All are seen from a harassed and frenzied playwright's viewpoint. That doesn't make his portrait of them any less truthful or accurate. It does make them more intense.

If you see yourself in these pages, too, don't be surprised. The struggle to succeed is a deeply human one. The theatre is perhaps the ultimate metaphor for us at our best and very worst as we try to Come In. No one is in between in these pages, least of all James Kirkwood. His book, like his life, is a lesson in going for broke.

TERRENCE MCNALLY
May 28, 1989

CAST LIST

CAST OF *LEGENDS!*

Mary Martin	*Leatrice Monsee*
Carol Channing	*Sylvia Glenn*
Annie-Joe	*Aretha Thomas*
Gary Beach	*Martin Klemmer*
Eric Riley	*Stripper*
Don Howard	*Policeman*
Roxy Rokker	*2nd Aretha Thomas*
Vincent Cole	*2nd Stripper*
Barbara Sohmers	*Standby for Miss Martin & Miss Channing*
Natalie Ross	*2nd Standby for Miss Martin & Miss Channing*
Gwendolyn Shepherd	*Standby for Annie-Joe*
Sheila Ellis	*2nd Standby for Annie-Joe*
Garry Q. Lewis	*Standby for Vincent Cole*

PRODUCTION AND CREW

James Kirkwood	*Author/Typist*
Clifford Williams	*Director/Anecdotist*
Mike Nichols	*Phantom Director*
Ahmet Ertegun	*Producer (Aka The Dread Turk)*
Kevin Eggers	*Producer (aka The Shopper, The Terminator)*
Bob Regester	*Producer*
Cheryl Crawford	*Producer*

PRODUCTION AND CREW *(Continued)*

George Yaneff	*Financier*
Alan Wasser	*Original General Manager*
Doug Baker	*Working General Manager*
Steve Meyer	*Production Stage Manager*
Randy Buck	*2nd Production Stage Manager*
Alex Holt	*Company Manager*
Jim Bernardi	*Stage Manager*
Freddy Wittop	*Costumes*
Harry Curtis	*Assistant to Mr. Wittop*
Doug Schmidt	*Sets*
Tom Skelton	*Lighting*
Jan Nebozenko	*Sound*
Steve Shull	*Sound*
James Cabel	*Wigs*
Bobby Fryer	*Managing Director, Ahmanson Theatre*
Trish Garland	*Choreographer*
Peter Gennaro	*Choreographer*
Edwin Gifford	*Publicity*
Michael Gifford	*Publicity*
Charles Lowe	*Husband & Manager to Miss Channing*
Keith Baumgartner	*Saviour to Miss Martin*
Tom Davis	*Left Hand to Miss Martin*
Susan Grushkin	*Girl Friday to Miss Martin*
Ann Amendologine	*Assistant to Mr. Eggers*
Terry Brown	*Assistant to Miss Channing*
Jonathan Bixby	*Assistant to Miss Channing*

FRIENDS TO THE COURT

Esther Sherman	*Agent to Mr. Kirkwood*
Elliott Lefkowitz	*Lawyer to Mr. Kirkwood*
Floria Lasky	*Lawyer to the Producers*
Milton Goldman	*Super-Agent*
Naomi Buck	*Wife and Unofficial Assistant to Mr. Buck*
Jerry Paonessa	*Shoulder to Mr. Kirkwood*

FRIENDS TO THE COURT *(Continued)*

Jody Paonessa	*Shoulderess to Mr. Kirkwood*
James Leo Herlihy	*Best Friend & Guru to Mr. Kirkwood*
Arthur Beckenstein	*Supporter to Mr. Kirkwood*
Kecky Kirshenbaum	*Supportress to Mr. Kirkwood*
Jim Piazza	*Friend & Court Jester*
Larry Hagman	*Relative to Miss Martin*
Maj Hagman	*Relative-in-Law to Miss Martin*

(JEANNE TRUDEAU)

INTRODUCTION

I don't remember when the idea struck me to write a play about two feuding actresses, legends in their time, who were somewhat over the hill, down at heels, had made one film together that was a box-office hit but represented personal hell during the making. Having worked on *A Chorus Line* and helped document the lives of chorus "gypsies," helped to answer why the calling, why the persistence, why they endure the struggle of a professional life-time devoted to rejection on a most personal level, I suppose I thought about the opposite end of the theatrical spectrum: those who became stars, how they stay at the top or fall from glory and what keeps *them* going.

At any rate, each idea, be it for a novel, a play, a screenplay, enters the consciousness at some time, is tossed about in the creative part of the brain, and either falls away because of lack of true interest or else rattles around, constantly coming to the fore during a walk, a movie, a game of tennis, or when one is simply plopped in a chair, daydreaming. If it persists, a certain itching begins. It itches slightly at first but then, as time goes on, the itch becomes more and more intrusive, until finally you are overcome by a rash and you simply have to sit down and scratch it. The scratching, for me, becomes the writing.

Here's major news: writing is not easy. But it can be fun in a perverse sort of way. It's a challenge. I say to myself: "Oh, Christ, I don't think I can write that!" I muse that one over for a while, then say, "Well, maybe I can, I could certainly *try*, no one's going to kill me for that." (They might kill me after, and have!) And I make a game of it. I play "Let's pretend" or "What if?" That is to say, I begin with: "Let's see, what if one of them, Sylvia, that's a name that always carries a certain weight, an image of a fairly chilly, ambitious—well, bitch. What if she always played the Joan Crawford parts, the one who started out scrubbing dishes in a diner and was going to make it to Chicago if she had to step over her mother, twelve orphans, several politicians, and twenty-three lovers. She was going to get there and end up owning her own office building as well as a collection of broken hearts. And suppose the other was named Leatrice. She was a sweet, dear thing for all outward appearances, fresh, scrubbed, usually played nurses, saints, and nuns. But underneath she had a streak of steel, the kind of actress for which the term Iron Butterfly was coined. Loretta Young, Joan Fontaine, Debbie Reynolds."

I decided the two of them always loathed each other. They made one movie, which was a scandal; Sylvia stole Leatrice's husband. Now they're close to seventy, and both no longer wanted by Hollywood. They're living in New York, and a brash young producer has a new play that he wants them to star in. Alone, neither would mean that much, but together, because of their past, they'd be big box office. By various shenanigans, he forces them to meet, and the meeting is the crux of the play. Are they going to tear each other apart or pull it together and do what they know how to do best: agree to do the play, entertain, put on a show?

That was the gist, the bare-bones idea.

I finished the first draft of the play in the fall of 1983. It turned out to be a comedy, but I also hoped the audience, if one there would ever be, might empathize with the ladies, care about them, root for them to bury their respective hatchets and get on with their careers.

If anyone, at that time, had told me I was going to end up with two real legends like Mary Martin and Carol Channing playing the leads, I would have leapt across the Hudson River with joy.

It is now 1988. Putting on this play has been the most bizarre roller-coaster experience of my life. I had meant to keep a journal during the making of *A Chorus Line,* but I didn't, fool that I was. After finishing the first draft of *Legends!,* I vowed I would keep a daily journal, take constant notes, and perhaps, if the material were rich enough, write a book documenting the theatrical journey of this play, come hell or high water. I stuck to my promise and, crazily enough, so did the fates, because hell and high water most certainly came—to say the least.

I cannot be objective, but I will try to be fair. Feelings will be hurt, bruises will be felt, some of what you read you may not believe—but my hand's on the Bible. You might easily say, "How weird!" You would be right. That's show business. Isn't it too bad it's not called "show art"? It's not, because it *is* a business, and a very tricky, undependable, fascinating one at that.

The only reason to be in the theatre is if you can absolutely *not* not be in it! If there is one iota of doubt, if there is even a lingering desire to become a pilot, a priest, doctor, lawyer, hooker, or, yes, an Indian chief, or just a plain person—follow that star and forget the theatre.

So let me take you by the hand, and come with me on a jungle-theatre ride. Theatre as civil war. And sometimes not civil at all. I hope you will find it fascinating. God only knows the participants you are about to meet, the circumstances they've wrought, have not bored me. They have at times driven me to thoughts of voluntary admission to Nutsy Acres, but it has not been boring. And I have pictures!

PREPRODUCTION

(CRAIG SCHWARTZ)

WHAT TO DO WITH THE BABY?

It's always difficult to let go of a play, book, novel, article. It *is* your baby, and you tend to be careful about sending it out into the world. You want it treated right; you don't want it to be an abused child. The first person to whom I gave the play was my agent, Esther Sherman. She was very enthusiastic about *Legends!* That made two of us. Esther is a thin, tensile tigress of an agent. She's a fighter, a worrier, and extremely protective of her clients. Sometimes her enthusiasm is not as wildly apparent as the Fourth of July; I believe this is because she knows how bumpy the road is in this business and that, theatre economics being what they are, it is not easy to get a play "on the boards" these days. It is not only not easy, it's nearing the miracle mark to have a play produced, let alone have it turn out a hit. For one thing, there are few independent producers left, producers like David Merrick who say yes to a play and then put their all into the realization of the vision they had when they first read it. Most producers now are real-estate moguls; they look for "product" for their theatres, but they rarely have a love affair with a play, which is what should happen when all hands signal they want to climb aboard—director, actor, set designer, whoever.

So Esther and I talked about who might be attracted to the play, who we felt was right for it, where it might possibly be done, etc. I belong to the Playwright/Director Unit of the Actor's Studio, and we spoke of having a reading there. I had reservations, because the response of the members to what is thought of as a commercial comedy is not usually overwhelming. That does not seem to be the forte of this particular bastion of the theatre. They are not huge laughers, tend to dissect with much more relish and enthusiasm projects that are more serious in form and intent.

I gave the script to a friend and fine film director, Frank Perry, also a member of the unit. He was extremely enthusiastic and offered to organize a reading of the play so we could have a look at it, hear how it sounded, find out if it was really a comedy—or not.

In the meantime, a friend of mine, Bob Regester, had read the play, liked it very much, and said he'd like to produce it, possibly in London. I had met Bob there years before, stayed at a lovely home he shared with Neil Hartley when both of them, though Americans, were working in the theatre and film in England. Neil was producer for many of Tony Richardson's films. Bob had been more active theatrically in London than in the United States and thought it might be a marvelous idea for Maggie Smith, Diana Rigg, or some other good English actresses. We'd had several meetings by the time the idea of the reading had come about, but Bob never actually offered to option the play, which means to have a contract drawn up and pay an advance. As a friend I was loath to say, "Hey, Bob, if you like it so much, why don't *you* option it?" One doesn't want to go begging.

Frank snagged two excellent ladies for the reading: Eileen Heckert for Sylvia and Frances Sternhagen for Leatrice. We got a fine black actress, Rosetta LeNoire, for the part of the maid, and a very good actor, John Rensenhouse, to play Martin Klemmer, the brash young producer. One of my best friends, Jerry Paonessa, with whom I've worked on several film projects, flew from the coast to be on hand.

Readings are very important in this business. An author can get a fairly good idea of what he's wrought by listening to his words brought to life by actors and—equally—listening to the sounds of an audience.

Monday, March 5, 1984

Snow, sleet, turning to freezing rain. We gathered at the Nat Horn Theatre on West 42nd Street. The Actor's Studio was being renovated. Thought no one would show up on this arctic day, but by two o'clock we had a wet, packed, buzzing house. Members of the unit and a lot of the bigwigs, Elia Kazan, Norman Mailer, Joe Mankiewicz, Sidney Kingsley, Cheryl Crawford, and on and on. Enough to give one dry-throat.

The first scene, with Martin Klemmer, the producer, trying to finagle the author, the Shuberts, Paul Newman, and the two stars into doing the play, got huge laughs. Whammo. We're off and running. I caught Jerry's eye; yes, it was a comedy. One never really knows until the sound of an audience laughing is heard, and what a lovely sound that is.

Things got bumpy from time to time, because the cast had not even had time for two read-throughs prior to facing an audience, so this was more or less a cold reading, certainly not a heavily rehearsed one. It's difficult to time the reading of lines when the actors have never had an audience; they can never be sure which lines are going to get laughs, which moments are quiet ones, and which ones are even touching. It's flying blind over the Rockies.

Intermission, and we all straggled out to the lobby. Arthur Whitelaw, a producer who had done the West Coast production of *P.S. Your Cat Is Dead!*, raced up to me and said, "Jimmy, it's terrific. I want to do this play, I really want to do it. Does anyone have the rights?" I told him it was free. "Fine," Arthur said, thumping me on the back, "I'm going to do it, we'll talk!" (I never heard from Arthur, whom I am fond of, again. Not a word, and he's a nice man. But that's show business.)

People came up with encouraging words; they seemed to enjoy the play, although the reading was a little rougher than I'd hoped for. At one point Heckie and Frannie passed me and Heckie said, "Jesus, I didn't know the whole world was going to be here, Kazan and —"

"Oh, they're just members of the unit." She gave me a look that said: Some members!

The second act began, and there were bumps here and there, a few fluffs, but Heckie and Frannie are fine actresses and they plowed ahead like the true professionals they are, as did Rosetta and John. At the play's end, much to my surprise, there was extended applause.

Frank and I took chairs for the critique. Criticism is a touchy ingredient to swallow. As I heard Noel Coward declare at a party once, "The only criticism I respect is an absolute rave." Critique this day was mixed. A gaggle of members jumped on me for my "black humor." They took exception to the dialogue between the maid and Sylvia (Eileen Heckert), saying it was racist, in bad taste, etc. I tried to explain (without springing to a *violent* defense) that their relationship was one in which a maid and a movie star had known each other for so long and so well that there were no boundaries limiting what they could say to each other. They were more like girlfriends than maid and movie star. My explanation did not fly, although my mother was a movie star and had a maid/secretary and the two of them rapping together would have caused a fly on the wall to drop and roll about the floor laughing.

Joe Mankiewicz went off on a tack that no one quite understood. Other comments knocked me for being too commercial. (The Actor's Studio, with its new leadership under Frank Corsaro, is now, I'm happy to say, much more hospitable to comedies than several years ago.) Norman Mailer and Elia Kazan were the most supportive. Norman, who is candid and, need I say, extremely bright, said he enjoyed the play very much and would like to call me the next day and drop an idea on me. Kazan, whom I also find warm and caring, said he hadn't heard so many funny lines in one play in a long time. Both felt it was a most promising—yes, commercial—play. So did Bob Regester and my friend Jerry Paonessa. The baby was alive and had taken its first step.

MIKE NICHOLS

Theatrical quiz. What director does everyone send his or her script to? Right—Mike Nichols. I believe that if an *Eskimo* wrote a play he'd put it on an ice floe and shove it toward Mike Nichols. I phoned Mike on a Thursday in August and asked if I could send him a script. The answer was yes. Mike and I have known each other casually over the years; he had once—here's that word again—toyed with directing *P.S. Your Cat Is Dead!* We always say how much we'd like to work together, but it had not come to pass.

It is wise in this business, when one gives out a script to be read, not to get overly concerned with waiting by the phone for an immediate response. It can take weeks, sometimes longer, sometimes forever, so I was surprised to receive a call two days later, on Saturday morning, in East Hampton from Mike. He was extremely chipper, said he liked the play very much right off the bat, and then dropped the bomb:

"What about doing the play with Harvey Fierstein and Betty Bloolips?" I was so goggled I could not reply for several seconds. "Do you know who Betty Bloolips is?" Mike asked.

"Yes."

"Don't you think she's terrific?"

"Yes." Betty Bloolips is part of a brilliant but little-known drag troupe from Britain that I'd seen Off-Broadway several times. He/she, the leader of the troupe, is sensational in timing, looks, and delivery, but I had written the parts to be played by two legendary ladies, not two men in drag.

"Well, what about that?" Mike finally asked.

I went into my "Wouldn't this be happening to me!" mode. Mike Nichols likes the play and wants to do it with two men in drag!

Mike said, "Thirty percent of those ladies are the fantasies of their hairdressers. They are, in fact, drag queens." I countered with: "But we all know ladies like that in movies, in the theatre—in real life." Mike went on about how such women were more or less human sacrifices. Then he said, "There has to be a serious idea at the center of a play. There is a core missing, and that core seems to be at the center of all the plays I've been doing lately."

"What is that?" I asked.

"Well, I think it might be—screwing."

"Screwing?" My ears were feeling oddly numbed.

"Yes—screwing," he said with certainty now. "I can do plays I don't particularly like, like—oh, *HurlyBurly.* But that has to do with screwing. Then I can do plays I like very much, like *The Real Thing,* and that also has to do with screwing. There's no screwing in your play."

Knowing Mike has a highly developed sense of humor, I thought of saying, "All right, at the end of Act One, instead of having the two ladies tear each other's wigs off and fight—I'll have them screw." Or "When the producer shows up at the end of Act Two, they'll have a three-way." Instead I admitted that there was no screwing in the play and went on to say, "But there are many viable plays that don't particularly have to do with screwing."

"I know," Mike said, "but lately everything I do seems to have to do with screwing."

"Well, maybe you should take a break; you'll get tired."

He laughed, went on to say, "If there isn't a serious idea at the center of a play, certain trivialities take over; if there's a core lacking in a play, then there's a core lacking in you." I tried to explain what the serious idea in the play was. "It's about this business and what it does to people—in this case, two lady stars— what it turns them into, how it affects their entire lives, their beings." I then attempted to get into talk about serious—as far as I was concerned—casting.

Mike went along with me and mentioned Elaine Stritch and Angela Lansbury (yes!), Julie Harris (yes!), and then got into English ladies, bringing up Maggie Smith, Joan Plowright, and Vanessa Redgrave (odd, considering Bob Regester). "But," he went on, "I'd do the play with Harvey Fierstein and Betty Bloo- lips. I'm so glad you like her; I helped her get her green card."

I went back to the other ladies until Mike finally asked, "Why aren't you responding to my notion?"

"I don't know; it's such a stunner, it takes time."

We went on to say, again, how we would like to work together. Toward the end of our conversation he said he'd read the play again and we'd meet in town the following week for a further discussion. "I'll put you through hell," he warned.

"I'm up for it." Yes, please put me through hell, Mike, please!

We finally ended with love from Annabel, his then wife, and love back to her. His last thought was: "No matter what happens, you'll make a lot of money with this play. There are endless ladies who can do it."

If he really believed there was an endless number of ladies that were right for it, why wouldn't he choose to do it with two of *them* instead of Harvey Fierstein and Betty Bloolips?

I called Mike again about setting up a meeting a week or so later, but by the time we'd exchanged amenities I could tell from his tone that it was going to be a no-go. I was right. "Jimmy, I like the play very much, but I have to do my next movie, *Heartburn,* and then another company of *The Real Thing,* and maybe one of *HurlyBurly.* I would rather not string you along for months and then finally say no." Mike said he thought the play would make a lot of money, that he would probably invest in it. Again he said he hoped we'd work together, wished me luck—over and out.

It was a comedown, but at least it was not a protracted one. I liked him for being a mensch and being honest.

Then I sent the script to Tom Moore *('Night Mother, Grease),* whose work I admired and whom I'd met several times.

ELVIS PRESLEY REARS HIS HEAD

And then it was sent to Ellis Rabb and Gene Saks and—to be a playwright now, you must use a quart of skin toughener a day. Directors, the right directors, are hard to come by, because there are so few of them that are considered bankable; "bankable" is the word for getting a production on that's going to cost a million dollars.

Now we come to producers, that obsolete breed, those vanish-

ing Americans. How did I get one? By luck, by chance, by seren-
dipitous occurrence. In retrospect, by means of the devil himself.
In late April I got a call from Esther Sherman. Would I be interested in doing a musical based on the life of Elvis Presley? Not
really; I had my own material to focus on. Days went by, and I
got another call. Ahmet Ertegun—the president of Atlantic Records, one of the big men in the record business—and a fellow who
worked with him occasionally on projects, Kevin Eggers, still
wanted to meet with me about a show based on Elvis, according
to Floria Lasky, his lawyer, and a prominent, powerful theatrical
one she is. Finally, at Esther's urging (and the nudging of several
other friends), a luncheon was arranged for the following week.

Wednesday, June 6, 1984

Ahmet, Kevin Eggers, Floria Lasky, Esther, and I assembled at
"21," certainly a classy meeting place. Right off, Ahmet's
mogulity struck me, the slick thinning hair, the pinstripe suit, the
manicured nails, the deep raspy voice that could have resulted
from barking his share of orders.

Kevin Eggers, a short, not overly thin—in fact, chubby—
chipmunkish energetic man who could be anywhere from thirty-
six to a young forty-five and had been an agent and a record
producer and commissioned the book *Elvis* to be written by Albert Goldman, was there as Ahmet's working partner and also as
a man claiming to have access to many Elvis sources. Floria, a
strong, striking woman, lots of suede and gold chains and a reputation for not being averse to engaging in battle—in fact, rather
doting on it—was on hand as moderator, along with Esther as
agent for the typist, me.

Ahmet has his share of fascinating stories regarding the
music industry, of which I know little. Soon we got into talk of
Elvis. I leveled with them: I'd not been a wild fan of Elvis, I'd
never seen a film of his or an in-person performance, although of
course I'd heard his music and seen him on the tube. I said I
thought there were other writers they should investigate who
understood the milieu better than I and had stronger feelings
about Elvis and his music. I suggested a few. There was the usual
talk that perhaps just because I was not a huge fan, did not know

that much about the true Elvis, I would be more objective, more likely to soak up fresh knowledge of the subject. The luncheon lasted a few hours. We had some interesting talk. I was fascinated by Ahmet, *am* fascinated by these kinds of men and their power. It was clear that money would be no problem for the project. In this day and age, that's inducement for many to work out a deal on a napkin at lunch.

Kevin Eggers I liked off the bat. I liked his enthusiasm, his energy, his dedication to getting what he wanted—which was a musical based on the life of Elvis Presley, using the Goldman book as the main but not the only source. He gave off the aura of a hustler, which is not all that bad if the hustler is hustling for you. Kevin has an easy smile, bright eyes, a good sense of humor, and an infectious "machine-gun" laugh that falls easily on the ears.

By luncheon's end, I was still suggesting other writers and had given my opinion of the ingredients needed to make a successful musical. I was happy to have met with them but really felt I was not the right choice. Ahmet and Kevin asked if I'd mind reading the Goldman book, seeing some video cassettes of Elvis' movies; not at all. Outside, on the sidewalk, we shook hands, and Kevin promised to get an "Elvis package" sent to my apartment. We said our goodbyes, and the three of them jumped into a limo. When they'd pulled away, Esther looked at me and said, "Well, I've heard writers talk themselves out of jobs, but never like that, baby!"

As I walked her back to William Morris, we laughed about the meeting. I said, "You wait, I bet you get a call from them by late tomorrow afternoon saying I'm the only one to do it."

She looked at me with disbelief. "You think so?"

"Yes."

"How—after *that* lunch?" She paused, then: "You want to do it?"

"No."

"Then why do you say that?"

"Just a hunch," I replied.

The next afternoon Esther phoned me at around four o'clock, her voiced tinged with wonder: "Well, you called it. Floria just phoned and they want *you*. They're sending you a lot of material and they want to have another meeting as soon as you've digested the

Goldman book and seen some of the films. How do you feel about it now?"

"I don't know." And I didn't.

I also didn't know the die had been cast for the most amazing episode in my life, bar none.

THE PRESLEY/*LEGENDS!* GAME

While I was doing rewrites, working on a few other odd bits and pieces, I read Albert Goldman's book and found it extraordinarily well written and researched, fascinating, with all sorts of information I had never imagined.

Over the summer I had several talks and meetings with Kevin, who turned out to be a bulldog. He was determined I would do the book to the musical. I talked to Jerry Paonessa and Esther about the project often. After a while I began investigating an approach to the Elvis story I thought might work for me—although I was still not saying yes, mainly because the idea of doing a musical is pure hell. The component parts, the egos, the personalities, the battles, the differences of opinion and vision, the timing, the time it *takes* to achieve the right collaboration. The mounting of a musical, especially a successful one, is a major miracle.

So caution kept me from commitment, even when I came up with ideas that titillated me and intrigued Kevin as well.

On September 6, 1984, I had lunch with Kevin to continue our talks. He said he and Ahmet were anxious to get going and wondered why I would not simply jump in the pool; I explained I had a play I'd just finished a rewrite of and that was number one on my schedule. He asked if he could read it.

Oh, fateful day!

Several days later Kevin phoned to say he liked the play very much, thought it extremely funny and also insightful about the lives of two aging stars. "It should really have a classy production," he said, and went on to praise the play further and ask if he could give it to Ahmet to read.

On September 21 Kevin phoned to say Ahmet also liked the play very much and might just consider producing it. He was going to read it again over the weekend, but Kevin was pretty sure Ahmet would take it on.

On Tuesday, September 25, Esther informed me that Floria had called to say, "Ahmet wants to go into contract on both *Legends!* and *Elvis.*" I told Esther I would rather go into contract on one at a time and wondered if *Legends!* was simply a way of piggybacking me into *Elvis.* Esther said that might well be. Kevin called to confirm Ahmet's enthusiasm about doing *Legends!* I said I didn't mind going into contract on *Legends!* because it's all there, down on paper, but I wouldn't want to take advance money on *Elvis* until we'd had more meetings and defined the show. Also, we'd not spoken about who would do the lyrics for the original music or the original music itself, who would direct, choreograph, etc. Kevin agreed but said, "I think Ahmet will be much more liable to go right ahead with *Legends!* if you sign up for both."

I quickly phoned Esther, Elliot Lefkowitz, my lifesaving lawyer and father figure, and Jerry Paonessa. For the first time I felt heavy pressure from Kevin, as if they were dangling a carrot *(Legends!)* in front of me in order for me to agree to do the BIG ONE, *Elvis.*

Kevin had liked my ideas and thought I was not far away from settling on a format for the musical. I still did not want to commit myself to a project I was not one hundred percent sure of. I had another meeting with Ahmet and Kevin at Atlantic Records, a very impressive Chinese lunch served in the boardroom, gold records hanging all over the place. Ahmet was most complimentary about *Legends!* and played "good cop" about *Elvis*, not pressing too much, letting Kevin be the "heavy cop."

Esther and Floria kept talking as the days passed, and Tuesday, October 2, Kevin phoned again and for the first time I felt not only pressured but that he was being a bit scurrilous. He said, "I told Ahmet everything was set, we were going ahead with both projects, and I'd hate to back down now. After all, Jim, he is our bank." When I still hedged, he said—slyly hinting, if this is sly—"Jim, I really feel it would be best for *Legends!* if we went into contract for both. Listen," he added, "it would just be for a first draft." First draft, my kishkas. If I signed a contract and accepted an advance, I'd be glued to it for eternity. I was leery of having my arm bent.

After enough phone calls and meetings to settle the Afghanistan problem, it was finally agreed we'd go to contract for *Legends!;* Floria and Esther would sort out what the terms might possibly be for the musical at the same time Kevin and I would continue investigating a scene-by-scene outline.

It was suddenly time for Santa to have his annual hands around our throats. Christmas. I had promised myself for years to remove myself from the scene of Bloomingdale's, drunken Christmas parties, sad-assed Santas ringing bells on rainy corners while hundreds of people who can't afford it race around madly looking for gifts for people they barely know, let alone love. That together with a nomadic childhood, split between parents who would fight either over who would "get Jimmy for Christmas" or, in many cases when their love affairs or professional lives took precedence, over "who would *take* Jimmy for Christmas" or "Where can we send him, what about Aunt Peggy and Uncle Leonard in Elyria?"

Christmas is fine for kids, for young people. All of which is to say that this year I'd planned ahead for a joyful holiday. I booked a safari in Kenya for three weeks. A dear friend of mine, Arthur Beckenstein, who is a graphic artist and has designed several book jackets and theatrical posters of mine, and I zapped off to see the lions, elephants, natives, warthogs (my favorites), water buffalo, rhinos, etc. We had a terrific holiday, taking the night train from Mombasa to Nairobi, waking up in the morning to see gazelles and giraffes racing the train, the curtains blowing in and out of the paneless windows on the 1930s dining car. Taking a hot-air balloon ride over the jungle, landing on our side, having a champagne breakfast right out on the veldt, watched warily at a distance by various fauna, and tossing the remains of our breakfast up in the air to be caught by hawks and vultures.

Gareeat Christmas, the best ever. Hardly knew it was happening. Returned to New York with enough wildlife photos for an exhibit and found that the contracts for *Legends!* were in reality being gone over by Esther, the lawyers at William Morris, and my very own Elliot Lefkowitz.

Criminentlies, we are really a go project! Now we're really about to jump into deep and shark-infested waters. The theatre—the only reason to be in it is . . . I've forgotten.

To quote Shakespeare—and everybody does—I felt like "a valiant flea about to eat his breakfast on the lip of a lion."

MIDDLE MESS

Before I went to Africa, I had a talk with Bob Regester, who'd returned from England with nothing definite set up for *Legends!*, although he had been investigating Maggie Smith, Joan Plowright, Vanessa Redgrave, and several others. I told him that I had a producer who wanted to do the play and I'd agreed to an option. Bob was extremely upset and said, "But you know how much I love the play and want to produce it." I told him he'd never once made an offer; he asked why I hadn't said something. I explained I didn't feel it was up to the author to *ask* someone who liked the play if he wanted to take an option—it's up to the prospective producer. He was extremely upset and asked if I would please write Ahmet a note explaining his interest and suggesting they consider him as coproducer. I did this just before I left for Kenya and had a brief answer from Ahmet saying he'd be glad to meet with Bob but at this stage he couldn't do anything without consulting with Kevin Eggers.

I arranged for Kevin and Bob to have lunch in mid-January. Kevin reported on it, saying they'd gotten along fine; Bob confirmed his total enthusiasm for the play and said he had access to money enabling him to go into a coproduction deal with them. Then Kevin asked, in a nice way, if Bob was for real. I told him he had producing credits in England and that as far as I knew he was; I reassured Kevin that it was up to him and Ahmet to decide whether or not to take him aboard.

At the end of the month Bob called to say he'd had a final meeting with Ahmet and Kevin; it had gone well, and he was joining the team. "We're going to do it!" Bob shouted.

Kevin and I continued to meet about the musical. At Ahmet's request, I also arranged a meeting with Bobby Fosse—we had appeared in a musical together years ago—a talented friend whom Ahmet was interested in as director. There was one funny moment when Ahmet insisted there was no reason to do a musical in this day and age that didn't have at least three hit songs to boost it into the firmament of megahits. Bobby nodded his head as Ahmet rather proudly announced, "I've been talking to Andrew Lloyd Webber, and he's extremely interested in writing the score for *Elvis.*" There was a perfect beat of silence, and then Bobby said, in a beautiful flat reading, "Well, that's *one* hit song!"

I had to control myself from roaring with laughter; at that time, Bobby was dead on: "Don't Cry for Me, Argentina" *(Evita);* "Memories" *(Cats);* etc. The session ended with everyone vowing to keep in touch; when I had a complete outline, I'd call Bobby and we'd meet again.

During the winter scripts were sent to agents, actresses, directors, scenic designers, lighting designers, costume designers. I called the *Chorus Line* crew—Robin Wagner, Tharon Musser, and Theoni Aldredge—but they were all off to England to do *Chess* with Michael Bennett and were unavailable.

Toward the end of February we had a meeting with our general manager, Alan Wasser, a large affable teddy bear of a man who had his head screwed on with regard to the business end. When not dealing with tried-and-true professional producers, one often depends upon a general manager to act as line producer and fullback in handling the intricate workings of gluing a show together. I liked him, his humor and demeanor, right off the bat. He also liked the play, which made me like him even more. Joe Hardy, who has a wicked sense of humor, was on hand as prospective director, together with Bob and Kevin. Bob was phoning Maggie Smith that afternoon. She had been toying with the idea of doing the play, but always seemed to have another project on the fire, or her husband was sick, or she was late for a matinee and couldn't talk. Elizabeth Taylor had not been heard from. Scripts were going off to all sorts of long shots—Shirley MacLaine, Julie Andrews, and on and on.

On March 11 I went to the William Morris Agency to sign the *Legends!* contracts. It had taken months for them to be finalized. Esther and I thought of smashing a bottle of champagne over each other's heads, but then we thought better of it. We drank it instead. Contracts had begun last September 25. More casting lists were made up, more meetings were held to bandy about names like Celeste Holm, Gwen Verdon, Irene Worth, Greer Garson, Eva Marie Saint, Carol Channing (to which most people said, No, no, she's become too much of a caricature). The name of Mary Martin had been brought up. Someone mentioned that Floria Lasky had handled her in years past and was very close to her. We thought she might be very right for Leatrice, in the event she wanted to work again after her years of retirement. This connection was to be investigated. On Wednesday, April 24, Floria Lasky sent a script to Mary Martin in Palm Springs, and we were off on one of the most frustrating, fascinating, fervid, farshnoofkaed woman hunts of our lives.

CHASING PETER PAN

Everyone rapidly became quite excited about Mary Martin for the part of Leatrice. She was certainly a "legend," albeit not a motion-picture one, she had the right reputation and qualities for the character, and audiences have always adored her. Of course, we were still pursuing other names, because being in the theatre does not mean putting all your leading ladies in one basket. They tend to fall in and out of line way too easily.

On May 2 Kevin phoned to say Floria Lasky had received a call from Mary Martin, who'd read the play, thought it was funny and touching, and said, "If only Ethel [Merman] were alive and we could get Pearl Bailey to play the maid," and on and on about the play, but actually felt she wasn't up to moving east, coming out of retirement, and doing eight performances a week again.

Kevin urged me to phone her. I didn't have her number, so I called Floria, who said she'd try to find out where Mary had phoned from—she wasn't sure whether it was San Francisco or Palm Springs (Rancho Mirage, where she lives). Floria confirmed Kevin's report that Mary did indeed like the play but just didn't have the inclination to come out of retirement at the age of seventy-two.

Some days later I received Mary Martin's address but no phone number. It was obvious they didn't want to subject her to a crazed author bent on casting his play during his own lifetime.

About two years before this I had participated in a tribute to the producer Cheryl Crawford. I had done a scene from *Oh, Men, Oh, Women* with Anne Jackson, and Mary Martin had sung a song from *Lute Song;* both shows had been productions of Cheryl's. I had been introduced to Miss Martin, and we'd had a photograph taken together. I found it, and on Monday, May 13, 1985, I wrote her the following letter.

Dear Mary Martin,

Now that I have my own Canon PC photocopier I can make my own stationery—thus the reduced foto we had taken together a couple years ago at a celebration, I believe, of Cheryl Crawford at the West Side Arts Theatre.

   Floria Lasky told me that you'd liked LEGENDS!, a new play of mine that we sent you and that you'd said it's too bad Ethel isn't here. Oh, how I could see the two of you playing together.

   At any rate—and I hope I don't fall into indecent

begging or groveling—I would give anything, my abyssinian cats, my collection of baseball cards, my new tap shoes, to see you on Broadway again. And so would everybody else. Whenever I have mentioned your name, like when people say they've read the play and like it and who would I envision as Leatrice—when I say my first choice would be Mary Martin. Well, I cannot tell you the "Ohh's" and "Ahh's" and the excitement and love that pour out of anyone at the very words "Mary Martin." It's extraordinary and the "Ooh's and Ahh's" are always followed by "Now there's a Legend, wouldn't it be wonderful if she came back to light up Broadway!"

So I'm writing to you to say several things, foremost of which is: I don't really think you've said goodbye to Broadway yet. You're too vital, too much you, too much a part of our theatrical history to do that at this stage of your life and of Broadway's life. I really believe this, I just intuit it. Secondly, as long as you like the play, what if you did it for just six months. That's not a long time and, of course, if you were having a glorious romp of it—any extension would be up to you. Also, there are so many other ladies who would be right for Sylvia. Who would you like to work with: Celeste Holm, Vivian Blaine, Irene Worth, Alexis Smith, Uta Hagen? Or a Legend of your choice?

If you would only give it consideration. We could have such a good time, it could be such a delightful, funny and, I hope, touching evening because it's about the business and all of our lives and what the business does to us and how much we want to entertain.

I can only hope that my pleas might intrigue you enough for us to have a meeting. I would hop on a plane, a blimp, get out my big kite—I might even jog—so that we could have a talk about this. And if it turned out you felt it was out-of-the-question I would not sulk or break an ashtray or make a Mary Martin doll and start poking pins in it—I'd just come home and KILL MYSELF. No, I wouldn't, I'd be sorry for not having you in LEGENDS!, but I'd be eternally grateful for your consideration and for whatever time we could spend together. My phone numbers are included and Floria would always know how to reach

*me. I would so appreciate your giving this consideration
and so would everyone I know, to say nothing of THEATRE
LOVERS EVERYWHERE.*

*With love and admiration,
James Kirkwood*

*P.S. I know how to get to airports quickly and easily and
I love to fly!*

I sent a copy of the letter to Floria, urging her, in the event she
was in touch with Miss Martin, to keep pushing for a meeting. I
received a note from Floria saying she thought the letter was
excellent and might open the door for further talks. She'd talked
to Mary, who would be in town soon to be one of the hostesses on
the Tony Award telecast.

On Friday, May 31, I got a phone call from Floria, who said
Mary Martin had checked into the Wyndham Hotel. I was on my
way to East Hampton for the weekend, but I dropped the following note off at the front desk as I drove out of town.

May 31, 1985

*Dear Mary Martin,
I would love to take you to lunch or dinner or dinner or
tea or shopping or riding through the park in a horse-
drawn cab Monday or Tuesday, if you have time, and talk
EVER SO GENTLY about* Legends!

*We could play "What if . . ."—that meaning, what if
you did decide to do it for just six glorious months at the
height of the season and all the fun and lovely times we
could have. I will phone you if I may.*

*Have a happy stay in New York,
Love—James Kirkwood*

The very next day, in the afternoon, the phone rang and a man
introduced himself as Tom Davis, Mary Martin's manager, and
said she would like to speak to me. The next words I heard were
delivered in that memorable sweet, warm-fuzzy voice. "You
know, I just have to meet you," she said, "because you write

such funny letters. They really are so funny. I'm going up to Max Showalter's house in Connecticut, and then the following weekend I'm coming out to stay at Tom Davis' house in Southampton. Now, I'm told you're not far from there, so perhaps we can meet."

"Yes, I'd like that."

"Good. Because I simply *must* meet you. Even if I never do a play again, I have to work that first letter you wrote into something for the stage." She went on and on about the funny letters—I hadn't meant them to be all *that* funny, more persuasive—and that's why she wanted to get to know me. We talked for a while and she said, "Even if I don't do the play, we might be able to work together sometime. Now, I'll be out there next weekend and we must meet." I was given all of Tom Davis' numbers, and we said goodbye. She had been warm, and I felt good after talking with her. I also felt the burden of convincing her to do the show was on my shoulders and there was a good chance I could foul it up. When I phoned Kevin to tell him a meeting would be set up for the following week, he said, "Terrific! Now, go out there and get her!" Of course, that's what we usually have producers for—to put the pieces together.

Early that week I received a phone call from a friend, Jeremiah Goodman, who has a lovely house in East Hampton. Jerry said he'd been asked to invite me Saturday night because he was having a dinner party and Mary Martin and friends would be there.

During the week I spoke to Kevin several times and Bob in London, and they both said, "Okay, it's up to you, you can charm her into it. Go—you can do it!"

By the time Saturday afternoon arrived, I felt as if I were opening on Broadway that night. I had the opening-night sweats. I knew the meeting would either go in the right direction or end the matter once and for all. How do you rehearse a meeting? It's difficult; you don't know what the other half of the script says. You just take a hot shower, dress well, splash on some cologne, and pray to God your mind doesn't shut down and your mouth puts together the right words. Saturday night might be a delightful dinner party for everyone else, but for me it loomed ahead like a summit conference.

MEETING PETER PAN

Still, when I was getting dressed in the late afternoon, I had to admit I feel fairly at ease in social situations, so I arrived, all done up in my summer best, at Jeremiah Goodman's around seven for drinks and dinner. Elaine Steinbeck (John's widow) was there; she's a fascinating woman with an amazing amount of energy; she kept the conversation going at a lively pace. With her was a former actor, Bob Wallsten, who'd worked with my mother in a play, and several other people.

We had drinks and soon there was a rustle in the halls leading to the living room and it was the star herself, Mary Martin, looking terrific. She was accompanied by Tom Davis, who seemed to be an amiable man and certainly in charge of protecting Mary. Mary and Elaine had known each other way back when they were girls in Texas, so there was a big reunion, but before long Mary caught my eye, immediately came to me, and said, "And you must be—"

"I am!" I said, immediately giving her a bear hug and the words "Welcome back to Broadway!"

"Oh, now, you're terrible!"

"I know, I can't help it."

We all had a round of drinks; Mary was gracious, talking to everyone, including everyone in the conversation. She is one of the spiffiest dressers around; she looked absolutely smashing in a luscious white summer skirt and a brocade jacket. She was sitting on a loveseat, and after the initial greetings and a bit of chitchat, she patted the seat next to her and said, "Come on over and let's talk."

There is still that tinge of Texas in her voice; it's extremely appealing and disarming. I obeyed and moved to sit next to her. "You know why I just had to meet you?"

"No."

"Your letters, I just love your letters, and I said to myself,

I just have to meet that young man." She looked at me, said, "You're very attractive. Now we must be friends."

"We'll have to be as long as we're going to work together."

She gave my hand a playful slap. "Stop that, now, I didn't say anything about *that*. But we'll be friends, I know it."

We talked about Broadway, about the Tony Awards. She told me she thought my play was extremely funny, then went on to speak of her last Broadway experience, which was a translation of a Russian two-character play she did in 1977 with Anthony Quayle, *Do You Turn Somersaults?* "I don't think the play was really all that right for me, but we opened in Washington at the Kennedy Center, and Roger Stevens insisted we bring it to New York. It was a big mistake. We opened on the night of the big blizzard, and people had to get to the theatre on skis."

I noticed as we spoke that Tom Davis, from across the room, was keeping a keen eye on me. He looked as if he might have to spring into action to abort a kidnapping.

"I can't stand the prospect of opening in anything on Broadway for Frank Rich," she said.

"Well, nobody likes that," I said. "But you can't really make your career fit one critic's—what—choice, pleasure? It's the audience we do it for, and if they like it—"

"Oh, I think the audience would love this play, it's so funny."

"Then—"

"Have you ever thought of doing the play in England?"

"Oddly enough, we have, yes. There's been a lot of talk of doing it in London first."

"Hmnn, now, that might interest me. I love England." We talked about the English theatre, the economics, the audiences, and finally she said, "Well, I'm renting a house in England with a couple of chums for July and August. Maybe we should talk more about doing it in London." She wanted to know about the producers. I told her Bob Regester was doing a play there now with Vanessa Redgrave and she should meet him when she arrived in England.

Then Mary spoke up. "You know, there are some words in the script that I could never say."

"We could make changes. There aren't many, you know. I mean, the part of Leatrice, she's the goody-goody, and she only says one or two really—well—strong words."

Then I was taken completely by surprise when Mary asked, "Leatrice? Did you say Leatrice?"

"Why, yes . . ."

"Oh, no, I thought of myself as Celia."

"Celia?"

"Yes," she said.

"There isn't any Celia. You mean—Sylvia?"

"Oh, yes, Sylvia," she said. "Oh, I think I'm much more right for Sylvia."

"You *do?*"

"Yes," she said, "don't you?"

"No, not really."

"Why?" she asked.

I suddenly found myself, after all this time, in an *Alice in Wonderland* kind of muddle. After all the chatter and letters and communications—we were talking about the *wrong* part? I couldn't believe it, especially since I had mentioned the role of Leatrice so many times.

"No," Mary said, "tell me why you thought of me as—how do you pronounce her name?"

"Leatrice. Like Leatrice Joy, who was married to John Gilbert."

"Oh, yes . . . but why would you think of me for *her?*"

"Well, because she sort of—or perhaps you sort of fit that image."

"What image?"

I felt about to hoist myself on my own petard, but I had to continue. "Well, you've always had a rather sweet image, an image of a total professional, who doesn't swear or carouse but who's still been rather canny about her career, and that's Leatrice. Of course, there are other layers to her, but the basic character is you, your persona."

"Isn't that funny, I was thinking of the wrong one?"

"Yes," I said, forcing a smile, a giggle, and a silent prayer that the *Bismarck* had not been sunk by a simple misunderstanding.

She laughed lightly, then patted my knee and said, "Maybe I should read the play again."

"Yes," I practically screamed. I was about to suggest that

I'd be glad to read it to her when we were called to dinner.

And a fine dinner it was. Conversation was lively. Elaine Steinbeck spoke right up, God bless her, and said, "Mary, I hear you're coming back to Broadway."

"Oh, no, we're just talking, just talking—"

"Well, you should, you really should."

Mary went on to ask if anyone there had read the play; no one had, of course, and when she went on to praise it her interest seemed to rise again, and she said, "If only Ethel were alive and we could get Pearl Bailey to play the maid!"

I stifled a laugh, because I know Pearl and have for ages and I wouldn't even want to be within a mile of her if someone handed her a script and said, "Pearl, darling, look at the maid's part." Conversation eventually drifted away from the play. We all sat around the table for hours, drinking wine and telling tall tales, theatrical and non-. There was a fair share of gossip. Mary struck me as being down to earth, eminently likable, fun; beneath the exterior and the reputation, there seemed to lurk a slight bawdy streak. My mother would have described it as "Naughty—you know, underneath she's got a naughty little something, and it's delicious."

Every now and then she'd return to the play and London, and at one point she said, "If I did the play, would you play the young producer?"

Immediate "Yes!" I undoubtedly would have said I'd play the German shepherd if there'd been one in the play.

"Good," she added, "you'd be perfect for that part."

I didn't dwell on whether or not that was meant as a compliment. The producer is a lowlife hustler who would do, say, or promise anything to get his way.

Mary and I talked some more about the play. She promised she'd read it again, and then, when she said she'd like to get to know me better, I suggested she read some of my novels, most of which are autobiographical to an extent. She said she'd love to, so it was arranged with Tom Davis that I'd phone late morning and drop them off, because they had to go to Cheryl Crawford's for lunch or brunch or whatever it's called if it's on Sunday.

Mary left about one in the morning, hugs and kisses all around. A great party, great evening, so glad we could all get together, and "I'm mad about this author."

The rest of us stayed on for a postmortem. Most were of the opinion that Mary just might finally agree to do the play, probably in England rather than on Broadway. Bob Wallsten was going to London; he promised to press our cause when he saw her over there. Elaine Steinbeck came up with a sharp remark or two that made us laugh: "I loved her saying, 'If only Ethel was alive!' If Ethel *were* alive, she'd have never said that. When they tried to repeat their fabulous Ford television show of the fifties, Ethel wiped up the TV screen with her, and Mary would never forget that. She'd never do a play with her, you can bet your life on that."

When we had all said our good nights and I was driving home, I thought, Well, the first contact was made and whatever it was, it was not a disaster.

Sunday, June 9, 1985

Woke up and had juice, coffee, and trepidations about the meeting today. It's the uncertainty of this game that gets to you. Always reaching out for a commitment from someone else to enable *you* to perform *your* work.

In the morning I gathered up a smattering of my books; decided to give Mary *There Must Be a Pony!, Good Times/Bad Times,* and *Some Kind of Hero.* That would be a fair sampling and enough. There was probably too much explicit sex in *Hit Me with a Rainbow* and too much of the bizarre in *P.S. Your Cat Is Dead!,* and *American Grotesque* should only be read when someone's bedded with flu for two weeks. Phoned Tom Davis late morning and was told Mary was still sleeping, to come around three, because they were off to Cheryl Crawford's for drinks and an early supper around four-something. The story had changed from brunch, and it was obvious my visit was to be a quick one.

I arrived at three on the dot. Tom Davis has a main house in Southampton which is rented, so he and Mary were staying in the pool house behind it. Very nice, with an extra little house on the other side of the pool that is like a combined sitting room and kitchen. Mary was up, again beautifully dressed, gave me a hug, and complimented me for being on time. I dangled a bag of books in front of her: "Anyone wanna buy any books?"

She peeked inside, then asked how many books I'd written.

I told her six. "How could anyone so young write that many books and also *A Chorus Line* and—how many other plays?" "Four." She turned to Tom: "Isn't that amazing for someone so young?"

I'm not young, but why destroy people's illusions, no point in that. At first Mary and Tom were in constant movement, as if they were about to take their leave. Mary said, "I ended up last night thinking, Oh, why not do it in London . . ." My heartbeat increased until she added, ". . . but I've got so many commitments. After we finish our London trip, then I have to do a benefit, and I represent Fieldcrest Mills. I design for them and travel around doing—"

"Presentations," Tom added. "That's who I work for. They're like industrial shows. She's our ambassadress of good will."

Mary got back into my prodigious output as far as writing is concerned (it isn't, really), and said I must have been born into it. I did not want this meeting to be brief, so I leveled with her, told her I'd never thought of writing early on, and then launched into what amounted to my life story. She had to sit down for that, and so did Tom. They were a good audience as I filled them in on my early acting career then dropped the remark that I'd been known as "the body finder" and told them about the five dead bodies I'd found (by accident) in my teens, one of which was eventually the source for *There Must Be a Pony!* When I came to the end of that episode, Tom asked, "Would anyone like a Bloody Mary?"

We all jumped at that, and I figured there was a chance I was in for the long haul. We talked on, until Tom finally suggested whipping up some food for us. While he did that, Mary and I went on exchanging stories, until I finally led around to the play once more. When she mentioned London again, I asked if she'd read the Sunday *Times* yet; she hadn't. "Then read the Arts and Leisure section, because, oddly enough, there's a long article in it all about the number and quality of American plays being done in London."

"Isn't that an amazing coincidence?" she asked.

She said it as if it might be a conspiracy. "Yes—and I didn't write it," I assured her. "Now, suppose you did decide to do the play for a while. What other actresses would you possibly want to work with?"

"Oh, there are so many fine actresses."

"What about Celeste Holm?"

"Umm, she's a very good actress . . . she is. . . . There's just something about her personality that doesn't sit that well with me. I like her, but onstage—there's just something, I don't know."

"What about Vivian Blaine? I worked with her in *Panama Hattie* in Dallas; she's read the play and likes it very much. She's very good and, well . . . you must have seen her in *Guys and Dolls.*"

"Vivian Blaine," Mary mused. "Yes, of course, I know of her and I know she's very good, but I've never seen her onstage."

"You haven't, not even in *Guys and Dolls?*"

"No, Jimmy, you see I was working myself all those years. I hardly saw anything. It was getting up around noon, breakfast, the mail, maybe a little shopping, then getting ready to go to the theatre, doing the show, then supper and home to bed. I really didn't see much theatre, didn't have the chance to, because I was always working. So I don't know Vivian Blaine all that well. Oh, I know she has a good reputation, but . . ."

We went over other names, and Mary finally said, "I like Eve Arden."

"So do I, and she's got the right bite and sarcasm for Sylvia."

"Yes, she does." Apparently the part of Leatrice was not bothering her today. We talked about Eve Arden, who'd just finished writing her autobiography. She'd sent Mary a signed copy; Mary said they were friends though not all that close, but she liked her very much. Then, after a while, Mary remarked, "Yes, she's a very good actress, but she's awfully large, don't you think?"

"How do you mean?"

"Well, wouldn't she be . . . just a bit big?"

"No, I don't think so, she's tall, but—"

"But I'm so small, she just might be too big."

I mentioned Irene Worth and Mary gasped, "Oh, I think she's marvelous, she's really one of the all-time great actresses."

"I think so, too. And the critics are crazy about her."

"Yes, oh, she'd be perfect!" We talked about Irene Worth for a while until Mary eventually sighed and said, "But, you know, she's not really a . . . what you call a *legend,* and . . . I'm not so sure I could hold my own against her. She's a marvelous actress, but . . ." A few more actresses bit the dust, and then Mary said, "Wouldn't it be great to get a real *legend?* Now, I know you might think this is a strange idea, but when I hosted the talk show in San Francisco, I got Alice Faye to come on, and she was so hesitant, nervous, you know about doing it, but when she did, she was just marvelous. She talked and talked, told funny stories, she's got a good sharp sense of humor, and . . ." Mary went on for a long time about Alice Faye, ending up with "So perhaps you should meet her."

We chatted on over lunch—well, it was going on four-thirty by then—and it struck me that Mary didn't really want strong competition from a stage actress. She also mentioned Ginger Rogers, but I pulled back from that somewhat. I have nothing against Ginger, except I wish she'd cut her hair; I just couldn't imagine tons of electricity zizzing back and forth across the stage between Mary Martin and Ginger Rogers.

By the time I got ready to leave, it was agreed I'd send off another script to her address in London, that she would meet with Bob Regester there, that perhaps I might even make a trip over. She'd read through the play again and think of whatever other actresses there might be. When I left I gave her a hug and a kiss and said, "I do hope we can do this together; we'd have fun, we would."

"I know it, and I'm feeling . . . well, fairly good about it all now. Thank you, darling, for the books; I can't wait to read them." With that, Mary and Tom left for Cheryl Crawford's.

Our second meeting went well. Down deep inside I thought, Mary will meet with Bob in London, he'll charm her, he knows how to do that, she loves London, and I bet we might just get a production there. The path ahead seems fairly simple.

THE SUMMER OF MY DISCONTENT

Mary went off to England about the time Bob Regester came back to the U.S. I sent off a script to her with the following letter.

June 12, 1985

Dear Mary,
How terrific it was to get to know you, even if for just a few hours. You are a nifty lady and I appreciate the time spent with you. I'm picking up YOUR book tomorrow from the Gotham Book Store and I look forward to reading it.

Here's a copy of the script. When you're reading it, give a thought to Leatrice. I would think that would be such fun for you. But if you feel strongly about Sylvia, let me know. Also think of London for a few months. And the applause you'd get. And then they'd be saying, "Isn't that fellow on Dallas Mary Martin's son?"

Of course, think about you and what you really want to do. But think of ME and MY CAREER! Don't you want to help your new best friend's career out a little? A Chorus Line *is on its last legs, soon there won't be any royalties coming in and you don't want me to have to go to the Motion Picture Home, do you? Think about it. And we could have such good times and I would play the producer if you wanted me to. Six months, in and out, and we'd have a whole other glorious chapter to write about in our memoirs.*

Have a wonderful stay in London. If you want me to bop over for further discussions, let me know. I'll be in touch with you anyhow. Think about Eve Arden and/or Irene Worth. I will be thinking about you.

Love,
Jim

A day or so after Mary and Tom Davis had gone to visit Cheryl Crawford, I got a phone call from Cheryl. "You know that play you had read at the Studio? Have you done work on it?" I told her I had; she said she'd liked it very much at the time and would like to read it again. Not a mention of Mary Martin, which tickled me. I dropped a script off at her house in Sagaponack a day or so later. Still no mention of Mary, which now tickled me even more. I told her the play was optioned; she'd vaguely heard of Ahmet, but didn't know of Kevin or Bob. I said if she was interested I was sure they'd be agreeable to a meeting and a possible coproduction. Although she hadn't mentioned Mary, I knew Mary was why she'd asked for the script; I also knew Cheryl had produced one of Mary's hit musicals, *One Touch of Venus*, and that she could be instrumental in snagging Mary if she truly liked the play.

Cheryl phoned a few days later, said I'd done extremely good work on the script, and asked if I'd come by for a drink, which I did. We had a good talk, and for the first time she mentioned Mary, saying, "You know, Mary Martin came by one day when she was out here, and she said she sort of liked it." Cheryl also spoke about Irene Worth and Constance Cummings in the event a production was done in London. She also mentioned Clifford Williams as a possible director. I liked him. When the Robert Stigwood Organization had *P.S. Your Cat Is Dead!* under option, Clifford was going to direct it; we'd been through auditions together before Stigwood dropped the project. Clifford had directed *Sleuth* in New York, *Pack of Lies*, and the recent revival of *Aren't We All?* So, although we'd still been talking to Joe Hardy in the case of a U.S. production, a London presentation would probably best be served by a British director. This meeting with Cheryl was at the end of June.

The next day there was a message to call Mary Martin in London. Whoever answered the phone said she was dressing to go out and asked who was calling. James Kirkwood. "Oh, wait a minute." In a few seconds, on came Mary, all warm and affectionate. "Oh, Jimmy, darling, I've been reading your books and I just love the way you write; you're a wonderful writer, you really are."

"Thank you, that's good to hear."

"You have such a personal touch, it's really quite wonderful."

I edged into the play, told her I'd had a meeting with Cheryl, who liked it and thought it would be so right for Mary.

"Now, I received the script but I haven't had a chance to read it again"—Please, I thought, read the play, skip the books!—"but I'll read it again soon."

I took the plunge. "Oh, come on, let's just do it for six months in London and have a great time."

"No," Mary said, "you said for three months out of town and three months in town."

"No, Mary, I never said that."

"Yes . . . you did, too. . . ." This read like a little girl.

"No, I didn't." And I hadn't, either—we'd never spoken of any time span like that.

Mary giggled as if she'd caught me in a lie and then went on to say Irene Worth was over there doing Shakespeare; I asked if she was going to see her. "Oh, no, I won't go to see her in Shakespeare, I've seen her enough in Shakespeare. I loved her in the Noel Coward things." It was left that she'd read the play again soon and I'd phone her in a week or so. We'd had a good conversation, and just before we hung up she said, "I keep thinking about the play and I can't get it out of my mind—so we'd better talk."

That was most encouraging. About this time I realized that I was the principal involved in all these meetings and calls; after each one I would dutifully report to Bob and Kevin and would be verbally patted on the back, encouraged to follow up with the next step. Frankly, it began bugging me. I was acting as producer. I invited Bob and Kevin for lunch around this time and told them of my feelings. They assured me it was only because I'd met Mary first and had gotten involved before them, and because I had a certain reputation as a writer, but now they would start pitching in themselves. Especially Bob, who said he would turn on all faucets in pursuit of Mary when he went back to England. I also asked why Ahmet, with all his power and connections, couldn't pick up a phone and call someone we were seeking, be it a director or star. "Oh, Ahmet will come in when we need him," Kevin said. I said, "We need him now."

Clifford Williams arrived in New York around July 9 for a few days of casting for the American tour of *Aren't We All?* I spoke to him on the phone, told him of the play and a possible London production with Mary Martin. He was only in America for a few days, then off to France, back to England, and then here in September for rehearsals of the *Aren't We All?* tour. I said I'd have a script sent to the Brooks Atkinson Theatre; he'd phone me if he had a chance to read it before he left, or he'd be in touch later.

Immediately after this, long distance from Mary in London. Again, speaking as if we were old friends, she told me what a grand time she was having, how much she loved London, being with her friends, and going to the theatre. "Why, just last night we went to see Lauren Bacall in *Sweet Bird of Youth,* then out to dinner and . . ." On and on. Now, I can smell a turndown a mile away. Finally Mary said, "I love your writing, and you know I love the play. I just don't know if the public would accept me in a role like that in your play. I wouldn't want to do anything to hurt the play—I think it's wonderful, and I just wouldn't want to do anything to harm it."

"You wouldn't," I reassured her.

"I would if the public didn't accept me."

"But they would. You're perfect for the part of Leatrice, the character is so much you—with a little twist."

She kept talking about her theatrical image, going back to the play she'd done with Anthony Quayle. "The audience didn't accept me in that Russian play, because I only sang part of a song and they didn't allow for applause and the audience wanted me to sing more and they wanted to applaud."

We went back and forth, my point being she was a legend and she was playing a legend who, although not written specifically for her, was very close to her persona. Mary even said, "You know, the other night, when I went to the Drury Lane, I realized that, yes, I *am* a legend. So many people came up for autographs and asked, 'When are you coming back to the Drury Lane?' and on and on!"

"Exactly," I said, "you have all these fans and they haven't had enough of you."

"But, darling, you see, I have this goody-goody image and the audience simply will not take certain words from me."

"Mary, Leatrice doesn't swear all that much, just a couple of times, and then she's more than provoked by Sylvia, and I'm sure an audience would love it all the more coming from you. It would be a change; *I* would love it if I went to the theatre and you—"

"But you're different."

"No, I'm not, I'm a good audience and I'd love it."

"I just don't want to harm your wonderful play by saying—well, certain words."

"Mary, I've told you, I'll make changes."

"But the play's so delightful the way it is; that would be hurting it."

It was Catch-22. She loved the play and its "naughtiness," didn't think it should be changed, but thought it was too naughty for her.

"Mary, you're an actress. The way you talk, you couldn't play

Lady Macbeth because you're not a murderess."

I felt in my gut she'd made up her mind to turn it down in this conversation. This was to be the kiss-off. But I fought on: "All right, I guess I'll just have to dust off my passport, get a new summer suit, a club, a *cage*, and come after you!" She laughed, told me how much she loved me, and said, "We have to work together sometime."

"But this is the time, this is it!"

"I really don't think they'll accept me."

I reminded her Cheryl liked the play, thought she'd be perfect for Leatrice, and would be coming to London toward the end of July. Mary said. "Oh, of course, I love Cheryl, but I don't know if I'll get a chance to see her. We're going to Venice and then to Belgium and . . ."

I was wearing myself out, so I decided it was best to end this conversation soon. Just as I began telling her I'd phone her whenever I felt like it, she said, "You know, in reading the play again, the other part, Sylvia, has many more lines, and—well, she's really the stronger of the two."

Now Mary was wearing *me* out. I simply didn't have the gumption to pick up on that thread of thought. If the audience wouldn't accept her as Leatrice, they'd stone her and burn down the theatre if they caught her playing Sylvia. She repeated, "I'm sorry, but it's only because I don't want to hurt your wonderful play."

One last shot: "You'll kill it if you don't say yes."

She giggled; we said goodbye and promised to keep in touch.

Milton Goldman, one of the top agents in the business and an old friend, was on his annual pilgrimage to London. I knew he handled Mary for theatre, although she'd been dormant in that area for a long time, so I phoned around until I found out where he was staying and called him. I wanted to verify my hunch. When I got him on the phone, I asked if he'd seen Mary, and immediately Milton said, "Oh, yes, I was with her last night."

"You know we're trying to get her for my play?"

"Yes, of course. Mary loves you, loves the play, but Tony Quayle came over to have cocktails with her and she gave him the play to read. He liked it very much but told Mary the audience would *never* accept her as one of those women!"

"I knew it, I knew it! I knew someone had told her that."

"Yes," Milton said, "but she adores you."

"Yes, but—goddamnit, Milton, will you please try to talk to her?"

Milton promised he'd try to help, and we hung up. Immediately I began swearing, ranting and raving, throwing things about. A friend of mine from Chicago, Carolyn Kirschenbaum (hereafter known as Kecky), was downstairs with Arthur Beckenstein, and they both wanted to know what the problem was. "I'm going Quayle hunting, goddamnit. I'm going to kill me an Anthony Quayle!" I shouted. I filled them in on the latest. "Jesus, wouldn't she have to give it to Anthony Quayle? I'll bet if there was a good part for him in it the audience would accept Mary. Why wasn't he off in Scotland shooting plaid, or in Italy eating pasta? The perverse serendipity of it is too much! Why did she just happen to give it to him, of all people? It's like climbing Mount Everything in greasy sandals trying to get this phuquer on!"

A week later a lunch was arranged in Bridgehampton so Kevin and Bob could meet Cheryl. After introductions, we all sat down and I filled Cheryl in on our latest roadblock; thereupon followed massive battle plans on how to achieve the Tony Quayle Solution. Bob was to leave for London in a week, where rehearsals were under way with Vanessa Redgrave in *The Seagull*. He would call Milton and urge him on in our behalf. Also Josh and Nedda Logan were in London; they were extremely close to Mary, and their aid would be enlisted. Bob would give Josh the play to read and, if he liked it, ask him to advise Mary to do it. Cheryl would be lecturing her way over on the *QEII* toward the end of the month, so she and Bob would be in London at the same time. They would combine forces in a final campaign to snag Peter Pan, short of breaking her knees, but only just short. Bob and Kevin asked me to write Mary yet another letter; I said I felt it would be better for me to sit in the backfield for a while, lest I go into overkill.

Cheryl told Bob and Kevin she'd like to come in as one of the producers. It was agreed they'd talk with Floria Lasky and, if Cheryl could be of real help in getting Mary, some sort of arrangement would be worked out. Cheryl also happened to mention that Shirley MacLaine kept an apartment in Cheryl's building in the city; she would get a script to her, and asked me to write an accompanying letter.

Bob phoned me from London Saturday, July 20, to say he'd had a long phone call with Mary, who said he sounded just like me with regard to power of persuasion. He said they got along fine on the phone, but she vowed she wouldn't do the show, repeated her story of realizing she was a certain kind of legend and what the audience would and wouldn't accept her as. He wanted to meet with her right away, but she was off to Venice in a few days and promised to see him when she returned to London on August 10, at which time Cheryl would also be there. He suggested I write her a letter which would be awaiting her upon her return from Venice.

The following Monday, Cheryl invited me for a drink; she was about to depart herself, so we had a farewell visit. She also urged me to drop Mary a line, and the next day I wrote the following letter. I had to crank it out, and it reads that way.

July 22, 1985

Dear Mary,

So what did you bring me from Venice—my very own canal? And a lot of pigeons!

I had drinks with Cheryl last night in Bridgehampton. I like her so much, love her forthrightness and candor. She will be in England by the time you get this. Cheryl is very high on LEGENDS! and that pleases me.

I talked to Bob Regester who said he'd spoken to you on the phone and would hope to see you when you have returned and also wanted to invite you to his production of THE SEAGULL. You will like him very much.

This is—in a way—a little final utch for you to play Leatrice. I know you are a legend yourself, but I don't understand, if you like the play as you say you do, your reticence to portray a legend that is based largely on yourself. I don't see how that could in any way be construed as not acceptable to an audience when, in fact, you would be playing a lady who has your reputation for being adored, a hard worker, a real pro. Also someone who always played "the good gal"—which is why it burns Sylvia so much. Because Leatrice always had the good reputation and she had a bad one. Now that time has passed in Leatrice and

Sylvia's careers, we find that things have changed and Lea-
trice, though still an angel, has had some rough blows dealt
her in her personal life—as you have—Richard's death
and the accident and Ben's death. These things are bound
to make a person change somewhat and I know the audi-
ence would love seeing that Leatrice can hold her own
against Sylvia. They would root for you standing up for
yourself and standing up against Sylvia's taunts. That
would be the joy and fun of the play. They would also root
for the two ladies to pull it all together and do a play, do
what you do best, and take that chance, not play it safe, not
give up and simply dwindle away. You said yourself people
in London keep saying, "When are you coming back to the
stage?"

It's true. People want to see you. And I don't believe for
a minute they think you're going to repeat SOUTH
PACIFIC, SOUND OF MUSIC OR PETER PAN. That
would be dull and you've done that, it would simply be
repetitive, you are beyond that.

How exciting to take a step further and do a play about
the business you've spent your life in and about actresses
who are at the age when they can come up with some de-
lightful surprises.

I know Anthony Quayle said he thought the audience
wouldn't accept you in such a part. I think he's dead
wrong. I think they would eat you up with joy. I've done a
lot of research on the play you did with him and from all
I've read and heard, and from people I've talked to who saw
the production, it was not really that good a play to begin
with. It was not an audience pleaser; I think LEGENDS!
will be.

Of course there are other actresses who could play the
part, but you are absolutely so right in every way for it.
Your image is perfect, your reputation, you are a survivor,
you look stunning, you are the right age, it is patterned
AFTER YOU—so I urge you to think about it seriously and
talk to Cheryl and Bob and me and, most of all, YOUR
PERFORMING SOUL and give it consideration. It could be
such a triumph for you. There would be absolutely no rea-
son for me to press you if I didn't truly believe this is true.

As a matter of fact, it would be counter-productive for my
own play. I only press my case because of my absolute
belief you and the play are meant for each other. Everyone
else I talk to who has read the play agrees. Everyone. There
must be something right about the combination. Why else
would everybody latch onto it so?

If you would like me to swim over there for a drink and
a talk, I have my water-wings all dusted off and blown up.
Think about it, dear Mary. And do talk to Bob and Cheryl.
And remember me and that I love you.

xoxoxoxo
Jim

When Mary returned from her trip to Venice, Bob arranged
to take her to lunch. His report to me was this: "I think she's
ninety percent committed to doing a tour of the United States."
After our history, I took this with a carton of salt. Also he'd talked
to Clifford Williams, and Clifford "is really committed to direct it."
Another carton of salt, because I'd never heard from Clifford since
sending him the play, not a word. (The way we treat each other
in this business!) Calls from Cheryl: "If only she hadn't given it
to Tony Quayle!" "But Bob says she's ninety percent committed
to . . ." And on and on. I was pressured into writing one more letter
to Mary, yes, yet another. I cannot find a copy of this one, but it
was in the form of a suicide note and I covered it with blood
(theatrical blood mixed with a bit of catsup). This one earned a call
from Mary saying how much she'd love to produce my letters as
a play. And we must get together when she got back to the States
in September. Very funny, Mary.

Alan Wasser, our general manager, sent the play to Bobby
Fryer (director of the Ahmanson Theatre in L.A.). Bobby phoned
me, full of enthusiasm about the play and the possibility of playing his theatre with Mary. He said he'd like to join with the
producers or invest in the play; I welcomed him aboard and suggested he talk with Floria. Toward the end of August, Bob Regester, who had been lunching and wining and dining Mary, like a
terrier refusing to give up a bone, phoned to say she was once
again talking about the part of *Sylvia!* Also, she wanted the name
of Leatrice changed, and no matter what part she played she

wouldn't say the F-word at the end of Act One and she wouldn't say the S-word and . . . would I please phone her and reassure her that those little matters would be changed?

I said I'd phone her in a day or so, but after I hung up I thought: Oh, F-word, I can't go around begging on my knees anymore, it's just too F-wording boring and demeaning. But I'd promised. So several days later I did phone—twice—but got no answer, which was a relief.

Soon everyone would be back in the United States. I did finally get Mary on the phone, and she raved on about the suicide letter, ending up with "I can't make up my mind about doing the play until I get back home; then we'll talk."

Amen, I say unto thee.

I did have in early September an amusing encounter with Shirley MacLaine. If I've mentioned actresses or directors regarding *Legends!* and then never mentioned them again, it's because I never heard back from them. At any rate, after sending the script to Shirley MacLaine, we never heard from *her.*

When I was a doorman at Grauman's Chinese Theatre in Hollywood at the age of seventeen, a fellow doorman was Thomas Hammond. Tommy is now a lawyer and also a personal manager. He's managed Bernadette Peters for years and invited me to attend a preview of *Song and Dance,* in which Bernadette was starring. As we approached the theatre, there was Shirley Mac-Laine trying to make her way inside, besieged by autograph hounds. I thought of running up and shouting, "Hey, I'm Jim Kirkwood, did you ever get the play and letter we sent you?" But, of course, I didn't.

Bernadette was the entire first act all by herself, and brilliant. During intermission Tom and I were making our way through the lobby and there was Shirley, standing and talking to another woman. As we neared them Tom said, "Why don't you speak to her?" "No, this is not the place." The next moment he called out in a loud voice, introducing me to Andrew Lloyd Webber's man-ager, saying, "Do you know James Kirkwood?" As we shook hands, Shirley looked at me and I looked at her.

(We'd met years before—I'd had lunch at her house in the Valley [L.A.] with mutual friends when I was acting in an indus-trial show, singing ballads to Buicks—but she would have no reason to remember my face. Yet there we were, face to face.)

"Jimmy?"

"Shirley?"

We bussed each other's cheeks and laughed. "Did you ever get the script Cheryl sent you?"

"Yes, but I haven't finished it. I've been on this book tour and I didn't take the script with me. I'll finish it now, though. You're so talented, such a good writer."

"Why, thank you."

Then she said, "Darling, it *is* a play, isn't it?"

"Yes," I said, "it's a play," thinking: She hasn't *finished it?* She hasn't *opened it!*

"It's not a movie?"

"No, it's a play."

"Oh, I want to do a movie."

"Well, why don't you finish reading the *play,* because it's going to be a movie after." I don't know where those words came from, but they seemed to fit at the time.

"All right," she said, "I will, and I'll call Cheryl tomorrow."

After the show Tommy and I went backstage to Bernadette's dressing room. Shirley was already there; we all heaped praise on Bernadette, and since Tom and I were having supper with her, we stepped outside after a while so Shirley and she could talk alone. When Shirley came out, she headed straight for me. "Could you get me another script tomorrow?"

"Of course. If you like it, why don't you do the play for six months? Then we'll get a preproduction deal and you can do the movie."

Her eyes lit up, and she threw me again when she said, "I got as far as when the two ladies are in the apartment and the one finds out the apartment doesn't belong to the other but to a friend."

Now, that's toward the end of the first act, and still she'd asked, "Is it a play or a movie?" Oh, well . . . she *had* cracked the script. I whispered for her to lean over.

"What?" she asked.

"If you don't read the script this weekend—I'll have your legs broken!"

She laughed, we kissed goodbye, and she left.

By mid-September everyone was back in the U.S., and it was

obvious that as far as this season was concerned things would have to pull together soon or else fall apart. I wouldn't have bet a nickel either way.

CLOSING IN ON MARY

On Saturday, September 14, many of us were in the Hamptons. Kevin has a house in Amagansett, next to East Hampton; Cheryl is in Sagaponack; and Milton Goldman weekends in Bridgehampton. Bob Regester was back from London and houseguesting with me. We held a war council at Cheryl's in the afternoon, hashing over all the yeses, nos, maybes, and what-ifs.

We had about twelve numbers for Mary on the coast. It was decided to put in a firm call, get a definite yes or no, and end this purgatory. She was not to be found at any number. We only had about four numbers for Clifford—the same. Not being able to reach anyone, we dispersed: Kevin, Bob, and I returned to my house, and I'll be a son of a bear if there wasn't a message that Mary had called not more than five minutes before we arrived.

We manned the phones. Bob and I were to be the talkers; Kevin monitored, as usual. When we got Mary on the phone, she was breathless and as disingenuous as I'd ever heard her. "Oh, I've been traveling so much I don't even know where I am, and my grandchildren have to tell me what day it is, and—oh, am I in Malibu? Or—oh, I just don't know." Bob and I both chatted with her; my leg was doing the Irish jig, as it does when I attempt to rein in my patience. Finally Mary said, "Now, I've always said I couldn't make up my mind about doing a play until I was back home, and I guess that's Rancho Mirage—I think—I'm not sure anymore."

I explained to her about Bobby Fryer's interest, which she'd been apprised of. "I understand," Mary said, "and I adore Bobby, and I know he has to announce his season, and I don't want to screw things up, but—"

"Ah-ah," I cut in, "you said 'screw'—why, Mary, I'm shocked."

She laughed. "No, no, we use that in Texas and it means— well, like screwing in a screw."

We talked for a long time; either Mary was pretending to be completely frazzled from her travels, or she really was, or she was stalling. Finally, she said as soon as she had a good visit with her son, Larry Hagman, and his wife and got settled in at Rancho Mirage, she'd make a decision.

On Wednesday evening we all met in the city. Bob; Kevin; George Yaneff, a partner of Bob's investor group, a mild, pleasant man who could easily be taken for subconsul to some foreign country; and the recently arrived Clifford Williams, whom I hadn't seen in years and who looked much younger than I imagined he would. There was a good opening for us at the Ahmanson Theatre, about ten weeks, if we could only cast the goddamn thing. I was surprised to hear Clifford say he thought we needed another big name to go with Mary; he had no idea of her popularity.

Eventually we repaired to a nearby restaurant for dinner. Clifford was to leave for San Francisco Friday for the opening of the tour of *Aren't We All?* We talked in general about the play, and when I excused myself to go to the men's room, Clifford followed. "Jimmy, are they for real, these guys?"

"How do you mean?"

"I mean, are they real producers, do they have real money?"

"Bob's done things in London, but Kevin hasn't really been involved in the theatre. However, he's backed by Ahmet Ertegun, who does have real money. I wish our general manager, Alan Wasser, could have been here, because he really knows the business down to the last T."

The next weekend I went back to East Hampton, where I got a call from Bob. He'd spoken to Mary again, and the new word was she'd given the play to Larry Hagman for his reading pleasure. "Jesus," I said, "by the time it's read by all of her advisers and relatives, we'll all be too old to do it." Then he asked if I would fly to San Francisco for the opening of *Aren't We All?* Mary would be coming up to stay with friends, meet Clifford, and see the play. Then we would fly south with her and spend a few days at her place in Rancho Mirage. I said I would, as long as Mary herself approved of this plan.

Several days later Mary phoned. And we had quite a conversation. After the amenities, she said: "You know, I've had a strange relationship with my son. It was not good for years when Richard [Halliday, her husband] was alive. But then we made it up, and I never want to do anything ever again to ruin it. So I finally gave him the play to read, and he and his wife, Maj—well, they both think it's so funny, they loved it! Larry said if he wasn't so busy right now he'd buy it and produce it as a film. He even kidded me, he said, 'Mother, I don't see why you can't say every word in that script.' "

"Good for him," I said.

"He also told me he was going to give me my first hashish brownie. Larry's a great kidder." (The ladies eat them by mistake in the play.)

"Save one for me!"

"Anyhow, darling, all signs are pointing for me doing your lovely play."

"Well, I couldn't be happier."

"Now, could you come out to San Francisco for Clifford's opening on Friday? Bob will be there, I'll meet Clifford, we'll see the play, then fly down to Los Angeles and spend Saturday with Larry and Maj in Malibu—he's dying to meet you, loves your writing—then we'll drive down to my place in Rancho Mirage on Sunday and Monday."

"It's a date."

"So," Mary said, "about the only things to be worked out are where and when, and the other gal."

We said goodbye. I phoned Bob, Kevin, and Alan Wasser and told them this news. We all acknowledged it looked as if the show might actually pull together. Mary Martin had been sent the script last April. It was now the end of September. And Mary was just one "element." How do plays ever get on?

That evening James Leo Herlihy, probably my oldest and best friend from days of yore, phoned from Los Angeles, where he lives, and said, "Jim, where the hell have you been? I haven't had a letter or a phone call from you all summer. What have you been up to?"

"I'm sorry, Jim, but I've spent months chasing Mary Martin all over the globe trying to snag her for *Legends!*"

There was a long silence. Then I heard Jim say, "Jesus Christ, I hope you don't catch her!"

WELL, WE DID

Thursday, September 26, Bob and I flew to San Francisco and checked into the Huntington, atop Nob Hill. The next afternoon, before opening night, an hour was set for Clifford and Mary to meet for the first time. Mary was staying with Dickie Quayle, no relation to the dread Tony. Dickie has a lovely apartment overlooking the bay and the Golden Gate Bridge and had been with Mary in London that summer. Bob and I arrived before Clifford to find Mary all done up like a movie star. She seemed a bit nervous at the prospect of meeting Clifford. After a while I was certain she was. When he arrived, we had tea and chatted. Clifford was not being the social-anecdotal Clifford as much as the observant professional. I'd brought my camera, so photographs were taken, as if we were recording a momentous occasion. We talked for an hour or so, and although the meeting held a tinge of the unease that accompanies a summit conference, we got along well, spoke of various actresses for the part of Sylvia and the play in general. Once or twice Mary used the "if" word: "If we do it . . . If we can find the right . . . If it's finally arranged. . . ." The "if" word unsettled me, but by this time almost anything would have. Soon it was time for everyone to leave to get dressed for opening night.

When Bob, Clifford, and I got out on the street, Clifford said, "Is Mary Martin really that big a name here?" I told him I thought she was. "Umm," he said.

That evening, in the limousine on the way to the theatre, Mary handed me an envelope with two tickets. "You'll sit with me," she whispered. I was delighted. Opening nights in San Francisco are very dressy. The Curran Theatre was packed with the elite of the city, and when Mary made her entrance everyone waved, shouted, clutched at her. She caused quite a stir. Had Clifford seen this display, he would have been reassured of her appeal.

The show creaked a bit at first, but soon picked up. The production was a perfect replica of the sort of urbane play *Aren't*

We All? had been in its time. Claudette is amazing for her age; Rex, although he foomfs a bit, is so full of stage charm he's irresistible to an audience. After the play, which Mary adored— "It's so civilized!"—we were taken to the restaurant on the top floor of the Bank of America building for a supper party given by the Shorensteins—"Why, they practically own San Francisco!" a bejeweled lady told me. "Practically, or do they *really* own it?" I asked. The party was delightfully old-fashioned; there was a reception line as you entered the main dining room, and we all shook hands with Mr. and Mrs. Shorenstein and their daughter, Carole. "They gave her the Curran Theatre as a plaything," the same lady told me. "Some plaything!"

The view was magnificent; there were two large tables in the VIP section, each seating twelve or fourteen. When the stars arrived, all hell broke loose. Mary was photographed with Claudette and Rex, and after the hubbub we all found our place cards.

Claudette Colbert and my father had starred together in London many years ago in a play called *The Barker.* This evening she spoke warmly of him—unlike the first time we'd met, when she'd said, in a matter-of-fact way: "You know, dear, your father was a fine actor, but he was a bastard!" "Yes," I'd replied at the time, "I know, he was my father!" I took no offense at her remark at all. This evening she said, "Now, you get Mary to do your play." My response, of course, was "You tell her that, you're sitting right next to her." And she did. Mrs. Shorenstein, who sat to my left, said, "I hear you're starting out at the Ahmanson. You should really begin your tour at the Curran; San Francisco is Mary's city. You think of that."

Saturday, September 28, 1985

Dickie Quayle drove Mary, Bob, and me to the airport for the short flight to Los Angeles. Mary and I sat in the front row of first class, right by the bulkhead, and chatted over a Bloody Mary. Bob sat right across the aisle. Guards seemed to be down; no one was playing games anymore.

We had a most perky stewardess. As we got ready to land, the stewardess strapped herself in; as we touched down and the plane bounced several times, she exclaimed, "That was about a three-flapper!"

"How do you mean?" I asked.

She indicated the john, which we were sitting right behind. "We class our landings according to how many times the toilet seat in there flaps up and down. This was a three-flapper." Mary, Bob, and I howled at that.

We were met by Larry Hagman's driver and limo, complete with champagne and a basket of goodies to nibble at on our way to Malibu. There is something about Malibu that brings back a rush of childhood memories; I remember in the last year of my parents' marriage—I was five—when they had a large beach house right about where the Colony is now, they threw a wild party one weekend. I was awakened by my nurse and carried out of the house just as dawn was breaking to stand on the beach while the house burned down in front of us. I remember there not being enough water pressure, and garbage trucks were brought in, and the garbage was dumped and hurled at parts of the house in an attempt to save something, but it was no use. Although both parents kept checking on me, reassuring me everything was all right, I remember them fighting, blaming each other for the party, which had gotten out of hand, and the fire, which had *really* gotten out of control. I have no further memory of their being together except in a nasty court battle over me.

Later, when I was a broke adolescent living on the coast, whenever I had to bike up from Santa Monica to see friends, I used to hate Malibu and those million-dollar shacks, which represented everything my parents had had and lost, including career, marriage, and happiness.

Any trip to Malibu brings that back. But today I felt on top of it. We were greeted warmly by Larry and Maj. Most of the houses in Malibu don't look nearly as big or sumptuous from the road as they do once you're inside. True of the Hagmans' house, too.

We were given a quick drink and then the grand tour. On the outside it's a smooth sort of beige stucco; inside it's an incredible array of different angles, walks, ponds, trees, plants, irregular-shaped rooms (on purpose, Maj's designing), an enormous kitchen, a living room, and an outside eating area facing the ocean. Guest bedrooms, their master suite, a great office for Larry decorated with memorabilia that could keep you gawking for an entire day.

Larry was wearing a very short robe, a Hopi coat actually, and under that a pair of the briefest shorts. And sandals. He is solidly built, with legs like a soccer player's. It occurred to me that if he really got angry he could kick someone all the way to Catalina. We're talking major legs. He's immediately likable, a bit crazy right under the surface, and there's a wicked gleam right behind the eyeballs. Maj, his wife of thirty-some years, is blonde, has lots of large, very white teeth, a natural, weathered, *gemütlich* face that indicates she spends a good deal of time in the sun. From this brief day spent with them, I imagined them to have a solid, healthy marriage. Mary dotes on Larry, and he treats her with charming, respectful, loving disrespect.

We finally settled in the outside dining area, which was sheltered from the sun by a huge purple satinish cover that was retractable. We all got along easily; there seemed to be no shyness on anyone's part, no layers that had to be worked through. There were no servants parading about, but one felt there were probably one or two on the premises. While Maj cooked the entire meal—grilled tuna steaks and mushrooms, put together salads and vegetables—we all talked of the play.

Larry said he liked it enormously; his enthusiasm was a joy to hear. "I'd love to do it as a movie if I weren't so busy. I'd love to play the producer—that's a great part."

Mary eventually got around to the language. In the original version, at the end of the first act, when the two ladies start fighting physically, the maid cries out, "Wait, wait—what if Mr. Klemmer [the producer] shows up?" I had both ladies shout out, "Fuck Mr. Klemmer!," then go at each other like wildcats as the curtain fell.

Larry said, "Oh, Mother, come on, you can say that. It's a great curtain line from two stars who are pretentious. You only say it once, and you say it with the other lady—you say it together."

"No, no . . . I could never." Mary giggled. She looked at me and said, "Oh, I *know* all those words, I've heard them all—especially with a son like this—but I've never said them on the stage and I don't think I ever could."

"Sure you could," Larry said.

"I couldn't."

"You just have to learn," he insisted.

"How could I learn to do *that?*" she asked.

"Mother, darling, just hop out of bed every morning, rush to the window, open it, and shout, 'Fuck! Fuck! Fuck! Fuck! Fuck!' " Her hands flew up to cover her face as she giggled again and said, "Oh, you're terrible, just terrible. No, I couldn't do that, you know I couldn't!"

"All right," Larry sighed, "start in easy. Hop out of bed, open the window, and start shouting, 'Duck! Duck! Duck! Duck! Duck!' and work up to it."

We all laughed. As we started to eat, Mary said, "And I can't say the S-word." I took that to mean "shit," although there was no place in the play where her character was required to say it. "But I'll tell you what I do say instead." She was looking at me.

"What?" I asked.

"Oh, plop!"

"Oh, plop!" I shouted. "No, no, please, not while I'm eating."

"Why, what's the matter?" she asked.

"That's horrible," I told her, looking around the table and asking for a consensus. "That's much worse than the word itself, it's so graphic. Please . . . people are eating."

She didn't seem to understand, and although most everyone else agreed we soon got off the subject, because we were, in fact, eating. "Oh, plop!" indeed.

At one point Mary used the "if" word, and Larry immediately said, "Oh, Mother, stop. I know what it is: you're afraid the maid will steal the play."

"No, no . . ."

"Yes, you are." He turned to me. "It's a terrific part; she could walk off with it, if you got the right one."

"Well, it's a good part, I think—"

"You bet it is!" This from Mary.

Lunch was excellent. We spoke of the theatre, films, Larry's series. Then we returned to the theatre and he dropped in one sentence to Mary: "You should only do six performances a week, you know."

Bob and I looked at each other, choked down whatever we were eating, and both started another subject at the exact same moment. We were not going to get into that area.

All in all, it was a perfect afternoon. We left in Larry's limo about five-thirty for the drive to Rancho Mirage, which is just past Palm Springs.

Bob and I sat in the back seat, with Mary between us, and told stories of our lives in and out of the theatre. Mary and I held hands for a while as she whistled favorite songs. She whistles like a warbler, incredibly well. "You could have had your own radio show," I told her. She patted my hand. "Well, I guess we're on our way." Riding along as the sun set, I thought: Isn't it amazing? Here I am sitting in the back of this cushy limousine holding hands with Mary Martin. She's whistling songs from *South Pacific*, which is one of the first musicals I saw, and when I sat there that night, mesmerized by the sheer theatrical magic of it all, if anyone had told me one day "that lady" up there would be in a play of mine, I'd have said, "You're totally insane." Yet here we were.

We arrived late at her lovely house, which is in an entire section of equally lovely houses—low-slung, three bedrooms, all white-carpeted, pool and Jacuzzi shared with the house across the pool, which was empty now. A beautifully planted yard and terrace in the back, and—again—tons of memorabilia. Most comfortable.

Mary claims not to know much about running her house. I thought of all those celebrities who say, "Oh, I can't even boil water," or "I don't know how to balance a checkbook," and you soon find out they can serve a seven-course meal and must know how to balance a checkbook because they own their own TV station. But this evening I began to believe Mary, because of the following incident.

We had drinks in the living room, which contained a bar area complete with ice maker. Soon we moved into the kitchen, where Bob began to whip up an elaborate omelette. By then Mary suggested we replenish our drinks. I said, "I'll do it." "Fine," she replied, "you know where the ice is, over in the bar area." At that time we were both standing right by her refrigerator. I opened the freezer door and, sure enough, there was an ice maker and a heaping bin of cubes. "There's ice right here!" I said.

"Where?"

"Right in here."

She peeked in and spoke with wonder, "Why, there is, isn't

there?" I said something about how she must be kidding. "No, I always get ice from the bar in there." Bob and I threw each other a glance that said, "Well, I'll be dammed," just as Mary said "Well, isn't that good to know!"

After dinner we went in the outside Jacuzzi, where we soaked a while before jumping into the pool. It was a clear, starry night, an easy night to let yourself be swallowed up in optimism. I went to sleep cloaked in it.

Mary had phoned her retired stage manager, Steve Meyer, to meet us the following day. Steve had worked with Mary on two shows, *The Sound of Music* and *Jenny*, and Mary wasn't sure he wanted to play theatre again. By the time our meeting was over, however, Steve had agreed to work on our show as production stage manager, and he was to begin the very next day, helping Mary learn her lines. We celebrated with a drink and a huge *salade niçoise*.

In the early afternoon Bob and I packed for the ride into L.A., where he was to investigate actresses for Sylvia. I was flying back to New York to do likewise. Driving back in the cushy limo, Bob said, "Well, Jim, we're finally on a roll, do you believe it?"

"Yes—and about bloody time!"

HELLO, DOLLY!

Back in New York, the serious search for Sylvia was on. Some actresses we couldn't locate; some were already committed to other projects; others didn't want to sign for a long enough period.

Reports came in from the coast: Mary was learning her lines, working with Steve Meyer every day; also, she didn't feel like a "Leatrice" and would like a simpler, more American name. She was getting utchy about who was going to play Sylvia. Bob got in touch with Alexis Smith, arranged a meeting, and gave her a script without making a definite offer. He said she looked terrific, was totally charming, funny, so right for Sylvia, and was looking forward to reading the script. He felt obliged to tell Mary he'd met with her, and when he did she said, "Well, of course, I don't want to stand in the way of the play . . . !" At which Bob had to say quickly, "No, no—back up, back up, it's you we want." "Well, then," Mary muttered, "I keep thinking about Carol Channing."

Carol had been mentioned before. God only knows the lady was acknowledged as being talented, but the consensus among everyone connected with the play was that she had become almost a parody of herself, a bigger-than-life Lorelei Lee/Dolly Levi doll with that strange high baby-voice and those enormous eyes that seemed to be in a constant state of surprise, as if asking, "What—what did I say that was so funny?"

Years ago I had seen her in *Lend an Ear,* in which she was brilliant, and I knew that, beneath whatever she had become, there was a fine, multitalented actress. I had the least resistance to Carol of any of our producing team. Mary and she were good friends and, according to Mary, they'd always wanted to work together. I could also imagine a chemistry existing onstage between the two of them, exactly because they *are* so different.

I had known Carol when we were both handled by the same agent, Barron Polan, when I was working in nightclubs as part of the comedy team of Jim Kirkwood and Lee Goodman. We often spent Sunday nights with Barron and other clients. However, I'd not seen Carol in some time.

On Wednesday, October 9, 1985, the big push for Carol came. We were once again handled by the same agency, William Morris, so I called up Esther Sherman and asked if she'd get a script over to Carol. I phoned Carol in the late afternoon to see if she'd received it and got her husband and manager, Charles Lowe, who sounded jolly and said Carol was out but would read the script that night, and should she call me late that evening or in the morning? I said in the morning—no reason to pressure anyone.

Charles, whom I'd only met a couple of times, is a legend in his own right. He is known to attend every one of Carol's performances, to start standing ovations, and do everything in his power to back up his star. He has a reputation as a nudge, but I had never worked with him, so this was only hearsay.

The next morning the phone call that awakened me was from Carol Channing. "Jimmy, darling, it's been a long time since we've seen each other, but listen—I love the play, I'm mad about it, I want to do it, but first I want to have a meeting with you so you can tell me what *you* want. Sylvia's a marvelous character and I want to know exactly how you see her." I told her I was delighted by her reaction and we made a date to have lunch at her place at the Regency on Sunday.

One of the quicker reactions! I was way up, phoned Bob on the coast and Mary and Kevin—all parties concerned. Everyone else was suddenly way up, too, and again I was given my orders from Bob and Kevin about how to conduct the meeting.

Sunday morning I cabbed it to the Regency and was greeted most warmly by Charles Lowe and Carol. Both had read the play and were high on it. Carol looked wonderful. On stage she wears a strange makeup with a red line drawn across the lower bridge of her nose, a high blush, an overly made-up mouth, and—well, enough makeup to make you feel you could carve your initials in it with your fingernails. In repose and without the clown makeup, it's a very pretty face.

Charles was exceedingly professional; he stayed long enough to order our luncheon and get through the amenities, then took his leave with "You and Carol should talk about this alone; I'll be back later."

Once we were alone, Carol went on most enthusiastically about the play and the part of Sylvia Glenn. She spoke highly of Mary and what a presence she was onstage, how they got along like gangbusters and even put each other on.

Then she slipped into talk of all the imitations she could do as Sylvia. I played dumb, because I didn't know exactly what she was getting at. After a while she asked how I saw her in the part. I told her I hoped she would play the part differently from Dolly or Lorelei, but as a rather strong, bitchy survivor of the movies, and I thought it would be terrific if she got rid of the blond wig and wore a dark one, which would make her resemble the kind of actress Rosalind Russell was, or even Crawford. She went for that immediately and with glee. "Yes," she said, "I'd love it. You see, Mary's hair is sort of a fuzzy orange-blonde, so I could wear a black wig like one of those old-time dames."

"Well, not black—that might be too much—a dark-brown one."

"Yes, almost sable, that would be good."

Then she said, "You know, at the end of Act One, when I snatch Mary's wig off, well, I think it's only fair if she yanks mine off. Because, you see, she'll have her orange fuzz underneath, and then with me you'll see this sort of gray fuzz and maybe one of those bands that hold down my own hair."

"Great!"

The meeting was going along fine until she once again went into the idea of Sylvia doing impressions of Louella Parsons and Hedda Hopper and Dietrich and "all those other ladies." I know what a good mimic Carol is, but I didn't quite see how that would fit into the play. I finally said, "I don't think we have to get into too many impressions. We don't want to stray from your character and confuse the audience." Finally Carol said, "You're right, the hell with them." Relief.

Over lunch we spoke of Sylvia and her relationship to Leatrice, her past, her husbands, her underlying drive, and we were in agreement. We spent from twelve-thirty until after four o'clock. Good food, good talk, serious, intense, but with its share of fun and laughs.

Charles came in toward the end, and there was a tinge of heaviness in the air when he started talking about the producers and who they were, what their track record was, and how important it was to have strong producers who knew exactly what they were doing every step of the way. I found it difficult to defend our group, because, although we had Bob with his London credits, it was obvious Cheryl would not be on deck as captain because of her general health, and Kevin had done nothing on the stage. They were pleased that Alan Wasser was to be general manager; he had managed *Sugar Babies* when Carol toured it with Bobby Morse, and even though it turned into a disaster, they apparently liked Alan.

Charles said Mary would undoubtedly want Irene Sharaff to do the costumes and she'd already gotten her own stage manager, so who would do the sets and lighting? "Lighting is terribly important," Charles said, "especially for a comedy." It was almost as if they were adding up who had who to do what. There was nothing outright dangerous about this talk, but I knew there would be forthcoming suggestions. They were both interested in which theatre we might play in New York. I told them there'd been talk of the Imperial. Their eyes lit up at this: "Yes," Carol said, "we should play a large house, because Mary and I are both used to that. The Imperial would be perfect." I saw dollar signs in their eyes. They never give up, Carol and Charles; they want to work and earn big bucks, and that's the way it will be until they're dragged away. God bless them!

All in all, it was a most pleasant meeting, and Carol was especially funny when I was about to leave. "Now, Jimmy," she said, "Mary's not going to want to fly around the stage in this one, is she?"

"I hope not."

"And, dear, she's not going to wash her hair onstage, either?"

"No, we'll turn off the water and hide the soap!"

"Good," she said, "because if she does—I'll do my impressions!"

HURDLES

Finally the production was pulling together, tours were being mapped, contracts were being ironed out, etc. On Thursday, October 17, I was lecturing at a university in Kentucky, and early in the morning I turned on the TV and there was Mary Martin being interviewed by Jane Pauley—there was to be a huge tribute called *Our Hearts Belong to Mary* the following Sunday at the Shubert Theatre—and Jane Pauley, after talking about that, said, "But the most exciting thing, I hear you're coming back to Broadway in a new play!" Mary was definitely curt. "Well, we're talking about it." Jane went on about what a joy that would be, but Mary remained resolutely mute. Oh my God, I thought, something's gone awry!

Back in New York, I made calls to Bob and Kevin; things were proceeding apace with only minor hitches: we'd lost our set designer, Tony Walton, because of a Mike Nichols project and were now considering Santo Loquasto or Doug Schmidt. But we had Irene Sharaff for the clothes, and they were thinking of hiring Johnson-Liff for casting. This coming Sunday was the tribute to Mary; we were all going, and the next day, Monday, a summit meeting was set up at Mary's hotel with Carol and all the producers. This would be the first time the production people—particularly Kevin Eggers, who up to now had kept a *very* low profile—would meet the stars.

Saturday morning, October 19, I received an early call from Charles Lowe about Mary and Carol and the benefit. "Well," Charles said, his voice deadly serious, "Carol goes on first, and then Mary and Nancy Reagan, so that means *two* standing ovations to start, one for Carol and one for Mary"—and the President's wife, one supposed. Charles wanted to be sure that I remembered and that I was to take an active part in starting them. Then he said, "There's some good news and then some other news."

"What does that mean?"

"The good news is that Mary has rented a place for Carol right out near her in Rancho Mirage so they can go over their lines in November. The other news is that Mary has some arrangements that have to be ironed out with Floria Lasky. I'm pretty sure they'll be worked out, and I think it has to do with matinees."

I told Charles I'd seen Mary on the "Today" show and she was extremely offhand about doing a new play. I told him I thought the perfect time and place for an announcement of their forthcoming costarring vehicle was obviously when they were onstage together at the tribute Sunday. Charles indicated this would be taken care of. Then he came forth with this: "Don't you think it would be a good idea for Carol and you to have lunch together on Tuesday, so you can discuss the meeting we will have had the day before, on Monday?"

Although that threw me a bit I said, "Well, yes, if Carol would like that."

"Yes, she would. Now, would you like to have lunch with Carol Channing at her apartment, or would you rather have lunch with Carol Channing at The Russian Tea Room?"

Suddenly the formality of "Carol Channing" struck me as odd; it had always been, until that second, simply "Carol." Now we were suddenly into this "Carol Channing" mode. Before I could reply, Charles said, "Yes, I think it would be better if you were seen at The Russian Tea Room with Carol Channing."

My impulse, of course, was to say "Not THE CAROL CHANNING!" but I merely agreed and we signed off.

The next day was *Our Hearts Belong to Mary.* I had asked Dina Merrill to go with me. I am most fond of her; she's as lovely inside as she is beautiful on the outside. We both have houses in

East Hampton, and a few summers ago had played husband and wife at the John Drew Theatre in a play I'd written entitled *Surprise!*

I was so looking forward to Carol and Mary announcing their comeback to Broadway in *Legends!* We met Bob and his date, Jill Fuller, for a drink at Sardi's, and then moved across the street to the Shubert, where *A Chorus Line* was having its night off. The theatre was packed, all very formal, posh, black-tie.

The show started with a spotlight on Mary and Nancy Reagan appearing together in the stage-left box. They kissed and hugged, big applause all around, had their picture taken; then the show proper began. The Yale Glee Club, John Raitt, Robert Preston, followed by Carol and Jerry Herman doing a funny takeoff to the tune of "My Heart Belongs to Daddy." I thought at the end of that perhaps Carol would make an announcement, but she said not a word. They showed the filmed part of the Ford Anniversary Show, with Mary doing her fashion number, a filmed section of *Peter Pan,* and a wonderfully funny filmed salute from Larry Hagman in which he was attired in a beautiful suit, standing in a rather formal room, delivering warm words to his mother, at the end of which he simply fell forward on his face into a roomful of water, which had not been discernible at all when he was standing. The last shot of Larry was of him floating face down, still clad in his suit. It was hysterical.

Soon Mary was onstage, receiving an ovation. She sang a duet with her beautiful daughter, Heller Halliday. Then Nancy Reagan came on; she had actually appeared in a small part in one of Mary's hits, *Lute Song,* and this evening she wobbled through a version of a number from that show, "Mountain High, Valley Low."

All evening everyone who appeared said how much Mary was missed on Broadway, and I kept thinking, especially when Carol and she were standing side by side during the finale, that Mary would raise her hand for quiet and say, "Actually, I will be starting rehearsals in a new play, costarring with my dear friend Carol Channing." But not one phuquing word.

After the show we all trooped over to the Marriott Hotel, a monument of bad taste, where we were ushered to assigned tables in the ballroom. Jerry Herman and I flanked Carol; then there was Dina on my other side, Bob Regester, Jill Fuller, Radie Harris, Charles, of course, and several others. I immediately asked Carol why Mary or she hadn't announced the play. Carol said, "Oh, damn, I know, but it was really up to Mary; it would have been such a good time!" Mary made a grand entrance, standing ovation from all. About a half-hour later a man from *People* magazine asked if I would mind having my picture taken with Mary and Carol, so I joined Carol at Mary's table. As the three of us scrunched together for a photo, Mary chirped, "Oh, here's our dear author."

"You wouldn't know it," I said. "I was hoping you'd announce the play tonight."

"Why," Mary said in mock surprise, "we're having our big meeting tomorrow!"

What did one have to do with the other? I had my picture taken, went back to my table, and would have sulked the rest of the evening except for the cheerful presence of Dina and Carol, who was exceptionally funny. She's got a curt tongue on her and does not easily suffer fools. When Dina and I left, I kissed Carol good night and we said "Till tomorrow."

"I can't wait," Carol added.

Neither could I. I smelled a troublesome ingredient but couldn't begin to put a finger on it.

ONE TINY LITTLE HICCUP

We were all to meet at Mary's suite at the Wyndham at three. We bumped into Alan Wasser in front of the hotel and had just gotten into the elevator when Carol and Charles breezed in. Introductions all around, Kevin and Bob's first meeting with Carol. We talked about the incredible space given to Mary and Nancy Reagan in the papers: they were on the front page of the *News* and the *Post*.

We were let into Mary's canary-yellow suite by dear Dickie

Quayle, only we had to negotiate floor space. All of the papers had been opened to pages containing either pictures of or feature articles on Mary and Mrs. Reagan, and the floor looked as if it had been prepared for an enormous puppy-training session.

We all made our way, with some difficulty, to seats, trying not to step on either the President's wife's face or Mary's. Soon Cheryl arrived, and in came Tom Davis with a rather shit-eating grin, I thought. Then Mary made a star entrance, dressed beautifully, as always. "What a night last night, wasn't it? Oh, it's so exciting, and today we went to lunch at '21' and everyone came over and— oh, we had such a good time!"

More introductions. After all these months, Kevin finally got to meet Mary. Carol and Mary sat together on a loveseat; I'd brought my camera, so I had a picture taken with the two of them which would be my Christmas card if things worked out: "Merry Christmas from the Kirkwoods!" Mary and Carol giggled and joked about the house Mary had secured for Carol in Rancho Mirage. It was a model home, and everyone kidded about how Carol would have to expect tours to be conducted through the house, and what if she were taking a shower? Maj arrived, looking healthy and happy and strong. Small talk continued, and suddenly there we all were, sitting, awaiting official notification of the forthcoming production of this play. Finally I motioned for Bob to step into an adjoining bedroom with me.

"Hey, Bob," I said, "is anyone going to officially announce why we're all here, are we going to celebrate or what?"

"Yes," he said, "I'll start that right now."

We walked back into the living room, sat down, and Bob said, "Of course, the reason we're all here today is to celebrate—"

Mary cut in with: "Well, *if* we do this together—"

She got no further than that. Bob and I immediately stood, headed for the nearest windows, opened two of them, and started to climb out as I said, "I cannot hear one more 'if.' Mary, if you keep this up, you're going to be on the front pages again tomorrow: Playwright jumps from Mary Martin's window."

Everyone laughed, someone came over to pull us back in, and Mary giggled, saying, "No, no, everything's all right." Just as everyone breathed a sigh of relief, she added in a little-girl voice: "There's just one little hiccup."

"Hiccup?" someone asked.

"Yes," she said, still using the baby-girl voice, "just one tiny little hiccup, that's all."

Our faces registered varying degrees of shock, curiosity, annoyance. I glanced at Carol; she looked somewhat stricken, and I couldn't blame her.

"What kind of hiccup?" I finally asked.

"Oh, let's don't talk about that now. I hate to be in on the business side of all this," Mary chirped.

Tom Davis spoke. "Yes, we'll all have a meeting tomorrow morning, and then I'll tell you."

No, no. No one wanted to wait out another day to find out what this hiccup meant. Tom said no, they'd get into that tomorrow, and not in front of Mary. Everyone insisted a meeting be held immediately. So Cheryl, Bob, Kevin, Alan, and Tom stood and said they'd go down to the bar right now and talk this over. I demurred. I was stunned that at this late date, after we'd all been called together to celebrate the finalization of months of "what if"s, the bedsheets were still pied, preventing us from all hopping in together.

They took their leave, and I was left sitting there looking at Carol and Mary and Dickie; Maj had disappeared. Carol and Mary went on talking about this and that, and Mary kept saying, "I just *hate* the business side of all this, don't you?" Finally Mary looked at me and said, "Would you like a drink, dear?"

"No, thank you," I said, standing. "I really have to go home now." I kissed Carol goodbye on the cheek; then Mary walked me to the door. I sighed deeply and said, "Christ, I hope this thing finally works out; it's getting to me now." She kissed me on both cheeks and said she hoped so, too.

The minute the door closed, I was livid, wanted to ring the bell and when the door opened, clip Peter Pan's wings. How dispiriting to pull this delaying tactic, to let Carol sit there with egg on her face, to play the little girl who just didn't want to get involved in nasty business details.

Bob Regester had said he'd leave a message on my machine that evening if there was news—good, bad, or otherwise—about resolving the mysterious hiccup. There was no message.

OTHER PROBLEMS, ETC.

Next morning, calls from all parties. The hiccup turned out to be this: Mary—and I imagined this to be a dictum of Larry's—would do the play but she would only do seven performances a week, as opposed to the usual eight. This not only meant renegotiating my contract as an author, but, more important, it cut the weekly profit down enormously and put us in jeopardy. For instance, if the weekly "nut"—break-even that the show must make each week to keep it operating in the black—was $165,000, the loss of that eighth performance could add up to between $25,000 and $30,000, which, on a so-so week, might easily bring us below the $165,000 mark and put us in the red.

Besides that, the cast, the crew, the theatre, the staff were all being paid on the basis of eight performances per week, but the show would accrue the income for only seven. Not a healthy deal, especially for the backers; that eighth performance could mean the difference between profit and loss.

We were all frustrated. Bob called, nervous and agitated, and asked me to meet him at Alan Wasser's office, where we found Alan on the phone to the Ahmanson; everyone was manning the computers trying to juggle the subscription list and shuffle it around to fit a seven-performance schedule. Alan was doing everything to make it pull together.

Late that afternoon Bob, Esther, and I met for a drink, and it looked as if Alan had finally made an arrangement by which Mary would play seven performances one week, eight the next, back and forth during the L.A. engagement; then all other theatres would be locked in to a seven-performance deal.

Bob said Mary was returning to California the next morning and asked if I would call to say goodbye. I finally dragged myself to a pay phone, hoping she'd be out and I could merely leave word that I'd phoned. But Mary answered, all breathless. "Oh, I've been out shopping; we've been having such a good time." She went on as if there'd been nary a hiccup in a carload; I was rather silent. Finally Mary said, "Darling, I wasn't trying to be difficult at all,

I really wasn't. It's just that I've never missed performances. I'm older, but even so, I don't want to start missing them now. I love you and the play, and won't Carol be absolutely wonderful, and I adore her, and—" I finally squeezed in a goodbye and turned the phone over to Bob.

The next day I met Bob and Kevin for drinks at Sardi's to talk about setting up casting calls for the other parts, meetings with the set designer, etc. Just as we were sitting down—Bob excused himself to go to the john—a woman turned to her companion at the bar and said in a very loud voice, "I don't care, Mary Martin is one of the nastiest people I've ever met in show business." I was so amazed to hear this bad review that I didn't say anything, but after a beat or so Kevin turned to me and said, "Yes, I heard that, too." We did not feel it imperative to pass this on to Bob when he returned.

The following week was a busy one. Clifford Williams arrived; we met with Jeff Johnson, Vinnie Liff, and Andy Zerman (Johnson-Liff), who would be our casting people, and set up readings. Doug Schmidt was now going to do the sets; for some reason we had lost Irene Sharaff or she had lost us, and both women now wanted Freddy Wittop to do the costumes; he'd worked with both Mary and Carol before. Another trip was also planned to California to search for a good black actress to play Aretha, the maid.

Steve Meyer phoned from Rancho Mirage to give me cuts or suggestions for changes from Mary. I told him I hoped there would be a minimum of this because it tended to undermine the authority of the director when the stars kept coming to the author for changes. Steve agreed but said Mary was adamant about learning her lines *before* rehearsal, so as many as possible of the changes and cuts that had to be made, should be made now. Clifford said, as long as we were going to Los Angeles to read black ladies, "Perhaps we should go down to Rancho Mirage [where by that time Mary and Carol would be going over lines] and pay a visit to some *white* ladies and set the ground rules." In other words, one doesn't want the two stars left alone with the script and stage manager doing excessive rewrites on their own.

Clifford and Carol had not yet met, so a breakfast meeting was set up at the Dorset for the three of us. The evening before, I went to Carol's to give her cuts and changes, which she took like a trouper. She'd had a small operation on her teeth or jaw, and her face was swollen; she didn't want to meet Clifford at the Dorset the next morning, not looking the way she did, although to me it was simply a slight swelling on one side of her jaw. I had to cajole her into letting me bring Clifford to her suite the next day.

"No, no," she said, "I don't want to meet him when I'm looking like this, I'll scare him." But I told her she looked fine and it was important for them to meet before she went to California.

So the next day Clifford and I went to the Regency in the late morning. Perversely enough, Carol, who was worried about her appearance, was wearing her bizarre stage makeup: a dark, dark base, very heavy on the rouge, and what I call "black-spider" eye makeup, that red line across her nose, and what she called her "Eva Gabor $8.95 wig." She was also clad in a white terrycloth robe, decorated by various stains. I could tell from the expression on Clifford's face the minute they shook hands that she had, in fact, terrified him.

When Carol spoke of her wig, she said: "The reason I can't get good real blonde hair anymore is that the nuns no longer shave their heads! That's how I used to get such good hair. Especially when I'm in London, I chase blonde women down the street—there are so many Swedes and Norwegians, and I try to buy their hair, but they won't sell it."

"Why don't you get hair from dead people?" I asked.

"Dead people?" Carol asked. "Mmn . . ." she mused, thinking it over.

"Make a deal with a mortuary, or get blonde women to sign predeath agreements!"

She laughed and then said to Charles, "Maybe we should investigate that."

She and Clifford talked about the play—Clifford saying it should be done with style and class—and it was clear she was no dummy, she has a brain and harbored a thought far beneath the surface that American comedy is much different from British humor. Implicit in this was the fact that she hoped Clifford thought so too.

When we left to go to readings, Clifford turned to me and said, "Good heavens, she looked so strange I had to remove my glasses. Does she always look like that?"

"Not quite," I said. "I think she was making up for her swollen jaw."

"That makeup would detract from anything. She doesn't wear that onstage, does she?"

"Probably, but under stage lighting it must look different."

"Let us hope so."

In a day or so there was a call from Tom Davis, saying Mary was delighted Clifford and I were coming out there to stay. "No, no," I said, "we're not staying."

"Oh, Mary thought you were coming to stay with her and Carol."

"No, we have to cast the rest of the parts, get understudies, go over sets and lighting and costumes. We're just coming down for a few days to lay the ground rules, see how Mary and Carol are coming along, read through the play, go over cuts."

The next phone call I received was from Carol, very upset. "Darling, those cuts! Now that I look over them, they totally diminish my character. My whole reason for being an actress. You can't do that."

"Well . . ."

"I mean it, dear. Jimmy, you have to come over to my place and let me tell you how I became Carol Channing. Then you'll understand why you must reinstate the cuts or I'll just have nothing to play."

We made a date for the following Monday evening. Clifford and I were immersed for several days in readings for Aretha, Martin Klemmer, and the stripper. There were good candidates for all parts, but no one had really struck lightning yet.

The next interesting phone call I received was from Tom Davis again. "Mary doesn't want Clifford to come down at all."

"But just a few days ago the word was that she was looking forward to us coming down there to *stay!*"

"She's changed her mind; she doesn't think they'll be ready. She doesn't want to read through the play for him either. She only wants you to come down—this should just be family. So would you please phone her and either give in or convince her to let him come down?"

I thought, Wouldn't it be amusing, for once, if one of the producers, Kevin, for instance, made one of these phone calls? But she'd only met him once, probably didn't even remember his name. So I phoned. "Mary, I talked to Tom, and Clifford is only coming down for one day."

"He doesn't have to, you know."

"I know, but it's only to get to know you better, to *talk* about the script, to become better acquainted."

"But we won't read for him."

"All right, I'll explain that to him."

"We won't be ready."

After I'd reassured her about three more times that she wouldn't have to read for him, she said, "Well, all right. But we'll see, maybe we will."

After I'd hung up it struck me: Is this the way it's going to be? Am I to have no peace at all, is this going to be a plague upon both my houses? It was at that moment I decided this was definitely going to be a unique experience and vowed I would write a book on it, no matter what the outcome.

HOW CAROL CHANNING BECAME CAROL CHANNING

Monday, November 4, 1985

Busy day, pouring rain for eight hours straight. By the time I got to Carol's suite at the Regency I was tired, hungry, feeling as wet and attractive as a sewer rat and about as cranky. As soon as Charles let me in I announced the mood of the evening, and when Carol heard me complaining she appeared from the bedroom, laughing and saying, "Oh, I love to hear that, that's honest." The two of them fussed over me, ordered a double vodka and dinner from room service, let me take off soggy shoes, and gave me a towel. They made over me like a stray dog that had wandered in from a storm; they were obviously trying to get me in the best possible mood, and they succeeded.

I put my tape recorder on, mainly so I'd get her complaints correct about the cuts and clearly understand the reasons for specific changes I might have to make.

After Charles had done everything he could to make me happy he disappeared, leaving Carol and me alone to talk about her character.

"Jimmy, this is the thing. I'm crazy about the script, I absolutely love it. But what got cut is the part that meant so very much to me . . . when you finally get to *know* the woman. I couldn't believe it! Here—" She opened the script to the part where Sylvia Glenn tells Leatrice about her childhood, where she describes her mother as telling her she might as well stay locked in the backyard even though she's lonely because, the mother says, "You're going to be lonely for most of your life, so you might as well get used to it." Carol's attitude was absolutely focused and intent on the parts that revealed the reasons for her character's behavior. "Now, look," she went on, "this is the part that made me break my heart. This is the first time she ever got up onstage—in school—and she got laughs and smelled blood and everybody noticed her. They didn't notice her when she was good, here on page two-sixteen. And she wanted her father and mother to notice her, and I want to know that. That's how she got to taking off her clothes [in public, later], because she wanted to be noticed and— that's how Bette Midler did and—look, I'm not a superstar."

"Yes, you are. You're a superstar."

"Well," she said in a throwaway voice, "yes, in your and my books, because we came up together."

"You're a superstar to the audience; they love you."

"No, what I mean is Joan Crawford and—"

"Oh," I said, "one of *those!*"

"Yes, and . . . Mae West. This is the thing. I'm not that, but the very thing that made me cry over them, the very thing that touched me . . . And I remember you saying one sentence when I said I'd do the play, 'I want to get a little more touching with these women,' and, by God, the first cut was about that, and that's the very reason I wanted to do it."

I argued that there was still a good deal of character exposition in the play, but Carol was adamant. She told me about her own mother telling her she was too tall, a stringbean, that she was no beauty and probably never would be. Drinks and dinner soon arrived, and we talked while eating. "You see," she went on, "thank God, we have the excuse after we eat the hashish brownies to *tell* about ourselves, and that's what I want to know. Look, you say in the script when she enters—she's a survivor. Survivors! I'm one myself, and you're one, too. Survivors never say, That's how my mother did me in. They say, Isn't it wonderful, isn't it great to find out the *why* of things! Not: Oh, poor little me, my mother did me in, and that's the end of that. Jesus, that's a loser. Not this woman, that's what I loved about her. Sylvia doesn't cry about herself; she says to Leatrice, It took me all these years to figure out why."

Carol was obviously on a roll, and it was a fascinating one. She was going to tell me how she became Carol Channing, and by this time I was hooked. "Now, all anyone knows is his or her own experience. As I said, *I* had a mother like this. Rose, Gypsy Rose Lee's mother. We all [in show business] had the same mother. We all look at Rose and say, 'Oh, there she is, there's Mommy.' We don't hate our mommies then; we don't have the perspective, especially if she has frailties or faults. My mother was just like this. I was never going to be pretty, I was too tall, I was . . . Look, somebody nominated me for secretary of the student body in school—I was eight years old, okay—and the procedure was, I had to get up onstage in the school auditorium and make my campaign speech. Well, I didn't know what to say. I couldn't say I was smarter than they were, I couldn't say I was better in any way, so I did an imitation of the principal of the school, saying"—and now she did their voices, all distinctively different, the chemistry teacher with a thick Russian-Yiddish accent—" 'Go to the polls and vote for Carol,' and then I did Miss Berard, 'Go to the polls and vote for Carol,' and then I did our chemistry teacher, who blew up the class on an average of once every term, 'Go to da polz und vote for Carol.' Well, by this time they were laughing. I heard that first laugh. Aha! And I thought, They're coming toward me, not away from me. Not a word my mother says is true about me, not one word. Suddenly you're soaring, you've got these wings and you're flying, and they're coming toward you and you're going toward them and the tennis ball is going back and forth and the bubble burst and the illusion that you're going to be lonely, locked in the backyard and kept there and told you're going to spend the rest of your life lonely because there's something very wrong with you, down deep *very* wrong. You're revolting, and on top of that you're not even very feminine and . . . because Daddy loves you so dearly. Because my father did adore me. So Mother's sitting there drumming her fingers because she's nothing like you. Because, if a mother gets a Mary Martin or a Carol Channing, she's got this mushroom coming up under her and it's very frightening and disconcerting, because she doesn't know what to do. She can't rescue you, because you're not a cripple, so she *makes* you a cripple. 'Goddamnit, you're going to be a cripple!' And, woman to woman, they beat you up.

"So suddenly you're onstage and you find out the whole thing's a lie, it's not true, and on top of which, although I'm not the cutest girl in class, never was, and very tall and . . . I could *act* like Marjorie Gould, and I did Marjorie Gould for them and—" now Carol's voice switched to sexy babytalk—"and I did Marjorie Gould for them, and I swished my ass around that stage like Marjorie Gould never *thought* of doing, and it was so exciting and so sexy, and I did it *better* than Marjorie Gould! Well, naturally I got elected. I found out I could be anyone I wanted to be on the stage. I could create the illusion, and people would say to me, 'You know, offstage you don't look like much of anything, but onstage there's something funny about you.' "

Carol's eyes were bright and gleaming, and those are some eyes to begin with. "It's the elation! I could feel—I can turn into Marlene Dietrich if I want, I can be Gracie Allen, I can be Harpo Marx. I can be funny, I can be anything I want. When I got offstage I ran, I ran—they didn't want to let me go, naturally—but I ran into the cloak closet and I prayed and I thought, I'll do anything in the world to get back on that stage again. Anything! Anything in the world. I'll crawl across the desert. I gotta get back on that stage again, because this is the only truth there is, because there's this miserable home life.

"But it's that kind of mother most theatre people have, or they wouldn't have to soar, they wouldn't have to go through the top of the tent. I never *didn't* get elected; I got to do every faculty member and got to say the minutes and make the motions like every kid that had made them. I had to get re-elected, so I had to stay good and nice to everybody, and it got to be a holy performance. Talk about unhappy childhoods—I had an enchanted childhood. I created it right up there onstage. It was enchanted, and I did it because I had to get away from my *mother*. That was the only truth there ever was. And suddenly—God, wasn't I fetching and attractive and so girly-girly and anything I wanted to be, and boys asked me to dance with them because they believed that illusion up there."

Carol sighed. "And that's how you get to be president of the class, because they sense your whole life is dedicated to them. The cruelty of a mother to a Mary Martin or a Carol Channing. And finally it takes until this age to realize she was frightened. She was frightened of losing her husband. She didn't have anything, so she was forcing me to be like she was, and because I was an only child I thought I had a mother like everyone else's, but she forced me to soar, to go over the top. And that frightened her."

She went on to praise her father, who was a religious worker, very high up in the Christian Science Church. Carol absolutely worshipped him, but she would always go back to her mother. "Do you know what she did when I got my first really starring role, in *Gentlemen Prefer Blondes?* She came backstage after opening night and, oh, she had a good one, the only thing she said was 'You know, Carol, you hit one note wrong. I can't remember where it was, but it jars the whole audience.'

"Well, I was—I asked, 'Is it in "Little Rock"?'

" 'I don't know,' she said, 'but the whole audience goes, Oh my God! Now, it could be the second, it could be the third number—actually it could be anywhere.'

"I said, 'Could you come back to see the show again so you can tell me where it is?' So, anyhow, I went to our musical director, Milt Rosenstock, and I told him what my mother'd told me, and he said, 'Tell your mother to go fuck herself! I would tell you if you hit a wrong note.' What it did, it made me so tentative on the second night, when all the reviewers were there, so I said to Milt, 'You have to go over every note with me.' He said, 'There *is* no wrong note!' "

When Carol paused, I said, "What a devil she must have been. I'd love to have a look at her."

"Charles said she had the meanest face he ever saw. But, do you know, most people thought she was a lovely, cultured Christian Scientist. She just sat there viciously hating my father. She was vicious because she was frightened and jealous of everyone else."

Of course, after all this hype, I agreed to restore most of the cuts that referred to Sylvia Glenn's (née Carol Channing's) childhood, and we went over them in detail to make sure we got them straight. We also talked about the cuts and name changes Steve Meyer had sent on that Mary had made. Like me, Carol could not understand Mary's reluctance to use the names of anyone she knew. As Carol said, "It's not Mary Martin talking about Bob Hope or Henry Kissinger—I mean, I know them, too. It's Leatrice Monsee." Again the tone dropped to conspiracy. "What about the name thing?"

"Well," I told Carol, "a week or so ago, when I talked to Steve, he said Mary just couldn't see herself as a Leatrice Monsee and I'd better think up another name. So I've been thinking of dumb little all-American names like Daisy, June, Mitzi—"

"Oh, I hope it's Leatrice Monsee. That's so ridiculous and silly for Mary Martin to be Leatrice Monsee, it's something Sam Goldwyn would hang on her. Like Bernard Delfont [the English producer]—he named himself Bernard Delfont, he doesn't look like a Bernard Delfont. It's a long Russian name. But 'Daisy,'" Carol said with disgust, "if I call her Daisy, that's not funny, but Leatrice Monsee, for Mary to be Lea-ah-trice, that's fun."

"Well, the last time I talked to Steve, I started giving him a list of these other names and he said, 'Wait a minute, don't give her any other names to play with now.' I asked why, and he said lately she's been calling herself Leatrice Monsee, keeps referring to herself as Leatrice."

"Oh, good," Carol said. After a while—it was getting late—Charles came back to join us for the wrap-up. I told him, "My God, I've never seen such energy in my life!"

"Yes," he agreed, "and you caught her at the end of the day. Wait'll you get her in the morning!"

We laughed and started to say our goodbyes, but Carol wasn't quite finished. "Now, tell me about Clifford Williams. Has he ever directed an American comedy? These two ladies are strictly American types, these two ladies are not British. Now, Freddy Wittop [our costume designer] lends himself to the individual, so with me he's bigger than life—the buttons, the lapels, everything has to be bigger. Clifford Williams at one point said, 'But we want it elegant, don't we? Always in good taste.' And it scared me. All actors are touchy. I had a bad experience once with Lindsay Anderson. 'Ah-ah,' he'd say, 'not too far out, she goes overboard, watch her!' But, Jimmy, if I'm not bigger than life I'm a failure. When Clifford was talking about 'not too bizarre,' I sat there and I got so hurt. I've failed before." Now she did a piss-elegant British accent. " 'The first time in your life you're going to give a rhally distinguished pahformance!'—that's what they're always saying to me. When I did *Bed Before Yesterday!*—'You're going to do it this way'—because some bitch told him I go too far; somebody said, Watch her, she goes overboard. If I'm not that, I'm nothing. The English worship American actresses, but they don't know what makes them. We grow Jimmy Durantes and they grow Ralph Richardsons. They call it 'bizarre,' but it's native with us. I could see it in his eyes." Then she aimed her eyes at me. "Does he go for our type?"

"Yes."

"Does he go for a sense of fun?"

"Yes, of course, he has a great sense of humor."

"You know him?"

"Yes." I told Carol how we'd met, when Clifford was origi-nally going to direct *P.S. Your Cat Is Dead.*

She was like a dog with a bone. "But does he go far out?"

I felt I was on the witness stand and my testimony was being taken down for use against me in case the waters ever became troubled between them, so I tried to change the subject. "The way you're talking to me tonight, I'd like for you to talk in the play."

"How do you mean?" Carol asked.

"The way you told me about your mother—that's Sylvia."

But I wasn't changing any subject; she had the bone in her mouth and she wasn't letting go. "If they don't want me to be bizarre, what the heck do they expect me to be? He's got to let us go ahead and be as trashy as we are. Two trashy movie stars. And you know him, and he understands Americans?"

"Yes." The grill was getting hot.

"You know, Claudette Colbert is not like Mary Martin; you know that?"

"Yes, I know."

"And Rex Harrison—they're within a certain type of draw-ing-room comedy, and that's quite different from us."

"Of course."

Her eyes remained on me; the judge and the jury were all hanging in there. "And he has a great sense of fun?"

"Yes, he really does."

Finally a sigh and: "I could tell he wanted to get along with us."

I quickly said, "It's late, and I have to get up in the morning, Carol. I'll see you in California with Mary. And Clifford will—"

"We won't do it for Clifford," she said. "We won't be ready. We'll do it for you, but we won't be ready for him."

"We'll just be there together, to celebrate and get to know one another better."

I gathered up my things, we said our good nights; I thanked them for their hospitality and Carol for her stories, which I totally enjoyed. On the way back I fell asleep in the cab.

CASTING

The day Clifford and Carol met for the first time, he and I went on to auditions and struck gold. Our casting people set up readings for us at a small Off-Broadway theatre on West 42nd Street. The three of them are enthusiastic, knowledgeable, considerate theatre folk.

The two parts we were vitally concerned with were Aretha Thomas, the maid, and Martin Klemmer, the producer. On this day we saw and heard many fine black actresses for the part of Aretha—a tricky role, because we needed someone both funny and warm and an actress who would not be *acting* the maid but would throw herself into the part wholeheartedly and *be* the maid, understand the kind of old-fashioned relationship a lady like that would have with a legend/star, in which they like each other so much they can joke about Sylvia being a broke actress and, on the other hand, Aretha can play the part, in front of Leatrice, of the archetypal black maid—with humor and without taking offense.

We were looking for someone who could, at Sylvia's request, play a modern-day version of Hattie McDaniel with a highly developed sense of perverse humor. Hard to find. On this day we'd read perhaps twelve actresses, and we were all heading out of the theatre, a bit the worse for wear, putting on our coats, gathering up the eight-by-ten photos with résumés we'd collected, when

Vinnie Liff said, "I'm sorry, but one actress just arrived and I think you should stay and see her."

Clifford said, "She's way late, and we really ought to go."

"But," said Vinnie, "she's come all the way up from Birmingham, Alabama. She's been visiting her father, who's ill. She was sent a script, loves the play and the part, and flew all the way up at her own expense to read. Won't you please see her?"

Well, of course, we'd see her. Annie-Joe Edwards was ushered in. A large black lady who'd been in *Ain't Misbehavin'* in London and several other shows. She apologized for being late and then completely knocked us out by whipping through two scenes with humor, energy, compassion, warmth, and, sometimes, an offbeat, sardonic slant to a line that had us roaring with laughter and elbowing each other in the ribs.

When she finished, the verdict was unanimous. We'd found our Aretha. What a joyous occasion, and an unusual one at that, when six or seven people can exchange glances and say, "Yes, that's it, that's her."

We shmoozed in the lobby of the theatre, and she handed us her picture with her résumé on the back, a further knockout. It read: "Vocal Stylist, Pianist, Conductor, Choral Arranger, Costume Designer, Hair Stylist, Writer, Composer, Fine Artist (Paints, Pencil Drawings, Greeting Cards), Cook, Yodeler, and *Performs full split.*"

The yodeler and full split got us. We could not imagine this huge lady doing a full split. I thought she might be dissembling and asked her if that was true. "Oh, yes," Annie-Joe said, "I do a full split!"

I was tempted to ask if she could do a full split and yodel at the same time. "We'll have to use it," I said to Clifford.

Finding Martin Klemmer was not as easy. We needed someone brash and comical, yet attractive and likable. Not an easy bill to fill. Several good actors were vying for the part, but there was not the unanimity we all felt about Annie-Joe.

The stripper was not an easy part to cast, either. We needed someone to arrive and deliver a "strip-o-gram" by mistake, an actor/dancer who could be sexy and outrageous without being in the least bit smarmy. The strip, intended for Aretha's about-to-be-married niece but mistakenly performed in front of Aretha,

Sylvia, and Leatrice when the party was called off, had to be done with a wide-eyed innocence and great brio, or else it could come off as dirty.

This part was extremely hard to audition for, because there was no set script for it outside of the opening dialogue. All the candidates had to work up their own routines, which were highly amusing, widely varied in style and content, and delivered with every attitude one could imagine. For obvious reasons, there was also an added embarrassment for these actor/dancers who were called upon to appear at a rehearsal hall and asked to perform an exuberant sexy striptease in front of six, seven, sometimes eight serious-looking, owl-eyed men sitting behind a long table, staring at them as if they were so much beef-on-the-hoof.

They came in all sizes and shapes, and with a variety of musical tapes, props, tambourines, drums, and costumes that attested to the actor's ingenuity. Naturally, many of them asked if they could perform to one person, and as the author I would be asked to come out from behind the table and sit in a straightback chair, to be played to and have a series of breakaway garments, G-strings, posing straps, and other beaded or fringed items draped about my person. I didn't know whether to laugh, cry, blush, shit, or go blind. So I tried to keep a version of the Mona Lisa smile plastered on my face while being seductionized by these talented dancers.

Sometimes I could not help bellowing with laughter. One fellow, working down to the nitty-gritty, flipped off his G-string, whipped it around, and flung it up in the air, only to have it catch on an overhead studio light and dangle there. We had to call a janitor with a ladder to retrieve it for him. Another handed me a pair of maracas, which I dutifully shook during his entire routine, going offbeat now and then, when my attention was pulled by whatever he was doing.

There was an extra added embarrassment in the situation. When these dancers finished their audition, they could not just walk out after the usual "Thank you very much, that was terrific, we'll be in touch." There would be such an array of clothing, boots, bandanas, G-strings, jockey shorts, and other oddities strewn about the studio that the dancer was forced to gather all this up, put on clothes in front of us, so that it was difficult to talk about his performance until he'd gone. We were all left in the awkward position of making small talk, such as:

"Where did you get that outfit?"

"My grandmother made it for me."

Or: "That was very good, very original."

"Thank you. I'm not a real stripper, you know. I was in *The Wiz* and *Hello, Dolly!*"

"Oh, yes, we know you're not a *real* stripper. Oh, I didn't mean you didn't do it well, you did, but . . ."

One day we had auditions at the Minskoff Studios, across the alley from the Shubert Theatre on one side and across the street from a busy office building on 44th Street. The dance studio had huge glass windows, and we could see tons of people lined up in each window of the building opposite, gazing in at seven men staring at an entire lineup of athletic black men stripped down to next to nothing, and wondering what sort of midday bacchanal was taking place.

Almost everyone auditioning had a good sense of humor, which didn't mean to say it wasn't an ordeal.

One fellow had a bit of "attitude," and when he finished, as he was gathering up his clothes—it was a gray, rainy day—he turned and said, "You all have some racket, sitting there having guys come in and strip for you."

"Yes," I said, "and we don't even have a show!"

He looked at me incredulously. "What?" he asked.

"No," I said, "I live in Connecticut. I'm very rich. Every few weeks I get bored, so I phone them"—I indicated the others sitting there—"and call for auditions."

For a second I had him; then he caught on and burst out laughing. We'd gone that far, so I added, "No, really, you were very good. Really excellent. Oh, by the way . . ." He was just going out the door now, stopped, and said, "Yes . . . ?" After which I asked, "You wouldn't be free for dinner tonight, would you?"

He howled, said, "You are definitely too much!" and took his leave.

These auditions were amusing for a while, but they also tore at my guts. The actor/dancers had to invest so much time in preparation. They had to scurry around, find appropriate music, work up a routine, and spend hours and hours—to say nothing of the energy and ingenuity it takes—putting together this one-man show, only to be told, "Thank you very much, we'll be in touch with your agent." There was a sadness about it. Especially now that there is so little theatrical work to be found. Many of them had backgrounds of distinguished professional credits.

On a day in mid-November, we hit the daily double. We found the perfect Martin Klemmer, our stripper, and an actress to stand by for both Carol and Mary. The stripper turned out to be Eric Riley, who'd appeared in *Dreamgirls* and *Ain't Misbehavin'* and also played Richie in the national company of *A Chorus Line*. Eric has a disarming smile, a great body, and a joyful innocence in performance that said, "Hey, lookit what I'm doing!"

Just as we hit the jackpot with the last lady of the day when we found Aretha, so did we with the last gent of the day when Gary Beach appeared late in the afternoon and gave a comedic reading together with some improvised shtick for the overseas phone call at the beginning of the play that included hiccups, squeaks, squawks, beeps, bloopers, and a raspberry or two. Gary is attractive, great smile, a wicked gleam in the eye, and eminently likable. He'd appeared in *Doonesbury* on Broadway and put in several years as Rooster Hannigan in *Annie*.

After weeks of searching, we completed our casting. As standby for both ladies (a job that would require incredible memory, nerves, and the stamina of Helen of Troy) we settled upon Barbara Sohmers, an attractive lady who'd recently returned from Paris, where she'd lived and acted for years. When someone asked me what would happen if both Mary and Carol were sick on the same day, I could only reply, "Barbara Sohmers is going to be one busy lady out on that stage!"

We chose Don Howard to play the cop at the beginning of Act II and also understudy Gary; Tim Johnson, another alumnus of *A Chorus Line*, to stand by for both Eric and Don; and Gwendolyn Shepherd to stand by for Annie-Joe. By the time we'd finished, we felt secure with our company, and especially fortunate in having found Gary, Annie-Joe, and Eric. Some playwrights claim the success of a play is due ninety percent to the right casting. I do not disagree with them—well, perhaps eighty-seven percent.

Having the right people up on that stage can make all the difference.

COUNTDOWN

Things happened fast now. Rehearsals were set to begin the first week in December in Los Angeles for a January 6 opening in Dallas, then ten or eleven weeks at the Ahmanson Theatre in Los Angeles, followed by other dates and eventually, if Mary agreed, Broadway for a limited engagement.

The prerehearsal meeting between Mary, Carol, Clifford, and me was still on at Rancho Mirage in November. I flew down to Palm Springs and received a surprise reception at the airport that bowled me over. I was greeted by an entire war party. Mary and Carol were all dolled up, carrying signs, and playing kazoos. There were photographers, a huge sign proclaiming *Mr. Broadway*. A big fuss. Everyone at the airport recognized Mary and Carol, but I think they were confused at the bearded fellow these two stars were serenading. We were whisked back to Mary's for a celebratory luncheon outside in her garden with Charles Lowe, Steve Meyer, and several others. Photographers snapped pictures and it was all very festive.

After lunch the place cleared out and Mary and Carol, with the help of Steve, read through the play for me. They did a fairly good job, too. Carol was fine when she didn't let her voice slip up into the ditsy Lorelei Lee register but kept it down to a nice low growl. Mary was really quite good; she underplayed, and came across with reality. I was cheered after the reading. Afterward we sat going over corrections, deletions, chatting about certain lines and cuts and possible additions. We were all awaiting Clifford's arrival the next day. In the evening Eugene, Mary's right hand, cooked dinner for us, we watched television, and then Mary put me to bed in her guest room. There was something sweetly legendary about her sitting on the edge of the bed, Peter Pan putting one of the lost boys to rest, asking if I wanted anything to drink, to read—I chose Ethel Merman's biography by Bob Thomas—and kissing me good night.

The next day Clifford arrived in a drenching downpour; after lunch we settled in Mary's living room for a readthrough of Act

I. Mary sat on a sofa, and Carol took an easy chair right next to her. Clifford and I sat opposite them. I noticed they leaned in toward each other and occasionally touched each other; they appeared to be doing this for mutual support. They were both obviously nervous and played the act much too friendly toward each other, whereas they are meant to be adversaries. I tried to brighten up the atmosphere by laughing, hoping this would relax them and allow them to go at each other. However, Clifford sat there mute as Mary and Carol clung to each other as if they were on a life raft going down the Colorado River.

When they finished, Clifford cleared his throat. "You know, you must keep in mind that these two ladies are complete opposites, and they loathe each other. If one doesn't feel that, see it, it doesn't work. You were a bit too cozy with each other. I know it was just a readthrough, but always remember, the more we see of their feud, the more fun we have, the better it works."

Strangely enough, both Mary and Carol jumped at this: Oh, yes, what a marvelous suggestion. Of course, they must fight, they don't like each other, etc. They accepted his comment as a revelation. This surprised me, because the play was certainly not subtle in that regard. Undoubtedly it was nervousness on their part. Then, as we talked, Clifford warmed to them and was his charming self, and I could tell they were taking to him. Instead of reading through Act II, we talked more of the play in general and the characters, and by the time Clifford left I felt he'd established a rapport with them and they had relaxed their resistance toward him.

The next day I went over changes and corrections in Act II with Steve Meyer; then, after lunch, Mary and Carol read through the play again for me. They gave it much more spirit and pizzazz than the day before. I was encouraged, because they had almost three more weeks to work before official rehearsals began.

When I returned to New York—we were still going over final sketches for the set, costumes—I had a phone call from Kevin that unsettled me. We had meetings scheduled for the next afternoon with Doug Schmidt, our set designer, and Freddy Wittop, costumes, and Kevin said, "Why don't you and Bob and I have lunch first? I think we have to have a little meeting."

"About what?" I asked.

"Well, there are certain things we have to talk about."

"What sort of things?"

"We have to go over some figures."

"Figures?" I asked, sniffing an area I never like to get into in person with producers.

"Yes," Kevin said.

"Figures—are you talking about percentages?"

"Well, yes."

"My percentage?"

"Yes," Kevin said, "we really have to renegotiate. It won't work this way, with Mary only doing seven performances."

I blew up, not at the idea that I would have to lower my percentage but that Kevin and Bob wanted to get me alone and work this out. "Kevin, stop right away."

"Stop? Jim, I'm telling you, with only seven performances—"

"And, Kevin, I'm telling you, don't ever discuss money with me. It will ruin our relationship. Please, please, call Esther, that's what I have an agent for. I'm sorry to sound like this, but never talk money directly to me. It's unhealthy, it doesn't work, I won't discuss it."

Kevin persisted, reinforcing the germ of an idea that he was not truly experienced in dealing with theatre people at all. "But the Shuberts said they haven't negotiated a contract like this for an author in nine years—"

"I don't give a fuck if they haven't negotiated a contract like this in *ninety* years. Call my agent, call my lawyer. This is not to say I won't be reasonable, but you musn't talk money to me directly ever, ever again!"

And slam went the phone. Esther did, of course, renegotiate. I came down from ten percent to eight percent, courtesy of Mary. The next day we decided on one of two models Doug had built. One was what would be called a regular box living-room set; the other was more of a triangular corner, which was more interesting in its angles and appealed to us over the traditional, so we chose it.

The next thing I knew, it was Thanksgiving. I got a funny phone call from Mary around this time. She started off by saying she was getting nervous about rehearsals; then she giggled. "Now, darling, I'm going to tell you a story, but I don't want *you* to be nervous."

"I promise."

"All right. You know what I have for breakfast? Well, I fixed my bran with yogurt on top, and I was about halfway through when Eugene walked in the kitchen and said, 'Mary, why are you eating your breakfast from the dog's bowl?' "

"The dog's bowl?" I asked.

"Yes, the *dog's bowl!*" We both roared. "Isn't that something, does that tell you anything about my condition?"

"Mary, were you down on your hands and knees on the floor?"

"No," she hooted, "of course not."

"Well, darling, when they catch you eating breakfast out of the dog's bowl on the *floor*—then I'll start getting nervous!"

We laughed and talked some more. "Carol and I don't know our lines cold," she said, "but we're getting glib with the script." She said she missed me and was looking forward to our all being together.

There was another call from Carol and Charles saying they'd heard that Kevin had hired Ed and Michael Gifford (Michael is the wife, Ed the hubby; they confuse everyone at first) to do the publicity for *Legends!* I said I'd heard that, too. I'd known them for years but hadn't seen them since they'd done some publicity and promotion for the publication of my second novel *Good Times/Bad Times,* which came out in 1968. Carol and Charles sent strong signals of disapproval concerning this decision; they thought the Giffords were not at all right for us and predicted trouble.

Toward the end of November I got a strange feeling in my stomach, a strong presentiment that we should be rehearsing in New York instead of Los Angeles. The decision to rehearse in California was in deference to Mary. Rehearsal halls, the madness of theatre, the *Sturm und Drang,* the entire climate of New York, the adrenaline of the city—the very air is conducive to theatrical rehearsals. California is too much of a lethargic swamp. Creative energy does not abound there, regardless of the Motion Picture Industry. I put these negative thoughts out of my mind, because the die was already cast. We were California-bound—like it or not. At least a production of the play was about to take place—not an easy feat in itself, these perilous theatre days.

ACT I

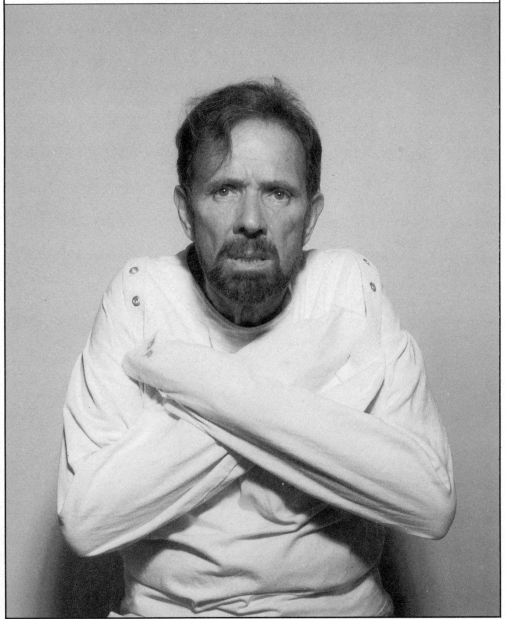

(JIMM ROBERTS)

LEGENDS!/
N.Y. TO L.A.

Monday, December 2, 1985

To Kennedy in a pouring rainstorm. American, first-class. On my
way to rehearsals of a new play, what with nerves, a packed plane,
it seemed the way to go. Especially when the destination is California. I mean, if you're on your way to hell, you might as well
be as comfortable as possible during the ride. California—never
a favorite place of mine, even though I was born there. I could
count the reasons into the hundreds, but it's mainly my childhood,
my parents and their sad careers, their many marriages and di-
vorces, finding dead bodies strewn about, and the foul Motion
Picture Industry, which is so full of bullshit, false promises, and,
I'm afraid, egotistical buffoons. (And yet I love going to the movies, so they must be doing something right.)

The place is stuffed with *Day of the Locust* memories, living in that scuzzy court on Argyle Avenue with my father and his fifth wife. The smell of that place was one of ingrained urine, damp mildew, and just a touch of car exhaust fumes, smog, and unfiltered Camels for class. As Bette said, "What a dump!"

Years ago, whenever I had to travel back there, I'd begin to feel sick to my stomach as the plane landed at LAX. Now I have a certain sense of humor about it. My stomach still does a slight Immelman turn, but at least I can summon up a smirk as I think, I don't believe I'm returning to the place of my birth, and why hasn't it fallen into the sea? How great if Arizona took over as beachfront community.

On the plane I had a few Bloody Marys and just let myself relax into it all. Met by Jerry Paonessa at the airport, always good to see him. Drove to my apartment at the Oakwood complex on Barham Boulevard, right off the Hollywood Freeway. It's a huge apartment complex, many buildings three stories high, the barren purple hills of Hollywood up to the right, then, looking down and toward Burbank I can see the old Warner Brothers studios.

Tuesday, December 3, 1985

Spent the day picking up rental car, getting settled. In the evening met Clifford for dinner at a mediocre Italian restaurant, during which he dropped a bit of distressing news. According to Steve, who's been cuing the ladies in Rancho Mirage, Mary is still very fond of Carol but she feels Carol's "getting a bit like venison."

"Come again—like venison?"

"Yes, you know, her presence and energy are a bit high! Mary does like her, but she's getting a bit fatigued by her. Most ominous of all, both ladies are having definite problems learning their lines." I'd been getting good telephonic reports, but Clifford maintained Steve had sent up orange flares today.

Clifford is displeased that the entire cast isn't assembling tomorrow, that it's only going to be Mary, Carol, and Annie-Joe; the rest will be coming on in a week or so. This is being done to save money, but for all-round team morale, for a big beginning-rehearsals-send-off, it's not what you'd call a hearty atmosphere. Also, out of a whole passel of producers, not one will be on hand for a few days either.

Clifford had been on the phone to Kevin and Bob and had been getting slight tremors about the possible risks of booking us into San Francisco or Chicago after Los Angeles. Clifford: "The only reason we were going for two old warhorses was that everyone would trot out to see them. Now there's all this doubt. If they won't, we should have gone with two solid actresses, like Rosemary Harris or Carol Shelley, and have done with it." We talked about Carol and Mary and who might trot out to see them and who wouldn't and why and what if they didn't and—I ordered a double nightcap.

OFF AND RUNNING

Wednesday, December 4, 1985

Day of the first reading! Awakened early, as if I could have slept. With my tape recorder, briefcase, script, camera, etc., I jumped into my Toyota for the ride to the Los Angeles Music Center, comprising the Ahmanson Theatre, the Mark Taper Forum, and the Dorothy Chandler Pavilion. I had freeway instructions, but it had been a while since I'd freewayed it; juggling lanes was not as much fun as I'd remembered, although I consider myself an extremely safe-dangerous driver, which is to say I drive fast and mean but I've never—since the age of twelve, when my mother used to put a pillow under me so I'd look taller and therefore older behind the wheel—had a major accident.

Downtown Los Angeles these days, because of the many freeways, is extremely frustrating. You can see where you want to go, but that doesn't necessarily mean you can get there. You run into dead ends, underpasses that lead to nowhere, streets that refuse to go where they promise, and most everything is one-way, so that, once embarked upon an error, you are forced to follow for quite a ways. It took me over a half-hour to reach the Music Center. The last block gave me a chuckle. A huge concrete wall rose up along the left side of the street. Someone had spray-painted on it in enormous letters JESUS SAVES US FROM HELL. Artist number two had altered this by spraying out an "s" and adding a few other letters, so that the sentence was amended to read JESUS SAVE US FROM HELLO DOLLY REVIVALS.

I was still laughing as I locked the car, until I realized that Carol and Charles would have to see it every day as they came to rehearsal. How far does a theatrical sense of humor stretch?

The Ahmanson Annex is a large two-story structure right across the street from the stage-door entrance of the Ahmanson Theatre itself. We had a large rehearsal room on the ground floor. By the time I walked in, most everyone was there. Hugs and kisses all around.

The first thing an author notices is the mock-up of the set—that is to say, the tapes on the floor outlining the doorways, the walls, windows, and the odd bits of furniture that have been recruited to sit in for the elegant Park Avenue setting we would eventually wind up with. My God, you think, here we go!

Present were Mary, Carol—without Charles, I presumed because Clifford had passed an edict forbidding him to attend rehearsals—Clifford, Annie-Joe, Steve Meyer, overall production stage manager, Jim Bernardi, our stage manager, Freddy Wittop, and Freddy's assistant, Harry Curtis. There were a few other people around.

First order of the day was to go over costume sketches, swatches of cloth, color charts, etc. Freddy had designed a dove-gray peignoir for Carol, and the sketch looked terrific for someone playing Elvira in *Blithe Spirit,* but it did not please Carol, who, after holding it up to the light, said, "Now, I'd look like a piece of dead meat in that!" She turned to Freddy and said, "If you have to use that color, put it on Anne Morrow Lindbergh, but not me!"

Mary was relatively quiet as sketches were shown, commented upon, discarded, or put in the "possible" group. Carol was outspoken. Almost everything met with her disapproval. They were mostly subtle "off" colors. We had spoken about making this a classy production; therefore bright, harsh colors were being avoided, so that we would not end up . . . well, garish.

The morning dragged on and on, and I could see, after a while, the impatience in Mary's eyes as Carol persisted in turning down most everything she was shown. I was also getting anxious—today was to be our first readthrough. Finally I asked Carol what color she liked. "Vivid colors," she said. "Reds, yellows! Mary can get away with those strange colors—puce, corals, things like that—but I'd look like a corpse, I'm telling you." I looked to Mary but saw only a slight smile on her face, nothing else.

"Red—I'd like a red suit!"

Everyone rebelled at that, but she kept on. "What kind of red?" Freddy asked, trotting out samples. "No, no," Carol said, "that has too much orange in it." Another one, two, three were shown, but none seemed to please her. "Carol," I asked, "what would you choose if you had your druthers?"

"Chinese red!"

"No, no," Clifford said.

Carol eyed him. "Yes, I'd like a real red suit; it makes me come alive."

Freddy Wittop commented that she couldn't clash with Mary, who might be into pink or coral, and also the color of the set had to be considered. Other reds were trotted out, and even a few yellows, which I was against. Then everyone started chattering about clashing with Mary, the set, that it had to be classy, etc., and I finally got utchy. I also realized that in the first scene of the play Carol is on with Aretha only and changes into another outfit before re-entering for her first confrontation with Mary. I pointed this out, but there was still much hemming and hawing, and it was getting on toward noon. Finally I heard myself shout, "Oh, for Christ's sake, let her have a red dress." Silence. Everyone looked at me. "Well, she's not on with Mary at first, so she can't clash with her. Get her a fucking red dress and shut her up!"

Several people laughed. Someone said, "All right, it's a red dress or suit for the first scene!" And that was it. Carol was ecstatic and threw her arms around me, parroting my words, "Get her a fucking red dress and shut her up!" She cooed in my ear, "Oh, thank you, dear Jimmy, thank you."

So we moved on to serious business, the readthrough. In place of Gary Beach, I read the part of Martin Klemmer, the producer who inveigles them into taking a meeting. Jim Bernardi read the cop and the stripper, and now and then Clifford would chime in. It was sounding good.

We broke for lunch, sandwiches and salads ordered in for everyone except Carol, who is allergic to almost everything and has special organic food and drink brought in in a variety of silver-plated containers; bluefish is a special favorite.

After lunch, Clifford became very chatty. He told delicious stories of other plays, other rehearsals. It was good to lighten up the atmosphere, but it got us a late start on the second act. We all got sprays of flowers from the producers to wish us luck, with little cards saying they were sorry they couldn't be there. As I sat listening to the end of the second act, I was feeling optimistic. Mary was going to be very good as Leatrice, and Carol was going to be an excellent Sylvia, especially if she could keep her voice from slipping up-register and didn't pop those huge expressive eyes, but kept them decently placed in their sockets. Annie-Joe had spunk and spirit and knew how to punch a laugh line. At seven o'clock we called it a day—a first day, and a good one at that.

As Carol hugged me goodbye, she once more laughed and said, "Get her a fucking red dress and shut her up! Oh, thank you, dear."

OFF AND STUMBLING

Thursday, December 5, 1985

Awakened by a phone call from New York and could barely honk. Voice totally gone. I was excused from rehearsal and stayed home most of the day, drinking tea doused with honey and taking massive doses of vitamin C. I went to bed early, really early. I don't want to be sick.

Friday, December 6, 1985

Feeling better, voice a little honky but at least I can honk. I drove down to the rehearsal hall and caught them during their lunch hour. As I walked up to the Ahmanson Annex, I saw Mary and Carol eating their lunch, sitting out in the sun on chairs like we used to have in school, with a little writing top attached. Mary called out, "We've opened Chez Leatrice!" and we all laughed. (In the play, Mary's character tells a story about falling in love with a young Frenchman who talked her into putting up money to open a restaurant called Chez Leatrice and then ended up taking most of the money and leaving her.)

Susan Grushkin, who assists Mary and drives her around, gave me some of Mary's lunch, and I sat out on the sidewalk with them. It was a kick. A huge trailer truck pulled up, the driver recognized these two famous ladies and called out to them, "Hey, Carol! Yo, Mary!" Every so often a car would cruise by, someone in the front seat would spot them, and the brakes would be hit. "Oh my God, look who's sitting out on the sidewalk!" Once they were obliged to go over and sign autographs. Neither one seemed to mind; in fact, they appeared to get a boot out of it. So we officially announced the opening of our sidewalk café, Chez Leatrice.

Over lunch, both Carol and Mary confided their concern about learning their lines and asked if they couldn't work longer hours. I said I'd speak to Clifford, searched him out, and told him what they'd suggested. Clifford shook his head and frowned. "I don't know. I think their powers of learning and concentration diminish as the day goes on. It might be counterproductive. Let's keep it this way for the time being."

When we all gathered in the rehearsal hall, ready for work, Carol spoke up. "We don't really have to take the full lunch hour, you know." Jim Bernardi said, "Equity rules say you do." Carol disagreed. "No, no, not once you've reached star status, you don't have to stick to those rules." Just then Annie-Joe waddled past in character, mumbling, "Un-uh, nothing to do with me, not taking away *my* lunch hour." As she walked over to the ledge by the windows, Carol, an excellent mimic, did a perfect imitation of her.

Clifford was finishing up a rough blocking of the first scene— getting it on its feet, with moves, exits, entrances, bits of stage business. Carol had a good handle on her lines, but Mary didn't. After a while they went back to Carol's first scene with Annie-Joe. Mary sat on a chair, off to the side, watching. It occurred to me that it was a waste of time for Mary simply to watch, so I suggested that she and Susan go into the lounge and run lines. Mary agreed and they stepped outside. Clifford worked over the first scene, trying to define it, set it, find the right moves.

When I left the rehearsal hall, things seemed to be going well. Slowly but well. They'd gotten past the scene with Carol and

Annie-Joe, and Mary and Carol were inching their way into their first scene together.

As I was walking the long block to the parking lot, one of those strange, lanky, gaunt, lost creatures you find roaming the streets of any large city, dressed in what might be called eclectic rags, held up his hands as we passed each other and said, "Beware the Ides of March." I was feeling fairly perky, and he didn't appear to be the violent type, so I countered with "Relax, it's only December." He stopped dead, turned, and put his hand on my arm. "Beware anyway!"

Saturday, December 7, 1985

When I awakened and glanced at the Los Angeles *Times*, I realized it was Pearl Harbor Day. I had no idea, however, it was really going to be PEARL HARBOR DAY.

I spent the morning buying necessities for the apartment and then hit the freeway for rehearsals. When I arrived at the Annex, there were Mary, Carol, and Clifford all sitting outside on the sidewalk at Chez Leatrice, having lunch. They all looked shipshape and seemingly pulled together. Seemingly.

Toward the end of lunch, Clifford and I walked off to have a chat. "I wish the fucking producers were here," Clifford said. I agreed. "How did it go this morning?" I asked. Clifford hesitated a long moment before answering. "A little dicey. I'm concerned about Mary. Maybe it's just an off day, but—I don't know. You'll see."

I did see when afternoon rehearsals resumed. They were running the end of Act I, and, indeed, Mary seemed out of it. She was confused, appeared lost, and didn't remember her lines or moves. Clifford was extremely patient, as was Carol. They would go over one small section five or six times, but Mary could still not absorb it. They would continue, and Mary would finally get it. Then, after a five- or ten-minute break, work would resume, and it was as if it had never been rehearsed. Mary looked terribly confused, almost frightened.

In midafternoon a chill came over the rehearsal studio. Not so much physical as the chill of doom. People avoided looking directly into each other's eyes. Every so often Mary would stop and say, "I don't know what's the matter. I never had this problem before, never."

"You'll get it, darling, you'll get it," Clifford would say. "It's early on. Just relax."

At one point I went out into the hall, and Steve Meyer was on the phone. When he finished I took him around the corner to the lounge area. "Steve, I'm worried."

"So am I."

"Is there anything you can think of that we could do to help Mary?"

He shook his head. "I've tried to think of everything, but I can't come up with anything. It's just not sinking in."

"Do you think it will—eventually?"

"I don't know."

We walked back toward the rehearsal hall. "Well, if anything occurs to you, let me know."

He said, "I will," with about as much hope as if the *Titanic* had already hit the iceberg and only the stern were sticking up.

During another break, Mary came up to me and said, "Jimmy, I'm just so upset about all this. Maybe you'd give Larry [Hagman] a call and see what he might suggest." I tried to allay her fears, put an arm around her shoulder, and walked her over by the windows looking out toward the Ahmanson across the street. "It's been a long time since you've worked. I think a lot of it is just letting yourself relax into it, trying not to tense up. You'll get it, you'll see."

"I don't know." Suddenly Mary seemed like a little lost girl.

They went back to the beginning of Act I with the hope of running through it roughly. Again it was as if Mary had never seen it. It was frightening to us, especially frightening to Mary. Cues had to be thrown for almost every line, and she barely remembered a move. In the midst of one muddled section Mary said, "I have to work on Sunday. I know it's my day off, but I have to have someone to work with."

Later, during a break, Carol came up to me and said she'd worked with a coach, Jimmy Dobson (an old friend of mine from acting days), when she'd done a "Love Boat." She said he was very good, and we set about having someone find him to see if he could work with Mary on Sunday. Later, during another break, Carol came up to me once more. "Darling, Jimmy's very good, but

I hear he likes to have a drink every now and then, and I'm worried it might get into a social thing. Make sure they just keep to work."

It wasn't getting any better as the day wore on. Clifford and I went for a little walk, and I told him Mary suggested I call Larry. He asked me to hold off for a while, lest everyone get thrown into full panic.

Although rehearsal was scheduled to go on for another hour or so, Mary was so discombobulated that Clifford broke at five and told me he'd go home with Mary and have a drink and chat and try to reassure her. By that time Jimmy Dobson had been contacted and was set to work with her on our day off.

When I left the rehearsal hall, I had that terrible childish feeling that I didn't want to drive alone. I wanted someone in the car to console me. Freeway traffic is not consoling.

I stopped off at Jerry and Jody Paonessa's for a drink and, undoubtedly, to unload some of my fears. They both tried to diminish them, reminding me we had several more weeks of rehearsal and that it was probably just a momentary block, nerves, etc. "Yes, but Mary's had the script for a couple of months, and I know she's been working on it every day."

That night, when I turned off the lights, I could only think about Mary. Amazing how the road signs point to trouble ahead but you ignore them until one day you turn a corner and realize you're facing an impending catastrophe. If the dear lady is unable to learn and retain lines, what can be done? Is it simply beginning nerves? The result of her terrible San Francisco taxi accident? Is it her age? A chemical imbalance? What? Or a combination of all these? And who is to know that—and, even if you know, what can be done?

Sunday, December 8, 1985

I woke with my fears in strong possession of me. An early phone call from Carol, who confided her deepest concerns to me. "Jimmy, yesterday, in the morning, before you arrived, we were working on the first act, had gone nowhere near the second. We stopped to straighten out some little bit of business, and when we started again, Mary jumped right ahead, smack into the middle of the second act, without even realizing it. Well, we kept on, you know, thinking she'd stop any second, but she didn't until some-one, Clifford or the stage manager, stopped her. She had abso-lutely no idea where she was."

"Jesus."

"Yes." Neither of us spoke for a second or two. Then Carol hit me with this: "Have you thought of anyone else? What about Julie Andrews?" I near shit. I mean, that was out and out saying "Whooaaa!" and seemed premature to me, if not downright out of line. She went on: "I know Julie's been dying to do a play; maybe you should get in touch with her." I told Carol we'd investi-gated Julie Andrews early on and the word came back strong and clear that she didn't want to do a play or leave the West Coast under any circumstances.

Carol and I consoled each other, completely backtracking and saying everything would be all right, and hung up. Just the idea that Carol would bring this up so early put me off my feed. But bring it up she did.

There were also calls from Clifford and Kevin. Clifford had gone back and had several drinks with Mary the night before; he tried to give her all the reassurance he could. He was happy she was willing to work lines on her day off. Kevin had finally arrived in Los Angeles; he was sorry he hadn't been here earlier, but the last week in New York had been an extremely nasty one because of the financial situation.

"What do you mean?" I asked, thinking all that had been straightened out: we were already in rehearsals!

"Well," Kevin said, "I don't want to demean Bob or embar-rass him, but Bob's group did not come up with their full share of the financing as promised. That's why neither of us could be here. There was just too much hassling going on."

"Is it all settled now?"

"Yes, sort of. But I don't think Bob will have the power he would have had."

Later on Bob phoned from New York; he didn't mention specifically what the problem was, but apologized for not being on hand. I told him about the problems with Mary. "Listen," Bob said, with great energy, "I'll be out there by Wednesday for sure, and I'll stay up all night with her going over lines, don't you worry!"

"Bob, you can't make a seventy-two-year-old lady who hasn't

worked in years learn her lines by keeping her up all night. I don't think that's the solution."

"Look, I get along with Mary fine. I'll work with her, help her out. Don't worry, we'll do it."

There was nothing more to be said. I got to thinking about stories I'd heard of hypnotists who'd helped actors retain lines. I put in a call to Mildred Newman (my psychiatrist—What? A writer needs a psychiatrist! Are you mad? Yes!) in New York and told her of our problem. Mildred, warm and concerned as always, gave me the name of a psychiatrist out in L.A. who might know of someone. I finally reached the doctor, who sounded like a nice fellow and had had experience working with various movie actors with memory problems. I told him a bit about Mary. Of course he knew of her, but I filled him in on her accident, the fact that she'd had the script for two months, etc. We spoke of Alzheimer's disease, and I said I didn't think it could possibly be that, because she is extremely lucid about current events and tells very funny and explicit stories of her past life—Alzheimer's would preclude all of that.

I made an appointment for Mary to see him at six o'clock on Tuesday. I was wondering how to broach the subject of hypnosis and wondering even more if she would go for it. I was also wondering why I had written the goddamn play in the first place. It was Sunday; perhaps I should go back to the church. "Dear Lord, if you'll only help out, I promise never to touch myself in a 'bad place' again."

Monday, December 9, 1985

Awakened to the sorrowful sounds of the California mourning doves. Their coo-*coo*, coo-*coo*, so repetitively grieving, always makes me imagine about eight doves sitting on a branch looking down at one of their family, dead, lying on the ground, legs stiffly up. The others are coo-*coo*ing over what the hell they could possibly do about it.

Down at rehearsals, Mary was still shaky. I knew I had to bring up the subject of hypnosis soon, because the appointment had already been made for the next day. I wondered when and how the best opportunity would arise.

Around eleven o'clock Carol had to leave to have her sinuses blown out. She was getting a trifle honky. I asked Mary if she'd like me to stand in for Carol and read the part of Sylvia. She said yes with enthusiasm, so, while Clifford was out of the room going over production details, Mary and I began in the second act. We went over and over and over it. She began to get a little rattled that it was not sticking; I suggested we take it two pages at a time. And we did. But she was still having great difficulty combining lines with stage moves. I finally said, "Mary, just take it easy. We'll go section by section, move by move. Try not to think of the thing as a whole."

Gently, calmly, we went over it page by page, then put two pages together, and finally an entire section, and I would stop to ask her a question when she seemed confused. "Mary, now what are you going to do?"

"Ah—I'm going to leave Sylvia's apartment?"

"So what will you have to do in preparation for that?"

"I don't know."

"Get your coat and purse and script."

"Yes, that's right. Where are they?"

I would point out where they were, and we'd start running it, and after about an hour or so Mary was responding to the more or less calm atmosphere I tried to create as I gave only lip service to Carol's lines, instead of the energy she imbues them with, which tends to panic Mary, making her afraid of not being able to keep up. Rehearsing in this rather low-key fashion seemed to pay off, and after a while we were able to get through eight or ten pages, perhaps only giving Mary a hint here and there. "Oh, this helps so much," she said to me just before we broke for lunch.

"Good. Anytime you want to run sections with me, let me know. You're doing terrific."

When Jim Bernardi called an hour for lunch, Susan, Mary, and I set up Chez Leatrice out on the sidewalk and, sitting in our little school chairs, ate our salads and got a bit of sun in the bargain. The rehearsal room, for some reason, even on a warm, sunny day, was chilly. I was eagerly awaiting some little opening so I could launch into my speech. I got it when Mary suddenly said, "We have so little time left; we'll be going to Dallas January first."

"I know." Then I jumped into my story, some of which was made up. "You know, a couple of years ago, I wrote the screenplay for a novel of mine, *Some Kind of Hero.* Paramount made it, and I asked to play a small part in it, that of a bartender who gives Richard Pryor some information about Margot Kidder and later tells him how to get in touch with the mob. Not a big part, but I wanted to make some sort of cameo appearance in my own movie. Anyhow, I'd also written a one-act play, *Surprise,* that Dina Merrill and I were going to perform in a program of one-acters at the John Drew Theatre in East Hampton. The film was behind schedule, and I finally had to give up the cameo and leave California for New York. These delays cut my rehearsal time drastically and"—here's where I went from fact to fiction—"I had so little time to rehearse and learn an entire rather talky one-act play, I tensed up and found it difficult to retain lines. I called up my psychiatrist, and do you know what she recommended?"

Without a beat, Mary said, "Hypnosis."

I could have fallen off my chair. "Yes!" I said, so loudly you'd have thought I'd just won the sixty-four-thousand-dollar pyramid. "Yes . . . I mean, how did you know?"

"I don't know, I just guessed and . . . well, I have heard of it helping."

"It really did the trick for me." (I had not gone to a hypnotist.) "Mary, what if I call my psychiatrist and see if she has the name of someone out here who does that sort of thing?"

"I suppose I should try anything if there's a chance. Except," she added, "I hate to take time away from learning lines, from rehearsing."

I assured her the time would be well spent if it provided a solution to the problem. She agreed to give it a try. During an early-afternoon break, I told Clifford about the hypnosis ploy and asked him to support it when the subject came up. "Yes, of course," he said, "anything, anything at all that might help."

I left rehearsal early, not wanting to be in on the angst of the next scene Clifford was about to block, the scene in which the ladies, now feeling the effect of the brownies, demolish the apartment more as they set about cleaning up the destruction wrought during the fight begun at the end of Act I. This involved so much physical business that I knew it would be a pisser to stage.

LIFE UPSTAGES ART

Tuesday, December 10, 1985

Awakened by a friend I'd been in the service with. "Hi, Jimmy—Lomax here. Are you watching the 'Today' show?"

"No, I was sleeping."

"Oh, Jesus, that's too bad!" He then went into an absolute paroxysm of laughter. "Damnit, I hoped you had it on. Gene Shalit just gave the movie of *A Chorus Line* the worst review he's ever given any movie! It was just brutal. You didn't see it?"

"No, I just told you, you woke me up."

"Oh, Christ, I wished you'd seen it, it was just terrrrrible!"

Now, Lomax Study is a good friend of mine. Why or how or what in God's name had given him the idea that I would have gotten such an early-morning kick out of hearing the worst review Gene Shalit had ever given a movie, when it was of *A Chorus Line.* Even though I had nothing to do with the film, still . . . I ended the call as quickly as possible, saying I was just so sorry I'd missed it that I'd better go back to sleep. People! FRIENDS!

Raining all morning, which to me is a joy in California. A change from the usual hazy, garish, sunny, brain-damaging, boring days.

At rehearsals, Mary was extremely shaky again, which in turn made Carol, Annie-Joe, Clifford, Jim Bernardi, and me shaky. I gave Susan and Mary the information about the appointment with Dr. Stolar, time, place, directions, etc. Now that it was all set, Mary tried pulling back from it, saying again she hated to take the time away from rehearsal. I had Clifford come in and say, "Oh, come on, Mary, give it a try. It only means breaking an hour or two early." So it was on.

Jimmy Dobson, whom I hadn't seen in years, had come to be at rehearsal with Mary. We talked about old times. I told him Mary had said she'd had a good workday with him last Sunday, and that she liked him. Jimmy said he liked her, too, but then confided to me that he didn't really think he could help her all that much. When I asked why, he said they'd gone at it steadily from ten in the morning until six, and she'd only gotten six pages of Act II down cold. That was not reassuring.

A new person came aboard today, Keith Baumgartner. Very nice, tall, happy chap, full of energy and efficiency. He's going to put the current script on a computer disk for himself, so he can keep up with changes and have new pages printed up every evening for the next day. He's also going to have a special script printed for Mary, large type and double-spaced, because, I was told, a lot of the problem of rehearsing, even with the script in her hand, is that she can't really see it all that well, even with glasses. Why she didn't say anything about this before, I don't know.

Rehearsals were bumpy again. Things that had been set tended to come unglued, fall apart, had to be put back together again. Carol had a good grip on her lines, but Mary had to leave by four-thirty to get to the doctor's. After Mary left, I rehearsed part of the second act with Carol and Annie-Joe. It went well. When it was time to finish, Carol said what a help it had been to rehearse with me. I was looking forward to the full cast and company being on hand tomorrow.

From rehearsal I drove to Jamie Herlihy's in Silver Lake. We'd planned to have dinner. When I got there I was feeling bushed, a little beat. I had some tea, we talked, and I called in to check my answering machine at the Oakwood for messages.

There were quite a few, but it was the last two that were stunners. "Hi, this is Lee Thompson"—wonderful gal that always looked in on my eighty-six-year-old aunt Peggy every day, shopped for her, etc. "Please call me at my house in Key West." The next message, voice very shaky, stopped me cold. "Jimmy, this is Bobby"—Peggy's son, my cousin. "My mother passed away this evening, and I'm going to Key West in the morning. She slipped away peacefully, according to Lee Thompson. Please get in touch with us. That's all."

That *was* all. She was more than an aunt to me, she was my second mother. Whenever either one of my parents was getting married or divorced or embarking on a new romance or ill and out of commission or broke and unable to take care of me—which was a lot of the time—I would be shipped off to live with my mother's sister, Peggy, and her husband, Leonard (now dead), and their two children, Lila (named after my mother) and Bobby. She treated me like a son, and although she was older than my mother, when my mother went through sieges of illness—TB, a terrible burn accident, and other misfortunes, which later included stroke after stroke—my aunt came to live with her in Key West to take care of her. She'd been down there for perhaps fifteen years, and I'd been more than happy to support her and even buy a little house for her to live in after my mother died. I built a second story for me to live in, and Peg was what was left of my close family. I adored her.

Instant tears. It seemed so right to be with Jamie when I got the news. We'd been close friends for years, had been through the deaths of our parents together, had even been through a flop play that we'd written together, *U.T.B.U. (Unhealthy to Be Unpleasant)*.

After the tears stopped, I made phone calls to Bobby and Lila, who fortunately was still in Florida (from Ohio) visiting friends after having spent Thanksgiving with Peg in Key West. They were going back to take care of arrangements. I felt it was impossible for me to leave, what with the entire cast assembling in the morning and the problems with Mary. There was nothing I could do anyway. Peg would be cremated and the ashes buried next to my mother in Elyria, Ohio. When I called Lee Thompson in Key West, she said she'd gone by to check on Peggy and found her simply sitting in her favorite chair with a breakfast roll in one hand. Peaceful. No sign of pain on her face.

Peggy had been perky, said exactly what was on her mind. After I got off the phone, I told Jamie that, knowing Peggy, her last words could easily have been "Well, this is one roll I'm not going to eat!"

When I got back there was another message on my machine, from Mary. She said she'd had "a lovely experience" with the doctor and I could call her at home if I wanted to. It was after twelve, and I didn't want to wake her up. I did call Clifford and told him about my aunt. He was compassionate, and I said I'd be a little late for rehearsals and the press conference that had been arranged by Ed Gifford at ten with the whole cast present. I also asked if he'd tell the company that I'd suffered the loss of someone extremely dear and important to me and advise everyone to take it easy, not to offer sympathy or talk about it, because that could only cause the dam to break again. He promised he'd take care of that.

I didn't have a good sleep, kept waking up thinking, Did I dream Peggy died or—but no, it was all too clear. This dear, spunky, brave, funny, independent, stubborn lady was gone. And does this major loss that reminds me, of course, of my own mortality—does this in any way diminish my silly fears about a play called *Legends!?* No, oddly enough, not really. Am I strange, or is everybody strange?

Yes.

Wednesday, December 11, 1985

Many morning phone calls about Peggy, arrangements, obits, etc. I arrived about twenty minutes after ten to find an entire battery of photographers, reporters, TV and print, set up facing Mary, Carol, Annie-Joe, and Gary Beach, just arrived, seated on the sofa in front of a barrage of microphones. For all the hoopla, flash cameras, clickings, they looked like a bunch of hostages who'd just arrived home. When they saw me they all yelled, "There's our author!" I was urged by Ed Gifford to join them. And did. We all answered questions for about fifteen minutes, then broke up into smaller groups, some reporters going after Mary, some Carol, and a few me.

When the press finally left, Clifford had Gary read through his first telephone scene, in which he (supposedly) talks to Paul Newman, the author of the play, the Shuberts, and both ladies, trying to get them together for a meeting to discuss appearing in his new production: *Star Wars—the Play.* Gary is a natural comedian; he then read through his last scene with Mary and Carol, when he arrives at the apartment and throws them curve after curve. I could tell both ladies liked him. This was a relief.

The atmosphere was much more what it should have been with everyone present. Even though my mind kept drifting to thoughts of Peggy—that awful, persistent, morbid "Are they cremating Peggy now, is she no more?"—I was grateful that not one person had placed a paw on me or whispered a word or two of sympathy.

When we took a break in midafternoon I said to Clifford,

"Thank you for calling off everyone about—"

"What?" he asked, rather distractedly.

"Thank you for telling them about my aunt's death so I haven't had to—"

His retort was very offhand. "Oh, that—oh, I forgot about that. Sorry." With which he walked away to speak to one of the production staff. I was annoyed with him, more for his abruptness than for having forgotten. I certainly was not going to tell anyone now. This made me think even more of Peg, of course. In the late afternoon I began to feel a bit blue, especially when Mary and Carol were running a section that has to do with death.

> LEATRICE
>
> Why'd you ask if I ever got lonely?

> SYLVIA
>
> Because I do. I get lonely. That's what I hate most—I really think—loneliness.

> LEATRICE
>
> You don't give that impression at all. You always act as if you're not only giving the party, but you're all the guests as well.

> SYLVIA
>
> Not true, that's just whistling in the graveyard. Speaking of which—that's what I hate most about dying.

> LEATRICE
>
> What?

> SYLVIA
>
> Everyone's always sounding off about how we have to die alone. "You come into the world alone, you leave the world alone." I always thought it would be kinda nice if we could all hold hands and jump together!

> LEATRICE
>
> (Giggling, imitating Davis-Crawford, Baby Jane)
> Well, yah can't, Blanche—yah can't!

> SYLVIA
>
> What's so funny about dying? Aren't you afraid of it?

> LEATRICE
>
> I'm not so much afraid of death anymore. I mean, of leaving my body. I just hate to leave it in such a mess!

They went over this section several times, until I decided to go home. I suddenly found myself thinking, with renewed annoyance, of Clifford's forgetting about Peg's death, and realized I was doing what I usually do when death touches my life: I turn the sadness to anger. I am angry when death takes away someone I love. I am angry with whoever runs the whole works and whoever thought up *death*. What a miserable concept to dangle in front of us all our lives until we finally meet it head on.

What a joyful little perverse surprise to await.

Thursday, December 12, 1985

After lunch Clifford began staging Gary's first scene; Gary is going to be excellent. When Mary arrived she was in a good mood, spirits up. Susan said Mary's second visit with the doctor had gone very well and "she likes him enormously." She and Carol went into a smaller room down the hall to run a scene with Steve Meyer on book. Indeed, when Jim Bernardi went to fetch them from the room to come into the main rehearsal hall, he came back and reported that Mary was going through a scene with Carol *sans* script and it was going so well he didn't want to disturb her. We all looked at each other and sighed. Perhaps it was going to click back into place after all.

In midafternoon I got a call from Biff Liff, one of Carol's agents and also, although Esther Sherman handles me at William Morris, one of mine, too, since I am signed to the agency for plays. Biff, always warm and concerned, had heard about the problems Mary was having memorizing; he was calling to tell me of a hearing device that actors can wear in their ears. Offstage, preferably in a cutout part of the set so that sender and receiver can see each other, somebody with a microphone is stationed with a script and can, when the need arises, feed the actor lines. He said perhaps we should investigate this right now.

I told Biff I thought it was too early to dangle something like that in front of Mary. Such a suggestion might easily push the panic button. He was understanding but said not to dismiss the idea, and promised to send me information on it that very day.

After we'd hung up I went back into the rehearsal hall. Things were coming along fairly well. Mary was stumbling but she was getting through it with some cuing from whoever was on book. I got to thinking about Biff's suggestion but I felt, today, that Mary would finally get it just about the time the first-night curtain went up in Dallas—only weeks from now. (Gulp!)

Friday, December 13, 1985

Met Carol in Hollywood to do Carl Princi's radio show; Carol was gussied up to the tits in one of her wilder outfits. She had gotten all jazzed up, thinking it was a television show, and she was a bit out of sorts to find she was only going to be heard, not seen.

She's a superb plugger, knows how to do her public relations to a T. She talked about how terrific it was to be working with Mary Martin as if their relationship were totally tension-free. She whips through an interview like a tornado, one path in mind, and that is to plug whatever she's currently doing.

Thence to rehearsal.

Trish Garland, who is to choreograph Eric Riley's strip routine, arrived, looking smashing. What a figure; her physical presence alone perked up the rehearsal studio; also any new energy brought into the group is a shot of adrenaline to the rest of us. She looks much more glamorous than when she was playing Bebe in *A Chorus Line* years ago. A pianist arrived, a real old-time rehearsal thumper, and Trish took Eric into another studio to begin work.

Outside of that, nothing unusual happened at rehearsal today . . . or so I thought.

Saturday, December 14, 1985

Awakened by a jangling phone call from Carol. A rush of disturbing words struck my ear. "Jimmy—Carol. I just thought I should tell you, Mary's leaving the show."

"WHAT?"

"That's what she said."

"When?"

"Yesterday, at lunch, she said she was not going to be able to open in the show, that it was your fault because—"

"My fault?"

"Yes, because you sent her to this doctor and he'd opened up a whole new can of peas about her life and times and now she realized she was completely alone. No Richard [Halliday, her deceased husband], no Janet [Gaynor], no Ben Washer [longtime friend and manager]. And she'd had a concussion when she'd had the accident and couldn't think of anything else, and that's why she isn't learning her lines, and she's getting Larry Hagman's publicity man to figure out some kind of press release so she can get out of the show and still be a heroine and not take the blame."

"Carol, you learned this yesterday?"

"Yes, at lunch."

"Why didn't you tell me this yesterday?"

I heard a combination between a sarcastic burst of laughter and a derisive snort; her next words stunned me completely. "Tell *you?* Hah! I wouldn't tell you *anything,* not the way you looked at me yesterday! With that hatred!"

"Hatred? What are you talking about?"

"Oh, don't give me that. You were looking at me with hatred in your eyes. Every time you looked at me I could see it."

"Carol, you're crazy! I don't hate you."

"Oh, yes, you do. Your eyes, just full of hatred and—"

She went on and on until I finally screamed: "Carol, will you shut the fuck up and listen to me for a minute!"

"No," she said, "don't try to get out of it, I can tell—"

I screamed again, really screamed for her to be quiet and listen to me. "Why in God's name didn't you tell me this yesterday? Why did you wait to wake me up this morning with all this good news?"

"Well," she said, calming down somewhat, "I didn't want to tell you in front of the whole cast. That wouldn't have been—"

"Then why didn't you tell me toward the end of the day, when I said good night to you in the corridor? You were sitting there marking your script, and I kissed you good night, and we were all warm and friendly—"

"Oh, no, I wasn't going to tell you *anything,* the way you looked at me with such hatred, not when you're in a mood like that. Oh, no. I—"

"Carol, now, you listen to me. I don't hate you, I'm delighted to have you in the show, you're terrific. I refuse to have this conversation on the telephone this early in the morning. I will not talk to you anymore when you're saying such ridiculous things. But I'll see you at rehearsal at ten o'clock, and what I have to say I don't want to say in front of the company, either. Now, let's not go on like this. It's terrible and destructive and—"

"Well," she said, in a more controlled voice, "I would have called you last night, but Charles was in the hospital."

"Oh, I didn't know that. I hope it's not serious?"

"No, just a minor . . . But I couldn't call last night."

"I'm sorry, but I'll see you at rehearsal, and we'll straighten this out. But remember—I do not hate you, I am very happy you are playing Sylvia."

With that exchange, we hung up. Things were getting messier and messier. I tried to call Larry Hagman but couldn't get him. Then I phoned Mary's doctor. This report of the reaction to Mary's second visit confused me totally, especially since Susan had made a point of telling me how well it had gone and how much Mary liked him. I asked him if it were true that Mary felt a whole new can of peas had been opened and she couldn't go on.

"No, not at all." I told him what Carol had reported. He seemed confused, too, adding: "She did spill out a lot of the past and said she'd never dealt with it in detail, but she never indicated it would inhibit her now or prevent her from going on. She said these were things she'd avoided dealing with head-on and perhaps she'd have to face up to them someday, and I agreed that that could wait until a later date and tried only to relax her about this current problem of memorization."

After I'd spoken to him, I was still not sure exactly how Mary had reacted to their meeting; she'd said nothing to me the day before. I did think I should fill in both Kevin and Bob, who'd just arrived in California, about the gist of what Carol had told me: that Mary had said she would not be able to open in Dallas. I phoned both and asked them to pitch in, to get to the bottom of this latest report of distress and to help bolster her morale.

Arriving downtown, I found Mary and the rest of the group calmly beginning rehearsal. I took Carol by the arm and said, "Step outside a moment." We walked out to the sidewalk and I closed the door behind us. "What was all that about on the phone?" I put my hands up to her neck, almost around her throat, and said, "Look into my eyes and tell me if you think I hate you. Just look at me. I am so happy to have you in this part, to feel your professional presence here, I can't tell you. Now, is that hate?"

"No."

"I swear to God, Carol, if I ever find myself hating you, you'll know it, I'll let you know. But for now can we forget that kind of paranoid crap and get on with what we're doing?"

I wondered what people in passing cars thought of the bearded man with his hands around the neck of Dolly/Lorelei Lee standing out on the sidewalk in this frieze, and relaxed my grip.

Carol went on: "This play means a lot to me, and I'm not able to play the character because Mary won't let me, and neither, for that matter, will the director. He doesn't know anything about comedy, especially American comedy. Don't you know that William Morris is looking for anyone they can find that could possibly replace her?"

"Carol, let's not panic. The play means a lot to me, too. Did you ever think of that?"

"Of course it does. I know that, but—"

"Then let's try to get on with it and do the best we can right now. Let's try not to be so paranoid. Come on." I took her hand. "And you don't believe I hate you, do you?"

"No, of course not." Thank God, I thought, until she added, "Not if you say so."

We went back into the rehearsal hall; I felt I'd already had a full day. I was a basket case.

Rehearsal was a basket case. Trust me.

Sunday, December 15, 1985

My awakenings these days are not my usual sort. No more the Boy Scout who bounces out of bed, hits that bugle, and gets the troops moving. Rather, I crawl out, anticipating the jarring freeway drive and the chilly rehearsal hall with its chillier results.

Got down there in a bad Sunday mood as they were setting up to go through Act I and—surprise!—Mary was unusually perky and did not carry the script at all. Today, for the first time, there was a glimmer of hope that she might just come through. Nothing spectacular, no *Peter Pan* or *South Pacific*, but there were whole beats, moments, scenettes in which she showed the old moxie. She'd get on a roll and everyone in the rehearsal hall would look at each other with widened eyes and the sort of hope that one felt about the little engine going up the hill—"I think she can, I think she can, I think she can!"

At the lunch break Clifford and I walked a block down the street to a bar/restaurant and had a Bloody Mary in celebration. "We might have an opening in Dallas after all," I said. We both knocked on the wooden bar. We had a bite of lunch and discussed various problems and possible solutions. Clifford was beginning to feel Carol's disapproval of him as a director of American comedy. As much as he didn't relish attempting to direct Mary, he felt Carol was an equal, albeit different, problem. Mary was directable if she knew the situation and was comfortable with the moment, understood it. Carol tended to argue a point more. She also played out front to a greater degree than Mary.

Clifford's opinion was consolidated by a contretemps that took place right after lunch. He had been trying to get Carol to play one scene in which she prayed to a crucifix so that she more or less directed her attention to it, as she spoke to God. Carol would start the speech and then immediately lower the crucifix and deliver the rest of the speech out front. He stopped her once, twice, and asked her to please give the crucifix her attention when she spoke. She would nod, start the speech to include the crucifix, then lower it and continue as usual. Clifford sat at the director's table with one hand up to his forehead, looking down at the script. When she finished the speech, Clifford said once more, "Carol, please look at the crucifix more, I've asked you—"

"How could you tell what I was doing?" Carol asked. "You weren't even looking at me."

"I could hear the way you were doing it."

"Aha," Carol snorted, "then perhaps you should be directing—radio!"

We all sat frozen waiting for war to be declared, but Clifford waited patiently for a few moments, sucking in his breath, and moved on to other business.

The afternoon was mostly spent finishing the runthrough of Act I. Again it went relatively well. The result was, we climbed all over Mary, telling her, Yes, by God, it's coming, you're getting it, it's just going to be terrific. She shared our relief; she grinned and appeared pleased.

I also made a point of petting Carol, stroking her, and telling her how good *she* was. Because she's having a rough time rehearsing with Mary, no doubt of that. When they were getting ready to leave, Carol said, in front of Mary, "Oh, yes, I know her type. Doesn't know her lines, where she is, what scene she's in, and then—on opening night—we're all terrified for her and blow our lines and she walks off with the play. I know that type. I'll be a total wreck, and Mary will sail through it like silk."

Mary just smiled. I hope Carol's right, not about her part, but about the Mary part.

Later on Trish arrived to work with Eric, the pianist, and also with Annie-Joe, who can actually do a full split at the end of the number, when Eric gives her a hip-check. To see this woman do the split is akin to the eighth wonder of the world. She not only did it but performed it with aplomb and a certain grace.

Trish was not all that happy with the four-four beat of "Bye-Bye Baby," which I had chosen for the number and for which I had written a set of parodic lyrics. She felt it wasn't really suitable and lacked a solid strip beat. Clifford also felt it wasn't black or funky enough.

They were still working when I left around six to go home, where I got a phone call from Larry Hagman. We had a good talk. I told him his mother was coming along, that we'd had a good day today, and he was quite optimistic. He'd been bolstering her up over the telephone, especially when she'd had a few low days, reminding her she'd been away from work for a long time and that it was, after all, only the first ten days of rehearsals. He said he was winding up filming his "Dallas" series this coming week and would drop down to rehearsals and lend support. That I wasn't sure was a good idea: it could backfire and cause more pressure.

Then Clifford called. He'd stayed late at rehearsal, where he and Trish, Eric, and Annie-Joe had all started singing black songs and stripper numbers. Clifford clearly felt we should search for another song, one that would have more oomph in it and a more dynamic beat. We set an afternoon meeting for tomorrow—our day off—to investigate this.

That evening Bob Regester finally arrived, and the production team took dinner at a Chinese restaurant. Kevin now had an assistant with him, Ann Amendologine, a slight, gamin girl given to short skirts. If Ann had been French, her perfect mother would have been Edith Piaf. Kevin and Bob expressed concern over obtaining bookings that were to follow our Los Angeles run. Again Clifford voiced his thoughts about why we'd gone with Mary and Carol in the first place: because he'd been told everyone would turn out to see those two. When Clifford had mentioned other actresses he'd rather work with, he'd been told we couldn't get bookings because they weren't "hot road names." It seemed to be a Catch-22.

Overall, however, it had been an optimistic day and held out hope. My Chinese fortune cookie read: "With hard work your efforts will be rewarded." Most predictions, including this one, bring to mind a string of four-letter words. I like the odd specific one, like: "If you play your cards right you will get laid on Wednesday evening." Still, tonight I gladly settled for the cliché.

Monday, December 16, 1985

Clifford, Kevin, Ann, Annie-Joe, Trish, Eric, and I spent two hours in the Colony Record shop poring over every possible number that might serve us. Everyone had his or her own favorite. We ended up with six contenders, brought them back to Kevin's suite, and played them over and over. Toward the end of the session, it seemed that Aretha Franklin's recording of "Respect" was the favorite.

As we sat at Kevin's, going over the pros and cons of each number, it occurred to me that the strip routine was by far the least of our worries. I thought about Mary and what she was doing on her day off: If she was relaxed enough to learn her lines. If she actually considered quitting. If all she'd gone through in her life had given her a tough little knot in the middle of her stomach that would somehow see her through the darkness in which she was most certainly immersed.

When I left Kevin's, I drove to Sunset and on into Hollywood proper. As I got near the Blessed Sacrament Church—where I used to be an altar boy, and where my father, although divorced five times, worshipped every Sunday until his death, and from which he was buried—I pulled the car over, got out, crossed the street, and entered.

It looked the same. I walked down the center aisle, genu-flected, knelt, and said a few Our Fathers and Hail Marys and a special prayer for the play. I walked to a statue of the Virgin Mary, lit a candle, and said another prayer: "Dear Mary, mother of Jesus, please take care of your namesake Mary Martin, restore her memory, and give her the faith to continue."

As I was leaving the church, a part of me felt silly for having done this. Was I really serious in these prayers? Stepping outside into the late-afternoon sunshine, I had to admit I didn't feel all that silly. In fact, I was deadly serious.

Tuesday, December 17, 1985

Despite the prayers of yesterday, I had a hunch it was going to be a corker of a day. Arrived at rehearsal around eleven. Mary was off having fittings, due to arrive around one. Carol and Barbara Sohmers were going over lines and moves in Act II. Clifford was sitting at his table, watching in a vague sort of way.

Mary didn't arrive until two. When she did walk in, all dressed up, hair recently done, and looking terrific, she took us completely by surprise, saying, "Oh, I feel awful, I have a headache, I'm completely worn out."

After we gave her sympathy, she said, "Well, all right, let's begin," and grabbed hold of the script.

"Mary," I said, "try it without the script. You know most of it."

"I'll just use it awhile; I'm tired."

I began to go on, but Clifford gave me a look that said, Don't push your luck. The cast started in the middle of Act II, and even with the book Mary was confused. She kept losing her place, not being exactly sure of which section they were in. Even Gary, who is so good, did not have a firm handle on his lines when he came in for his scene toward the end, and Annie-Joe ambled through her lines, delivering them one at a time, slowly, and being rude to boot. I whispered to Clifford, "Can't you starch them up? This is so sloppy." He made a gesture that indicated: Patience, wait a bit.

When we took a break, I got Clifford to walk away from them so we could talk. "Clifford, you're being too lax with them; they need to be pepped up. They're being very sloppy."

"I realize that, but it's difficult with Mary in such a state."

"That's what I'm talking about. You can help snap them out

of it. Raise your voice, give them a little speech, wake them up. I would yell at Annie-Joe and—"

"That's not my way."

"What is your way?"

"Not that. If I ever start to yell, it would be far too loud and far too much."

We were at a standoff, and rehearsal soon resumed. Finally he did say something to Annie-Joe: "Come on, dear, pay attention, pick it up. You know how to do it." She gave him a dirty look and said, "I'm trying to find my character."

They went back to an early point in Act II, when Mary is threatening to leave the apartment; she had no idea what to do with her purse and other props. "Aren't those moves written into your script?" I asked.

"No."

Jimmy Dobson had neglected to transfer her moves to her new, double-spaced script. I looked to Jimmy; he said nothing. Clifford said, "Let's go on."

We did. But eventually we got to a place where there were cuts and changes that had also not been incorporated into Mary's script. We had to stop again. I turned to Clifford and said, "I don't understand why nothing's been—"

Clifford interrupted me: "No, no, don't pursue this, not now."

At that point, I thought, Oh, I'm not going to sit around like some petulant child, tugging at the director's sleeve, not only egging him on but wanting to egg them all on. This is obviously annoying to Clifford, and it's infuriating to me. As they resumed, I made a point of not sneaking out, but of simply packing my briefcase, getting my jacket, standing up, and walking out of the rehearsal hall. I wanted my displeasure to be known by all. I vowed not to come back tomorrow. It's total masochism to sit there and allow the Chinese Water Torture to be performed for my benefit time after time.

Wednesday, December 18, 1985

Great to get up and not go to rehearsal. But *Legends!* caught up with me anyhow. In the late afternoon the phone rang.

"Jimmy—it's Carol."

Oh my God! "Yes?"

"I just got back from my fitting and, darling, wait until you see my costume, my red suit. It's perfect, I love it, I love you."

"Good, I'm glad."

"I owe it all to you. I'm so excited, I can't wait for you to see it. Now, they showed me a couple of sketches for the dress I change into when Mary arrives, but I said no. Really, you should see what they had in mind. I told them, I said, 'Listen, I am not playing a certified public accountant in this play, I'm playing a *movie star,* for God's sake! Movie stars don't run around in drab rags like that!' "

I asked how rehearsals were going. There was a pause, a sigh, and Carol said, "Well, dear . . ."

I cut her off, saying, "Gotta go, see you tomorrow." I looked at our schedule. Soon, like it or not, the Christmas holidays would be interrupting the regular flow of rehearsals. Time gallops by. Christmas, then New Year's, and we're off to Dallas. I took a Valium.

Thursday, December 19, 1985

Another grand day! Returned to rehearsals. It was decided to have a go at Act I; it stumbled along in its usual stop-and-start way.

The critic/reviewer from the Dallas paper was due in town and wanted simply to ride in Mary's car on the way to rehearsal. But she nixed even this—and all publicity, interviews, or anything that would interfere with rehearsal time. I am to do an interview with him, but he had recently tangled with Carol over her last *Hello, Dolly!* tour and felt he shouldn't write a feature article about her.

When we broke for lunch, Clifford and I took a walk around the parking lot, both very concerned about Mary's lines. I asked if he couldn't urge her on a little more; he felt it would be counterproductive. "I can't push her any harder, can't figure out any better schedule." Jimmy Dobson is no longer going to work with

Mary. Susan said that on this last trip to Rancho Mirage very little was accomplished. It was mostly social. Mary is now going to work with Keith Baumgartner, who is really on his toes and pays strict attention to business, and Mary likes him. He will work with her at night and also at rehearsals.

As Clifford and I were pacing the parking lot, exchanging this information, he suddenly turned to me and said, "Well, Jimmy, even if the play is a disaster in Dallas, it won't hurt you that much, will it?"

If I'd been standing on a cliff, I'd have taken a header. His remark threw me totally. I could only reply with a rather simple "Yes, of course, it would."

"Really?" Clifford said. "Oh, I don't think so."

What could he be thinking of? As director he can walk away from it, another play, hit or miss, but he hasn't been glued to it for two solid years as I have, gone through the planning, the writing and rewriting of it, the incredible wooing of Mary—I was so taken aback I just let the subject drop, but was not all that cheered when Clifford went on to say, "Kevin and Bob are making noises that ticket sales in Dallas are soft."

I thought, Wouldn't it be terrific if something good happened right out of the blue? Just to break the monotony.

After lunch the second act was tackled. As the day goes on, Mary gets weaker and weaker and really can't remember much of anything. I wish she'd continued with the doctor, but she's adamant about not taking time out for anything, even though it might help. Every time Mary stops and says, "Now, am I eating this here or have I put it down?" or "Do I take a drink here?" I know she's lost for the next line. It's the actor's way of stalling when the mind won't cough up the words.

I feel so sorry for her and so impotent just sitting watching, unable to come to the rescue, except every now and then to trim a speech by a line or a line by a few words. I feel equally sorry for Carol, who is hard put to work up to full throttle with all the stops and starts, like trying to drive a car when it keeps stalling. Around three o'clock Mary just stopped cold and said, "I have to have the book. I'm holding Carol up, I'm holding everyone up, and it's embarrassing." The impulse was to say, "Mary, the only way you'll get it is by doing it without the script." But there was such desperation in her plea that no one uttered a word. Keith got up in silence and handed her the script. There was a fuss about finding the right place, and for a second I thought she'd burst into tears, but she didn't. They went on until a break. Then Clifford, and wisely so, brought Trish in with Eric to show us the strip routine.

It isn't quite finished but it's perky, bouncy; the music is much more suited to it than my takeoff on "Bye-Bye Baby." It's a little rough, but one can feel it going in the right direction. It was also such a divertissement from our "problem" that we all relaxed into seeing it. Trish and Eric were both concerned about our reaction, but we were all pleased, including Clifford.

The ladies resumed, while the rest of us were summoned to a production meeting with all department heads: Doug Schmidt, our set designer; Freddy Wittop's assistant, Harry Curtis; Bob and Kevin; Bob Saltzman, our prop man; David Masacek, our carpenter; and on and on. Lots of talk about when the trucks would be leaving L.A. for Dallas, the load-in, the setup, the tech rehearsal, etc. Everyone was talking strictly go-ahead, gung-ho; no one was acknowledging that none of this would matter a lick if Mary couldn't step out on the stage and say the lines.

I started to enter the rehearsal room late in the afternoon but stepped right back out when I heard Carol say to Mary, "No, dear, that's in the first act; we're toward the end of the play now."

"Oh, I thought—"

"No, dear, this is where you say—"

Check please!

Friday, December 20, 1985

Or, to be more precise, BLACK FRIDAY.

By the time I arrived at the rehearsal hall, the atmosphere was intensely fractured.

Carol had been rehearsing outside and up by the cafeteria with the understudy, Barbara Sohmers, and Annie-Joe; Mary had been closeted in the rehearsal hall with Keith. When I peeked in there, Keith gave me more cuts Mary had requested/made. Now Leatrice says nothing about her early life as an orphan, moving from one family to the next, which means her character's reason for becoming an actress and for searching for love, for wanting to please everyone, is totally missing. When Mary asks for these cuts, it's difficult to refuse them unless one is ready to say: All right, we made a mistake, *don't* do the play. With this daunting alternative, we whittled the play away, cut by cut.

Another edict: Mary is so embarrassed about not knowing her lines, she doesn't even want the understudies in the rehearsal hall. No producers, no understudies, no one connected with the cast unless they're in a scene with her. Just Clifford, me, Keith, the stage managers. And Carol, of course. There are too many people sitting too close, watching her tumble. Mary said to me, "It's much easier to rehearse with Keith than Carol; she makes me so nervous." Mary said this in front of Keith, and later I asked him if he'd be willing to don a wig and high heels and play Sylvia, if it came to that. "Sure!" he said. "Anything for your play!"

Clifford said they'd have a go at Act II again after lunch. I asked if he could please persuade Mary to try it without the script. But when they began, there it was in her lap.

Just as they got going again, Annie-Joe, who had a line in response to Sylvia's "You mean, at the party—your friends take dope?" stopped cold. Her next line, as Aretha, was "Honey, black people take anything they can get!"

Annie-Joe turned toward me and growled, "I'm not going to say that line, I'm tired of that black stuff. It could get very offensive. I won't say it," she muttered. "I'll just say something about . . . my friends take anything."

I have no problem with an actor feeling a line is unsuitable or objectionable or anything, but there is a way to approach this, and Annie-Joe had not taken it. She should have spoken to me during a break and simply stated her case, instead of stopping during rehearsals in front of the cast and, to top it off, telling me what she *would* say in its place. There was silence for a moment, and Clifford only looked at me, as if to say, Well?

This was no time for a major confrontation on rehearsal manners, so I only said, "Say anything you want to!" I gathered up my things, stood, and walked out of the hall.

Steve Meyer was sitting outside by the phones. "Not going

off angry again?" he asked. "Yes, I'm afraid so, see you in a few days, *if* I'm up to it." I turned the corner, walked past the lounge area where Gary, Don Howard, Barbara Sohmers, and Gwen Shepherd were sitting, talking and laughing. They stopped, said hello to me; I mumbled goodbye and left. Wondered if they were, deep down, as doom-riddled as I was.

As I walked to the car, the truth struck me like one of the tablets hurtled down from the mountain. Mary was not going to be able to bring it off.

Saturday, December 21, 1985

Typing the date sends me into a mini-panic. The date of reckoning fast approaches. Already December 21. Haul out the prayer rugs. I took the day off; nothing I could do but sit there and make Clifford nervous and perhaps, by eye contact alone, transmit to Mary my cold fear and even chance a knee-jerk blowup by crying out: Jesus, Mary (and Joseph), listen to what's being said to you. Just listen, instead of staring at the printed page, and you can't go that far wrong.

Tom Davis should be arriving today, and he'll put that ear-bug idea into Mary's head. Clifford told a story about Ralph Richardson using an ear device in London. He had one line at the end of Act I and just couldn't get it. It was a line like "I think someone left the front door open." When the stage manager whispered into his microphone to transmit the line to Richardson's ear device on opening night, the actor merely cocked his head and said, "What?" So much for ear devices.

Sunday, December 22, 1985

Another glorious day of not going to rehearsals. Spent the time addressing Christmas cards. (This year's card is a photo of me with one arm around Mary and the other around Carol, saying "Merry Christmas from the Kirkwoods." The year before, the photo was with Liz Taylor. All say "Merry Christmas from the Kirkwoods." People seem to look forward to them.)

By evening I realized that each day away from rehearsals is like missing the Spanish flu.

MARY CHRISTMAS

Monday, December 23, 1985

Called Clifford, who said things were going better and claimed that Mary could get through the first act without the book. I suggested perhaps I should stay away altogether: my absence could mean good luck. He laughed and said no, no. He'd put the striptease into the first act, and both Mary and Carol were being integrated into it toward the end. He said the ladies enjoyed it thoroughly. I replied that I was sure Mary was enjoying it, because she didn't have any lines to say for about three minutes. Clifford asked if I was coming today and I said no; as long as things were going smoothly, I'd stay away.

He did ask me to come tomorrow; rehearsals were beginning at ten, but at one o'clock he was going to attempt a stumble-through of the whole play. That promised to be more fun than a tree full of owls, so I agreed to be on hand.

Tuesday, December 24, 1985

Christmas Eve day. Odd to wake up to a sunny, warm day and realize it's Christmas Eve day. If one *has* to go through it—give me snow and Vermont and sleighs, the whole bit. Drove down to rehearsals around eleven. I could tell by the tense looks on everyone's faces that the hour before had not been a winner.

"Clifford, how's it going?"

"Oh, so-so."

"Oh, shit."

"Umm."

After lunch Jim Bernardi and Steve set up the props and we prepared for our runthrough. Tom Davis is here now to back up Mary. I don't know that he's the best support system. He does not tend to have an optimistic look on his face. There's always a slight wincing expression, as if he knows something is going to go terribly wrong but he's not quite certain *when*.

Today he didn't have to wait too long. Whatever was going well before was not going very well now. The first act was not too bad, except when Mary asked to have the script toward the end. We begged her to go on without it, and she agreed. Between acts she conferred in a corner with Tom Davis. Act II started off fairly well; the cop scene, albeit a short one, breezed by, but then the stumbling and foomfing began. I wrote a note on a scrap of paper and slipped it to Clifford: "Is this worse than working with Claudette and Rex?" The answer came back printed in large letters. "I thought nothing could be worse than that. I was wrong. This is twice as bad."

Mary Christmas.

By the middle of the act, things started falling apart with alarming regularity. Mary did add one enormously surprising ad-lib bit of business right at the curtain that killed us all. When the two of them hear the doorbell ring and realize the press is at the door, wanting to come in and get the lowdown on the fight they had at the end of Act I, the two ladies decide to give them what they want. So, although they've made up and have decided to do the play, they pretend to fight, insult each other, and use this opportunity to get a little pre-production publicity. They tell Aretha to "let 'em in."

With that the door opens and Tim Johnson, Barbara Sohmers, etc. (as reporters), come in, led by Gary. They carry flash cameras. This afternoon, as Carol started to chase Mary around the room, screaming insults at her, Mary suddenly stopped in front of the sofa, turned her back to Carol, lifted her dress, and mooned her. The photographers flashed pictures and the stage manager yelled curtain. We all howled with delight; it was so impromptu, so funny-on-the-spot, that both Clifford and I shouted, "Keep it in!" The idea of Mary Martin, our little Peter Pan and Maria von Trapp, mooning Dolly Levi struck us as hysterical. She did it well, and she also has great legs. She wears a body stocking, and her behind looked firm and pink and pretty. There was nothing smarmy about it. Mary was delighted at our reaction and agreed to keep it in for the final curtain.

This took some of the edge off the shaky day it had been. Actors are survivors, and touching ones as well. As soon as rehearsals were over, Carol put on a Santa Claus beard and passed out bottles of champagne; Mary gave out beautiful books. A ten-million-calorie mud pie was wheeled in with some other sweets, and before we knew it Annie-Joe was at the piano playing Christmas carols, Tim Johnson stood beside her playing the flute, and everyone was gathered around singing.

I quickly walked to the men's room and found myself wiping tears from my eyes. It was a combination of the play, Christmas, the death of my aunt, and God only knows what. I mopped myself up and went back into the rehearsal hall. They were now singing with a sort of vengeance, as if the noise alone could drown out the fears we all held inside us. I wanted to join in, but I could only sit over in the corner and watch, incredibly saddened by this frenetic display of Christmas spirit and determination: We will not let this rather sticky wicket we're in get us all down. We won't. I left at the height of the so-called festivities, kissing them all, wishing them Merry Christmas, saying I'd see them Christmas Day at the dinner party Bob Regester had kindly arranged to throw for the company.

Driving home, I played out the worst scenario that might emerge from this Christmas season. We all knew Mary was spending the day with Larry and Maj and assorted grandchildren at Malibu. I thought Mary might easily have a drink or two and suddenly, snug in the warmth of her family, say, "Larry, I'm just not getting it, I'm not going to be able to do it. It's so humiliating." At which point Larry would say, "Oh, Mother, come on, now, you're a pro. You've been away for a long time; it will come back, you'll see." Then Mary would suddenly burst into tears and virtually collapse, crying out, "No, no, I can't. I don't know why, but I just can't, it's torture." Larry would take a deep breath and say, "Oh, well, fuck it, then, Mom. Don't do it; it's not worth all that; you don't need the money—get out of it now."

And that would be it. The scenario was not that inconceivable, not at all.

Christmas Day, December 25, 1985

Cut to: the evening, and Bob Regester's Christmas dinner for the cast at Neil Hartley's. The house itself is of Spanish influence, charming, huge living room with a terrace overlooking the lights of the city blinking through the tops of trees rising from the slope below. Dining room adjacent, lower floor with bedrooms and baths. Excellent view, a good party house. Bob knows how to entertain and does it graciously.

Everyone gathered early in the evening except Gary Beach, Clifford Williams (who was dropping in after dinner), and Mary, who was also stopping by on her way back from Malibu and her day with the Hagmans.

Carol arrived, all dressed in red, everything red, shoes, stockings, lots of bows and bangles, and that huge blonde wig. She looked like an immense Christmas doll, one that could be stuck on a tree. Of course, the imagination wavers when considering the size of the tree she'd fit upon.

We all stood out on the terrace having drinks at first, taking snapshots, talking Christmas talk. No one discussed the play until Bob summoned us to go in for dinner. As we were all filing into the dining room, Carol suddenly chirped out, her words sailing on the end of a long sigh, "Oh, isn't it just lovely that Mary isn't here?" Oddly enough, it was said with humor and a certain warmth. We all laughed and looked at each other, wondering what the impetus was for that one-liner.

Carol sat at one end of the table; I sat next to her. After a moment she said, "Isn't it also nice that our famous *comedy* director"—sarcasm dripping now—"Clifford Williams, is also missing?" No one responded to that. We all sat focusing on the food, which was terrific. But Carol went on: "Clifford doesn't understand anything that goes on in this play, he really doesn't. James Kirkwood's characters are not Noel Coward, they're bigger than life, and you can't stifle them."

I attempted to change the conversation, because I did not think this was particularly morale-building Christmas Day talk. But Carol was on a roll. She was letting off steam with anyone whose ear she could get: Keith Baumgartner about Mary and her lines and rhythms, constantly switching back to Clifford and his lack of any comprehension of American comedy. Oh, yes, and she was not at all pleased about her participation in the strip routine. She wanted to enter into the dance number much earlier than Clifford thought wise. She was being humorous about much of this talk, but the sharp edge of a cutting knife was present, and there was no doubt at all that stormclouds were not that far from the horizon.

Mary arrived with Susan and Tom Davis soon after dinner. She seemed to be in an excellent mood; the scenario I'd rehearsed had obviously not taken place. Now, this is what struck me: As soon as Mary came in, everyone made a big fuss over her, Carol came over, they embraced, had their pictures taken hugging each other standing by the mantel. Immediately after, Carol went out onto the terrace, followed by her coterie, and Mary stayed in the living room with her group, and they did not speak again until Carol left.

I think Mary had had several glasses of Christmas cheer, and why not? It seemed to loosen her, because she focused on me with narrowed eyes and snapped: "Well, if only you wouldn't write so many lines that are almost the same but they're not the same, they're just a little bit different. So many of them are *almost* the same. You do that, you know!"

"I do not," I replied.

"You do, too!"

"I do not!"

We sounded like kindergarten children. I thought we could probably go on for hours and then end up sticking our tongues out at each other.

"Well, I think you do."

"Then you're crazy!"

Thank God someone laughed at that point and we ended this little round before it fell over into the ridiculous. Carol made a speedy exit, Mary stayed on for a nightcap, then left, saying she'd see us all at rehearsals. The others soon drifted away, and I was alone with Bob, congratulating him on a lovely dinner party.

Clifford arrived, and we told him Mary was in good spirits and apparently all had gone well in Malibu. Bob said, "We all have to stick together, we can't panic. If one person tips the boat, she'll walk, and the whole ship will sink. It's going to be murder in Dallas, but that's what Dallas is for; it's our out-of-town. If Keith has to be down behind the sofa on his hands and knees throwing her lines, then that's what it's going to be."

We agreed that, come hell or high water, Mary would probably get through it, and we'd all be gibbering idiots. But it just might possibly pull together around the end of the second week in Dallas, and we'd all say, "What in the fuck were we worried about?"

THE FINAL PUSH

Thursday, December 26, 1987

In the morning everyone was a bit slow in pulling it together after Christmas. Each was rehearsing in his or, rather, her own favorite way: Keith and Mary in the rehearsal hall; Carol out in the sun with the understudies. It occurred to me that's probably the way they'd like to *do* the show eventually. A new avant-garde theatrical gimmick. The audience could watch Mary with Keith up on the stage, then take a break and hit the patio to see Carol do a scene with the understudies. I thought of buying Clifford a pair of roller skates for a joke, so he could more easily commute between rehearsal places. Only this was no joke.

After lunch we started to run the second act, beginning with the cop scene. Mary wasn't able to come in with her first line, which is "Brilliant!" The second line had to be cued, then the third and the fourth. Ice water in the veins.

They ran the cop scene once, twice, three times, and then started in on the meat of the second act. Mary constantly asked for lines or was thrown them without asking, and suddenly she just broke down: "No, no, I can't go on, it isn't fair to Carol or the rest of the cast, it's not fair to Jimmy and the play and Clifford. I just can't do it! I'll have to quit—"

"No, Mary—" This from about six people.

"No, no, it's just not fair, it's not right, I simply cannot do it, I'll have to quit."

Quit. The first time the ultimate word was uttered. It was out in the open now. She was standing, we all huddled around her as if she were a disabled athlete and we were trying to comfort her out of some temporary injury.

She began to cry, not big loud boo-hooing, but there were

tears in her eyes and she seemed so very tiny with all of us surrounding her and throwing out dumb little incoherent lines like "No, Mary, listen . . . ," "You'll be just . . . ," "Hey, everybody goes through . . ."

All sorts of mixed feelings, from "Oh, God, come here, you poor frightened little girl, it's going to be all right," to "Well, for Christ's sake, if you'd only start thinking and *listening!*" The latter was drowned out by sympathy. It had to be so humiliating for her. Here was Nellie Forbush and Peter Pan and Maria von Trapp—falling apart, all of them collapsing in on Mary Martin. In public.

It was obvious rehearsal for the afternoon was over. After a while, lest we suffocate her, we all backed off a bit, and soon Annie-Joe put an arm around her with great compassion and led her out to the parking lot for a prayer session.

Clifford and I stayed in the rehearsal hall, not wanting to aid or abet—by any word, deed, or expression—a complete rout. Carol went off in the corner and nibbled at some of her silver-dished goodies. Everyone else disappeared down rabbit holes.

Eventually Annie-Joe walked back in with Mary, who sat down in the chair outside the rehearsal-room door, near the phones, with Tom Davis. I walked over to see if she was all right. It was then Mary started talking about a rash she'd discovered underneath her breast the night before, when she was undressing for bed. "It had bumps; they were red, about the size of my small fingernail. They itched and were peeling and I couldn't really get a good night's sleep. It might be shingles."

Clifford had joined us during this description. The signs were up: medical withdrawal. Susan was asked to call Mary's doctor. He was on vacation (of course!). Another doctor was found, an appointment was made, and soon Mary was getting her things together. We all hugged her, told her it would be fine, nothing to worry about, relax. She had a costume fitting at five; someone mentioned it, but no one went on about whether she'd go or not. She left with Susan, Steve Meyer, and Tom Davis. We all waved goodbye as if she were sailing away on the *QEII*.

The minute she'd gone, there was total silence in the rehearsal hall. The air seemed dead; all the oxygen had been sucked out of it. We wandered around in limbo for a while. I said to Clifford, "Do you think we'll ever see Mary again?" He shrugged and then asked Carol if she'd like to go on rehearsing with Barbara Sohmers. "Oh, yes, that would be a great help, yes, let's do that."

They did, and, of course, Barbara had all the lines down cold, and one couldn't help thinking: If we could only do a memory transplant. By the time rehearsal finished Carol said to Barbara, "Oh, thank you so much! That was a great help." Carol turned to us. "Wasn't it?" Yes, yes, we all agreed. No one was putting his mouth on the main subject. They had gone through the rehearsal as if nothing was wrong, and I was amazed they'd managed it so well. My mind is so bloody one-track, I could not help thinking: Now Mary's going to the doctor, now he's examining her, now it's shingles, now he's saying, "You can't go on." Now they're calling. . . .

Clifford and I met at Bob's in the evening. We were both convinced Mary would not make it to Dallas, or if she did it would be analogous to President Kennedy's visit there. A phone call was made to alert Kevin, who'd gone back to New York for a few days, to the imminent danger we faced; we asked him to start thinking immediately of a possible replacement. No, no, not yet, Kevin said; that would send up too many red flags. We'd talk soon.

Bob phoned Tom Davis and they had words. Mary had seen the doctor; it wasn't shingles, some other rash; and she was resting. She'd gone to her costume fitting, and she was planning to go to rehearsal the next day, but Bob had better cancel Dallas. She wasn't going to play Dallas. Bob tried to avoid any further conversation about Dallas until Kevin was back with us.

We called Kevin back immediately and got on different phones to give our considered opinions. Clifford and I were of the darkest. I asked again if they had insurance on Mary, and neither Bob nor Kevin was sure about the terms, what exactly it covered and what it didn't and how much. I again suggested they'd best find out. Kevin and Bob insisted a cancellation of Dallas was out of the question; they faced lawsuits, huge losses of money, the backers, etc. We said then they'd better reverse their decision—forget about red flags—get on the phone and start investigating the availability of other actresses. It was finally agreed that Kevin would call Johnson-Liff and find out who was doing what and where and when. Or, rather, who was *not* doing anything at the exact moment.

Friday, December 27, 1985

The day began with phones ringing. Andy Zerman at Johnson-Liff had come up with a list of names, but Kevin was terrified this might leak, and if Mary found out about it, that would be her out. We were going underground. Andy had made up this list: Jean Simmons, Frannie Sternhagen, Debbie Reynolds, Celeste Holm, Tammy Grimes, Shirley Jones, Gerry Page, Carol Burnett, Estelle Parsons, Jayne Meadows, Kim Hunter, Eileen Brennan, Teresa Wright, Nancy Marchand, Maureen O'Sullivan, Nanette Fabray, Coral Brown, Florence Henderson, Eva Gabor, Greer Garson, Claire Trevor, Vivian Blaine, June Allyson, and Jane Wyatt.

The real contenders seemed to be Debbie Reynolds (because of her name on the road), Celeste Holm (because she'd be so right), Frannie Sternhagen (because she'd be so good), and Eva Gabor (because she's the right age, has glamour, and can do comedy). The rest were put on hold for the time being. Celeste Holm was available. Andy said it was lunchtime back East, International Creative Management handled Debbie, and he hadn't been able to reach anyone yet.

The Giffords had set up a luncheon for me with the main critic from Dallas, Dan Hulbert, of the Dallas *Times-Herald*. I dreaded it—the irony of an interview with a critic about a play starring these two legends when we were seriously thinking of replacing one, was freezing.

Arrived at the rehearsal hall to find all the principals working together on the first act, instead of off in their separate cubicles. No visible panic, Mary seemed pulled together, in a businesslike spirit. Tom Davis grabbed my arm to say that Mary didn't want to meet with the Dallas critic, and could I help get him off her back. He'd wanted a full interview and that had been turned down, so someone had suggested that he simply drive with her from her apartment in Hollywood to rehearsal in the morning. Tom said she didn't want to do that, either. I told him that was not my venue; it should be done through the PR people. He also wanted to engage me in the "Cancel Dallas Campaign" to keep Mary from quitting. I told him that was not my decision to make, it was up to the producers. And tried to explain to him the ramifications of such an act. "All right, then—but she'll quit." All of this by way of cheering me up even more before my luncheon with Hulbert.

—Which was scheduled for twelve-thirty at the Itchy Foot, a restaurant/bar of mostly Italian persuasion a few blocks down the street. And there was Dan Hulbert, a bespectacled, nice enough young man, probably no more than thirty-two, if that. He was very friendly (they can be when caught out of print; the venom is saved for the pen) and extremely excited that *Legends!* was going to have its world premiere in Dallas.

Though he was going to be seeing Carol later on in the day, after rehearsal, all he wanted to talk about was Mary Martin. "Mary's been off the stage for such a long time—is it a problem for her to come back now at this age?"

"Oh, no, she's a trouper; once a trouper, always a trouper."

"What about learning lines. It's a large part, isn't it?"

"Learning lines takes time, but that's just the basic requirement. She's just so right for the part of Leatrice. I'm so happy we actually found two legends to play legends."

He was a little like a terrier with a bone. "Yes, but doesn't she have any problems, any barriers to overcome?"

"Well, no, not really."

"You mean things are going that smoothly?"

"Well, you have to realize," said I, "that all stars have their little idiosyncrasies"—like learning lines!—"you know, little things they feel uncomfortable doing or saying. Sometimes you have to invert lines, change the rhythm slightly, but that goes with the territory, that's part of the package."

"For instance?"

"Well, you know, Mary doesn't like to say certain words."

"Like what?"

Then, trying to be humorous, I laughed and said, "Well, you know, 'shit' and 'fuck' and the C-word." Let's get off the subject, I prayed as I rattled on, finding myself forced into a performance and going with it. "I feel so lucky, it's such a happy company. We have no lemons, isn't that odd? You see, usually every company has at least one lemon that everyone dislikes and picks on. Not with us. What a happy ship. Yes, I know it's unusual, but it's true." When he did a little more digging, which indicated this sounded a little too good to be real, I leveled with him to a certain extent. "Listen, no show is ready to open, ever, until it's forced to open because people are in the theatre and the curtain *has* to be raised. We'll have a bumpy time in Dallas, but that's par for the course. There will be changes, the audience will tell us things." Slight laugh. "And undoubtedly you will." And on and on.

It was a good interview. He was not hostile but very enthusiastic, and I presumed he was one of those critics who are scholarly, perhaps in the extreme. Who knew? We'd find out. I did feel a bit sullied in having to lie so much, but it would have been suicide even to let anyone spy a chink in the armor at this stage of the game. How can you deliberately pull your finger out of the dyke and sink your own play? You can't. He hoped he could ride in the car with Mary to rehearsal. I said I hoped he could, too. We said goodbye, see you in Dallas. I had wanted to ask him about his qualifications for being a critic and how did he feel about having that kind of power over the lives of approximately fifty people and the fate of a million-dollar investment? But I had done that once at a luncheon with Dan Sullivan of the Los Angeles *Times* and it had gone over like a dead mouse in a punch bowl.

Back at the ranch, I told Mary I'd had lunch with Dan, that he seemed nice, very eager to meet her, not a killer, and I thought she would find fifteen minutes or so with him a pleasant experience, not taxing at all. She barely responded.

Rehearsal began in the afternoon with the first act again. They got to the part when Carol asks Mary to say the speech from *Rainbow's End,* the picture for which Mary (Leatrice) won the Academy Award for playing a woman who regresses to a little girl, rather as Cliff Robertson did in *Charley.* She refuses Carol, but when Annie-Joe (Aretha) begs her to, she finally agrees. Sitting on the sofa, she folds her hands in her lap and begins speaking like a little baby girl. Her first line is "Her knows her won't see Donny again, her knows her would wike her own baby, but her knows her can't, can't ever."

They reached that point, and Mary couldn't remember the first line. Suddenly Carol gasped, "I know how you can remember it."

"How?" asked Mary.

"Well," Carol said, with great excitement, "if you can't think of 'knows' I'll point to mine."

Mary—and the entire room—looked confused. "What do you mean?"

"Don't you see," Carol went on, "*I* know your line, so I'll point to my *nose.*" She put a finger on the tip of her nose. "Like this. And that will give you your cue—'knows.' And then once you have *that,* you can go on with 'Her knows her won't see Donny again.'" Mary only looked at her. "Well," Carol went on, "you hate the way I make it up with that line across it, so that should really help you. 'Knows'—'nose'!" She put her finger on the tip of her nose again and giggled. "See?"

"Oh, Carol," Mary sighed.

"Well," Carol said, addressing the rest of us, "if she can't remember anything—"

Clifford cut in and said, "All right, let's go on now."

Around four, Mary started to get very shaky again, and suddenly she stopped. "Can't we rehearse on a stage?"

"What?" someone asked.

"A stage," Mary said. "I have to be on a stage. You're all so close to me, it's difficult." Since we were in a rehearsal hall, it was true that Clifford, the stage manager, Keith, and I were seated no more than ten or twelve feet from her; the proximity can be a bit off-putting, but that's the way rehearsals are. "I really have to be on a stage, I never saw my audiences for forty years, I only heard them, and I don't want to see them now. I want to be on a stage!"

It was obvious this was no whim, she meant business. There was a confab, and Steve Meyer was sent out to forage around for empty theatres in the L.A. area. Mary went on: "I've never rehearsed in a rehearsal hall like this." Clifford asked where she'd rehearsed her last play, *Do You Turn Somersaults?* "In a loft," she replied.

The obvious solution was "Fuck it, get her a loft." But that would not have flown, as they say. Many rehearsal halls are lofts and vice versa, but at this stage of the game, if Mary wanted to rehearse in a covered wagon we'd have gone for it.

As rehearsal resumed, Tom Davis dragged me outside by the phones. "I told Mary if she wasn't ready the night of the first preview in Dallas, she wasn't going on. And if she's not ready the second night, she's not going on. And if she's not ready for opening night—well, that's it." It's such a psychological help to keep getting these bits of information poured into one's ear like so much arsenic.

Back in the rehearsal hall, they approached the strip number with Eric. Shortly after I returned, toward the middle of the number, Carol suddenly got up and entered into it, frugging and swinging and swaying.

"No, no, Carol," Clifford said, "not yet."

She stopped dead. "You've put me in for only the last couple of bars, and that's not right. You don't understand the vulgar part of a Hollywood star, and I don't think you understand American comedy, either."

"Now, Carol—"

"No!" Carol pulled herself up to her full height and strode offstage as she snapped, "If I'm not put in that number earlier—I walk!" Just then she turned and aimed this one at Clifford: "And so should *you!*"

All quiet on the western front. Carol went over to her corner by the standup piano like a boxer waiting for the gong to ring for the next round. Mary simply sat in her chair, looking weary but slightly relieved. This little exchange certainly took the heat off her. Clifford stayed at his table, and then for a while he and Carol muttered several phrases at each other from across the room, but it was obvious the war was to be kept limited; no atomic weapons were going to be dragged out unless one of them went just that inch too far.

Eventually a temporary truce was achieved, and rehearsal continued until Steve Meyer returned in the late afternoon with word on theatres. There were two choices: the Pasadena Playhouse, or the Variety Arts in downtown L.A. "Both theatres have not been used for a while, both are dirty, ill lit, cold, and damp," Steve reported.

"Great," I said, "let's make a choice!"

Mary said she really didn't know the Pasadena Playhouse, and eventually it was agreed to use Variety Arts, because it was not too far away. Rehearsal was called for ten in the morning with Keith, Mary, Gwen, and Barbara. Clifford would work early on with Annie-Joe and Carol on their first scene.

Clifford and I repaired to the Itchy Foot for a drink and hashed over the mess that had been this day. We both felt Dallas should be canceled. "But, on the other hand," Clifford said, "we're going to have to shove her out on the stage no matter how long we postpone; maybe we should simply shove her out as early as possible." We talked about other casting possibilities, kidded again about where we should hide Keith to prompt her— either behind the sofa or up the chimney. "We used the chimney for Rex in *Aren't We All?*" Clifford said. As we walked to our cars, Clifford stopped abruptly, put a hand to his chin, and mused in his delightful British way, "How did we happen to get so many cunts in one cast?" There's something about a British accent that removes the curse from certain words. "How many?" I asked.

"Four, I believe."

"Four? Who?"

Clifford rubbed his chin in thought. "Well, let's see, there's Mary and Carol and Annie-Joe and—" He paused, thought a moment, and said, "No, wait a moment, I was certain there was a fourth."

We roared with laughter. Nerves were making us punchy. It was obvious we should say good night—LEST WE GO TOO FAR???? Before getting into our cars, we agreed that rehearsing in a theatre was probably not going to be the panacea we needed. I said, "Tomorrow we'll probably get a request to rehearse in a 747 because Mary will feel too earthbound!"

Saturday, December 28, 1985

At noon I drove down to the Variety Arts, in a strange area of downtown, 9th and Figueroa. The theatre itself is a gem, it reeks of period—1924, when it was built. Terra cotta on the outside; on the inside it's a treasure, great cushy lobbies, posters, nooks and crannies all filled with memorabilia. The theatre is the kind they don't build anymore, the kind that promises a good time, instead of those cold, institutional monsters that seem to indicate a meeting of the school board is imminent. Good sight lines, a large proscenium (stage opening), and just the right size, about fourteen hundred seats, perhaps a few more.

A good facsimile of the set furniture had been arranged on the stage, and everyone seemed to be in a good mood except Tom Davis, who was lurking around waiting to trap the producers or whoever else he could snare to fall under his rather shifty-eyed spell and drop auguries of doom upon, "Won't go on, better cancel Dallas, quit!"

I took Carol aside in the lobby and gave her some cuts in her "ass monologue." (When she falls under the influence of Aretha's hash brownies, she loosens up and starts talking about when she was a child and her mother came into her room by surprise and caught her looking at her behind in a mirror. Carol/Sylvia says, "Well, you should have heard the commotion, she got right on the phone and called up my father at the office and said, 'Oh my God, Frank, you won't believe what happened, I just caught Sylvia looking at her behind in a *mirror!*' Well, I didn't see what the commotion was all about. I mean it was *my* mirror and it was *my* ass and I wanted to see what it looked like. I wasn't doing anything to it, I was simply *looking* at it." It's a long section in which she describes her childhood, loneliness, etc., and ends up saying, "I was so mad afterwards I went straight up to the attic and killed every fly I could find, then I spelled my whole name out in dead flies!")

Carol took the cuts well, and I also gave her some line readings. Most actors balk at them, but sometimes they're the quickest way to convey the author's meaning to the actor. Carol didn't mind this, either, and we even worked on a new way of doing it before she was called in to rehearse with Mary again.

Mary seemed in good fettle. Trish was present, looking beautiful, to monitor the strip number. About two-thirty they started running through the first act. It actually went fairly well, until after the end of the strip number and Eric's exit. The number's going to be fine; he does it with style and joy, and the combination of Annie-Joe's exuberance and the reaction of "the ladies" serves it well. Also, there are about three glorious minutes when nobody has to remember any lines. Hallelujah!

Because of the size and darkness of the theatre, Bob and Kevin were huddled in the back row, like little mice keeping out of the way. Mary's ban on who can be in attendance has still not been officially revoked. During a break, I walked up onstage to talk to Mary. She said, "Darling, it's Carol's face, her expression, that keeps me blowing sky-high." I asked how she meant that. "Well, she looks at me with such intensity and . . . almost panic . . . and I know she wants to help but it's . . . not allowing for natural timing. It's that look of panic that throws me."

When rehearsal resumed, I sat about halfway back, next to Trish. Clifford sat behind us. What a joy to be able to sit in a darkened theatre and get rid of some of the steam we'd been holding in these many weeks by being able to mutter curses under our breath when something went wrong.

I growled my usual obscenities, and Clifford kept up a running commentary. When Mary was going through her "retarded speech" and came to the line "If only her mind had kept up wif her body," Clifford said, "A truer word was never spoken." I know this sounds like high treason, but it's a working situation, and when the work is not going well, it doesn't matter who's mucking it up. Even a legend. At one point, when Mary and Carol both came unglued and Keith was trying to find the right lines in the script, Clifford tapped me on the shoulder and said, "It's like doing a school play. Do you do school plays here in America?"

"Yes, of course!" I said, thinking it a simple question. Children all over the world do school plays.

"Well," Clifford whispered, "then you understand. It's like doing a school play with two elderly twelve-year-olds."

Mean as it sounds, Trish and I broke up. Clifford does have a way with a phrase.

They got over the bumpy spot, and things went along as smoothly as ever, if not more so. There were beats when Mary came alive and took stage with authority. One could see the beginnings of a performance. She was right; it *was* a good idea to rehearse in a theatre. It did give a certain lift to the proceedings.

Clifford said he thought the first act might run a bit long, and we should keep an eye out for possible trims. I went out into the lobby and made some cuts that I thought might help.

Bob and Kevin left early so as not to be discovered. After rehearsal I snagged Keith and we repaired to a ratty bar next door, where I gave him the cuts for Mary over a drink. He is so supportive, cares so much. Before we left, I let him know how important he was to us and how much we appreciated him.

When I crawled into bed, I felt there was a ray of hope today, prayed it would not be snuffed out tomorrow. We are really flying by the seat of our pants now. Where did that expression ever come from?

Sunday, December 29, 1985

A phone call from New York woke me up. "You all ready to go to Dallas?" *Mein Gott,* it was true: we leave on New Year's Day. I tended to a lot of business, took laundry and cleaning out, and got down to Variety Arts just as they broke for lunch. I ate with Kevin, Bob, and Ann. Asked Kevin about the Fairmont Hotel in Dallas; I hadn't been to the city in years. He said it was terrific, and I mentioned I'd had a letter from one of the managers saying they knew I'd be there for the run of the play and offering me a suite for the price of a single, $90 a day. The suite ordinarily would go for $150 or $165. Kevin and Bob were impressed. So was I.

Walking back to the theatre, I caught sight of Carol outside in the damnedest outfit I'd ever seen. She is not known for subtlety in dressing, but there she was in tight, high red boots, red pants, and a top quartered in hot pink, red, and orange. We greeted each other, and I suggested she come into the lobby. I thought if she crossed the street in that outfit she'd cause backup crashes all the way to Bakersfield. I'd just recently learned that Carol had not canceled a New Year's engagement in Las Vegas to do her nightclub act. I was shaken at hearing this; it meant today would be her last day with us until we met in Dallas. If there was any time we should all be working together, it was now.

Soon Clifford had both Mary and Carol going through their paces. Mary was in a happy mood. I stayed all afternoon, but made myself unobtrusive by sitting far back in the darkness of the theatre.

When Carol got to "the ass section," she did it without the cuts and just as she had been doing it, not as we had gone over it the day before. I got up and walked down the aisle, stopping the rehearsal. "Carol, remember when we went over this yesterday, we—"

"Oh." A hand flew up to her face. "Darling, I didn't know you were there!"

"*Darling,* where did you think I was?"

"I don't know, but I didn't think you were out front." She quickly addressed Clifford and me. "Oh, well, let me do it again right now. Right now!"

She stumbled through it, but it was obvious she was thrown, and she was caught improvising between the new and the old way.

Parts of it were right, parts wrong. Consequently she felt trapped, I believe, and had to blow off steam. "Why," she demanded, "does everything of mine get cut or changed around, and no one ever says a thing to Mary?"

Mary was sitting on the sofa not five feet away and answered in a perfectly calm, matter-of-fact voice, "Because they know I don't know a damned thing and there's no point in giving me notes or cuts or suggestions or—anything."

"Yes, I know." Carol went on working herself up about changes and cuts and "now I have to go away and we're almost in Dallas and it's not fair and—" Tears were forming in her eyes, and I had to shout her down.

"Now, Carol, don't—come on, you're doing fine."

"No, no—"

"Yes, come here." And I went to her; we took a little walk off to the side and I reassured her, telling her how good she was going to be, how we all appreciated her work and knew this had been an unusual (to say the least!) rehearsal period, not an easy one, God only knows. We ended up hugging, and she swore she'd work on that section and do it right the next time we got to it.

She's going to be good, but both Clifford and I are still concerned about her tendency to talk out front much of the time. This is especially noticeable in her first scene, when she is alone onstage, hoping to pull off the deceit that this is her apartment (not that of a friend, Dorothy Coulter) and praying she can fool Mary/Leatrice. It was a nice little speech and Carol did it well, but, again today, after crossing herself she clutched the crucifix to her bosom and delivered the prayer straight out front. I said to Clifford, "It seems as if God is sitting twelfth row center."

"I should hope so!"

"Then, if he is," I replied, "why isn't he helping us more?"

Monday, December 30, 1985

Drove over to Jerry's early. Then we went to Western Costume to pick out a shirt, celluloid collar, old-fashioned frock coat, and string tie. I had asked to have the author's picture in the lobby—this because I believe authors should be more identifiable. In England, France, and Germany, authors carry more weight than they do here. Often, when I go to the theatre and the play is by someone I'm not familiar with, I'd like to see a picture of the author so I'd know what he or she looks like. When I asked for this, to be pictured along with the cast members, the request was not met by confetti and cheers. Ed Gifford, I suppose to take the curse off my outrageous request, came up with the idea of having me in a sepia photograph somewhat similar to the ones the Messrs. Shubert used to hang in the lobbies of their theatres back in the twenties. They probably would prefer a photo with a paper bag over my head. But, after all, the author writes the goddamn play—at least he should be acknowledged along with the cast. What are we—ghostwriters? They hurl shit at us when we get reviewed; let's see who's getting hit.

Then down to Variety Arts, where Mary was struggling through the end of the first act with Annie-Joe and Barbara. After a break, Mary worked alone with Keith. Clifford sat in the lobby reading *The New York Times.* When I tried to incite him to go inside and have a look, Clifford gave me a rather weary "Jimmy, there's not much direction I can give to a woman who doesn't know her lines. Please."

Very quiet with Carol off in Las Vegas. There was no energy in the theatre today. The idea that we're to do our first preview a week from tonight is scary in the extreme. Decided not to stay around and watch Mary run lines with Keith. If the director wasn't sitting there, not much point of me hanging around.

I was rattled by the atmosphere today and kept thinking of how close we were to a public hanging. So this is how nerves manifest themselves. Got a phone call from Debbie Cartwright at the Fairmont Hotel in Dallas. She sounded upset and said they'd received a call from someone today on behalf of Bob Regester and Kevin Eggers, requesting the same rate for them as the offer that had been extended to me. Because of this, she said, the management was sorry but they had to rescind the offer. She was apologetic; they would offer me a suite at $150 a day instead of $90. I was staggered by this reversal and said thank you, but no thank you very much.

I immediately hit the phone and tracked Bob down at the theatre. I was livid, although Bob denied having made a call or having anyone make it for him. I had thought perhaps our company manager, Alex Holt, had done it. I told Bob to ask Kevin. He called back and said Kevin hadn't done it, and the word was that Alex hadn't, either. "Well," I said, "some stupid moron did, and I want to know who!" I was angry all out of proportion, but I couldn't yell at Mary or Clifford, so I aimed my anger at the most available target. After I'd exhausted a few four-letter words and hung up the phone, Debbie Cartwright called back to say she'd been talking to the management and the manager was aware of me and my accomplishments (???) and they'd offer me a suite at $110 a day. I was on a roll now; this infuriated me even more. "I don't believe this," I said. "Now we're haggling and counteroffering. This is terribly demeaning and embarrassing. I never heard of such a thing, for a hotel of that quality to solicit a guest, then turn around and take it back. Aren't you embarrassed?"

"Yes," she said, "I really am sorry this has happened."

"May I please speak to the manager *myself!*" Now I was ready to go to the Supreme Court. She implored me to let her handle it; she would speak to him once again and get back to me. She phoned in the late afternoon. "Mr. Kirkwood, I'm terribly sorry all this happened. We've all spoken, and the hotel will gladly stick to its offer of a suite for eighty-five dollars a day."

"Ninety," I shouted. "It was *ninety* dollars!" We both broke up. I thanked her and we made our peace.

Authors are driven to madness. It goes with the territory. I admit to it. Take me away—please!

Tuesday, December 31, 1985

New Year's Eve day. A certain stillness in the air. Everyone looked as if they'd been put "on hold." Down to Variety Arts, where I found only Mary, Annie-Joe, and Keith. Mary wanted it that way, quiet, not a lot of people, just going through lines. She was in good spirits, but still struggling with the end of Act I. Just can't seem to nail that down.

During a break she asked if I couldn't simplify it a little more, but I've done so much cutting already I told her we should make an effort to do it as it is now. At one point Mary put a hand to her head and said the magic word: "Dallas! Tomorrow—Dallas! I don't believe it!"

Visited with her for a while and then with Clifford, who was simply standing by. There wasn't much for him to do in the way of directing. It was really a matter of letting Mary become as secure as possible with the lines. He's discouraged, I can tell, and I don't blame him. He feels impotent.

Talked to all my near and dear ones in New York in the late afternoon—missing all of you very much, and as little chatter as possible about the show. Spoke to Esther who, I know, is empathizing with me. "I wish I could help." "I wish you could, too."

In the evening drove over to Jamie's for a festive, warm, cozy New Year's Eve. Ten or twelve people, all good friends of his. Drinks, some good cheer, and some of the best lasagna and salad I'd ever had, all sorts of sweets. At the approach of midnight, I walked down the steps of his terraced garden. I always feel embarrassed at the stroke unless I know everyone. It seems silly running around kissing people you don't know that well. Do they want to be kissed or will they back off—or what?

So I stood alone in the quiet of the California night, down the steep incline of the hill behind his house, which he's had made into a magical garden, rather the way the Chinese terrace their land. I felt removed when I heard the distant roar from the houses in the Silver Lake area as the clock struck. I took a moment to pray for Mary, first of all, which meant also for the play and everyone involved with it.

I went back up to the house, had a couple of nightcaps and some good talk, then drove home like a sensible person. The whole day I felt in limbo—like a soldier in Vietnam, waiting to "move out." Tomorrow we move out!

DALLAS, HERE WE COME

Wednesday, January 1, 1986

Jerry drove me to the airport. There was the *Legends!* company gathered outside the airline, and all our luggage, with little green bits of yarn tied around it. Said goodbye to Jerry, who replied, "If you need me I'll try to get to Dallas." I said, "Get on the plane right now."

We piled on, all of us in tourist. There was a comforting feeling about all of us being enclosed together in a DC-10. It gave us the feeling of being "a company" for the first time. We were, indeed, "pushing off."

I sat in the rear with Clifford. Cast members and crew were passing out *Legends!* buttons. Although no one thought we'd actually get the curtain up, you'd never have known it from the spirit on the plane. I believe it was just the simple fact of getting away from the mess that rehearsals had been. No more chilly rehearsal hall, no more of that dreary, enervating California smog-sunshine. I felt as if we'd all taken a shower and washed some poison off. All clean, we were now ready to jump into the frying pan. Theatrical folk, when traveling together, have a way of letting other civilian passengers know they're all "with a show." Someone stood up and called out, "Eric, why don't you do your strip for the people!" Much intraplane communicating going on.

Clifford and I talked very little about the play. Bob and Kevin wore grins: It was Bob's birthday. Also, I'm sure they, too, felt the escape from the City of the Angels; at least that part of purgatory was behind us. Clifford and I each had a Bloody Mary and held it up in a toast: "Well, here's to—" There was no point finishing the sentence, so we just laughed.

Dallas! I hadn't been there since I'd performed at the Dallas State Fair Musicals years ago in *Panama Hattie* with Vivian Blaine, Arthur Treacher, and Buddy Ebsen and *Wonderful Town* with Imogene Coca and Edie Adams. How the skyline has changed. As we drove in from the airport, the city gleamed, all glass and mirrors, greens and golds. Rising up in the middle of the plain, like the Emerald City.

We all checked into the Fairmont; we didn't discuss rates. I was in the opposite tower from Kevin and Bob, which was fine. Conferences would have to be planned, not a lot of running down the hall, banging on each other's doors, and shouting, "The piano should be painted green," "Cut Mary's last line in Act One," "Get them to turn up the sound!"

My suite was perfect, high up, good view of the Emerald City. Kevin phoned, asking me to come over to his suite and have a birthday drink with Bob. I cleaned up and joined Clifford, Ann, Kevin, and Bob. Spirits were, for some inexplicable reason, still high. I joined in. We all told stories of our days in the theatre, except for Kevin, who told tales of recording and agenting days, always prefaced by his trademark, "Now, let me tell you something."

Clifford tells the best theatrical stories. Apparently Rex Harrison cajoled Claudette Colbert into leaving her Barbados home to come to England to do *Aren't We All?* with him. Clifford said Rex waged a successful campaign, although Claudette was not all that anxious to do the play. Early on in rehearsal in London, they took a tea break. They were all sitting rather close together and after a while Clifford said, "All right, time to get back to work." Rex glanced vaguely around and said, with Claudette Colbert not ten feet away, "Where's the fucking French dwarf got to?" Well, of course, she heard it. There was dead silence in the rehearsal hall, and no one knew anything to do but get back to work, which they did. Clifford said that from that moment on, for two solid weeks, Claudette spoke only French to him during rehearsals. Clifford is married to a lovely French lady, Josiane, and is fluent in French. "It drove Rex crazy," Clifford said, "because he had no idea *what* she was talking about." What a lovely revenge. We drank and ate and wished Bob a happy birthday. By then it was time to go to bed. I left their tower and went to mine, feeling, in some weird way, "safely separated."

Our first night in Dallas. I wondered what we'd all be like when the last night came, and which night would be the last night.

Thursday, January 2, 1986

Great sleep, comfy, cushy bed, the kind that caresses without smothering. Continental breakfast, cleanup, and a good fast walk to the Majestic Theatre, only about ten minutes away, windy, fifty-eight brisk degrees.

First came upon the backstage entrance. Big trucks, much activity, unloading equipment, furniture, pieces of the set, etc. Major activity, electrical equipment hauled in, hammers pounding, orders shouted. You'd think the show was really going to open. Inside, the theatre is a jewel box. Crimson and plush and just about the right size, around sixteen hundred, I believe. Posh boxes lining the front of the mezzanine. Like a small opera house.

After a while the company straggled in for yet another rehearsal. The first act—okay. The second act is nothing but bumpy. I am writing this longhand, sitting out in the theatre. Mary has to be cued on almost every line. Clifford is sitting near me; he's taken to reading the labels on his new sneakers. During a break we had a meeting with the sound man, Jan Nebozenko, and his assistant, Steve Shull, both extremely nice professional men who obviously know their job. I heard Bernie Jacobs' (one of the two Shuberts) recording, which will be used in Gary's first phone scene, in which he talks to Bernie about getting a theatre and persuades the ladies to meet. Bernie's voice sounded authentic, and he had even rewritten a line or two, which made someone say, "Well, listen, they own almost all the theatres, so if he wants to rewrite a line—he'll rewrite it." It was also good of Bernie to let us use his voice.

I suddenly looked down from the sound console, which was located in a theatre-right stage box. I was amazed at the sight of this huge crew of men, hammering away, lugging scenery about, dragging furniture around. Kevin said he'd just commented to Bob, "My God, look at that—do you realize we're *paying* for all those people?" He said Bob paled.

Still more rehearsals—which went slower and slower as the evening dragged on. Clifford passed me a note: "I'm beginning to think we have a real problem." I printed back, "Help—get Debbie Reynolds!" He printed back, "Get anyone!" When I tore it off to keep—it was on his pad—he said, "Here, I'll take that." I think he thought I was saving it for this book.

After several hours, around nine o'clock, things turned hairy. Mary's energy started to flag—just as Carol's impatience escalated. Carol had that wild look in her great big Lorelei eyes, and soon chaos was upon us. Toward the end of the first act the dam burst. Suddenly Carol started jumping ahead, like a runaway train, ignoring Mary's lines, not waiting for her to find them, totally confusing Mary, until she had no idea what she was doing or where she was.

It was apparent they could not go on this way, with Carol racing ahead and Mary looking as if she'd been struck by a truck. We all jumped up, ran toward the stage and up the steps onto it, as Carol, eyes blazing, kept saying, "No, no, I'll learn this whole part as a monologue—so that when Mary forgets her lines I can keep the curtain up!" She said this in front of Mary three or four times in slightly different variations. "No, no, I'll learn all the lines, Mary's and mine, and I'll just keep it going—so no matter what she does we can keep the curtain up."

Mary was simply standing there, a bit dazed. Clifford was talking to Mary when Carol clutched my arm and said, "Don't you think that's right? I'll learn it as a monologue, yes, that's what I'll do, learn the whole end of Act One as a monologue, don't you think?"

I walked her farther away. "No, I don't," I told her.

"But what will we do if Mary goes up?"

I walked her a bit farther away. "Carol, what we have to do is remain calm. I know it's hard, but just try to calm down. Mary will come through. We musn't panic."

"Really?" she asked, almost the way a child would ask for reassurance that we are all going to heaven.

"Yes."

She thought for a moment and then said, "Yes, I guess you're right."

Clifford attempted to get them to run through the last beat of Act I, but it was no-go. They tried, but it got all fouled up. I knew Mary didn't have any gas left in the tank. Not a drop. And she didn't. Soon it was obvious she was going home for the night. No big scene, little whispers, people getting her coat and things, and soon she was leaving, apparently for the night. Or was she checking out for good? She disappeared, walking quietly offstage through the foyer of the set.

We were all greatly dispirited. We stood around for a while until Doug Baker, our general manager, assigned by Alan Wasser, suggested going to dinner at a Greek restaurant on the outskirts of town. We agreed: we knew there had to be a top-level meeting. Once there, we ordered drinks and food and dove into a postmortem. Everyone was furious with Carol for patronizing Mary to such an extent. Bob was livid; so was Clifford. He would gladly strangle Carol if he could. Kevin and Bob decided they would have a serious talk with Charles Lowe in the morning to try to get Carol to remain calm and not exacerbate the situation. I came home swathed in depression, which knocks me out as if I were hit by a hammer. Thank God, depression doesn't make me drink, or this production alone would turn me into a raging alcoholic.

Friday, January 3, 1986

There was a new presence at rehearsals, now that we were in a theatre. Charles Lowe was in attendance, sitting by himself down around the third or fourth row, always dressed in suit and tie, very dapper, with a briefcase and all the trades, *Variety, The Hollywood Reporter, Daily Variety*, plus *The New York Times, Daily News*, etc. He did not involve himself with creative matters yet (script, interpretation, direction, etc.), merely kept an eagle eye out for lighting and sound. But he was a presence.

Oddly enough, after the disaster that was yesterday, Mary showed up in good spirits and went through the first act fairly well. Carol was calmed down; everyone was minding his or her manners. But we sat through a dreary and shaky Act II. Wobbly as it was, however, Mary was laughing and joking through all the drek. She seems to love the mooning bit at the end of Act II. I know it's gimmicky, but there's no time to write or rehearse a new ending. All in all, it was bumpy—and only three days away from our first preview—yet morale was somehow good, at least on the outside.

Went back to the Sheraton and had drinks with most of the cast: Eric, Annie-Joe, Gary, plus Ann and Kevin. Saying good night these evenings is rough; we all tend to stick together like one big security blanket. One is loath to leave, for fear the entire ship will sink if we're all not talking about it staying afloat. It's when you pile into bed that waking nightmares start parading through your brain, along with corresponding headlines in *Variety:* "*Legends!* Closes Before Opening." "*Legends!* Bites the Dust in Dallas!" I went to sleep counting headlines instead of sheep.

Saturday, January 4, 1986

Had my continental breakfast while reading a feature article on myself by the critic Dan Hulbert in the Dallas newspaper. Not the best article, and a picture that looks as if I'd just been cut down from a hanging and then sprayed with gray paint. The article says I'm the author of the book and *screenplay* of *A Chorus Line* and other odd bits of misinformation, ends up denigrating my acting career. Thank you very much for the bad screenplay credit. Can't wait to read his review. Yes, I can.

Between three and three-thirty, they began running the get-on, get-off of Gary's office scene at the beginning of the play. It's a rollaway set that slides back and, by swinging open the fireplace of the living room, disappears through it on tracks during a blackout and remains backstage for the rest of the play. It was taking a long time, and I hoped there wouldn't be an interminable stage wait before the lights and curtain could go up on the Coulter apartment.

Then we returned to running through our *bête noire*, Act II. Again it was brutal. In attendance, besides "the regulars," were our company photographer, Kenn Duncan, his assistant, and a young girl we'd met in L.A. who had known my half-brother, Michael. Just as I was thinking it was embarrassing to have anyone not connected with the production see it in this shape, it occurred to me that the night after tomorrow there were supposed to be around sixteen hundred people paying good American dollars to view this debacle.

A top-level meeting was called for seven in the evening. I thought it was going to be for Doug Baker, Kevin, Bob, and me to decide which one of us would help the other commit hara-kiri. Shades of Yukio Mishima: I'll take beheading; no disemboweling, please. I was surprised to find it was for all department heads: props, sound, carpenter, stage manager, lighting, set, etc.

It was held in the basement below the lobby, and I swear to God the place looks like the enbalming room of a mortuary—gleaming white walls and bright lights, about twenty-five red folding funeral chairs, set in a semicircle with a rather high table in the center for the anatomy lesson of the corpse—the play.

The meeting was called to order, and all I wanted to do was plead for immediate postponement of two or three previews—or life—but that was not possible in front of the department heads. So I had to sit and listen to talk about what color socks the corpse would wear—not red (Carol), which made her red outfit look like a clown suit. There was talk of covering the front of the stage with black cloth, sound problems, the time it took to change scenes, and on and on, as if everything else was fine and dandy. I could tell by the way my knees were jiggling up and down that I was about to burst. I finally corralled Bob, Kevin, Clifford, and Doug in a corner of the room and told them I felt strongly that if Mary was forced to humiliate herself in front of an audience—by, say, being prompted eight or ten times in a row—she would suddenly face front, announce, "I'm sorry, I can't go on!" She would turn, perhaps with a bow to Carol, walk off, and we'd have lost her for good. I urged them to postpone previews. They talked about losing the preview money. I countered with: It's a matter of losing one hundred thousand or the entire million it cost to mount. No, they were adamant, the insurance wouldn't cover it, the Pace Group (partial investors and owners of the Majestic Theatre) would have at us.

We went over all the alternatives and possible scenarios—most of which were colored black. What if Mary got a doctor's certificate and we put Barbara Sohmers on with Carol? Would Carol play with her? Yes or no? Maybe she'd see herself as a heroine, saving the day. Or maybe she'd put her foot down: "No, I will not play without Mary!" Finally Doug said he'd try to get some alternative figures together in case of postponement and talk to the Pace people.

A runthrough of the entire play scheduled for eight-thirty. There was a lot of dicking around, striking the office set, trying to get the time down so we wouldn't have to play the entire score of *Parsifal* during the set change.

Nerves would not permit me to sit, so I wandered around aimlessly at the back of the theatre. After a while Bob and Kevin returned, with hints that we'd cancel Monday and Tuesday. They'd just spoken to Tom Davis and Mary, who was extremely grateful, and other calls were being made to see if this new game plan could be implemented. Ed Gifford said he would try to announce this postponement "due to mechanical reasons with the set, lighting, etc."—anything but blame it on Mary.

The word came down that we would postpone, but only one performance at a time. Try to bump ticket holders over into another night. Rumor now has it ticket sales are good.

At last began the runthrough around nine, with Kenn Duncan and his assistant sitting in the front row, attempting to snap pictures without the ladies' noticing. Fat chance. Gary's first telephone scene went well—a few little hitches, but he's solid and his energy is high.

Then came Annie-Joe and Carol. For the first time Annie-Joe was in her blue-sequined evening gown and fur coat, looking very jazzy. Also Carol made her debut in her brown wig. What a difference from the blonde $8.95 Eva Gabor. She looked terrific, like a slightly beat-up Joan Crawford. Now if we can only pry those goddamn red stockings off her so she won't look like the Red Express when she comes onstage.

On came Mary in her beautiful fur-lined cape, hat, gloves, and—cocktail dress, I suppose you'd call it. She looked spiffy. Actually they chugged along through the first act fairly well. Flubbed a couple of times, then got back on track without being cued, although, toward the end of it, there were a few lines shouted out by Keith from offstage. The end of Act I is still a mess. I believe Mary's having more trouble with that, because the pace picks up, the fight begins, there's quicker physical action, and she simply gets too rattled.

The second act was bumpy, stop and go. During one mixup, as Keith was straightening them out, Clifford, who was sitting right behind me, tapped me on the shoulder and surprised me with a totally *non sequitur* question in his quaint English way: "The American expression 'giving head'—does that mean you get *your* cock sucked, or does it mean you are sucking someone else's cock?" I straightened him out on that point, but he went on almost as if he didn't believe me.

"Hmn, I thought it meant you gave someone the head of *your* cock."

"No, Clifford, you give a cock *your* head."

"Hmnn . . ." He was still apparently pondering it.

Finally I said, "Look, Clifford, if you manage to pull this production together and get the curtain up—I'll show you how it works."

"Oh, dear, what a shame," he said. "I think I'm out of luck!"

We both roared with laughter. Act II had gotten under way again, and Carol glanced out front with a pleased expression, as if something that had taken place onstage had tickled the hell out of us.

The second act limped along after the cop scene, which always ran smoothly. Mary, although way off most of the time, was not in bad spirits. She simply plowed ahead, over hill and dale. Toward the end, just before Gary's entrance and last scene, she stopped and asked for the script. Everyone said, "Oh, no, you're doing fine, come along," and she continued without it.

But soon it was midnight, and union rules forced us to a halt. I flew up onstage and tried to stroke Mary, who tends, in all honesty and modesty, to pooh-pooh any praise. I felt a great surge of affection for her; she certainly was hanging in there, and the inner toll extracted every night when she went home had to be a mighty one. I also told Carol how good she is and how great she looks in the wig; I saved my campaign to get her out of the red stockings for another time.

THE DREAD TURK ARRIVES

Sunday, January 5, 1986

Stayed home—hotel is home?—until it was time to go to the theatre for what would be our dress rehearsal, at around five-thirty. Gary was running his scene, Clifford was tinkering with lighting. Trish Garland had arrived and said she'd sit with me during the dress. I could have used a large Swedish nurse, a cop, and my very own psychiatrist, Mildred Newman *(How to Be Your Own Best Friend)* to get me through this evening. There was not a good aura in the theatre. Gremlins were in the air; intangible, but they were there.

There was some talk that an electronic ear bug had been sent for from the East for Mary. The receiver could be inserted in her ear; there would be a separate battery pack located somewhere under her clothing, and then Keith would sit offstage with his own sender-mike and feed her lines when she needed them. For a part as large as Mary's—once onstage she's never off—it did not seem practical. How could anyone get through an entire play being cued for almost every line, especially in a comedy, where pace is of the essence? At any rate, it was not with us on this day.

But Ahmet Ertegun was. He arrived, immaculately groomed, sleek mogul that he is. The first time I'd seen him since a meeting perhaps six months before. Though Ahmet was the producer of record, he had very little to do with the actual putting together of "the piece." Now, rather like an impresario, here he was to see his baby. And this evening the baby was definitely retarded. Several of the Pace people were there, too. Outside of perhaps six or eight other folk, including Charles Lowe, of course, the theatre was empty and there was a chill in the air.

The runthrough began. Gary's scene just lay there; good as he is, without audience reaction or some kind of reaction it's a no-go. Annie-Joe started off her scene like a freight train, racing through it so that Carol, in order to keep up with her, began foomfing around, getting a bit rattled. Technically the gremlins had a field day. The FAREWELL DEAR ARETHA sign didn't come down on time, the balloons didn't pop right, Carol got tripped up with the phone cord as she moved it to the coffee table, etc., etc.

Then Mary came on and delivered a Christ-awful mélange of the first act—just dreadful. Every so often Trish would lean over and say something like "That wastepaper basket doesn't look good so close to the piano." I wanted to say: "THE WASTEPAPER BASKET DOESN'T LOOK GOOD? WHAT ABOUT THOSE PEOPLE TRIPPING ABOUT THE STAGE? DO THEY LOOK GOOD?" The end beats of the act were disastrous. The fight scene sort of dissolved in front of our eyes, and the curtain mercifully came down.

In the intermission, if one could call it that, we sat frozen in our places. Trish would squeeze my hand every now and then, as if I were sitting a death watch over a dear one and was simply waiting for the inevitable doctor to come out of the room and say, "I'm sorry, it's all over, Mr. Kirkwood. But at least she won't be suffering anymore."

I glanced around at Ahmet and whoever he was sitting with; my glance was not returned by anything that could be called human communication.

I prayed the Good Witch of the North would touch her wand to the second act and perhaps bring some semblance of life to it. My prayers for this went straight to hell. The second act was a total rout—total—endless prompting and fake business, and poor Mary seemed completely lost. Carol, though frazzled, carried on as best she could. When the curtain finally fell, there was applause amounting to the beating of a single crippled dove's wings. There we sat. Clifford and I looked at each other. Ahmet was mumbling to the people he was sitting with. Trish regarded me as if I'd just been handed the death sentence.

It had been so bad, it took time for people even to get up out of their seats and move about. I finally managed to haul it up and stand in the aisle. Ahmet rose and walked down the orchestra incline toward me. Approaching, he shook his head and mumbled something about there being problems with the *play!* He then started in with a story about the time he produced Eva Le Gallienne as Juliet when she was *sixty.* That set me back on my heels. I had never heard of Le Gallienne playing Juliet at sixty; I'd never heard of Ahmet producing a play, either, although I knew he had money in *Rachel Lilly Rosenbloom,* which closed in previews. He left in mid-story, saying he'd better go backstage and see Mary.

I couldn't bring myself to go backstage; I had nothing to say to anyone. Clifford and I were told there would be a summit meeting at the Fairmont Hotel, where Ahmet was also staying, and decided to walk back, but as we emerged from the stage door, Carol and Charles came along. Carol offered us a ride back in her car, which we accepted. We piled in, and there was only talk about "Isn't it nippy out?" and "There sure aren't many people downtown at night in Dallas, are there?" and before you knew it we were being left off, saying bye-byes, love and kisses. I suppose even touching on the events of the evening would have opened a can of peas the size of Brazil.

Waiting for the elevators, we saw Ahmet arrive with a pale-faced Bob Regester. We all went up to his terribly deluxe suite, a duplex, with private stairs leading to it. A huge Christmas tree was still up, sporting British flags; the rooms were enormous and plush.

We occupied a board room—long conference table, bar, paintings, the works. Soon Doug Baker and Kevin arrived. That was the group. Clifford and I sat next to each other, across from Ahmet, with Bob to our right, Kevin and Doug to the left. Ahmet was obviously chairing the meeting. Looking at him, all sleek and powerful, sitting there in his pinstripe suit, I could imagine him playing Scarpia in *Tosca.*

He led off talking about his meeting with Mary. "Of course, I've known Mary for many years." (If this was true, one wondered why Ahmet, in all the months we were pursuing Mary, had never once put in a phone call to her or written a note.) He quoted her as telling him, "I'm afraid I just can't do it. They told me all the previews were canceled—but I think the mind is gone and I just can't learn anymore. They talked me into it."

Ahmet did not hide his disgust at what he'd seen. He didn't like Annie-Joe, he didn't even like Gary, which surprised me, and he thought Mary looked, walked, and acted—well, he didn't give her any credit for acting—"like an old lady." He kept saying what a total disaster it was. He did like Carol, thought she was quite good. But he went on about Mary: "This old woman creaking about the stage, it's brutal." He turned to Kevin, his man. "Why the fuck didn't anyone warn me this whole thing was such a disaster!" He went on talking about his chat with Mary and insisted she really had no intention of going on for any of the previews, and wouldn't go on for opening night if she didn't know her lines. Ahmet wanted to know who in his right mind thought she might ever go on.

Clifford and I reiterated our fear that she would never step out on that stage with an audience in attendance, whereas Kevin and Bob, bless their optimistic hearts, were hanging on to their fantasies that she would. There was talk of Debbie Reynolds, and people were manning the phones, waking up Andy Zerman (casting) in New York.

Ahmet was a complete downer; there was no reason why he shouldn't have been, but he was not about to administer a drop of solace on any front. We could have used a bit of stroking—like "This must have been hell for all of you to go through," or "How do *you* all feel?" There was none of that.

The meeting went on for two miserable hours. Most of it was Ahmet dumping on the play, Mary, Kevin, Clifford, and me. Although he did not point a finger at us and actually say, "You stink," that was, as we say in the theatre, the subtext. Then he launched into stories of the recording business and finally touched on producing Eva Le Gallienne as Juliet at the age of sixty. Clifford was confused by this, too, but it turned out he had produced a *record* of her reading some lines from Romeo and Juliet. Aha, a record. That was not actually a parallel as far as our experience with Mary's stage performance was concerned. Clifford and I were visibly wilting, so around two in the morning, tails between our legs, we excused ourselves (for making naughty on the stage?) and left Ahmet, Bob, and Kevin alone.

As we were going down in the elevator, I said, "Now Ahmet can tell them how he *really* feels. He must be bouncing them off the walls by this time."

Monday, January 6, 1986

Not much fun getting out of bed this morning. I dragged myself to the theatre around noon, not knowing what to expect, or even *if* to expect.

Oddly enough, the atmosphere was humming. The ear bug had arrived from Minneapolis by special air, and Mary was going through tryouts on stage. She appeared to be intrigued with it. The sound fellows, Jan and Steve, were working on the frequency, the mechanics of it all. Keith was offstage with a microphone, throwing her lines, and she was hearing them, cocking her head this way and that. During a break I approached Mary and asked how it felt. She threw me a big smile and said, "I can hear, it's amazing. There's a slight hum, but they're working on it."

As the rest of the cast gathered, I could feel the excitement build. There was going to be an afternoon dress rehearsal, and Mary would be equipped with the ear bug. Clifford and I were not overly optimistic, but the mere idea of trying something new was enough to lift our spirits. Bob and Kevin were eagerly awaiting the outcome, and although I gathered the time they'd spent with Ahmet last night after Clifford and I made our exit could not exactly be called "happy time," they put up good fronts.

The afternoon runthrough went fairly well. There were moments: slight pauses when Mary was awaiting a cue from Keith, times when he wasn't quite sure whether her pause was simply timing or whether she'd gone up. But basically the ear bug was working. Carol played along with it very well. It must be frightening to act with someone who is not only attempting to listen to you, but is also listening to what amounts to a radio.

There was excitement backstage after: hugging by the sound people and Mary and Keith. Mary was a bit frazzled by the tension of this "new thing," but she was also heartened to have a backup. "It's a little hard on my ear; I wish we could make it more comfortable." So they set about trying to do that. Another dress was scheduled for the evening.

We broke for dinner, then went right back to work. Ahmet was again in attendance; because of the previous night's meeting, I avoided him like a Turkish jail. Also Maj, Mary's daughter-in-law, had arrived for the evening runthrough. Again Trish sat next to me, and again would offer a comment, like "The bottom of Carol's dress is wrinkled" or "What's that paper carton doing under the piano?" She's a dear, but my perverse mind, fueled by tension, prompted me to come up with all sorts of suggestions about what she might *do* in the carton; I refrained from expressing them in words.

Mary's performance was cautious, but there were no major calamities. Carol was quite good, she's getting away from Lorelei Lee and assuming another persona entirely. Except for a penchant for playing out front when she has a major speech, she's on the mark. Eric's strip is working well, Gary's two scenes whipped along. The main areas that need hammering away at are the ends of both acts.

Immediately after, Ahmet approached and asked if I thought it was any better this evening. I said "Oh, yes, don't you?" He only muttered, shook his head, and walked away. I hope he removes himself from the scene in the immediate future. His brand of pessimism does not fly at times like this.

Had a chat with Mary, who was excited and delighted that Maj, who seemed truly pleased, was there. Carol's spirits were up, too. Clifford asked if I was going to ask Mary if she planned to go on the next evening. I said no. As the author, I think I should keep our relationship clean and not pressure her. That's up to the producers.

Trish said she was going with Ahmet, Kevin, Ann, and Clifford to the Fairmont for drinks, and was I coming. No. I had taken a dislike to the man I began calling "the dread Turk."

Instead I went with Gary and the rest of the group to the Sheraton, where we all had drinks and played "I wonder if she's going on?" and "I wonder when?" and "I wonder what will happen when she does?" and "Things are looking somewhat up—aren't they?"

All I could do when I went to bed was send up another prayer. From all the prayers I'd been offering, I thought I might as well return to the church.

CURTAIN UP

Early call from Kevin—Mary's going on tonight. What? MARY'S GOING ON TONIGHT! That got me out of bed in a hurry. My hand shook as I tried to shave around my beard without shaving the dammed thing off. Gulped down a breakfast—during which about four other people called to say, MARY'S GOING ON TONIGHT.

The theatre was alive with the electricity of an impending performance. Crew working away at last-minute details; cast and understudies streaming in as if every one of them had just been injected by a massive dose of vitamin B-12. Or speed. I walked out to the front of the house. The phones were ringing and there were people in line, either buying tickets or exchanging them from what was supposed to have been our first preview the night before.

Mixed feelings. The night I'd looked forward to for so long was staring me in the face. Now I wanted to break into a chorus of "Hold Back the Dawn." Not so quickly into the breach. Maybe we'd better wait another day or three or four or—just go home.

In the theatre, Clifford was working with the ladies. Mary had her ear bug in place, and rehearsal went on all afternoon. Mostly Clifford was trying to clean up the ends of the acts. Both were difficult to set, even with the ear bug, because both required such heightened physical action.

Keith had not only to feed Mary lines but also to give her directions for the proper moves: "Run downstage of the sofa, shout, 'Every major star ought to have a telethon, you could do one for *bedsores!*' Then turn, run stage left and—" etc. There was also the danger that, when Keith gave her a direction, what with all the fast action and confusion onstage, she might, instead of saying a line, blurt out, "Then turn, run stage left, and knock over the chair downstage of the piano."

Spirits were up, though. There is a kind of adrenaline that takes hold when the moment of truth is mere hours away. On the other hand, there is a slight doubt that it's even a comedy, after so many runthroughs without any reaction coming from "out front."

After rehearsals, I went up and hugged Mary, told her it was going to be just fine and that I was proud of her. And I was. The burden she carried had to be cosmic in size, and the possibility of soiling a legendary career in public must have been terrifying.

I walked to the Sheraton with Gary and Eric; we sat down and were soon joined by Tom Davis. The idea that we were doing our first preview was mind-blowing to all of us, and I couldn't believe Tom Davis' main point of conversation, which went like this: "Now, the opening-night party—you know, they have this big promotion where we're all getting our own limousines. Now, Mary doesn't know she's going, but she is. She also doesn't know that Larry, if he gets here on time, is coming to the play and then he'll be at the party, too. But she doesn't think he's coming, just Maj. But—there are only going to be seven places at her table, and Larry will sit with her but Maj won't, she'll be at another table. Now, we mustn't let her know about Larry coming—that's a surprise—and the party—" And on and on. Until I wanted to scream, Fuck the party—what about the play, what about Mary and this first performance?"

I soon fled back to the theatre. Alan Wasser had arrived. It was good to have his presence there; he's a nice man and a real pro. There was a sound check for Mary's battery pack and ear bug; people were popping into dressing rooms wishing everyone "Break a leg" or *"Merde"*—anything but the forbidden "Good luck"!

I visited briefly with Mary, Carol, Annie-Joe, Don, Eric, and Gary. Then I walked outside the stage door, around to the front of the house; people were streaming toward the theatre from all directions. My heartbeat increased; the chatter in the lobby was loud and filled with anticipation. Too much excitement there, so I retreated backstage again, where half-hour had been called.

Everything was in high gear. I walked from the stage-left door to the interior of the theatre, climbed the steps, and came out on the far stage-left mezzanine, which curved around close to the proscenium and also housed the sound console. The audience was packing the theatre, and the noise level was high. This is usually a good sign that their reaction level will also be high. Usually, but we didn't know about tonight.

From my vantage point I had a full view of the entire house. I sat in a chair next to the sound console. Steve, Jan, and I all gave each other the high sign, thumb and forefinger in a circle. The curtain was held until every seat in the theatre was filled, a packed house, still very noisy, until finally the houselights began to dim; the noise rose for a second or two, then dropped in anticipation of the beginning of the play.

There was that special hum of the curtain rising, and the lights came up on Gary (Martin Klemmer) talking on the phone in his small, tacky (on purpose) office, taking up the small center stage and masked on either side by black cloth. This surprised the audience, who probably thought that Mary and Carol would be caught in a posh set, laughing and gulping down cocktails.

However, within seconds, Gary began getting his laughs as he talked on the phone first to Paul Newman (Paul's actual taped voice), then Bernie Jacobs, and finally his first phone call to Sylvia Glenn (Carol). At the sound of her voice, growling "Hellooooo" in a marvelous actressy phone voice, there was a buzz of recognition in the audience. Another hum of recognition when he first called Leatrice Monsee (Mary) and they heard her chirpy voice reply, "Yes, this is Leatrice Monsee."

He was getting laughs on every line that was meant to, and so were the ladies. I could not believe the reaction—way beyond happy. Later in his scene, Gary, now pretending to *be* Paul Newman, frustrated by a bad overseas call, with static and whole parts of words missing, which he did brilliantly, started to get a hand before the end of his last speech. He speeded it up and finished in a cacophony of sounds—raspberry, honks, hiccups—blackout, and a burst of enthusiastic applause.

A rather long time, during which music was played, while his set was trundled off in the blackout before the curtain rose on Dorothy Coulter's Park Avenue apartment. The set got a hand, and there was Annie-Joe, a mammoth blaze of blue sequins, and soon the front door opening and slamming could be heard and on came the red-stockinged freight train in the brown wig, Carol Channing. Huge hand. Her scene convincing Aretha to postpone the party for her niece so that she can use the apartment to impress Leatrice and the producer went very well. Several huge laughs. The scene is too long, but still it played well.

Finally came the announcement from downstairs that Leatrice Monsee was on the way up, and Sylvia made a quick exit into the bedroom to change into her silver-lamé evening gown. Annie-Joe got laughs picking up the bits of balloons Carol had popped and putting them down her front as she went to the door saying, "Who-wee, we're up to our asses in movie stars."

In came Mary. Another huge, extended hand; Mary is, after all, one of Texas' own. She looked terrific, all dolled up, and her first scene with Annie-Joe went smoothly, if a bit slowly, as Mary had to receive her lines via satellite. Soon Carol re-entered in her sparkling silver gown and got another hand. We had our two ladies onstage, and from there on out the first act went comparatively well; lots of laughs, a few little glitches here and there, but nothing catastrophic. Eric's strip went over wildly with the audience; they screamed and clapped and, toward the end, when he gave Annie-Joe a hip-check and she did the full split, they went crazy. The laughs provided Mary time, with Keith's assistance, to have the lines cued to her and then repeated without an obvious wait—in most places. When the dialogue was serious, sometimes the pace was noticeably slow. But, all things being relative, as they are in this life, it was a miracle the act ended to heavy applause and without a major hitch. The last beats were still unsteady, but even so . . .

I went backstage to say quickly how happy I was and that they should just "keep on going." Then raced out to the lobby, and all the comments I heard were good ones: Very funny, aren't they marvelous, the two of them, and do you realize that Mary Martin's about eighty (wrong), doesn't she look great (right); wasn't that striptease terrific!

Settling into my chair for the second act, I couldn't help thinking that if the audience had seen what took place on this very stage with these very same people two nights before, we'd have all been tarred and feathered, had gasoline dumped on us and been set on fire. What merriment the local folk would have had watching us run about trying to put each other out.

Lights down, and we were under way again. When the curtain went up, presenting us with the two ladies, one on either side of the stage, wigs off, Carol's dress torn, both in disarray, with Don, our cop, standing there with his book in hand looking from

one to the other—the audience giggled merrily. Don's first line—
"All right, ladies, I'll just put down here under ages—'indeter-
minate' "—got a laugh. The cop scene went very well, and so did
most of the act, taking into consideration slow pacing, a few fluffs
here and there, and what we called "the vacuum-cleaner scene"
(when the ladies attempt to tidy up the apartment and do more
damage than good, a scene that never had much chance of direction and was quite messy to boot). I wanted to get my hands on
that scene so badly and fix it, but priorities would not allow it at
this time. When the ladies ate the hashish brownies by mistake,
the audience went along with their merry ride. Although both
ladies were playing drunk more than stoned—because neither
lady had *been* stoned—they pulled the scene off fairly well.

When the two of them got serious, let their hair down, and
confessed their mistakes and misfortunes, the audience was quiet,
obviously touched by these two ladies finally becoming friends
and leveling with each other.

The big surprise was Gary's last scene. He comes in toward
the end of the play; the ladies think they've fooled him, pretending
they're riding high, but he's got the lowdown, knows exactly their
perilous condition. They believe they're going to Broadway in the
play with Paul Newman; he tells them not only has Paul fallen
through, but they're going Off-Broadway—not on—their salary
will be seven hundred dollars a week instead of ten thousand. He
completely pulls the rug out from under them, hands them a list
of other actresses who could play the parts in the event they turn
down the play, and finally leaves them totally deflated. After his
exit Aretha convinces them that, no matter what, they should do
the play together, and they do.

Gary is an extremely fine comic actor, and we all thought it
was a good scene. On this night, however, a chill came over the
audience as Gary went on demolishing the ladies' dreams of glory
on Broadway, and by the time he made his exit there was even a
mild hiss or two from the audience. I was perplexed in the extreme. Gary had played it beautifully, but the audience didn't like
it. The ladies got their laughs after he left, the mock fight went
well, if a bit sloppily, and the final curtain—when Mary suddenly
stops running in front of the sofa and moons Carol—got a big
laugh, and down came the curtain.

The applause was hearty, a standing ovation for the ladies,

many curtain calls, and a happy, chatty audience straggled out.

I went backstage, and there was a clump of people—half on the set, half spilling off—everyone hugging each other, laughing, backslapping. Carol said, upon seeing me, "Oh, darling, you've written a *comedy*, aren't you happy?" Laughter. Various people said, "Did you hear those laughs?" Like: No, I stuffed cotton in my ears. Mary looked, at the same time, deliriously happy and as if she'd swum the English Channel with a refrigerator strapped to her back. Totally exhausted, she was shaking, smiling, perspiring, and looking terribly small.

And soon there were Kevin and Bob beaming and Maj and the entire cast and production team acting like the crew at Cape Canaveral after a successful launch. It was pandemonium. People kept asking me what it was like to write a comedy. In the preceding weeks we had lost sight of that aspect of the play, what with all the angst. We stayed in a group, for fear that if we scattered, it might all vanish. We had to let it sink in that, yes, we had opened in Dallas and we were living to tell about it.

Soon Texans invaded the backstage area, and finally people dispersed to their dressing rooms. Ahmet, in his usual role of supporter, had not even stayed on to see the actual performance.

Before leaving the theatre, David Masacek, our carpenter, came up to me, shook my hand, and said, "You've written a very good play, very funny, you should be proud." I was touched by the seriousness of his tone. I went to see Carol, who was extremely pleased, and told her how good she was. Charles Lowe kept saying, "Did you hear those laughs? I haven't heard such laughs in—oh—I don't know how long. Those were *Neil Simon* laughs!" We'd all hugged and squeezed Mary for getting through it, but I felt Carol had been there all along, the anchor for the play up to now.

A pack of us invaded the Sheraton Lounge, drinks all around. Christ, the relief. Now everyone confessed thinking it was going to be a disaster of major proportions, but—whatever—for the audience, the play worked.

The one major disappointment was Gary's last scene. I could tell by the look in his eyes that he was confused and depressed, although he was too much of a gent and a pro to let that dominate his joy in the working of the play in toto. I assured him it was in no way his fault, he'd played the scene perfectly. The audience just didn't think it was funny. We asked other members of the company what they thought the problem was, and no one could come up with an answer. Gary and I vowed to find the key to making the scene work. Then we all got, as Noel Coward would say, "gloriously, deliriously drunk."

I don't remember getting back to my hotel, getting undressed, or anything.

I do remember waking up at four in the morning and thinking, By God, I've got it, I know why Gary's scene didn't work!

The ladies, by that time, have ingested the hashish brownies; they have become friends; the audience likes them and is rooting for them to make their big comeback on Broadway. Then in comes this rather brash, if funny, young, wildly ambitious producer to pull the rug out from under them—no Paul Newman, as promised, no Broadway, low salaries, a long list of other actresses. Gary played the scene lightly and humorously, and it had never occurred to any of us that even so the audience would resent him besting the ladies. Anyone who tells me the subconscious doesn't work will get a huge fight from me. I swear the solution occurred to me during a drunken, fitful night: have the ladies offer *him* a hash brownie, let *him* lose control and fight to maintain his professional dignity in front of them, only to make an ass of himself at various times—comedically speaking, of course. I was so high with the inspiration, so anxious to get to work on the scene, I left a call for nine o'clock and forced myself into the arms of Morpheus with a grin on my face.

The baby, though definitely a breech birth, nevertheless lives. The show is on the road.

Wednesday, January 8, 1986

Met with Clifford for breakfast at our second home, the Brasserie. There was a business meeting going on at another table: Doug, Alan Wasser, Kevin, and Bob. They asked us to join them in Kevin's suite after lunch.

Clifford and I went over cuts, and I told him my idea to have the ladies offer Gary a brownie. He agreed it might work out well. I swallowed my omelette whole, dashed up to my room, and began mapping out the new scene. This is one of the times you pray not to have writer's block. There's simply no time. The muse was with me; soon I was actually having fun, seeing it in my mind's eye. I knew whatever the eventual scene would be, this would be merely a rough outline, and all of us, working together, would fill it in.

By late morning I had enough to phone Gary. He was up for it and laughed as I dictated the lines to him. Although the day was officially off for the cast and crew, he was more than agreeable to meet at the theatre around four to rehearse.

Met with Clifford at noon and showed him the draft, which he approved. Then we went to a meeting in Kevin's suite with Alan, Doug, Kevin, and Bob. Everyone agreed we ought to have a backup system in the event Mary short-circuits on us. Two lists. One listing people who would come in on short notice and "save our asses" and another of those who could take over in the long run. Clifford was still doubtful that, despite last night's Miracle of Fatima, Mary would be able to continue, operating as she was—on batteries. It was incredible to us that an actress, any actress, could get through an entire play having to listen to someone offstage and pay attention to actors speaking to her onstage. No mean feat.

Hopped a cab with Clifford to the theatre. Gary had already memorized the lines and was walking through the scene. I played both Mary and Carol as we mapped out bits of business that would add to the fun. We all pitched in, gave the cuts and changes to Steve, Jim Bernardi, and Keith, who would need them to keep Mary on course in the event these changes threw her.

Gary came up with some delicious bits of tongue-tied talk, a terrific double take when he senses something is wrong with him, and a great self-conscious walk, trying to keep himself from going completely berserk. And on his farewell, a stumble up the step of the foyer, a turn, and then a flourishing exit straight into the wall, seeming to smash his nose against it.

Mary and Carol arrived about six, and we quickly went through the scene several times. They got a kick out of it, too, although Mary was praying the little extra bits wouldn't throw her. Still, she was game, and they were riding on the high of their reception the night before.

Besides, actors—stars—are vulnerable when in this tentative

position with a show; it's after they're welded into their roles, know where each and every laugh, tear, quiet moment is, that they become intransigent.

For our second performance I expected a big letdown. Usually the adrenaline is sufficient to carry the day (or night) of the first performance regardless of who knows what to say or where to be when it's said. Nerves and raw energy alone do the trick. The second performance is usually when the glue comes unstuck.

Again the buzz in the audience before the curtain went up signified a good house. Again the place was packed. The reception for the first act was even better than the first night. There were, naturally, little bumps, rough spots along the way, but it was playing. The first-act ending was shaky, but you wouldn't have known it from the audience's reaction.

Spoke to Mary, Carol, Annie-Joe, Eric, and Gary during intermission. So far the response to this second performance seemed to solidify the fact that, yes, we do have a viable play. I told Mary how proud of her I was. She grinned nervously and kissed me on the cheek.

Back for the second act. It, too, was moving along well, except for "the dread vacuum-cleaner scene." The closer we got to Gary's reappearance, the more nervous I became.

Then he makes his entrance, is offered a drink by Carol, turns it down, saying, "No, thanks, I don't drink." Mary adds, "Neither do I—how 'bout a gin on the rocks?" Laugh. Then, after a line or two, Mary, as Leatrice, loses her point and, in desperation to have *something* to say, asks, "Would you like a brownie?" Big laugh. Gary turns it down at first but later, when he mentions the list of other actresses who might play the parts, Carol growls, *"Other* actresses? On second thought, why *don't* you have a brownie? They're absolutely delicious!"

Gary: "I don't mind if I do. I haven't had a bite to eat all day long."

Now the audience is primed as he walks toward Annie-Joe, who picks up the plate of brownies and extends it without looking at him, glancing instead at her wristwatch in a comic countdown for the brownie blastoff. Big laugh as she performs this bit of business impeccably.

From there on we were in clover. They could hardly wait for the effects of the hashish brownie to take hold, and when Gary, at the beginning of a cross, did a little hop-kick-step, shoulder-jerk, then froze and looked back at what he'd done, they were hysterical. He played the rest of the scene like a dream, and upon his leavetaking tripped, stumbled, turned, and smashed into the wall—receiving a huge round of applause on his exit. My heart leapt like a frog. The scene, which had lain there the night before, was now, thanks to Gary's comedic talents, one of the high points of the show. All this within twenty-four hours.

The second-night audience gave them all a standing ovation. Backstage—joy, hugs and kisses all around. Clifford and I went to the Sheraton, where we had drinks with Gary, Bob Regester, and George Yanoff, who'd flown in to check the show for his investors. We were all in an optimistic mood. Small miracles do major miracles promise.

Opening night tomorrow!

ACT II

OPENING NIGHT

Thursday, January 9, 1986

OFFICIAL OPENING NIGHT. For the first time in a long while, slept until ten.

Worked more on the brownie scene, embellishing it, bending it to fit Gary's personality and style. Met him at the theatre and worked with him alone until our stars arrived late afternoon, when we all rehearsed together. They are pleased with the scene, because it adds a huge comedic boost toward the final curtain.

The air in a theatre is different on opening-night day. There is an underlying hush; despite all the activity that might be taking place onstage, backstage, and around the theatre on the surface, beneath it there is a layer of quiet. Is it prayer, hope, fingers and even breathing crossed? It's intangible, but it's there. Perhaps it's a limbo of nervous energy waiting to explode when the stage manager calls out "Curtain!"

After rehearsal I went back to the hotel, took a long hot shower, ordered a light meal from room service, made myself one drink, and tried to relax. While I was getting into my dinner clothes, my fingers trembled as I put in the studs and cuff links. We were told we were all getting limos as some promotion gimmick, so I asked to be picked up at twenty of eight. I didn't want to be standing around backstage or in the lobby with my nerves hanging out for all to view. Odd to see Steve Meyer and other members of the crew in tuxes. All very formal—and frightening.

The backstage area was filled with huge baskets of flowers, boxes of candy, bottles of liquor, telegrams, and other presents. All the folderol that goes with opening night and makes me all the more nervous because it accentuates how special this one particular night is and heightens one's fears that the play won't live up to all the fuss being showered upon it. It becomes an "event," which can turn out to be something akin to a public hanging or a coronation, instead of simply "going to see a play."

Quick visits wishing everyone *"Merde."* Mary and Carol turned out to be opposites (again) in their approach to opening nights. Mary expressed her strong wish never to be told who was out front—in terms of celebrities, friends, or family. Carol, on the other hand, got a boost from knowing that, say, "George Burns is coming tonight!"

I go along with Mary. As a performer, even a writer, I would rather not know who is there, for fear it would, at some crucial point, intrude upon my concentration.

I scooted out to check the lobby. Bumped into Larry Hagman, who was trying to hide his J.R.-ness. We exchanged nervous smiles and said a brief hello. This audience was much dressier, and there was not quite the same level of buzz as they walked in with more dignity and self-consciousness than the preview audiences. The atmosphere was cooler, not so charged with anticipation and warmth.

I made my way to the mezzanine, only to find the Pace people sitting where I usually sat, so I crossed over to the audience-left side, where I sat in a box next to Ann. I took this as an ill omen, wanting to sit right where I'd been when we'd had two relatively warm, responsive audiences. Superstition dies hard.

Glancing around the theatre from my vantage point, I thought the group that filled the orchestra section looked more like wax dummies than animated first-nighters. Whereas the preview audiences had packed the house, on opening night the second balcony was not full. This, too, gave me pause. As curtain time approached, the anticipatory hum was missing. People were either talking to each other, admiring their outfits, or sitting rather quietly gazing at their playbills. I wanted to shout: "Come on, everyone, wake up, we're going to have a party!"

The houselights dimmed, and there was a tiny rise in the noise decibel level and then silence. Gary's first scene didn't get nearly the number of laughs it had the night before, although he played it the same. Respectable applause after, then an interminable wait until his wagon set was rolled off and the apartment scene lit up. The audience was slow to warm to Carol's scene with Aretha. They were there, but it was not bank night by any means. Mary got a huge hand on her entrance, but the laughs were muted.

It wasn't until the raunchiest exchange in the play that the audience really perked up:

LEATRICE
I'm only having one [drink]. Also, I must admit, I was a teensy, tiny bit apprehensive about our meeting. I upped my insurance and left a sealed envelope with my lawyer.

SYLVIA
I love you. Teensy, tiny . . . that's one thing I never understood about you. One of the most ruthless characters in Hollywood and that's saying something and . . .

LEATRICE
(Immediate protest) Ohhh . . .

SYLVIA
Come on, this is Sylvia you're talking to. Sylvia Glenn, star of stage, screen and—

LEATRICE
K-Mart openings.

SYLVIA
That's what I mean about you. You've always had a wicked sense of humor, you can see it right behind the eyeballs. It was always visible to me. But, of course, you'd never swear or really drink or—

                    LEATRICE
Oh, all that's changed.

                    SYLVIA
I don't believe it. Prove it!

                    LEATRICE
No.

                    SYLVIA
I don't believe it anyway. I remember that swear box you used to keep
on the set. Anybody'd swear and they had to drop in a quarter. And
Ethel Merman came up to you once and said, "I hear it costs a quarter
everytime you say a no-no. Well, Babe, here's five bucks—go fuck
yourself!"

Big laugh from the semi-stuffed shirts. That's what they
wanted—dirt. Unfortunately—or fortunately—that's the only
time the F-word is used in the play now. It did warm them up
somewhat, but the first act was bumpy. There was one whole
section about a bomb film Carol had suggested Mary for, one that
almost ruined her career, that got completely fouled up and made
no sense whatsoever.

The first-act ending was messy; there was a decent laugh
when they ripped each other's wigs off, and respectable applause
when the curtain fell. However, during the intermission we knew
we had a tough fight on our hands. One couldn't help curse the
perverseness that landed this particular audience in our laps for
opening night instead of one of the two previous groups.

I smuggled myself about the lobby and heard generally good
comments, but people were not throwing confetti in the air.
Bumped into Bob and Kevin, and we all smiled and said the usual:
"Well, for a first-night audience they're not all *that* bad!" A quick
visit backstage to hear, "They're sure not as good as the preview
audiences, are they?"

"No, but we all know opening-night audiences are never all
that good."

"Right. But so-and-so or such-and-such a line got a big
laugh."

"They'll be much better for the second act."

Wrong. It was not necessarily the audience: the second act
was not played well. Carol went up a couple of times, and Mary

even pitched in to get things back on the track. But the strain caused Mary to wobble a bit, and the momentum was lost by this time. It was simply shaky. Toward the end Mary skipped one of her best insults to Carol: "You not only got to Chicago on your back, that's how you got in the motion-picture business in the first place—*on your back!*" This triggered other mixups, and it was a muddle. Curtain calls were all right. There was a standing ovation, but I believe it was because a lot of Mary's Texas friends were present and it was, no matter what, an official opening night.

I was extremely depressed and had no wish to attend the opening-night party. But one had to: one is not allowed to go back to the hotel and cry. One is, after all, an adult. Kind of . . .

The party was held at a disco, vibrating with loud noise. But there was a glassed-in side room where the cast and crew could escape and sit at tables. Soon everyone was present. Carol and Mary made their entrances to applause and the flash of cameras. Larry Hagman was also big news in Dallas.

We were all trying to put on brave faces, but one zillionth of an inch beneath the skin was a layer of depression. Clifford, Bob, Kevin, George Yanoff, and I were all hanging on to the theatrical cliché: Well, the regular, slow, dull opening-night group you always get. Many well-heeled Texan first-nighters were drinking it up, toasting Mary and Carol. No one paid much attention to the author, who didn't really want much attention. I was interviewed by one TV man, who was a bit patronizing, I thought.

At one point Larry Hagman herded Kevin, Bob, and me over into a corner and gave us a few opinions. Something about how Annie-Joe should begin her first scene singing before Carol enters. He also mentioned that when he'd first read the play he'd thought Mary should play Sylvia. That's all Mary would have to do, learn that whole first scene with Annie-Joe, accompanied by all the physical business of dismantling the apartment.

I washed these comments down with more vodka, but I finally told myself it was an awful fucking dreadful rotten opening-night party, jumped into my limo, and went home.

Luck, fate, chance, timing—whatever that theatrical magic is—was not with us this evening. And we had been tricked into believing it would be.

POST-OPENING ODDITIES

Friday, January 10, 1986

Many phone calls from both coasts, none of which I wanted to take: all were from well-wishers, but you don't want to whine about a bad opening-night audience. What's a fellow to do—lie?

Calls from Kevin and Bob, who wanted to meet with Clifford alone and then have me join them at the Brasserie for lunch. Done. Kevin began talking about a loooooooooong tour, up until and all through the summer, not even aiming at New York. Thought they could make a lot of money and possibly recast before trying Broadway. (This is not a nice business.) Kevin wanted Clifford and me to take off three days, go someplace and relax. Not now—we wanted to make cuts in Act II, because the running time of the show was too long for a comedy. After lunch Clifford and I went up to my room and started going through the script.

Call from Linda and Fred Hess, Aunt Peg's granddaughter and her hubby, who'd dropped down in Dallas on their way to or from someplace to see the play. Drinks with them before the theatre. Good to see them, good to talk about Peggy; in all this hubbub it somehow made Peg's death official. I'd ordered two tickets for them, thought they'd comp. me but they made me pay, the little devils. Why? We were sold out, for God's sake! And wouldn't this audience be the warmest yet! As Clifford and I were going over the cuts in the basement and listening to the reaction over the loudspeaker, we could hear it was going gangbusters. Tonight you'd have thought we were giving away free microwave ovens.

Clifford and I anticipated resistance from Carol over the cuts, but we knew Mary would welcome any slicing at all. "Hello, I'm Leatrice Monsee!" Curtain! We finalized them, and I watched the last fifteen minutes of the play. The audience was eating it up. Afterward Larry Hagman and Maj were beaming, as were Carol and Mary. We all cursed this audience for going bowling or whatever the hell they'd been up to the night before, when we needed them.

A bunch of us repaired to the Brasserie. Just as the mood was on the wild upswing, Ed Gifford stopped by Carol's table with advance word of the reviews, saying that Carol came off with high honors, they were kind to Mary . . . and then he looked at me and shrugged as if he'd just found out my legs were going to be amputated. "I take it I get it in the neck," I said/asked. Ed kind of winced, nodded his head (yes, I'm afraid it's the legs!), and walked away.

Saturday, January 11, 1986

Tried eating breakfast the next morning while reading the newspapers, which said how funny and charming the ladies were in this piece of drek. I paraphrase, of course, but that was the gist of my buddy Dan Hulbert's review. This was my first realization that I was, in fact, dealing with legends (Mary and Carol), whom most critics are loath to soil, so that leaves the author upon whom to dump. I quote him on Mary's entrance alone: "When Mary Martin made her entrance, stepping daintily in her fur-trimmed cape, peering shyly out toward the first theatre audience she's faced in almost a decade, it wasn't a momentous occasion. No trumpets blared. Rather, it was a hushed moment, a magical one, like watching a sunrise." The headline over Dan's review read: " 'LEGENDS!' WON'T BECOME ONE."

I thought of a sunrise I could imagine some two thousand years ago and felt myself on a cross, hands nailed, next to Him. The critic on the other paper, Russell Smith, was somewhat kinder, although full of qualifications. His headline read: " 'LEGENDS!' IS HALFWAY THERE." Underneath: "Act 1 looks good in premier, but Act 2 needs lots of work."

A public whipping is not pleasant to take, but you cannot say, "This is not exactly the play I wrote or had in mind, I was an abused child and never even went to college, and one of the leading ladies is being fed almost every line through an ear bug, and . . ." So you take a cold shower, an extremely cold one, and get on about your work. Which was picking up the retyped second act with cuts and traipsing off to the matinee, which, perversely enough, was sold out, and was by far our best audience. Mainly matinee ladies; God bless their souls, they were out for a good time, and that's exactly what they took it for and got. They roared through the whole bloody thing.

The cast was uniformly considerate about the reviews, most of them saying, "I don't care what they say—listen to those laughs." Gary said, "The critics—fuck 'em." "No," I replied, "not even with your dick." We laughed; we had to.

Saturday night sold out again and laughing to beat the band. Standing ovation and cheers. I listened to that, read the reviews again, and then, once more, got "gloriously, deliriously, deliciously DRUNK!"

Sunday, January 12, 1986

Woke up with a hangover that would fell a rhino. I had to get up at nine for a meeting with Mary and Carol at ten to go over cuts. I only had time to shower and cab over to Mary's suite, where, as the group assembled, I felt it necessary to make an opening statement announcing my physical condition. "I'm not feeling well, really not feeling well, so—please—don't let's have any trouble with the cuts, just write them down and accept them, please. But I can't even give them unless I have food."

Tom Davis said, "You can have orange juice, that's it."

"I'm sorry—either I get bacon and eggs, toast, jam, and juice and coffee, or I walk! It's that urgent. I'm a sick person."

Mary and Carol oohed and ahed, and breakfast was forthcoming. Then we got into the cuts with Keith, Clifford, Mary, and Carol. They took them all without a whimper. We knew Mary would, but thought Carol would balk at losing some of her "bits." Not at all—she was a lamb.

I saw Carol's real hair for the first time. She'd always had on either The Blonde Bombshell or the brown wig she wore in the show or a towel around her head, always saying, "You don't want to see my real hair, it's awful."

It was not awful at all; it is thick, dark brown, flecked with gray, tied back in a ponytail. "It's beautiful thick hair," I said, giving it a gentle tug. "I thought maybe you had peach fuzz under there, like a nun. It's lovely."

"It is not, it's ugly," she insisted.

I wondered why she didn't wear it that way, then thought: Of course not, no one would recognize her as Carol Channing.

Cuts given, I took myself back to my hotel and went to sleep. I barely made it up for dinner, then—bammo—out again!

Monday, January 13, 1986

Rehearsal at eleven with Mary and Carol and Annie-Joe at the theatre to go over Act II cuts and a few new lines. Carol was in her manic mood; her energy kept escalating until it would take an elephant tranquilizer to bring it down. With the new lines, Carol began saying, in front of Mary, "Well, if Mary doesn't say the line, I'll just come in with . . ." Or "Well, Mary won't remember that, she never does." I finally took Carol by the arm and asked her to calm down. "Darling, you know I have high blood pressure, and this kind of thing is not good for me."

"No, I didn't know that," she said, with what seemed real concern.

"Yes, it's true." And it is. But the idea that an author has to use that as a wedge shows what lengths we'll go to for a little peace and quiet during the work process. ("I'm sorry, dear, but if you don't take it easy and perform that scene exactly as written, I'll have a stroke!")

Released around three-thirty for a nap before the performance. Carol and Charles had arranged for a party of ten or twelve of us to see Charles Pierce, the very talented female-impressionist, who was playing in the main room of our hotel after the performance. We knew he did impressions of both Carol and Mary, and we all looked forward to this.

Sold-out house again, and a good one. The first act went very well, and the cuts will help in the second act when the ladies are secure; they are still unsure of them and the second act was sloppy.

I was not feeling at all like going to see Charles Pierce, especially after Clifford announced there'd be no general rehearsal tomorrow (after the mess tonight?!) but the ladies would rehearse Act II by themselves in Mary's hotel suite. A lion tamer with a whip and a chair is required. Having been a performer, I think I know how they feel and their need of someone with strength and authority, especially when things are shaky. When I said I thought the plan was wrong, all I got from Clifford was a weary "Oh, Jimmy . . ."

Soon a party of us had assembled in the Venetian Room: Mary, her assistant Susan Grushkin, Tom Davis, Terry (Carol's dresser), Keith, Gary, and me. Small house, Monday night, maybe five other tables. Charles Pierce came on and did a fine show. He did not actually do Mary, but at one point said, "And there's Mary Martin wearing the same darling little hat she wore in *The Sound of South Pacific*." He did do a good Carol Channing, but a tame one, as opposed to the way he nailed Bette Davis, Tallulah, Mae West, and Joan Collins. Played to our table a lot, and some of his material is extremely racy. Gary and I kept craning to see how Mary was taking it. In good spirits, it seemed.

After the show Mary and Carol went backstage to have their pictures taken with him. I was still upset about the rehearsal plans and said I thought it was strange, when they were so uncertain about the second act, that there was no rehearsal with the director. Tom Davis suddenly spoke up. "Well, I've had enough of this, I'm putting my fucking foot down, Mary's not rehearsing, she's tired." I said if she was that exhausted what were we all doing attending a late show in a nightclub? He told me to go fuck myself, and I told him where else he could put his foot, stood up, and went to my room. I was convinced Mary's nervousness was caused by uncertainty about what she was doing. There is no way I could imagine her wanting to go on exposing herself in front of an audience with an unsteady performance. She needed help, and I wanted to see that she got it.

Now we get into the Marx Brothers. I tried to sleep. Impossible. I finally woke up Bob Regester at five in the morning and told him if there was to be no rehearsal I would wash my hands of the entire play, go back to New York and NOT on to California. I said there was no point in my being around to witness the mess that was being displayed on the stage at times. He reminded me of the good audience reaction and said he couldn't very well phone Clifford at this hour but would call him at seven or eight. I was up for the night.

Tuesday, January 14, 1986

By seven or eight I'd heard nothing and phoned Kevin: I was told he'd gone on to Los Angeles for a day or so. I then phoned Jerry Paonessa, who was in New York on business, and told him I was coming back and why. He was upset and said, "Hold on, I'll phone Bob and Kevin and maybe even Clifford." I began packing. He got Bob, who had *not* phoned Clifford, told him I was heading east and why, said goodbye, and hung up. I finished packing and made a plane reservation. Jerry phoned back to say he'd talked to Kevin, who said he doubted I'd leave and throw a million bucks down the drain. That snapped it. I didn't want simply to disappear, so I called Charles Lowe to let him and Carol know I was on my way east.

That, as they say, put things in motion. "Jesus," Charles said, "you can't do that—you've been holding this whole fucking thing together. Wait fifteen minutes."

The phones continued. Charles called Tom Davis and other parties concerned and then phoned me back to say rehearsal had been scheduled for three-thirty at the theatre. I unpacked. Clifford then called and suggested a truce over lunch.

We talked the whole thing over, but Clifford was extremely pessmistic about Mary. I said, "I think she simply needs to know exactly what she's doing, to go over and over it, and then she'll relax." I thought he should be stronger at rehearsal. I could tell he did not like to hear this. I did not like to have to say it. We made a temporary peace and headed off to the theatre.

Carol arrived first, extremely happy that I'd not left. I asked if we couldn't have a quiet, thoughtful rehearsal. "Of course," she said. But as she got ready I could tell this comment nagged at her. Finally she turned to me and said, "Why do we always have to be so careful with Mary? Does she own the show?"

"No, but you know the problems she has."

"I have problems, too," Carol said, adding, "Do you know Mary went out shopping this morning? And she's been out shopping before. I would never do that, never, not at this stage." I tried to calm her down but she kept repeating, "If Mary goes shopping, how could she be so exhausted or concerned about the play?"

Mary arrived without Tom Davis, which was good, because I was ready to kill him on sight. We rehearsed the second act, but it was slow going and bumpy and Mary didn't even seem familiar with the material she used to know. Clifford suggested we run the ends of both acts, but Mary got confused and wasn't quite sure which act she was in at times. It is a puzzlement. The afternoon was discouraging, and it was at last decided to have Carol rehearse with Barbara, Mary go over her lines with Keith, and simply let the show play for the rest of the run in Dallas.

Just when spirits are at the bottom of the hill—surprise. After this afternoon, the performance this evening went extremely well—I believe all thanks to rehearsal of the second act. The ladies got through the cuts rather cleanly and the curtain came down at ten-twenty-five.

Lee Stevens, one of the heads of the William Morris Agency, and his wife, Liz, were on hand, and I was invited to dinner at the Brasserie with them, Charles, and Carol. And what a strange dinner it was, right out of *Alice in Wonderland*.

They were quite pleased with the show, and of course we started hashing over all the problems. Carol is a wild one. She went on about how she'd have packed and left if I'd gone back to New York. Then she lit into Clifford. "He has no idea at all how to direct American comedy, none at all—or American anything, for that matter. I take all my direction from Jimmy." Then she started talking about Mary. It was a totally schizoid conversation and had to be the result of the pressures Carol had been experiencing all during the rehearsal period and our time in Dallas.

Lee Stevens and his wife said they were surprised the show and performance were as good as they were after all the rumors that had drifted east.

"Well, it hasn't been easy," Charles said.

"It certainly hasn't," Carol said. "Imagine Mary spending all that time shopping and then she's too exhausted to rehearse—really!"

Charles: "Well, yes, but . . ."

"And of course she can't remember lines," Carol snapped.

"She goes home and gets drunk after the show, and the next day of course she doesn't know what act she's in!"

I said, "Oh, I don't think Mary drinks that much. She has a nightcap and—"

"Oh, God," Carol said, putting a hand up to her head. "The dear, I don't know how she's gotten through this, she's amazing. She really is. Think of the courage it's taken for her to get this far."

I spoke up, hoping to keep the conversation going in this direction. "I don't know how she can get through a show like this with a bug in her ear. Thank God for Keith, but even so—"

Lee Stevens said, "Well, it must have been an experience."

"Yes," boomed Carol, "you think it's easy working with an alcoholic!"

Both Charles and I were shocked; even Charles, usually totally on Carol's side, said, "Now, Carol—"

"Well, what would *you* call it?" Carol asked.

"Now, Carol, you mustn't talk like that." Charles broke into a chuckle and patted her hand. "You're just jealous because *you* can't drink!"

Total switch from Carol. "Oh, I just love Mary, I do, she's so wonderful to work with, so giving, so caring, and—oh, God—what a worker!"

I was getting dizzy and couldn't believe my ears, but there was something terribly funny about it. After a pause, Carol said, "Of course, it's not easy to work with someone who's practically—well, it's not senile, but it's—"

"Now, Carol"—a warning from Charles.

"Yes," said Carol, "she's an angel. I couldn't have done it, but here she is, and the show's going better every night! God bless her. I wish she wouldn't drink!" A burst of laughter. "And go shopping! My God!"

It was the Three Faces of Carol in the Brasserie, right in front of us. I'm sure Carol did not literally mean what she'd been saying; rather, it was the release of months of nerves that allowed the actress's already heightened dramatic view to bump into hyperbolic overdrive.

Charles soon changed the subject. "And we have no producers, none at all. We have *no producers*. Jimmy's been the producer, too. They don't know what the fuck they're doing! And what's all this talk about San Antonio and New Orleans dates? We have approval of where we play, and I'm going to cancel them out. And," he asked, turning to me, "what about Chicago, why not Chicago for Christ's sake?"

"I think they're working on that," I told him, not really wanting to get into dates and bookings with them.

"They're working on shit; they don't know what they're working on."

"I wish we could get Julie Andrews," Carol suddenly said, then she turned to me. "You know, I went into Mary's dressing room and told her you said I terrified her."

"Carol!"

"Well, I did," she said, fastening those eyes on me. "Told her you said I scared her, rattled her. She denied it!"

"Of course, she would," I said.

"But I went right in and told her," Carol repeated.

The evening taught me one thing—besides throwing me a bit off balance with the yin and yang of the total conversation—don't say a word if you don't want it eventually broadcast or in print.

Soon we finished our lovely after-the-theatre supper and I staggered up to my room with minor indigestion. I went to bed and suddenly began laughing at the conversation that had taken place downstairs. I roared, had to cover my mouth for fear of waking up other guests. Perhaps we are all getting near the cracking point.

MORE ODDITIES

Wednesday, January 15, 1986

Charles awakened me with a phone call saying he'd heard we got a good *Variety* review, didn't say we were exactly a smasheroo, but was extremely positive and promising, indicating we might well build into a hit.

Smooth rehearsal in the afternoon with Gary, Mary, Carol,

and Annie-Joe. They went over the cuts, and we put in a few new little iggies in Act II, plus some lines for Gary in his brownie scene. He is so adaptable, so innovative; every night he builds the brownie scene so that it's funnier and better. Sometimes he goes over the edge, overplays a bit, but one has to go out on the limb to see how far one dare go. Good evening performance.

Thursday, January 16, 1986

Woke up feeling optimistic, did some reading, lots of phone calls from the East. Had the *Variety* review read to me. Very good.

Then the usual mood swing. Arrived at rehearsal at one-thirty, just as Carol was getting out of a limo. Apparently the mayor and the city of Dallas gave a huge luncheon for Mary and Carol. Mary did not appear, and when asked why, Carol said something about how she hoped Mary was back in her hotel learning her lines. This has got to be picked up in the press. Terrific.

Mary arrived and a slight rehearsal started, very slight. Suddenly Mary was carrying the script and seemed completely disoriented, confused, and unfocused. After we'd gone over a few of the cuts again, she broke down, said she couldn't go on like this, she was holding everyone else up, couldn't remember where she was. She began sobbing, and then I heard something about "leaving the show."

Rehearsal came to a screeching halt as Clifford jumped up onstage and took Mary into her dressing room. This was all so surprising, because things had been going relatively well. Carol kept saying, "I don't know what's the matter with her." Then she muttered, "I wonder if it's the Dick Coe thing?"

"What Dick Coe thing?" I asked.

"Well, Dick Coe was here last night and saw the show—you said hello to him, didn't you?"

"Yes," I said. Dick Coe is the critic emeritus of the Washington *Post,* a very nice man and a theatre lover who unfortunately isn't reviewing much anymore.

"Well," Carol said, "he said hello to Mary backstage on his way out to see the show. Then this morning Mary asked what Dick Coe thought of it. And I told her—nothing. Mary said, 'Well, he must have said *something.*' And I kept telling her he hadn't, and she kept repeating he must have said something. So I finally told her he said he had to see the show again because he couldn't hear most of Mary's lines and the pace was so slow."

"What?" I asked in disbelief. "You told her *that?*"

"Well, it was the truth, that's what he said."

"I know, but you know Mary—you didn't have to tell her that."

"Yes, I did," Carol said, looking me straight in the eye. "What would you want me to do—lie?"

"Jesus, yes!"

"Well, I wasn't going to *lie*. What would I have said?"

"You should have said he thought it was fine, and that would have been that. You know how vulnerable Mary is right now."

Carol kept arguing the point, and I told her, please, for God's sake, to cool down and not say anything more about Dick Coe or any other critics, and not to pass on destructive news of any kind. I left the theatre while Clifford was still in with a weeping Mary.

I walked back to the hotel in a rage. When I got there, Clifford called to say he'd had a good talk with Mary and hoped he'd been able to calm her down. I told him about my scene with Carol, and he couldn't believe what she'd said. He also dropped the news that he was leaving for England this very evening, but would be back in Los Angeles.

My fury built as evening approached. I finally phoned Charles to tell him what I thought about the Dick Coe situation, and we were soon into a shouting match. Charles finally said, "Don't you think it might be wise to give Carol her release?"

"No!" I said, but I think he meant Mary, because later on he said something about Mary checking into a hospital to avoid any bad publicity about her leaving the show and her learning problems.

"Why do you always pick on Carol?" he demanded.

"I don't!"

"Yes, you do, it's always Carol!"

"It is not, Charles. Look, I'm delighted she's in the show, I couldn't be more grateful to her for being there, for being solid, for keeping it going."

"Then why do you always criticize her?"

"I don't, I'm criticizing her now about *this*, about what she said to Mary about Dick Coe, especially now. She should keep her

(ABOVE) *Stoking up for battle. Left to right: Clifford Williams, Bob Regester, the author, and Kevin Eggers.*

(BELOW) *Mary and Clifford meet in San Francisco. Left to right: the author, Clifford, Mary, and Bob Regester.*

(ABOVE) Ahmet Ertegun, Mogul.

(RIGHT) Kevin Eggers, Mogul in training.

(OPPOSITE TOP) O happy day in Malibu!
Left to right: Bob Regester, Mary, the
author, Maj and Larry Hagman.

(OPPOSITE BOTTOM) Holiday Wishes!

tons of love

Happy Holidays

the Kirkwoods

(ABOVE) Two spiffy-looking legends. (OPPOSITE TOP) Casting in New York. Left to right: Tara Jayne Rubin, Andy Zerman, the author, and Vinnie Liff. (OPPOSITE CENTER) First read-through in Los Angeles. Left to right: Freddy Wittop, Harry Curtis, Mary, Annie-Joe Edwards, the author, Clifford, Carol, Steve Meyer, and Jim Bernardi. (RIGHT) Lunching at Chez Leatrice. Carol and Mary with Susan Grushkin.

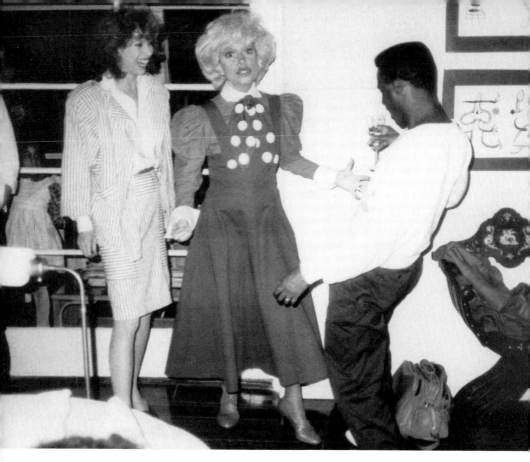

(ABOVE) "We know it's Christmas, but where did you get that outfit?"
Trish Garland, Carol, and Eric Riley. (BELOW) *"Step, kick, kick,
brush, kick touch . . . again!" Mary, Trish, and Carol.*

(ABOVE) The author—"I'm glad someone is!"

(LEFT) "My God, showbiz is fun!" Annie-Joe and Eric.

(BELOW) An author's life-support system: Front: Bobbie Lefkowitz, Esther Sherman, Jody Paonessa; Rear: Elliot Lefkowitz, Jerry Paonessa.

Please Do Not Disturb
Miss Martin Resting

(ABOVE) "So who did you take to the L.A. opening?" Shirley MacLaine and the author. (OPPOSITE TOP) Opening night in Los Angeles. "Why are these people laughing? Because they haven't read the reviews yet." Left to right: the author, Zsa Zsa Gabor, Ahmet Ertegun, and Carol. (RIGHT) Three-and-a-half legends. Carol, the author, Shirley MacLaine, and Mary.

(ABOVE) At Pat O'Brien's in New Orleans. "No matter what—we keep smiling." Left to right: Carol, Mary, Susan Grushkin, Charles Lowe, and the author. (RIGHT) "... and smiling." Mary and Carol in Philadelphia. (BELOW) James Kirkwood Day in Chicago, when Mary swiped my book. Left to right: the author, Mary, Mary Ella Smith (Mayor Harold Washington's assistant), Carol, and Gary Beach.

(ABOVE) *"We're taking six weeks off for vacation, then Mary and Carol and the company will go back into rehearsal for our Broadway opening at the St. James Theatre in New York in April, isn't that wonderful?" Roxy Rokker, Mary, the author, Zev Bufman, Carol, and Gary Beach.*

(BELOW) Carol, Zev Bufman, Mary, and the author with the famous ten-million-dollar cake.

(LEFT) A real lifesaver: Gary Beach as Martin Klemmer.

(BELOW) Act I, Scene 2. "A legend begs for help." Carol and Annie-Joe.

(LEFT) Carol and Mary:
"I thought we were both
dead!"

(BELOW) Carol: "I hope
she looks like Sam Jaffe in
Gunga Din."

(BELOW) Carol: "And Ethel
Merman opened her purse and
said, 'Well, babe, here's five
bucks—go fuck yourself!'"

(ABOVE) *Preparing to deliver a strip-o-gram.*
Carol, Eric Riley, and Annie-Joe.

(OPPOSITE TOP) *The world-famous split about to*
happen. Eric Riley and Annie-Joe.

(RIGHT) *Don Howard and Carol: "Could I*
please have your autograph . . . it's for my
grandmother, she was a great fan of yours."

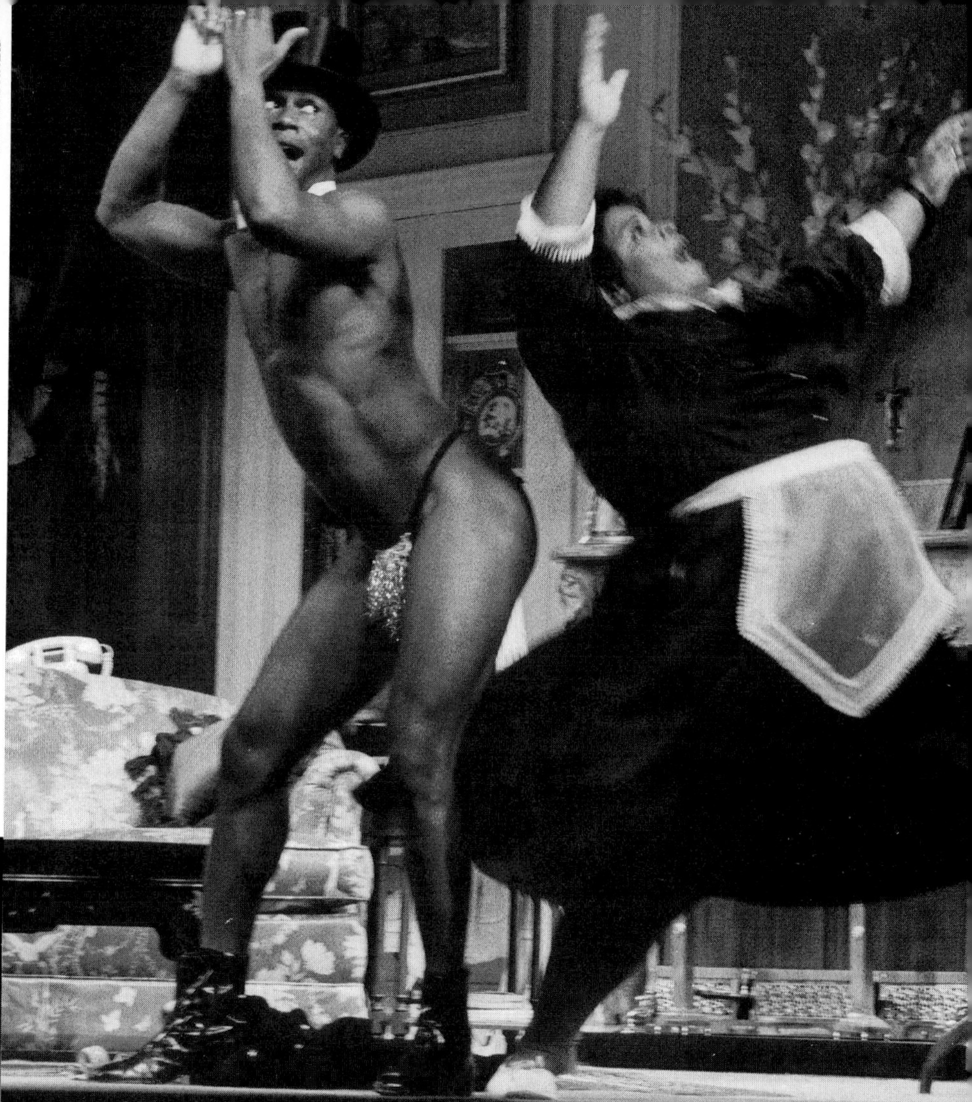

(KENN DUNCAN)

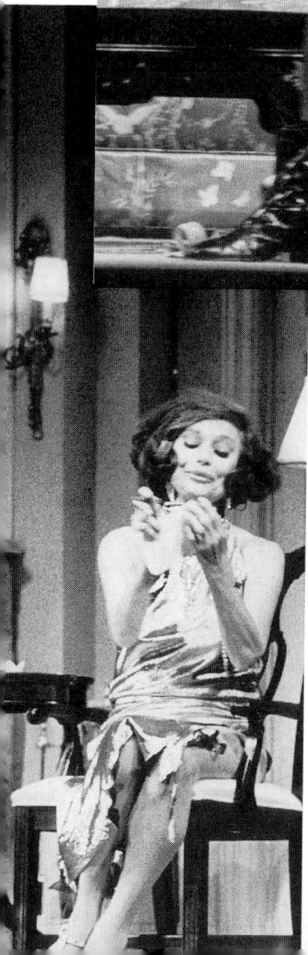

(GIFFORD/WALLACE INC.)

The end of Act I. "Go, ladies, go!" Annie-Joe, Mary, and Carol.

mouth shut and not pass on any distressing news to Mary. That only makes sense, if we want to keep the show going!"

He argued with me; it was as if he didn't hear what I was saying. Eventually I had to shout, "Charles, I cannot talk to you any longer on the phone or I'll throw up, I really will. You know exactly what I mean. Now goodbye!"

I hung up and looked for something to break. This mess, and Clifford gone. Seems as if we can't have two days in a row without some major hitch. Son of a bitch! Besides which, Dan Hulbert wrote a follow-up piece on the play called "TAKING A SECOND LOOK AT 'LEGENDS!'" in which he tells me how to rewrite the play— almost entirely, if you take the situations in the play he criticizes as artificial. On the same page in the Dallas *Times-Herald* was an article saying *"Legends!* has broken the box office record for the Majestic Theatre, grossing $440,000 for the thirteen performance run which ends Saturday."

Friday, January 17, 1986

Another whacked-out day. An afternoon of fractured rehearsals, then back to my hotel to meet Jerry Paonessa, who arrived about six. God, it's comforting to have an old friend on hand. Of course, the poor fellow had to hear all the tsouris, but he's a good listener and a sage adviser as well. We had dinner and jawed, then went to the theatre. This audience was all right, but not up to the response we'd been getting. The first act was played well, however, and Jerry seemed to be enjoying it. Bill Gile, who had directed me in the play with Dina Merrill, showed up tonight and came up to me during intermission, raving about the play.

Of course, that was during intermission, and we had the second act to go yet. And go it went, down the drain. The first part played beautifully, but then, after Mary's mastectomy speech, her ear bug cut out and she was not able to get her lines from Keith. I cannot describe what a muddle ensued. Mary dipped back into the first act for a while; Carol got that wild look in her eyes as she tried to keep the train on the track. And when the insults between the two ladies are supposed to fly at the end of the play, it was incredible. Mary would take the beginning of one insult and tack it on to the end of another, so that it made no sense at all. The play came completely unglued. I was angry and depressed.

Saturday, January 18, 1986

Cheryl Crawford, one of our producers, who had been missing completely, phoned from New York. She'd had an accident and hoped to be able to make it to Los Angeles. I told her I hoped she would. Cheryl is a professional producer, and that is what we need.

Jerry and I walked to the theatre for the matinee. I went into Mary's dressing room and showered her with outrageous compliments. She's amazingly resilient. No matter what's going on inside, she presents a bounce-back picture on the outside. A trouper she is.

Sure enough, our seesaw kept up. The matinee audience was the best we'd had so far, and the show played amazingly well. Mary seemed quite sure of herself. Go figure. Kevin nabbed me for a talk during the second act; he spoke more about lining up a longer tour. I told him Charles and Carol said they would not play San Antonio. This was one of the first times I realized what contempt Kevin held them in. "They don't mean a thing," he said. "It's Mary, Mary's the star."

"Yes, but so is Carol, she's the costar, and Charles—"

"Fuck them, don't worry about them, I'll take care of them." He went on to say we were dickering for an engagement in San Francisco, maybe Toronto and Washington.

The evening audience was packed to the rafters and jolly as could be. We had a fine farewell performance. Standing ovation, much hollering and shouting.

Sunday, January 19, 1986

Woke up early, finished packing. Then Jerry called to confirm our reservations and seat assignments. He turned to me and said, "They don't have anything."

"What?" I shouted, grabbing the phone. I do not usually fly off the handle about such things, but the tension of this play manifested itself in odd ways. I told the young lady I'd phoned several days ago, had confirmed reservations, and gotten two seat assignments, one by the window and one on the aisle.

"I have no record. Are you certain you called?"

"Yes. I'm certain. I have my ticket here, and I wrote down the seat numbers."

"I have no record of you and Mr. Paonessa. The plane is overbooked."

I decided to try the old "May I please speak to your supervisor?" bit. When I got the supervisor on the phone, I did not want to have to plead or beg or dicker. I wanted the two seats promised on the flight booked. "I'm sorry," she said, "but the flight is—"

"Now, listen," I said to the supervisor, "my name is James Kirkwood, and I'm the company manager of a play called *Legends!* starring Mary Martin and Carol Channing, which is—"

"Oh, yes," she said, "it's playing in Dallas, I read about it."

"Yes," I went on to say. "Now, as I said, I'm the company manager, and we're using American Airlines to fly from here to Los Angeles, then later to San Francisco, San Antonio, New Orleans, Chicago, Boston, Washington, and Philadelphia. I control the movement of our company of fifty-six people"—I don't know how I picked that number—"but if Mr. Paonessa and I do not get on this flight in the seats that I requested and was told we had, not one member of our company will ever again set foot on American Airlines!"

"Wait a minute, please. . . ."

I waited, Jerry standing next to me. When she came back on she said, "Mr. Kirkwood, I'm terribly sorry about this mistake. We can't give you the two seats you requested in tourist. However, I could give you two seats in first class, if you'd please accept them."

I graciously accepted. Why be a bad sport?

PREOPENING BUMPS, THUMPS, AND GRINDS IN L.A.

We were all terribly glad to be leaving Dallas. The nerves, the ups, the downs, the mood swings were so extreme, it seemed we'd been there for months.

There was a day off before we started dress rehearsal at the Ahmanson Theatre in beautiful downtown Los Angeles. We were told ticket sales had picked up a bit. The Ahmanson has a good subscription list, *but* we were booked in for a long spell, about ten weeks, our last week or so being off subscription and also being Holy Week, during which the theatre usually takes a holy beating. The pressure to get good reviews was strong, so we'd be assured of not falling into the red and being unable to continue the tour.

Had a call from Cindy Adams of the New York *Post* saying there were strong rumors in the East that the two ladies were beginning a major feud. I lied—I'm sorry, Cindy—I said they adored each other, which had been true in the beginning, although now nerves were frayed a bit.

However, no matter what I said, the good old reliable *Post* printed something. Within a few days the following clipping was sent me.

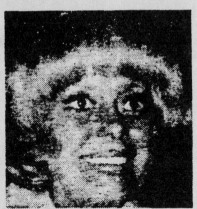

PAGE SIX

LIFE could be following art with Carol Channing and Mary Martin, the two stars of _Legends_, en route now to Los Angeles after a stunning opening run in Dallas. Carol plays Sylvia Glenn and Mary plays Leatrice Monsee, two aging moving queens who would cut each other's throat just to blunt a blade, reminiscent of the alleged feud between Bette Davis and Joan Crawford. Sunday, while being honored by the city of Dallas, Carol was asked, Where is Mary Martin? Quicker than you could say "putdown," she quipped: "She is in her hotel room learning her lines." As Carol stoked the fires, a spokesman for the show hastened to assure one and all: "Miss Martin has been word-perfect from Day One."

CAROL: upstage

Wednesday, January 22, 1986

Drove down to the Ahmanson around noon. The theatre itself is handsome at first glance, but much more suited to a large classical play or a musical, too big for a drawing-room comedy. Totally black side-wings bank the sides of the set, lending it a kind of funereal touch. The balconies are fierce and look as if they'd been designed to hurl Christians from. They also begin too far back from the proscenium.

The set was up, and when I first walked out into the theatre proper, Carol was wandering about the stage, saying she felt her voice was in a series of dead spots. "The sound isn't good, and the lighting is so dark—it's impossible to play a comedy in such darkness." With that she walked off the stage.

I was standing up by the first row and turned to walk back to the sound booth. Charles Lowe was sitting in about the eighth row and reached out to grab my arm. "Jimmy, the sound in this theatre is awful. You can't do a comedy with bad sound, where the audience can't hear your funny lines."

"I know," I said, leaning right down into his face, "I'm just going back to talk to them about it now."

Charles looked up at me and said, "What?"

I realized Charles wears a hearing aid and obviously I was not speaking into the right ear.

Just then Mary walked out onto the stage and immediately put a hand up to shield her eyes. She moved a few steps this way and that and then, still shielding her eyes, squinted out toward me in the orchestra and said, "The lighting is so bright on this stage I'm afraid it will weld my contact lenses to my eyes and I won't be able to see at all!" She quickly walked offstage.

There was a major character missing from our company: Steve Meyer was nowhere to be seen. I was told he had been let go, that our producers thought he was not being as helpful to Mary as he could have been. I was introduced to our new production stage manager, Randy Buck, a young, good-looking, extremely professional fellow who took over the job seamlessly. His wife, Naomi, was also a stage manager but, although she was soon with us constantly and a great help, she was not officially part of the production team.

Before our L.A. rehearsals began, Clifford and I were summoned to Mary's dressing room. She was suddenly acting quite the queen. She no longer wanted to lose lines to Carol; she wanted to think about changing the final curtain, the mooning bit, and I couldn't blame her for that, even though it had been her inspiration. She no longer had the little-girl-lost look or the "I'll do anything anyone wants" attitude. Perhaps this is healthy.

After the cast assembled for notes and small changes, a brush-up rehearsal began, and things were going along fine until Mary suddenly stopped and announced, "I won't say the ipecac line anymore."

Toward the end of the first act, when Mary finds out Carol has lied and it's not her apartment, they have an argument and Mary starts to leave, saying she'll be late for dinner at "21," which is her own lie. Then they had this exchange:

SYLVIA

Your compassion and generosity are truly touching. I hope you choke to death at "21."

LEATRICE

Thank you.

SYLVIA

(Calling after her) By the way it was me that started the fire in your dressing room trailer outside the set of *Daughters* [a film they'd made together].

LEATRICE

That's all right, it was my secretary, Peggy, who put five drops of ipecac in your coffee *every* morning!

SYLVIA

Ipecac?

LEATRICE

Yes, it induces vomiting.

SYLVIA

(Wailing) I was sick every morning all during that picture!

LEATRICE

I know and it was soooo very attractive. Goodbye!

I was sitting in the front row. "Why, Mary, what's wrong with it?"

"Nobody knows what ipecac means."

"But it's explained in the context in which you say it. Carol asks 'Ipecac?' She obviously doesn't know what it means, and you tell her."

"I don't care, I won't say it. I need another line, and I don't want an exchange of two things to say, I only want one line and then I exit."

I sat there for a moment, and then I thought, Well, what the hell, I can think up another line if it really bothers her, although it had been working well ever since we opened and getting a laugh. "Okay, Mary, I'll think up another line."

"Good," she said.

I looked down at my script, and then I noticed no one was speaking—they were not going on with the scene—and I looked up to see Mary and Carol staring at me, obviously waiting for a new line. I looked back down at my script and heard someone, I don't know who, say, "Well . . ."

Glancing back up at them all focused on me, waiting for a new exchange, snapped it. I stood, folded up my script, and said, "I've been rewriting this fucking play on my feet for the last seven weeks. I'm tired of it. Would you mind giving me an hour, or maybe even two, to come up with a new line?"

I did not wait for an answer. I went home.

Thursday, January 23, 1986

I stayed away from rehearsal to make my point. I phoned in some lines to Keith and said, "Mary can take her pick or leave them alone."

"When will we see you?" Keith asked.

"You won't," I replied. "I'm tired of I-won't-say-this, I-won't-say-that, I-won't-do-this-or-that."

"What are you going to do?"

"First I'm going to try to hang myself, and if that doesn't work I'll play tennis. You all can rehearse without me today."

And they did. And I don't think anyone burst into tears. Authors can be a pain in the ass, and I'm certainly no exception. Oddly enough, when I went down for the evening performance, all went very well. Mary was starting to cook this night, and the audience was responsive. Merle and Ron Mardigian (my film agent) were there, and we had supper after at the Hungry Tiger. They both said they'd enjoyed the play very much and thought it "had legs."

Friday, January 24, 1986

My friend Jim Piazza arrived from New York today. Good to see him and have a friend on hand. We drove down for rehearsal in the afternoon.

Now, the night before, Mary had really started to play the brownie scene, wherein the hashish hits her, very well. At one point, just before Carol launches into a virtual monologue about her childhood and her mother, Mary says, as she moves from the sofa to a chair, "Well, are you going to share it or just replay it in your mind?" Last night she said that line as she wobbled over to the other chair, grabbed hold of it, then suddenly flopped down as if she thought she might miss it. It was very funny and got a nice laugh.

This afternoon, when we reached that point, Carol suddenly said, "Is Mary going to keep in her Ben Blue bit?" Ben Blue was a well-known comic in films years ago, not averse to doing pratfalls.

"What do you mean, Ben Blue bit?" Clifford asked.

"When Mary makes that long cross over to that chair and sort of falls down," Carol said.

"Mary's always crossed to that chair," Clifford said.

"Yes, but not like last night," Carol countered.

"I don't know what you mean," he said.

"Yes, you do. She took forever crossing over, and what am I supposed to do all the time she's doing that Ben Blue bit?"

Now, Mary was sitting onstage all this time and did not say a word, simply sat there, straightening out her skirt. Jim was standing next to me and shot me a look of amazement, as if to say, You mean *this* is what goes on?

"Well," Carol said, "what am I supposed to do?"

"Just start your speech," Clifford said.

"Not while she's doing her Ben Blue bit," Carol snapped.

"Now, Carol—" Clifford began.

"All right," Carol said, in a loud voice, "if she's going to keep doing her Ben Blue bit before my big-ass speech, then I'll do *my* Ben Blue bit just before her mastectomy speech!" And on and on she went.

I finally stood up and clapped my hands together. "All right, Carol, that's enough now. Let's get on with it, we're losing a lot of time!"

She gave me a look that would have frozen Joan Crawford and they went on with rehearsal. Mary's energy now was low, and no wonder, and soon Annie-Joe was complaining about certain parts where she had no activity and didn't know what to do, mainly in the last scene, when Gary was talking. I suggested that she just *listen* and got a look that would have frozen Charles Manson.

After rehearsal, which did not end on the most pleasant note, Clifford said, "Annie-Joe can be a sullen cow when she wants. She was really winching."

"Winching?" I asked. "What's that?"

"Whining," he said, "only it's not congenital."

"I hope not."

That evening, before the performance, Carol and I had promised to make an appearance before a committee of 250 "founders" of the theatre, upstairs at the Dorothy Chandler Pavilion, where they were to gather for cocktails at seven, before attending our show.

I don't mind doing lectures, TV and radio, newspaper interviews, or even flashing, but I dislike these events where you have to speak in front of little cocktail groups, most of whom are terribly rich and lacquered and drinking.

However, at a quarter to seven, Carol, in a stained white terrycloth bathrobe and a towel wrapped around her head—a vision in high couture—Charles, Jim, and I were met by Rick Miramontez, the Ahmanson publicity fellow, and walked down the block to the larger Dorothy Chandler building. The room was elegant, the group exactly what I'd imagined—dapper men, beautiful, bejeweled, well-gowned women, all drinking and chatting and waving across the room to each other.

A microphone and stand were set up. I was asked to speak first and then introduce Carol. I began by waiting until they'd all quieted down, and then I said, with an extremely straight face and in a flat factual voice, "Good evening, ladies and gentlemen, my name is James Kirkwood, and I'm an alcoholic."

It got a laugh, and I went on and did some bits I do when I lecture at colleges. Carol, Charles, and Jim were standing a few yards off to my right. Jim had given me some one-liners, and after I delivered them I said, "It's so great to be here at the beautiful Ahmanson Theatre, where the line at the box office stretches around a reflecting pool, as opposed to New York, where the line would stretch around a few bag ladies and a dead horse. And speaking of dead horses—" I stopped, turned, looked to my right, and said, "I'd now like to introduce one of the stars of our show. Are you ready, Carol?"

It got a laugh, and Carol laughed; she does have a good sense of humor. But then I said, "Ladies and gentlemen, here she is, the star of *South Pacific, I Do, I Do, The Sound of Music, Peter Pan,* and—" The cocktail group was laughing, but I heard this frantic whispering and looked over at Carol, who was saying to Charles, "No, no, he's got the wrong shows! Those are Mary's!" I couldn't believe she got one joke, but not the other, so I quickly introduced her and got off. Carol walked up to the mike and did her usual excellent PR speech.

Jim saw the show for the first time tonight. The first act breezed along, and he was very pleased. I was, too, so much so I went backstage at intermission to tell Mary and Carol, but before I could reach either one, Charles dashed out of nowhere, grabbed my arm, and said, "Please come in and talk to Carol, she's terribly upset." With that he ushered me into one of Carol's two dressing rooms, where she was in a panic.

"Jimmy, I'm sorry, I was a mess, I couldn't even remember my *name* in the first act, and—"

I interrupted. "Carol, you were terrific, the act played beautifully."

"Ah!" she cried. "I was awful, just awful—and I don't even know if I can go on for the second act, I don't think I can! Isn't there someone in charge around here? How can they put a new *sofa* out there and not tell Mary and me?"

The sofa we'd had was covered in a shiny material that was a bizarre mélange of colors; it looked as if it belonged in an airport lounge and someone had thrown up on it to boot. I had complained until everyone agreed to have it re-covered. This night the sofa was re-covered in a simple blue-green material that minded its own business. I was fairly sure it was the same sofa, only re-covered, as Carol went on to say, "It's a different height, it affects all my body language, Mary's feet barely reach the floor. It's impossible, how could they—"

"Carol, I think it's the same sofa, they've just re-covered it."

"I beg your pardon, it is not, it's totally different. I tell you, it threw my whole performance, and I'm sure it did Mary's, too."

About that time, Jim Bernardi called five minutes and Carol said, "You'll have to hold the curtain; I can't go on with that sofa."

I told her again I was certain it was our regular sofa, but Carol would have none of it. She clenched her fist and fought back tears as she ranted on that no one had warned her so she could have tried sitting on it, working on it, before the show. "Where's the set designer, where's our *director*, where are the people in charge?"

"Carol, I'm sure—"

"For God's sake, Jimmy, you were an actor, you should know the difference—you *would* know, if you had to go out there and work on that dammed *thing.*"

Charles tried to calm her, and finally I said that if she'd go on for the second act I'd gather everyone together in her dressing room after the show and there would be an official explanation—either it was re-covered or they'd substituted another sofa while it was being done. After a lot of talk about the dreadful way the show was being run, Carol agreed to go on, if there would in fact be a summit meeting immediately after. I went back to my seat, where I told Jim what had taken place.

The second act began; despite the day *and* the sofa, both ladies were playing it well, and I could hardly wait for Mary's "Ben Blue bit." When it came, she took even longer than she had the night before, wobbling from sofa to chair, and added even a little more shtick. She did this in total silence as Carol stood frozen-faced, glaring at her, not uttering a sound until Mary was finally settled in her chair.

After the show Jim came backstage with me while I gathered Clifford, Randy Buck, Jim Bernardi, and others on the staff and we trooped into Carol's dressing room. She was still furious about the sofa. Randy and Clifford and a few others then assured her the sofa had merely been re-covered; it was verily the same one she'd always used. "Are you sure?" she asked. "Yes," they all replied. There was a beat, Carol sighed, then both she and Charles started complaining about the lighting and the sound. Randy promised to run checks on both, and we all finally straggled out.

Jim tagged along as I gave several notes to Mary and Annie-Joe and spoke to Gary. Carol had two dressing rooms, and when it was time to leave, about twenty minutes later, I pondered which one she might be in now, so I could avoid any confrontation. I picked my route, and just as we passed her other dressing room the door opened and out she popped, in street clothes, on her way home.

"Oh, Jimmy, darling," she said, throwing her arms around me and kissing me on the cheek, "thanks so much for all the help—mad about the sofa, wish I could take it home!"

With that she breezed away. I could barely mutter good night at this switch and walked out in a daze. After all that high drama, "Mad about the sofa, wish I could take it home!"

While we were driving home in the car, Jim said, "Would you like to stop off somewhere for a drink or a bite to eat?"

"No," I said. "Actually, I'm bushed."

"I don't blame you," he said. "This was quite a day."

"Not at all unlike most of the others," I added.

"You're kidding," he said.

"Not at all."

"Jesus Christ!" he exclaimed.

"Yeah," I said, "Him, too."

Saturday, January 25, 1986

There is a lovely lady named Conchita hired by the Ahmanson to organize our first-night opening and gala after at the Dorothy Chandler Pavilion. Because of the nature of the play, whatever legends can still walk, talk, or crawl were being corralled by the Ahmanson and invited to attend. I was asked if it would be possible for me to bring a Legend. Conchita mentioned she'd spoken to Shirley MacLaine, who was working on a picture but said she'd try to attend. She said Shirley had sent her love to me, so I asked for her number in Malibu and phoned, got a service, but left my number and asked her to phone me.

She did call a day or so later and accepted, saying she'd have to leave the party early to be at work the following morning. I told her I'd have a limo pick her up and we'd meet at the theatre. I'd have to be there early to pass out opening-night presents and go around wishing "Break a leg" and *"Merde"* and spitting on people's backsides for luck.

I received a call from a Mr. Philip Sinclair, Lana Turner's manager, who said Miss Turner would be interested in attending. I did not know Lana Turner, but I knew people who'd worked with her, and I'd heard her tardiness was practically legendary. Mr. Sinclair admitted she did not get A+ for on-time. I told him I'd be delighted if she attended, but I hoped she wouldn't come sauntering down the aisle fifteen minutes into the first act, thereby distracting the audience from the two legends on stage. I took a chance and said, "Would you please tell Miss Turner I'm an admirer of hers, but if she's not seated by the time the curtain goes up, I will attack her with a club like they do baby seals? I will bash her about the head and face."

There was a pause. "What was that message?" he asked.

I repeated it, and he asked if I wanted those exact words passed on. I assured him I did. He phoned me the next day to say, "Miss Turner accepts your opening-night invitation. She's seen those programs on television about the horrible treatment of baby seals and she will make every effort to be on time."

"Good," I said, and added, "Now, if she feels there's a chance she might not make it before the curtain goes up, for God's sake, tell her not to wear white. It could get messy."

"I will tell her," he said, "and we look forward to meeting you."

In the meantime there was word from Mary that she thought the show should end with her and Carol singing part of a song. It was difficult to imagine how they'd burst into song in that apartment after fighting all night, but it was, as Mary said, probably right that the audience would like to hear them warble, and certainly the present ending was a copout.

Monday, January 27, 1986

A meeting with Clifford, Kevin, and a few others at Ed Gifford's suite in which we discussed the possibilities of a song. With opening night only days away, we thought it best to convince Mary not to put it in before the opening—that would be too much pressure for both ladies. Then Ed looked at me and said, "Jimmy, I've got some bad news, but I have to tell you!"

"What now?" I asked, never expecting what he was going to hit me with at all.

"We're in big trouble with the NAACP!"

"What?" several of us shouted.

"Some Englishman came to see the show and took great offense to the relationship between Carol and Annie-Joe, especially in the first scene. He called the NAACP; they're all up in arms and are coming down to take a look at the show. We might have pickets!"

"Pickets!" I said. "Well, that's the only thing we *haven't* had!"

Kevin gave me an "I told you so" about the black humor, even though we had already mapped out cuts in that scene, removing some of the business that Kevin felt might offend, but which I still believed was not offensive because of their long friendship.

"Now the NAACP. I wonder if the CIA will be after us next?" I asked.

We all agreed there was nothing to do but wait and see what happened and put the minor cuts in. I think Ed, being a publicity man, had glommed on to the possible idea of pickets and—publicity.

Clifford then chimed in and said Duncan Weldon, the David Merrick of England, had been to see the show and liked it very much. He felt the play was not being served well in performance or pace by our ladies, but would like to do the show in London if he could find the right two ladies for a production over there. We were all pleased to have *some* good news.

Tuesday, January 28, 1986

Met early with Clifford, and then rehearsal with Annie-Joe, modifying the beginning scene and going over more cuts. Carol was adamant about some, saying sympathy for her character was being diminished if she wasn't allowed to keep in one or two serious speeches reflecting her feelings about the acting profession. "Look," she said, "I've taken all the 'fuck's and 'shit's and other words Mary won't say, and now you're cutting the heart out of my character. It's all wrong."

Adjustments and compromises were made. We kept in one or

two speeches she requested, and the rehearsal was brief and undisciplined. That evening the first act went beautifully. I went backstage to tell the cast how proud I was of them. I should have gone home. The second act was disastrous. The cuts had thrown them, and Mary and Carol were way off their marks. Backstage, both ladies were annoyed—nay, furious—that they'd screwed up, especially since we were getting very close to the official Los Angeles opening.

Wednesday, January 29, 1986

I decided to stay away from rehearsal. I was getting too utchy with Clifford. I also knew it could not be too substantive; there was a two o'clock matinee. I tried phoning Keith, who is the best one for me to approach to get through to Mary and Carol with my notes. Instead of getting Keith I got Clifford, and we had words. I told him I thought they had to rehearse the beginning of Act II, after the cop scene, because once they got off to a shaky start it spread through the act like brushfire.

"Oh, no, I'm not going to do that," he said, rather snappishly. "They're exhausted. You direct them, if you want."

"Gladly," I snapped back, and added, "I will also direct the production in London if it's done there."

"Go ahead!" he shouted.

We both realized we were acting like children, so we mellowed down a bit. He said Mary was really exhausted, hadn't even realized there *was* a matinee, and was very upset that there was a matinee and evening on Saturday when we were opening on Sunday night. "I think we just have to leave them alone, let them run things with Keith."

Though I didn't attend the matinee, I spoke with Keith after. He said it had been a good show, but in the last few performances Carol has been holding up Mary's dress after she moons and Mary had said if she did it one more time she would no longer moon. They'd lost a laugh at one point, and Carol had said, rather audibly, "Well, we killed that laugh, didn't we?" Mary does not like these onstage pronouncements, and I can't blame her. Carol had also said, regarding Mary's complaint about Carol's holding up her dress, "Perhaps we should be doing

The Sound of Music." Ladies, ladies, only a day or so and we'll
have opened.

Saturday, February 1, 1986

Esther Sherman, my agent, arrived from New York, as did Elliot
and Bobbie Lefkowitz and my dear friend Arthur Beckenstein.

Esther wanted to save her views for opening night, but Arthur drove down to the matinee with me. As we entered the
backstage, there were Carol and Charles, so I introduced them
and then said how well the second act had gone the night before.

"Of course," Carol said, "Mary wasn't drunk. Of course, it
played well then, but you never know. . . ."

Even Charles chipped in: "Carol, we're going to have to have
your mouth taped."

I was amazed she would say that in front of a perfect
stranger. We went into her dressing room, and Carol admitted
opening-night nerves were mounting.

Jerry Paonessa brought his daughter, Leigh, age twelve, to
the matinee, and she adored it, which surprised me. Jerry reported
that, as Leigh looked through the playbill and read about all the
shows both Carol and Mary had appeared in, she suddenly turned
to her father and said, "Boy, a lot of people are going to be sorry
when these ladies die!"

The Saturday-evening performance, the last before our opening, was packed, and the audience was typical of Saturday nights.
They'd eaten and drunk too much and were slow on the uptake.
They were appreciative but far from the best audience we'd had.
After, Carol was running around backstage crying out, "Oh, this
is the best omen of all, the very best, to have the worst audience
we've ever had right before opening, oh, it's just terrific, isn't it,
Mary?" Mary looked at Carol as if she'd lost her mind, and didn't
reply.

I repaired to the Paonessas', where Jody threw a late supper
party for me. A bunch of close friends; we all had several drinks,
laughed and scratched a lot. When people were leaving, all saying
what fun they'd had, Jody said, "Oh, I'm so glad, I wanted Jimmy
to have a good time on his last night!"

We laughed and howled some more.

THE LOS ANGELES OPEN

Sunday, February 2, 1986

Not a bad title for a golf tournament. The very phrase "OPENING NIGHT" strikes fear into the hearts of theatre folk, smites them a mighty blow to the bowels. And here it was.

Drove down to the theatre around five-thirty to make the rounds, spend a little time with each performer, not too much, give them their present and card, an encouraging word, and move on. The backstage area was awash in opening-night paraphernalia. Ahmet and Mica Ertegun were on hand; they barely spoke to me; we nodded and I spoke with an old friend of Nancy Reagan's and mine, Jerry Zipkin, who had flown out just for the opening. I presumed he was with the Erteguns.

I'd asked the stage doorman to keep a lookout for Shirley and the limo so I could go out and jump in, but, sure enough, in she walked a little before half-hour. She looked gorgeous, gave me a hug, and said, "Should I say hello to Carol and Mary?" I said I thought they'd gone into their preopening trances by now and it would be best to wait until after. Especially since I was aware of Mary's never wanting to know who was there, I thought it would be counterproductive to have Shirley MacLaine pop in. "What would you like to do now?" she asked.

"Have a drink."

"Well, come on, then." She took me by the hand and we walked out to the limo, which drove us a half-block to the Hungry Tiger, where I had two vodka Gibsons on the rocks. Shirley MacLaine takes a lot of ribbing from people, but I don't care if she was Hitler or his mother (did Hitler *have* a mother?) in a previous life, she certainly knows how to behave in *this* one when she's with an author on opening night. She was perfection. Warm, humorous, supportive. As I was downing my drink, she asked if I was nervous.

"Of course."

"Listen, Jimmy, you've done everything *you* could. There's nothing you can do tonight but sit there and enjoy it. Just relax into it, it's up to the gods now. Come on, we'll have fun, you'll see."

Soon we were back in the limo, driving around the long, long block to the front of the Ahmanson Theatre. Spotlights swept the sky, flashbulbs popped, limos were humping limos, causing a huge backup, so we had to get out a ways from the theatre and walk along the red carpet. When Shirley was spotted, an entire herd of photographers and reporters came thundering toward us. The flashbulbs literally blinded us, so that we had to hold hands to keep our balance. Took forever to reach the lobby. Shirley was besieged by autograph hunters, and I signed a few myself.

We could hear the gongs ringing as we entered the theatre and soon met up with Esther and Arthur, with whom we were sitting. I had asked for seats in row K, which is about one-third of the way back in the orchestra, where there is a large break between row K and the rows in front for walking across the theatre. This so I would have easy access to leave without crawling over people in case I felt I had to absent myself for whatever reason: bladder, seasickness, play-sickness, or all of the above.

As we settled in our seats, Shirley said, "Jimmy, isn't that Lana Turner sitting right there?"

I looked to my left and, seated in row J, right ahead of us and perhaps seven or eight seats over, was Lana Turner, in a beautiful black see-through lace dress, looking exactly like Lana Turner. I excused myself, walked over, and knelt down, touching her lightly on the shoulder.

"Hi, I'm James Kirkwood."

"Oh . . . it's so nice to meet you. Well, I hope you notice I'm on time; in fact, we were even early," she said, introducing me to her party. She wished me luck and said she was very glad to be here. I said I'd see her at the party afterward.

You could hear people whispering: "There's Ann Miller!" and "Look, there's Eva Gabor!" "No, it's Zsa Zsa." "Christ, look over there, they're both here!" "Oh, and there's Charleton Heston!" "Oh my God, and there's that 'Golden Girl,' Betty White!" As the houselights dimmed and the anticipatory buzz heightened, Shirley took my hand, Esther kissed me on the cheek, Arthur gave me a pat on the leg. And off we went.

To my surprise, the audience was warm from the curtain's rise. Gary's first scene got big laughs. Of course, it is about the business, and most of the people on hand tonight were in the business. Esther and Arthur had not seen the play in performance, so they were laughing, and Shirley was *really* laughing, loud and warm and natural. Carol and Annie-Joe's scene got laughs, Mary came on to an ovation, and the first act played well and had decent pace, as far as I was concerned. Of course, all things are relative, and I had witnessed some relatively dreadful performances.

I think because Shirley was so responsive I was able to relax into the evening right along with her. I could also hear Liz Smith, an old friend of mine, laughing down front somewhere. The end of the first act, where Mary and Carol tear each other's wigs off and begin to go at each other, earned a whomping laugh, and when the curtain fell there was a big hand and a high decibel level of sound as intermission began.

We walked out to a section at audience right where there was not a huge crowd, most people being gathered at the other side of the lobby. I preferred not to be in the midst of it all. My group was having a good time and thought it was going well. Soon we were back for the second act, which also played without hitches, although the pace could have been better. Gary got his usual quota of big laughs when struck by the brownies. All in all, it was a much better opening-night performance than I had hoped for. Standing ovation right away, big applause, and many curtain calls.

We all piled backstage, where everyone seemed pleased that the show had gone so well and the audience, above all, had not consisted of the usual opening-night stiffs. Bobby Fryer was grinning; even Ahmet and Mica seemed happy, although we kept our distance. There were quick visits with Mary and Carol, Gary, Annie-Joe, and Eric, and then Bobby Fryer led a group of us from the Ahmanson to the party at the Dorothy Chandler Pavilion, across the plaza.

As we walked, Shirley took my hand and squeezed it. "I really had a good time; I think it's great fun, and if it's ever made into a movie, I'd love to play Sylvia. Will you remember that?"

I stopped walking, turned, and locked eyes with her. "Darling, you're the one who'd better remember it. Don't worry about me—I'll remember it. *You* remember it!"

"I will."

We walked on and again bumped into the paparazzi, who blinded us with flashbulbs. Once we were inside the huge Dorothy Chandler lobby, a lady from "Entertainment Tonight" grabbed Shirley for an interview: Did she like the play? Was it funny? How were Mary and Carol? Shirley gave a good interview and then graciously said, indicating me, "And this is the author, Jimmy Kirkwood, right here." The lady glanced my way, sighed "Umm . . . ," went on talking to Shirley, then switched to someone else.

We were led up some stairs and down another huge staircase into an enormous room with a dance floor, a band, and many tables. A balcony circled half the room, lined with tables where others were seated. Edging the dance floor were tables reserved for Ahmet, Carol and Mary, and many other celebrities; when I asked if there was a table for the author I got a negative. I thought this rude, so we quickly nabbed one of several tables that held "A.E." signs. Ahmet's, but he had several others.

Shirley went for the food right away; she had to leave early, because she was working the next day. Soon a commotion at the top of the stairs caused the band to stop playing, the room dwindled to a hush, the band struck up "Broadway Baby," and there was Mary, in a dark draped evening gown, and Carol, in a white one, holding hands at the top of the stairs, smiling, waving, and making the daily double descent. The room gave them an ovation and photographers went into overdrive as they waved their way down the staircase; when Larry Hagman went over to embrace his mother, flashbulbs exploded by the carton.

At one point someone came over and grabbed Shirley and me, and the four of us had our picture taken together. Carol had eschewed her $8.95 Gabor wig and was wearing her onstage brown one, going all out to change the image. Good for her.

About that time I was snatched by someone, turned around, and found myself standing next to Ann Miller, Zsa Zsa Gabor, and Ahmet. After a picture was snapped, Zsa Zsa turned to me and said, "Oh, dahlink, I luff de play and the lines. I could play de part"—her smile turned to a pouty little frown—"only I'm too young."

"No, you're not," I said, in all honesty.

She looked at me, still frowning. "I'm not?"

"No," I told her, "you'd be perfect."

"Ohh . . ." she said, then turned away and went on about her business.

Shirley soon said she'd have to leave. I started to take her to the limo, but Bobby Fryer came along to walk with us, and Shirley said, "No, you stay here, it's your night, your party, and I'm so glad you asked me. And remember," she said, bussing me on the cheek, "if *Legends!* is made into a film, I'm playing Sylvia!"

I thanked her for her support and reminded her she was the one who had to remember, not me. Lana Turner's manager came over and asked if I'd join her table for a minute or two. The lady is still beautiful. Her figure is slim, and I was surprised at how tiny she is. I never thought she was an amazon, but she's really quite small, with delicate bones, and very gracious. She said she loved the play and wondered if we could meet for cocktails the next afternoon and have a talk. Of course. We chatted for a while, pictures were taken, and a time and place for a meeting were set with her manager and another man. I went back to my table and rejoined my friends.

All the time this was going on, an extraordinary drama was being played out that I was completely unaware of. I was filled in later by Ed and Michael Gifford, our PR people, and Kevin.

We were not definitely booked into San Francisco at this time, although negotiations were under way, so the critic from the San Francisco *Examiner*, Gerald Nachman, had come down to attend the opening of the play in Los Angeles. When Ed Gifford heard this, he asked Mr. Nachman if he could possibly bypass reviewing the play and merely report on the opening-night event, holding off his review for when we opened in San Francisco, at which time the play would supposedly be in better shape. This was agreed upon. Happily drinking and chatting with friends, I had never met Mr. Nachman and was totally unaware of his presence. I will let the article he wrote, which appears on the following pages, speak for itself.

Several small footnotes to the aforementioned. Apparently Mr. Nachman approached Mary during the evening and quoted her in another article as saying, "Oh, pooh!" (Notice Mary did not use the S-word! She did not even say, "Oh, plop!") "Oh, pooh," Mary went on, "what does *she* know?" In this same article he quoted Kevin as saying, apropos of Carol, "Don't listen to her, that's just big-star bull——. It's going to open in San Francisco."

GERALD NACHMAN

Well Hello, Carol
—So Long, Legend

T WAS RIGHT out of "All About Eve," with myself in the George Sanders role of critic Addison De Witt and Carol Channing playing the Bette Davis part of another famous Channing, Margo.

Our scene took place at a party at the Music Center following the Los Angeles opening of "Legends," the comedy in which Channing stars opposite Mary Martin in a show scheduled to open at the Curran in April.

There I was, innocently scurrying about gathering quotes from Charlton Heston and Mary Martin, when I bumped into Lee Solters, portly press agent to the stars (Sinatra, Streisand, Channing), who took me by the arm and said, "Say hello to Carol. She wants to meet you."

-- I blanched a bit — recoiled is more like it — aware that I am not Carol Channing's favorite person after a negative review of "Jerry's Girls," which later closed on the road, though I was nowhere in the vicinity. So when Solters took my arm and led me over to meet Channing, I had what you might call misgivings, but it seemed impolite to refuse. She was surrounded by admirers, led by husband Charles Lowe, a distinguished fellow who runs interference for her.

"Oakland," I said, injecting some levity into things.

"Well, San Francisco is my hometown," she smiled, "and I can't go back there because, if I do, you'll just smash me in the face."

At this point, sensing the paparazzi closing in, I walked away and collided with the show's New York press agent, Ed Gifford, a rumpled man with the pained smile of one who has seen it all. "Having fun?" he asked.

"Not yet," I said. "I thought you said the show is opening in San Francisco but Channing says she isn't going there." Gifford was aghast — a press agent's nightmare was unfolding — but, like a pro, be showed only a big grin, offset by stark horror in his eyes.

Channing's husband stomped over and said, "Who told you we're playing San Francisco?"

ILLUSTRATION BY JOHN BORING

"Gifford did," I said. Lowe (to Gifford): "Who told you?" Gifford: "Kevin did." Lowe grabbed a flunky and cried, "Get Kevin! Tell him it's very important!" Kevin is Kevin Eggers, a producer. In a nonce, Eggers appeared, a short round jolly chap who assured me the show is coming to San Francisco. "Did you tell him we're going to San Francisco?" snapped Lowe. "We can't

we shook hands (I
pretended to flinch, a small joke that got no reaction)
and exchanged opening banter. Channing fixed me
with those huge eyes when I asked if her show was
coming to San Francisco.

"I want to very much, but I can't because of you," I
quickly shot back something along the lines of "huh?"

"Did you see the show?"

I said I had. Solters jumped in fearlessly. "He's not
reviewing it, Carol, he's just covering the opening."

"Why did you come down here if you hate me so?"
she asked. "You don't like me for some reason, and I
don't know what it is. What have I done? Tell me."

She was a foot away, staring at me with eyes full of
unblinking anger, the famous wide Hirschfeld mouth
in a grim line. She wanted an answer, no, a guarantee.
"You seem to have a vendetta against me. Why is that?
I'd like to know." The tight knot of Channingites was
silent, leaning forward to hear, both shocked and
thrilled by the carnage before them.

Unlike Addison DeWitt, I had no sardonic
wisecrack, just dry-mouth dread and the sense of being
cornered. In 25 years of writing of and reviewing show
folks, this was a first, the sort of confrontation people
like to think occurs regularly. The odds had caught up
with me, as they did John Simon on that fabled night at
the Ginger Man in New York when Sylvia Miles
dumped a plate of pasta on him. I was there, in fact, and
was impressed that Simon returned in a crisp new shirt.

Channing wasn't armed with linguine, just her
husband, who kept tossing in asides from stage left
until drowned out by his wife's heated dialogue. "What
can I do? I can't play my home town if you're there."

"What do you want me to say?" I babbled. "I think
you should play San Francisco. Honest." "It's nothing personal. There's no vendetta."

"It's my hometown! Do you have a hometown?"

After feverish jawing, Eggers took me aside.
"Listen: We're definitely going there. No question
about it. Don't listen to them. You didn't hear anything.
Just enjoy yourself. You're our guest."

Taking his advice, I speared some melon off the
buffet and was searching for a quiet table. A man was
waving me to his table. It was Lee Solters. "Sit with us,"
he said pityingly. "Lots of room." I rolled my eyes at
him. Solters apologized. "I had no idea. Don't know
what got into her." Then he chuckled. "This is Carol's
table." As I leaped quietly to go, Solters pulled me back.
"Stay. She's busy mingling. Don't worry, she won't sit
down." Four minutes later, Channing, Lowe & Co.
marched over to the table. "Been a ball, Lee," I said.

"Don't run away," he said, grabbing my arm and
pinning me to the table. "Carol wants to apologize."

"Sure," I said, by which time Channing had
descended again, plunked herself down in the next
chair and fixed me with a hostile gaze. Lowe began:
"Carol feels you don't like her. We want to know why."

Carol again: "Did you see our show, Mr.
Nachman?" . . . Mr. N (again): "I did." . . . Miss C: "Can I
come to San Francisco? You tell me." . . . Mr. N: "People
are interested in the show and your fans want to see
you. I don't want to be in the middle."

Miss C: "Ah, but you see, you *are* in the middle. I
can't come there because you have this thing about me.
Mary Martin says you say wonderful things about her."
(To others:) "Do you know what he did to 'Jerry's Girls'?
Every Sunday, he put in this tiny review saying how
bad I was!" I explained that all major shows get a
capsule review and that the Little Man is not a prime
example of vendetta journalism. She was unconvinced.

I told them I hated to eat and run, and stormed off
in what I felt was a fine dramatic exit. With a little
warmer audience, I'd have got a big burst of applause,
but these opening-night crowds can be murder ■

I wished I'd been a firsthand observer of these festivities, but you can't hit all the numbers all the time.

The celebration began to dwindle, but we'd all been invited to a private party at Annie-Joe's, and most of us knew that would be *our* party, the cast party where we could all assemble and hash over *this* party and get down and dirty.

Annie-Joe's was fun—lots of food, liquor, and piano playing. Annie-Joe sang and played up a storm, and others joined in. Charles and Carol arrived also, which was nice of them. They grabbed me and started complaining about Clifford, who was leaving for England the very next day. They said they couldn't understand how producers would hire a director who was leaving the play the day after the Los Angeles opening. I found this hard to understand, too. But, then, nothing connected with this production went according to the rules of Hoyle.

Everyone present was riding a high, thinking how well the opening night had gone. Such are our delusions. The main thrust of this jolly mood might simply have been a reaction to the plain fact that we had actually opened, period.

LOS ANGELES OPENING FALLOUT

Monday, February 3, 1986

I drove to the Regency at noon, where a goodly number of our people were staying. Soon we were in the midst of a meeting in Kevin's room: Alan Wasser, Doug Baker, Clifford, Randy Buck, Kevin, and Bob Regester. I was pleased that Ahmet was not there.

Clifford was a bit hangdog about departing, although I don't think he was truly heartbroken. He knew he was leaving a show in trouble, and I think he'd had a bellyful of the ladies and undoubtedly me. He was off to London to do a production of something called *The Candlelighters*, which was written in 1600-something and was being done at the Barbican.

Clifford would come back for at least three days to put in a song with Mary, Carol, and Annie-Joe. It was now certain we would try an alternative ending to the one we had, and both ladies had locked into the idea of singing a song, or part of one.

Ed Gifford breezed in, wearing a pair of old turquoise bathing trunks. He was in the midst of making frozen daiquiris and said he had word of the reviews. There'd been, he said, one bad, one good TV review. The L.A. *Times* was a qualified negative (it turned out to be about as qualified as the word "NO!"), and a very bad one from the *Examiner*. However, the word was that the trades, *The Hollywood Reporter* and *Daily Variety*, were good. He could see the look on my face. "But," Ed said, "listen to this, and I'll have a copy soon. The front page, I'm not talking about the second page, the entire front page of today's New York *Post* is a picture of Mary, Carol, Shirley MacLaine, and Jimmy."

"The front page?" I asked

"Yes," he said, "the front page."

I shook my head. "Jesus, the world must have quieted down for a day, death takes a holiday; you mean there was nothing else more important going on than an opening of a new play in Los Angeles?"

"Not only that," Ed said, "but Liz Smith is devoting her entire column tomorrow to the show and the opening, and she liked it, you know."

Someone said, "Bobby Fryer said the L.A. critics really don't have that much effect at the box office out here."

I found this hard to believe. "Listen, if you get rave reviews, people tend to get in heat about seeing a show; if you get bad ones, they take their time. They do not stampede the box office."

There was talk of the tour, a rehash of Carol's confrontation with Gerald Nachman (which was the first time I'd heard about it). And now I was really getting on to Kevin's hatred of Carol. "She's full of shit; it's Mary that counts. Mary's the star."

I said I thought Carol was equal, that she'd been carrying the show for us, and she should be treated accordingly.

"Fuck her and her husband, they're just a pain in the ass!"

This seemed like an extremely unhealthy attitude to be embarking on a long tour with. We moved to other matters. A song would be investigated for them, we'd let the show settle for a while and play, we'd see how business went, and we'd pray to the gods and sacrifice a virgin—if we could find one.

I said goodbye to Clifford with as much good will as I could muster. The reality of a floundering ship with no captain from here on in hit me. I vowed, if he were not able to rejoin us, to press Kevin and Bob for help in getting another director.

I drove out to Century City for my meeting with Lana Turner. We met in the cocktail/tea lounge (lots of foliage) of the Towers. Very posh. Miss Turner arrived, with Philip Sinclair and another man. She wore slacks and looked terrific, except she had huge dark glasses on. When we'd settled into chairs, she said she hoped I'd excuse the glasses but she hadn't put heavy makeup on and—well, certainly I'd understand. She said she loved the play, asked about the TV rights, and indicated she'd like me to write something for her.

She said, "The Lana Turner story [for TV] is in great trouble; the script is god-awful."

"Miss Turner—"

"Lana, for God's sake . . ."

"All right, Lana, would you please take off those dark glasses? I can't tell who you're talking to or what your expression is. . . . Please." I thought I'd get an objection, but she immediately whipped them off and said, "There, no makeup, but . . ."

"You look fantastic, you don't need any."

"And you," she said, "last night you looked cute as a button."

I'd brought along a copy of *Hit Me with a Rainbow,* a novel of mine that Natalie Wood had optioned before her tragic death, about a movie star who more or less kidnaps a young man and takes him off to Mexico while she's being pursued by her insane opera-star lover, with whom she is finished.

She seemed intrigued and looked forward to reading it. She was fun and bright and seemed quite canny. She spoke of her firing by Jane Wyman from Miss Wyman's series, "Falcon Crest," saying, "I was very hurt by that," adding, "Of course, she didn't want any real competition." We spoke of other projects. She said that when she'd been interviewed the night before for "Entertainment Tonight" she'd been asked if she thought Hollywood treated its legends well. She said she'd paused for a moment and then decided to level: "No, they don't, not at all. We learn our craft, work at it, devote our lives to it, work our asses off, and then—just when we know what we're doing—they slam the door in our faces."

We went on talking about "the business" until a lady settled by a large arrangement of ferns and began playing the harp. This fractured our meeting; we had pictures taken, exchanged all sorts of numbers, and parted.

Later that afternoon I was sent a copy of the New York *Post* and, by God, there we were on the front page: "THE STUFF LEGENDS ARE MADE OF." "Four show business legends celebrate last night in Los Angeles after the opening of 'Legends!' a new play written for two ageless Hollywood stars, Carol Channing and Mary Martin. From left: Miss Channing; James Kirkwood, the 'Legends!' playwright; his date, Shirley MacLaine; and Miss Martin. The glittering details are on page 13." I thought it was kind of them to include me among the legends.

The reviews came out Tuesday. Dan Sullivan, who doesn't seem to approve of anything crassly commercial, was far from a qualified negative. Far from it. His headline was "STARS STRUGGLE TO SHINE IN 'LEGENDS!' " Richard Stayton, may he stir-fry in hell for eternity, was downright vicious. His review seemed to be a vendetta; in fact, many people asked if I'd ever tangled with him, crossed him, poured sand in his gas tank, burned his house down, or otherwise pillaged his life. His headline was charming: " 'LEGENDS!': FEAR AND LOATHING IN THE THEATRE. Martin and Channing deserve a better fate."

It was so spiteful, I must quote the first few lines:

In all honesty, playwright James Kirkwood should provide a subtitle to "Legends!": "The Night of the Living Dead."
Ha ha. Giggle. Giggle.
No? How about this subtitle: "A Corpse Line!"
Ho! Ho! Yuck, yuck. Sigh . . .
Just kidding, dear reader. Just dutifully straining to mirror the tasteless level of "humor" provided by Mr. Kirkwood in the Mary Martin/Carol Channing showcase that ambulated into the Ahmanson this weekend, fresh from its previous crawl in Dallas.

Not exactly what we call "constructive criticism." Who knows what makes the fuckers so mean.

But mean they can be. And hurtful.

Such as the reviews from *The Hollywood Reporter* and *Daily Variety.*

I reprint these to bring into the area of wonderment the question of who saw what play, who reviewed the proceedings that took place onstage, and who reviewed a play they *wish* they had seen but didn't. Perhaps Messrs. Sullivan and Stayton were looking for another play. Something much more highbrow. Much more Noel Coward, although even he was spanked soundly by many critics when his work first came out as "meaningless froth, plotless, silly, unsubstantial and just plain dirty."

And now I must tackle the nitty-gritty of it. The two actresses I wrote about are not based on Ina Claire, Lynn Fontanne, or Katharine Cornell. They are based on tough, claw-'em-up-to-stardom ladies like Crawford, Miriam Hopkins, Davis, and others of that ilk. Ladies who were, in a way, vulgar at times. And their vulgarity surfaced when they were threatened, either by the studios or each other. They swore like troupers and fought like cats. Perhaps critics could not adjust to the image of Mary Martin playing one of these women. Perhaps Tony Quayle was right when he said, "I like the play, but they'll never accept you in it."

But by this time, the die was cast.

Let me give you the ladies' reactions to reviews. Mary swore, absolutely swore, that since *The Sound of Music,* which got some fairly negative reviews despite its success, she had never read and would in future never read a review. I don't know if this is gospel or not. But that's what she said.

I worked with Tallulah Bankhead once in a show called *Welcome Darlings.* I loved the lady; there was a piece of work. But she, too, claimed never to read the reviews. Then, one evening, I was sitting in my dressing room at half-hour when she came storming in and began swatting me about the head and shoulders with a rolled-up newspaper, shouting, "You got a better review than I did from this bitch!"

"Aha," I said, ducking and dodging her blows, "I thought you never read the reviews."

"I don't!" she shouted. "Someone told me about it."

THE Hollywood REPORTER

55th year　　　　Hollywood　　　　February 4, 1986　　　Vol. CCXC, No. 32　　　75 Cents

Stage Review

'Legends'

Ahmanson Theater
Closes March 22

By DREW CASPER

Watching Mary Martin and Carol Channing in "Legends!" a new comedy by James Kirkwood, is like being at a fun party.

As a couple of feuding, financially desperate ex-screen goddesses brought together to co-star in an off-Broadway play, their bitchy ripostes and giddy skirmishes are as delicious as those in "Old Acquaintance" or "The Women."

Martin plays Leatrice Monsee, the silver screen's ultimate victim. Beneath the sweetness and light, she comes equipped with "a mean streak the size of Argentina." Somewhat unconnected at first, it takes Martin an entire act to warm up in the role. When she does, sparks do fly.

On the other hand, Channing as Sylvia Glenn, the movies' archetypical slut, is at white heat as soon as the curtain goes up. Her maniacal, shameless, sadistically prankish, brutally forthright ways that cut through any hypocrisy and cant (even her own) cloak a susceptibility within. Channing is so scintillating in the part that she completely eclipses the memories of Lorelei Lee and Dolly Levi and is chiefly responsible for the show's combustion.

Kirkwood's mongoose-and-cobra-in-a-cage conceit is peppered with side-splitting lines and situations, obviously inspired by the juiciest morsels from Hollywood history, as the Davis-Crawford "Baby Jane" confrontation or Loretta Young's on-the-set sanctions against her foul-mouthed confreres. Fascination tempers ridicule in Kirkwood's bits and pieces which, in the end, bring home the point that "three-quarters of show business is nothing but appearance."

The play is extremely generous with the supporting cast, each of whom makes the festivities livelier. Gary Beach is a high-pressure producer, an expert at sweet talk and double-talk whose come-uppance comes in the form of hashish brownies. Annie-Joy is a sassy, street-wise black maid, unafraid to bring the stars down to earth. Eric Riley is a male stripper from Chippendale's. And Don Howard is a cop, answering a "911," who possesses the gaucherie to ask the ladies their age.

Though Clifford Williams' loose direction respects Martin's and Channing's talents and star-turns, it occasionally results in a sluggish pace and some flat staging.

Freddy Wittop's costumes, featuring a mink-trimmed apricot cape and a backless silver lame sheath, are brightly satiric. Thomas Skelton intelligently lights Douglas W. Schmidt's set of a Park Avenue high-ceiling apartment with rose moire walls and a Chinese green lacquered baby grand with a sense of the day running down, a neat correlative of the status of the central characters.

Rambling Reporter
Robert Osborne

.... If you were keeping a flashbulb-for-flashbulb count out in front of the Ahmanson Sunday night at the "Legends!" opening, it was Lana Turner and Ginger Rogers who tripped the most cameras. ... Our own paparazzi seemed to go bananas with the bulbs when each lady (Lana with Eric Root) arrived for the Mary Martin-Carol Channing romp. .... And that's not to say the skies and forecourt didn't light up like New Year's Eve when others showed up too, like Larry Hagman with family entourage, Zsa Zsa and Eva in one Gabor package, with Wally Seawell escorting both, Ann Miller with James Doolittle, Shirley MacLaine with "Legends!" author Jim Kirkwood, the Hestons, the Michael Yorks, et àl. All in all, a good night for people with stock in Sylvania Blue-Dot, Westinghouse, Phillips and G.E.

DAILY *VARIETY*

VOL. 210 No. 41   20 Pages   Hollywood, California-90028, Tuesday, Feb. 4, 1986

LEGIT REVIEW

Legends

(Ahmanson Theater; 2071 seats; $32 top)

Attention, Broadway producers and New York theatergoers. There are a couple of ladies you're all familiar with who are starring in a show by a playwright you're all familiar with, and that show is headed your way.

The ladies are legendary, and playwright James Kirkwood is working on his legend-ermaine, and the play's name is "Legends."

Show itself is a vehicle for two "older actresses" (Carol Channing and Mary Martin) who play "older actresses" who are still stars but are down a little bit on their luck. Or, to put it in their terms, "financially fragile."

Producers Ahmet M. Ertegun, Kevin Eggers and Robert Regester (for EEE Ventures Ltd.), Cheryl Crawford and Pace Theatrical Group, in association with Center Theater Group Ahmanson, are all to be congratulated for casting these two ladies, a combo that many theaterphiles would want to see regardless of what show they were in.

But Kirkwood has come through, not only for the ladies, but for the producers and audiences.

Kirkwood, who wrote the book for "A Chorus Line," which is quickly becoming a legend in its own right, has written another showbiz story, this one from the other end of the spectrum from "Chorus."

This tale is from the point of view of the hustling producer who's ready to exploit Sylvia Glenn (Channing) and Leatrice Monsee (Martin), both of whom are in unintentional "retirement" — which means that they haven't worked in some time but have to keep up a semblance of what they once were.

The producer is excellently drawn by Gary Beach, who does a solo scene at beginning of show in which he sets up the ladies and playwright via telephone. Play he's putting together is called "Star Wars, The Play." He uses Paul Newman as the hook to get the actresses, who've publicly feuded for years, to get together.

His imitation of Newman calling from some remote location on a static-filled telephone is a gem of theatrical gimmickry.

The meeting of the stars arranged, Channing appropriates Manhattan apartment of a friend who she knows is out of the country. When she arrives, apartment is decked out for a party saying goodbye to Aretha. Departing Aretha is not singer Franklin, but maid of the apartment's residents.

Channing not only encroaches upon the planned revelry, she talks maid (played wonderfully by Annie-Joe) into trying to fool Martin, who'll be there any minute.

Once that's out of the way and Annie-Joe has intercepted her guests, Martin arrives, ready for lethal combat. The two square off for a bitchy fight to end all such fights, acid tongues lashing at one another.

Annie-Joe is able to detour the guests, but she isn't about to head off a gift partygoers arranged for her — a male stripper (Eric Riley), who sweeps in and does his act for the three unsuspecting ladies. This acts as an ice-breaker for the two ladies, and from there it's a matter of each peeling off the other's mask.

Channing has just moved into a spacious walk-in closet, and Martin has just been informed that extension of her unemployment benefits has been denied, but $240 in food stamps monthly has been okayed.

In a lot of good-humored bitchery (after a knock-down, drag-out fight that results in incorruptible officer Don Howard citing the pair for disturbance of the peace while getting their autograph) show sails to a wonderful conclusion. They take the show, but signing the contract doesn't mean they always have to talk civilly to each other.

Director Clifford Williams has staged the piece with all stops out, and that's the way Channing and Martin play it.

Channing, in a brown wig, has dropped all Dolly Levi characteristics, and Martin's "Sound Of Music" habit apparently has been sent to the cleaners. Only Channing mannerism employed is the itsy-bitsy voice she uses in imitating Martin, which, oddly enough, sounds like Channing imitating Channing.

Channing's vaudeville training is obvious and makes her perf a jewel. Martin is more limited by her musical comedy background, but that doesn't make her performance any less than marvelous.

There are a few places the show has to be trimmed or polished, but there's no major rewrite necessary. Needed are just a few changes in some of the jokes that don't work and situations that need shoring up or eliminating altogether.

Technicals are topnotch, with Douglas Schmidt's sets superb, Freddy Wittop's costumes top of the line and Thomas Skelton's lighting topdrawer.

Show is almost ready for New York and doubtless will be by the time it leaves here. Only question remains, is New York ready for Channing, Martin and Kirkwood?

Edwa.

"But you obviously have it right in your hand."

"Someone gave it to me!"

Ever since that episode I have been wary of actors who say they don't read reviews. Certainly your best and worst friends will tell you about them. I mean, it's their duty, and the excuse they usually give is they didn't want you to hear it from someone else and be caught by surprise, thereby risking a heart attack, so they start off by saying, "God, I hate to have to tell you this, but . . ."

Carol obviously reads them, but if the audiences are good, if they seem to enjoy the play and the performances, I don't believe she lets the reviews bother her too much. I'm sure when she gets a bad personal review she's furious. Gerald Nachman is proof. But they are hurtful.

I must say this about Carol. When a reviewer/critic dumped on me but said how funny and delightful and witty the ladies were—and if only they had a better play—she never failed to reply on a television interview or to a newspaperman, "Well, you realize that James Kirkwood wrote the funny, delightful, witty dialogue we speak out there on that stage. He really did. We did not make it up. If you could hear Mary and me talking in our dressing rooms, you'd go to sleep." She never failed to rally to the author's defense. God bless her for it.

I stayed away from the theatre for a few days, always remaining in touch with Randy and Keith about the reaction, the ladies, the morale, which seemed to be good, although some of the subscription audiences were less than hyperactive. Esther and Arthur went back to New York. Life calmed down for a while. A very short while.

I had been asked by representatives of Elizabeth Taylor if I would travel to Phoenix and emcee the Broadway Entertainment section of an AIDS benefit she was organizing there. I gladly agreed, and although I was only gone for two days, when I returned to Los Angeles there were four messages to call Kevin in New York. I phoned Esther to see what was up. Nothing, she said; Kevin had actually been in to see her and consult about getting an American director who would be on the scene. I was delighted. But then I phoned Kevin, and in the meantime, he said, he'd had a great conversation with Clifford in England. Clifford had gone over the script and made all sorts of wonderful cuts and suggestions, Kevin said, and would be special-delivering them to me and was looking forward to coming back and adjusting the play. This sent me into a tailspin again. It was decided I should come back to New York and make certain changes there and let the ladies play the play for a while without constant additions or deletions. Fine by me.

When I saw Mary, she suggested that Annie-Joe and Carol's first scene, before Mary comes on, be cut and made shorter. She also suggested that perhaps they pop in and out of doors, just missing each other, to set the mood for the kind of play it had turned into. Not a bad idea; I figured this might have come from Larry Hagman.

Now, here is an inherent problem with a play that gets its share of negative reviews. Regardless of whether the audiences are attending and enjoying it, everyone connected with the production thinks he or she can fix it by taking out this scene, that scene, this bit of business, that funny line which might connect with what someone has said is old-fashioned black humor, strong words that might be offensive to an audience, a speech that has to do with cancer (which Mary always performed beautifully and which did not detract from getting back into comedy immediately after). It's simply a case of too many cooks spoiling the broth. If you listened to each and every one, you would excise the entire script; there'd be barely more than a handful of lines left. Panic sets in, and everyone wants his idea to fix the play to be incorporated. All reason flies out the window, shatters into shards, and cannot be put together again.

Yes, there was work to be done, but there must be a captain, there must be a titular head. In my experience, the captain is usually the director; in default, the author. Or, in the best of all worlds, a coalition of the director and author, providing they are— mostly—of the same mind regarding the direction in which fixing the show should proceed. This work cannot be done by an entire crew of people most of whom have wildly divergent ideas.

I excuse Mary and Carol from the ranks of these armchair critics. Although they were the stars of the show, despite the aforementioned suggestion by Mary and her desire to sing a song at the end, they did not deluge me or the producers with ideas; in the main they went along with whatever was suggested. It was agreed that Mary and Carol would sing a bit of a song at the end of the show, and part of my work was to write a scene leading into it in the most natural way possible.

I was more than happy to say my goodbyes to the cast and crew, hop a plane, and fly out of the smog so I could work in peace and quiet for a while in New York. I thought. . . .

WORK, FEAR, AND LOATHING IN NEW YORK

I returned to New York on February 14. It was good to remove myself from the City of Angels and the scene of the crime. I got right to work, trying to "fix" the first scene with Annie-Joe and Carol and also shorten it, and write an ending that would accommodate their song.

While I was engaged in this work, I had a most frustrating experience with Kevin, who came over one day and insisted upon sitting right next to me and going through the script and my ideas—and *his* ideas—line by line. He would comment on every page or so about this word, that line. It was extremely frustrating and claustrophobic. I'd never had this experience with a producer—with a director, yes, but not a producer, especially one who'd never mounted a legitimate show before and was—or should have been—feeling his way along instead of attempting to take complete control. I was annoyed with him and told him this was not the way for an author to work on rewrites. "You cannot sit at my shoulder every second with total veto power; it's impossible for me to work this way."

I was allowed to continue my work for the time being, but then came a series of phone calls from Kevin, nattering about this and that to keep me confused and annoyed. There were also threats, veiled and unveiled, about Ahmet's closing the show if it were not better reviewed. And he said Clifford was sending over a script with his suggestions, cuts, and changes. It was beginning to be messy.

During this time Kevin was making some little cuts of his own and phoning them in to Randy on the coast. At first I was not aware of this. About the time I finished with my rewrites, Kevin called and came by with the script Clifford had put together. I found some of the small cuts arbitrary and detrimental to the rhythm of certain lines, some suggestions in the right direction, and some of them plain amateurish. Clifford did enclose a note saying he knew he was not a writer; his changes were meant only as guidelines for me to follow. As if this weren't enough, a few days later I received a script with *Kevin's* suggestions and rewrites. It was getting to be untenable, especially since neither one had actually read my own rewrites yet.

It all came to a screaming climax around February 24, when Kevin and I had an extremely abrasive phone call about who was doing what to which play and how and why. I'd just had my rewrites xeroxed and sent to Clifford in England and to Kevin in New York, but they could not have been read and digested by this time. I'd spoken to Clifford on the phone before sending them and gotten his approval of several of the main points. But I was beginning to feel about Kevin the way I'd feel if I were trying to write and a swarm of gnats was constantly buzzing about my head and face and short-circuiting my word processor. After he'd delivered a dozen or so persistent "Let me tell you something!"s, I hung up the phone.

The next day I wrote Kevin a rather strong letter, apologizing for hanging up on him but reminding him that he was not my coauthor and that I felt he should allow me the courtesy of reading my work before deluging me with nitpicking comments and copies of my script pasted together by anyone who happened to have scissors and Scotch tape.

Kevin wrote me back a very official letter expressing his concern that we were no longer working as a team and outlining five major points that had to be addressed or he feared we would face disaster and be forced to close. I phoned him and went over the five points.

The first was that we must remove all racial slurs and jokes. Kevin maintained we were on shaky ground by having a black maid with two white women. I told Kevin there were no racial slurs and his comment about us being in jeopardy having a black maid with two white women made no sense. If that were true, many plays would be totally invalidated. What should we have— two black women with a white maid?

Point number two: Kevin maintained that "we [I don't know who "we" meant] strongly support" Clifford's proposed cuts in Act I. He said there was no need for additional writing. I replied that a play cannot be fixed by making cuts alone; transitions must be written to bridge and smooth them out. Kevin maintained in point number three that Leatrice's cancer speech was too serious for a comedy, it must go. Mary performed this section beautifully, and it did not "bring the play down" at all but strenthened the relationship between Mary and Carol, because we finally saw the mutual trust in them growing. In point number four Kevin said the end of the play should be a coming together of the women with the hope that their lives will once again be rich and meaningful. This one I didn't understand: that's what the ending accomplished as it was. In point number five he'd gone on and on about removing all profanity, saying our audiences were older and couldn't take such offensive language.

"Kevin, there is hardly any profanity in the play. Carol, who says herself she plays tramps and bitches, uses the F-word once to great response from every audience. Mary doesn't swear at all. In talking about one of Mary's leading men and the way he treated her in a film, Annie-Joe says, 'Oh, yes, that man was mean, mean as cat-shit!" And when the doorbell rings, announcing Mary's arrival, Carol exclaims, 'Oh, Jesus, Mary, and Joseph, there she is now.' That's not swearing, she's a Catholic. I'm a Catholic and we use that as an exclamation. So I don't understand where all the profanity is you're talking about. My God, look at *HurlyBurly* or *Glengarry Glen Ross.*"

Although the conversation was civil, it was more or less a standoff; Kevin is not the best listener; he's a much better talker. In the days that followed, I tried to rally support from Cheryl, but she'd suffered another fall and was in no condition to do anything but try to make a recovery for herself. Bob was much more understanding of the creative situation than Kevin, but he was in California and had been going through a series of flu sieges, one after the other. I turned to our original general manager, Alan Wasser, but Alan admitted having great difficulty working with Kevin. He found him abrasive, a troublemaker, and said he was making life hell as far as dealing with theatre owners about future dates. He had given up on Kevin and was letting Doug Baker deal with him; Alan apologized for more or less dropping out.

So I was not the only one having trouble dealing with Kevin. Also about this time, I got a phone call from Carol and Charles. Charles said Kevin had been told not to speak to Carol until he wrote her a letter with a formal apology for telling Gerald Nachman she was full of bullshit. Carol then got on the phone and said, "Don't you think we ought to get a director who speaks American?" Outside of that, they said the show was playing well; Bobby Fryer had come to the Sunday matinee and was pleased with the way it was going; Charles added, "He said we're doing better business than Elizabeth Taylor did." Somehow I doubted this, but . . .

Despite my conversations with Kevin, he'd sent on some material of his own or Clifford's to Randy on the coast, because I got another call from Charles and Carol saying Carol would take rewrites only from me; they would not accept any cuts from Kevin, who, Charles said, "has been treating Carol like a chorus girl from the very first day."

It was clear now that the happy, chubby, freewheeling, accommodating fellow Kevin had been before rehearsals was turning rather quickly into a martinet, wanting to rule all phases of the production with an iron hand, regardless of his lack of experience.

The last day of February I tried to call Clifford in England, to no avail; by that time Kevin had returned to California and a conference call came from him and Bob. I told Kevin, in the nicest way, that he was not a writer and I found the latest paste-up version of the script appalling, as if some mischievous high-school kid had got hold of it. He admitted he wasn't a writer and neither was Clifford. "Then why," I asked, "are you both bombarding me with your versions of the play?"

Again: "Those are only meant as guidelines." But when we'd talk about the guidelines, Kevin wanted to adhere to them specifically. We began going over scenes and lines and speeches, and it soon became apparent this could not be done on the phone. It was agreed I would come out there Sunday, March 2, and spend the week going over all the new material, so that, when Clifford arrived for his week, the rewrites would be ready to be rehearsed and incorporated into the show. I felt, deep inside, that all the new work could not possibly be learned, directed, and put in in one week, and said so. No, Kevin insisted, if we were all ready for Clifford it could be done. A meeting was set up between us Sunday evening, the day I was to arrive. I asked that Jerry Paonessa, whom they both liked and respected, be present as mediator. I felt, in a way, I was being ganged up on, and Jerry is a calming influence in times of crisis.

And I smelled—crisis.

WORK, FEAR, AND LOATHING IN L.A.

When I arrived, there was a message to call Carol and Charles. Warm welcome; they were glad to have me back. Carol and Mary were having fun rehearsing "Accentuate the Positive," the song chosen to end Act II. Carol said, "Mary's doing all her trilling and I'm doing . . ." She lowered her voice and baritoned out, ". . . my bong, bong thing."

I said I was looking forward to seeing them and was on my way to a meeting with Kevin. From Carol I got a very flat "What for?"

That evening Jerry and I went to Bob's house and joined him and Kevin for drinks and dinner. We were none of us in an adversarial mood; we talked in generalities about which changes to rehearse first, until Kevin got on to Carol and Charles. "They're both troublemakers, that's what they are, no matter what."

"Kevin," I said, "we're all troublemakers. I don't care what you say, they're devoted to this play, and Carol's been doing yeoman work. I wish you and Bob didn't have this ongoing feud with them. I know you claim Mary's the star, but so is Carol."

"Carol's a troublemaker," Bob and Kevin both insisted.

I'd spoken to Randy on the phone earlier and he'd said, "The other night Mary flubbed a lead-in line so that Carol lost a laugh, and she turned to Mary right onstage and said in a loud voice, 'Well, thanks a lot for that one!' "

Kevin brought up this behavior. "Mary's getting tired of that crap. I tell you, if Carol keeps it up, Mary'll take a walk."

"But," I went on, "if you keep treating them like dirt—this sort of hostile relationship will only escalate into *major* warfare."

All in all, however, we managed a pleasant evening. Kevin and Bob are fun to be with socially; they both have a good sense of humor. It's only when the fur starts flying that all humor goes out the window. We agreed to meet the next day to go over more specific matters. Again I asked for Jerry to be there. I believe his presence this evening helped keep us on course.

The meeting the next day in Kevin's suite got a bit stormy. Everyone read over the new scenes. We were in agreement about the end of the play, which was important. In this new version the ladies sang their song and, by hook or crook, I got the policeman back in; Eric the stripper returned, having forgotten part of his costume; Gary was kept onstage; and they all backed up the ladies and Annie-Joe doing do-wops behind them.

Then we got into the first scene between Annie-Joe and Carol, Clifford's version of which I took exception to. "Clifford has merely ripped the first two or three pages off the beginning and made cuts through the rest. It doesn't have a sense of fun."

"That's for you to put in," Kevin said.

"I *have* put it in, in my version."

It's hard to deal with the kind of conversation that makes no logical sense. We got to Mary's cancer speech and a slightly changed version I'd written; I still thought Mary's original mastectomy speech was better, as did she, but I was trying to accommodate and not rock the boat.

Then we got into the schedule of what changes should be given them first. I thought it best to go to the new ending before giving Carol the rewritten first scene, from which a lot of material she liked was now cut. We all felt the best way to proceed was to give her the completely new material and have it accepted before getting her back up by giving her cuts she wouldn't like. Randy and the rest agreed with me, but Kevin was adamant.

"Listen, Carol's going to blow sky-high anyhow, so the sooner she does it and gets it over with, the better."

We could not budge him from this reckless attitude. I was also getting tired of hearing Kevin quote chapter and verse from Clifford, who had not been with us since the opening and didn't really know what the humor of the company was.

The meeting was soon adjourned, lest we start hurling crackers and cheese at each other. I had to fly to Atlanta for a lecture the next day but came right back on Thursday, March 6, and made it to the theatre toward the end of the matinee. Apparently the performance had been good; our ladies were happy. I could hear Mary trilling away by the piano, rehearsing the song. I went to Randy's office to discuss the logistical problems of when, where, how to rehearse the changes to achieve maximum effect once Clifford comes. He'll only be here for one precious week, and the actors are allowed limited rehearsal time. Randy and I were both concerned.

I was called out onto the stage to listen to them run through "Accentuate the Positive" with Annie-Joe at the piano. The lead-in comes after the ladies have become friends and decided to do the play together instead of staying in retirement. They start talking about the film they did together and the song they sang in it. What was it? they muse. Oh, yes, "Accentuate the Positive." "Yes," Annie-Joe says, "I remember that, I've seen you all in that picture six or seven times on the late, *late* show."

They give her dirty looks, Mary raises a hand as if to go after her, Annie-Joe laughs and starts to play and sing, and then the ladies join in, easily and sort of offhand, unrehearsed, until toward the finish, when they do a few kicks and end with their arms around each other. The song was fun; Annie-Joe's a good musician, and Carol and Mary's voices are so different—Mary is a canary and Carol a bass.

I was especially happy to see that Carol was in a noncombative mood, even though she'd been given the retyped script by Kevin, despite our pleas. After they'd rehearsed the song, Carol asked me questions about the reason for the changes. I explained that Kevin was adamant about diminishing whatever criticism we were getting for any humor that could be taken as racial. "Oh," Carol said, "don't people understand our *relationship?* We're old friends, we love each other, and that gives us the freedom to kid each other."

Annie-Joe cut in, "As long as I'm playing a maid, a black maid, there'll always be criticism."

Carol looked at her for a long moment and then said, in her deep Bankheadian voice, "Well, dear, would you like to play a *French* maid?"

Annie-Joe just looked at her.

After rehearsals Mary asked to see me in her dressing room. She admitted to liking the new speech I'd written for her but asked if she couldn't wait to put it in until after they'd incorporated the new ending. "I'd rather save my energy for the song for the time being." What could I say? She went on: "I think it would be good to get Trish Garland in to stage the song a little. Now, darling, you know, the song's going to be fun, but people aren't paying to hear Annie-Joe sing, good as she is, and the arranger is making out the arrangement for *her*. So, darling, this can't come from me, but someone has to make this clear to him. It's for Carol and me."

I love the way they always say, "It can't come from me." Why not? So I said, "Of course it can come from you. You're Mary Martin, you have every right to give your opinion about the arrangement."

"Oh, no, dear, it mustn't come from me. No."

"All right, I'll speak to someone," I promised.

Hooked again.

Clifford arrived on Sunday, and we all met at Kevin's; Clifford seemed a bit fatigued. I got no new burst of energy or adrenaline from him. He would like to put the song and new ending in on Friday. Monday was the actors' day off, so we all met again and went over all the new material, refining it, getting it ready for our first big day of rehearsal, Tuesday.

Tuesday morning I bumped into Clifford in the parking lot, and as we walked to the theatre together I asked him please to make a little speech at the beginning to get everyone's energy and enthusiasm up for these new changes. Yes, he'd planned to do that. However, once on the stage, we listened to the arrangement with Marc Shaiman, a brilliant musician and terrific fellow, although he's extremely expensive and way overqualified for this job. But Kevin wanted the best and most costly, and that's what we got.

Then we merely drifted into rehearsal—no statement from Clifford—and today it was Annie-Joe who was big trouble. She complained, stopped after every line, said she couldn't find her motivation with these cuts, and added, "My character has gone down the drain; my friends all like what I do and now it's all gone." (Annie-Joe had been the one during rehearsal who'd balked at some of the very lines and business we were removing now.) It seemed as though she was playing the role very dainty and white, giving what sounded like extremely arch readings. I hoped

Clifford would haul her to the carpet, but it was finally Carol who turned to her and said, "All right, you play Medea, I'll play comedy!" Good for her. Carol was fine most of the afternoon; she took direction—what there was of it—and we finally broke when rehearsal time was up.

That evening Clifford watched the show from the glassed-in sound booth, which tends to muffle the audience's reaction and the actors' voices. Jim Piazza and I sat in the orchestra, where you can feel the aliveness of it.

Cheryl Crawford had recovered enough to make the trip to California and was seeing the show for the first time this evening. The next day we all had lunch with Cheryl before rehearsals, and she gave us her candid opinion. She thought the play quite good but she was deeply concerned about the difference in playing styles between Mary and Carol. Although Cheryl is an old friend and producer of Mary's, she was disturbed by her performance (and I'd thought it relatively good, which goes to show what the word "relative" means). Cheryl wanted Mary to top Carol at times. We all did. Her overall comment was that Mary's performance was weak and damaging to the play.

Soon we left for rehearsal. Again I asked Clifford to make a speech in front of the cast, reminding them time was short and we must get to it. Again he said he would. Rehearsal began. No speech, nothing. Marc Shaiman began coaching the guys on their harmony, after which we again sort of drifted into rehearsal without any attack or leadership. Annie-Joe was still difficult, and didn't want to do this or that or anything that was suggested. Rehearsal began to fall apart, and as it did so I heard Carol mumble several times, "Do we have a titular head? Do we? Is there a titular head for this play?" Good for you, I thought. But she got no answer.

Carol got off a crack at Mary. Annie-Joe asked Mary, when they started going over the song, "Should I approach the verse of the song as text in the play, or as simply the song itself?"

"Yes," Mary replied.

"Yes—what?" Carol boomed out. "You can't answer a question like that by *yes!*"

"Well, you know what I mean," Mary said.

"No, we don't, none of us does."

During the morning I learned that Clifford was leaving for

England this Saturday. As rehearsal disintegrated again, I thought: Tomorrow's already Thursday, this is madness, nothing has been truly set. They'd read over the last scene twice and foomfed around with the musical number and that was it. I decided to stay away from the show in the evening.

The next day I could barely crawl out of bed. Heavy. Heavy. Spoke to Keith on the phone and was amazed to learn that Clifford had not even attended the show the previous night. He'd seen it his first night from the sound booth, and that was it. He was over here to clean up the show, give notes, rehearse the changes. What is going on? Clifford would be leaving in two days.

I phoned Kevin to say I was astonished to hear that Clifford hadn't even seen the play the night before. Kevin said in a lowered voice, "Clifford's here right now."

"I don't care, I'll tell him myself. I find it unconscionable. He has to have authority with this cast, and energy, and captainship. But he let rehearsal yesterday disintegrate into a slovenly picnic, and you all sat around and watched. What's the matter with you?"

Kevin said we'd all meet for rehearsal after the Thursday matinee and hung up. The phone rang immediately, and it was Charles calling to say Carol wanted me to know that last night Mary's energy had been way down and we'd best try to conserve it the next few days. She was worried about putting in anything new this week, because Rex Reed was coming to see the show Friday night and Helen Hayes was coming Saturday and General Westmoreland and Bob Hope and his wife were . . .

I managed to get off the phone without screaming, "Will everyone please shut up for one goddamn second, please, while I locate the arsenic!"

Here I'd been rewriting my kishkas off for weeks; we had this afternoon for an hour or so between matinee and evening and a few hours tomorrow and then—no director. Insanity. I could hardly wait to get to the theatre to see what surprises might be in store for me.

I was not disappointed. As soon as I arrived backstage, I was led to the chorus dressing room, where I was told by Clifford and Kevin that the ladies didn't want to do the ending we'd rehearsed the day before with the entire company. They'd decided they really want to sing the song together alone on the stage. Could I please go into another dressing room and write a scene that would incorporate this?

It was getting to be so absurd that I did just that. It took two hours and was ready to rehearse following the matinee, with Gary, Carol, Mary, Annie-Joe, and Marc Shaiman. The ladies seemed pleased. After rehearsal I went home to look over all the remaining material waiting to be put in the show.

Friday's rehearsal call was four-thirty. The day before, Annie-Joe had been heard to say she could play anything written down in an hour or so. However, on this afternoon she was in full sulk again and said it would take her a good week to learn the arrangement Marc had written out for her. Catch-22. The minute one shapes up, the other shapes down. After a while it's almost a conspiracy; you begin wondering if they all get together backstage during the show and say, "All right, I drove them crazy today. It's your turn tomorrow. And, Mary, you have a day off."

But the next day, Clifford's last, turned out to be the most brutal yet. There was a matinee, and I got a call in the afternoon asking me please to come down for a meeting at around half-hour to talk over what to do about future rehearsals, scheduling, changes. No warning of anything more drastic.

I appeared on time. As soon as Randy got the curtain up, it was suggested that Randy, Clifford, Bob, Kevin, Joe, and I all go down to the Hungry Tiger for a drink and a bite to eat. Now, one of the scenes I'd rewritten was Gary's last scene with the ladies and Annie-Joe, in which they give him a brownie, too. It played well as it is, but the new version was much richer. We'd never even gotten near it on this trip with Clifford.

So . . . on the way down the block to the restaurant Clifford came up to me and said, "Oh, Jimmy, what a matinee, and Gary's scene played brilliantly, the laughs and—what applause! I wish you'd been here."

"I've seen it many times, Clifford, at matinees and evenings, and I've seen it tear the roof off at times."

"Yes, but I didn't realize how brilliantly it plays," Clifford reiterated.

When we'd all gotten settled in the restaurant, ordered drinks and something to eat, the boom—as they say—was lowered. Clifford led off again with what a brilliant matinee it had been and how well the show played. I could tell from the way Randy was looking at me that he knew I was being ambushed and he felt for me. Then they all chimed in: they needn't put in the new version, the beginning scene with Carol and Annie-Joe could be inserted with Randy and me, not only should the vacuum-cleaner scene, which I'd rewritten, not be put in, but most of the dialogue should be cut out of the one that was being played now and just let them do the physical business. Which would, of course, make it seem more mechanical than ever. All that needed to be done was to rehearse the lead-in to the song at the end and leave everything else alone.

After weeks of writing and rewriting, it was all for naught. The week had gone down the toilet. I was struck dumb. When I only sat there looking at them in disbelief, with my mouth open, Kevin told me what good work I'd been doing and how I'd helped with the cuts and how much the play had improved and . . .

I could not believe this turn of events. When I could resume speech, I said, "Listen, if I'm doing such good work, if I'm being so clever, why am I not being listened to as the author? I've worked on these changes, and I think they will greatly improve the play; now they're just being tossed aside without even being given a chance. If you just want to cut, cut, cut with no other direction, no fixing, I might as well go home and let you have at it."

"Oh, no!" most of them said.

We left the table and began walking back to the theatre. Bob Regester tried to cheer me up. "Listen, Bob," I said, "the reason for this meeting and this course of action is purely and simply to accommodate no one doing any more work, not Clifford, not Mary—no one. And after all the rewriting."

"Yes," Bob said, "and it's all excellent, it's very good work, and we all appreciate what you've done."

"But it's to no avail, none of it will see the light of day. I'm totally and completely demoralized. First I'm told there are all these problems with the play—and there are. And now suddenly everything's peachy, hunky-dory perfect. It's ridiculous and sickening."

Back at the theatre, dear Randy tried to give me a few consoling words, but all I wanted to do was get out of the place without having to talk to anyone, without even goodbye to Clifford.

Jim and I drove back to the Oakwood. I was pacing around like a madman and had to let some steam off, so I phoned Clifford, who was packing to leave. I told him I'd decided to put in Gary's rewritten scene. I said I thought the meeting was shocking and felt the entire reason for the decisions of this evening was to relieve him of any more work. He took exception to this remark, but said he'd respect my wish to put Gary's scene in, ending with "Have a good sleep, Jim." I hung up, no goodbye, have a good trip, I hope the plane doesn't fall down, or anything.

When I went to bed, I felt a little better for having stuck up for one point at least. But overall I had ideas of turning—serial killer!

GETTING OUT OF L.A. THE HARD WAY

The day after Clifford left, Jerry Paonessa and I had dinner with Tony Fantozzi, one of the biggies at the William Morris Agency on the coast. He's also known as a great troubleshooter and for years has been handling all the impossible clients that other agents throw their hands and phones up over. Oddly enough, Tony represents Carol. He's a definite kick in the head, very funny, looks like a combination of Groucho Marx and Kukla, cigar implanted in mouth, a voice that issues forth extremely flat readings that have nothing to do with the often raucous libelous content of the sentence. "Kirkwood"—I get a boot out of that—"Kirkwood, I know the situation from Charles and Carol, and I think you should throw your fucking hat in the ring and direct the fucking thing. The show's an audience pleaser, you can have a big winner, but somebody's gotta have control. Now, Carl Reiner's coming to see it Thursday, but he's got a picture, so he ain't gonna do you no good. This Kevin guy doesn't know his ass; by the time you get to San Francisco the ship will have sailed."

We talked for hours and Tony ended up saying, "I'll back you up, I'll do what I can, but I think you should direct the goddamn thing." He took a puff on his cigar and added, "It's great for this wop to sound off about this and that—because you're the one that's in deep shit!"

Tuesday, March 18, 1986

We had our first meeting since Clifford's departure at Kevin's, with Bob and Jerry Paonessa present. The atmosphere was tense; I could not believe Kevin was still fighting me on putting in Gary's rewritten scene. I was adamant, reminding him of all the writing that *hadn't* been put in. God knows when the song would go in, what with Annie-Joe's fits of fancy. But Kevin was being willful. When I reminded him I had Clifford's okay, this was his comeback: "Clifford said, All right, go ahead, try it—because he's intimidated by you."

"By me?"

"Yes."

"You've already said several times he's intimidated by Carol and Mary and Annie-Joe, and now me, too. For God's sake, what a director to have." Kevin went on to say how talented Clifford was and that they'd been having meetings about doing another play together, a revival of *Dial M for Murder*, which, in fact, was the reason Clifford hadn't seen our show a night or two when he should have been taking notes. I finally blew: "Look, there are two alternatives. If you block me, refuse to let me have control over my own work, then I have to meet with the cast and say, 'Look, I'm the author, we are now without a director; I'm the only creative member of the company present, but I'm not being allowed by the producer to have any control over what goes in and what comes out. Therefore there's nothing for me to do but leave.' " I turned to Kevin. "If it comes to that, you're going to have an extremely demoralized cast on your hands. The alternative is to let me, in conjunction with Randy, who's good and whom they like, put in the scene as rewritten, and the lead-in to the song. Otherwise there's no way I can see we won't have a disaster, and I might as well pack and—"

Oh, no, Kevin and Bob said, you can't leave. Then Kevin dropped one of his "Let me tell you something"s.

I started to "lose it," stood up and paced the room. "Well, *let me tell you something,* I'm feeling angry and crazed, I'm at the end of my line or rope or whatever the fuck you call it, but I'm tired of being jerked around this way and that—"

Jerry spotted the approaching hurricane and quickly entered the conversation. "Look, what you're talking about is not that big a difference. Carol and Mary like Jimmy and Randy; why don't you at least let them help out? Then, if something doesn't work, you'll all be able to tell soon enough."

They wanted to know if I thought I could handle Carol above all. I told them yes. Finally, after Kevin had about five shotguns to his head, a cannon pointed up his ass, and me about to pull the pin of a hand grenade, he agreed. Rehearsal was called for four, and the two of them were going to be out front, watching.

Randy and I began with the song. Mary did not even know the words. She started singing, "You've got to accentuate the *negative.*" I looked at Randy; we could only laugh. Carol was in her all-black outfit, stockings, skirt, top, little black derby hat. She looked extremely pretty; without all that stage/clown makeup plastered on her face, she's really quite attractive. Jerry, Jim, and Bob were out front, watching. At first Carol was playful, but there was a manic something beneath the surface. Of all days, the exorcist was about to put in a guest appearance.

When we began the scene in which Carol and Mary are both affected by the hashish brownies, Carol came to a line in which she gets halfway through, loses her point, and turns to Mary for help. I was directing and she turned to me, standing right by the lip of the stage, and said, "Why don't I finish that line? Why do I turn to Mary and let her finish it?"

"Because, Carol, you've lost your point."

"Oh," she said, and I heard *tone* creeping into her speech. "I've lost my point, have I? And why have I lost it?"

"Because the dope is working and your mind is fuzzy and that's what happens, people lose their point and need to be reminded."

"Oh, is that the way it works?" she asked. Now a definite sarcasm was laid on.

"Yes."

"And you know that personally?" she asked.

The entire cast had quieted down. "Yes," I assured her.

"You mean you take dope?"

"I've smoked pot, yes."

"Do you do that all the time?" she asked.

"No, I don't, not much at all, but I've done it, and that's the way it affects people."

"Un-huh," Carol said, suddenly, for no reason I could fathom, ready for a major fight. "Well," she added, flinging an arm out toward the orchestra of the theatre. "Do you think all the paying customers out there know about this *effect* it has? Do they understand why I don't finish my line?"

"I think most of them do," I replied, trying to remain civil.

"I see . . ." she muttered. "Well, just in case, for those that don't, maybe we should have notes printed up in the program that explain—"

I'd had enough. "Carol, please let's get on with rehearsal. We're wasting a lot of time. No one's ever mentioned—"

"I beg your pardon, but lots of my friends have asked why I don't finish that line."

"All right, we'll talk about it later; please let us go on now."

"Fine. But remember, maybe you should write something for the playbill."

We continued until we got to a section where dialogue had been cut. Carol had a line that said, with regard to getting old, not working, and being alone, "I don't want to end up all lonely and forgotten, doing housework in a parsonage for a bunch of Catholic priests." Mary spoke up and suggested that one of Carol's lines that had been cut was actually funnier and should replace the above line. That line being "I don't want to end up all lonely and forgotten and go to sleep in a cramped studio apartment with a lighted cigarette in my hand. I mean, I want to be cremated, but I don't want to do it myself."

Well, yes, Carol thought that *was* better, so we reinstated it and took out the other; soon she was sitting next to Mary on the sofa as we went on, and when another question about a line came up, Carol looked at me and said, "Well, why don't I ask *Mary* if she'll approve of the line, and if *Mary* likes it, then—"

"Carol, don't go on like this, please."

"No, no, whatever Mary wants, Mary gets, so I'll ask Mary about anything I want and see if she approves."

Mary just sat there, not saying anything; the rest of the company was silent. The exorcist in Carol was on the move today; the green slime was oozing out and nothing could stop the flow, although I was determined not to end up buried in it. I allowed her one more "Well, let's ask Mary how she feels and—"

Then: "All right, Carol, that's more than enough. All right, here it is. I'm the author. I've been writing for you, rewriting, I've tried to accommodate everyone in the cast. I don't think I've been difficult, I've tried not to be. Now, the director—"

A big "Hah!" from Carol.

"—has gone back to England, and if you'd like, I'll leave, too. Do you want me to do that, Carol? Because if you do I'll simply pack up and go back to New York. Is that what you want?"

"Oh, no," Carol said, as if I'd misunderstood her entire tantrum, "no, you've written me the best character, I love this character. Don't you know that?"

"I certainly couldn't tell today."

"Oh, you know I do, I love her."

"Well, then—shall we continue?"

"Oh, yes . . ."

And we did, for a while, until Carol suddenly said, "Do you really want me to say, 'Let's give 'em the roller coaster, the funhouse, and the parachute ride!' "

"You've been saying it for months."

"I know, and I hate that line!"

"Well, Carol, why didn't you ever tell me? Surely in that time—"

Carol's eyes widened and she actually went on, saying, "Well, let's ask *Mary* how she feels about it."

I jumped up from my seat. "Carol, stop it now. I thought we'd settled all that. Look, I don't give a damn about that line. You want another line, okay, what about"—I was pacing like a tiger myself now—"what if you say, 'Let's give 'em a show they'll never forget, never, not in a million years!' "

"Oh, yes," Carol said, beaming, "that's much better, I like that."

"Good. Jot it down, then let's get on with the rehearsal, please, and let's not have any more—"

"You're right, we won't," Carol said.

And we didn't. After rehearsal broke, Charles came up to me and said, "Would you please come into Carol's dressing room? She'd like to talk to you."

The moment I entered, she burst into tears and grabbed hold

of both my hands. "Oh, Jimmy, I don't know how I could have treated you that way. You, of all people. I'm absolutely humiliated and embarrassed, and I'll never forgive myself." She burst into tears and threw her arms around me. I said it was perfectly all right, and when she pulled away mascara was streaking down her cheeks. "The only thing," I added, "I'd just had a rather spiky meeting with Kevin and Bob this morning in which I reassured them we could work together in harmony, so your timing was a bit off."

"Oh, my God! Oh . . . Oh, listen, get Randy, I want him to call the whole cast onstage and I want to apologize in front of them."

"No, no," I said, "it's all right, it's all over."

"No," she wailed, "it isn't."

Then Charles, who is always on her side, lit into her. "If you ever do that again, if anyone ever saw you act that way onstage— no director would ever work with you again! And of all people to pull that shit with—Jimmy. He's the last one, he's your ally, for Christ's sake."

"Look," I said, "there'll be other times when we disagree—"

"No," Carol said.

"Yes, there will, but let's not do it in public. There'll be times when we have differences, when I'll think your pace is too slow, or you're playing out front too much, and I'll come to your dressing room and we'll talk about it. But let's try not to have a knock-down-drag-out, okay?"

"Oh, you're a sweetheart." Hugs and kisses all around.

Jim, Jerry, and I walked down to the Hungry Tiger for a drink and some food, shortly followed by Bob Regester, who sat down, thanked and congratulated me for the way I'd handled rehearsal, and then, as my reward, launched into the following: "Oh, God, are we going to take a financial bath our last week here, Holy Week, off subscription, and there's no advance sale? We're going to drop so much money, we'll barely be able to get out of town."

"Bob," I said, "there's nothing I can do about that. I'm sure it's not as bad as you're predicting, but I've had a rather tough day as it is. Let me have a night's sleep, and then you can dump some more disasters on me when I'm fresh."

We went on rehearsing; Annie-Joe took her time learning the arrangement, and the song was finally ready to go into the show on a Saturday matinee, March 22. The day before, Kevin announced he was heading back to New York. I couldn't believe he'd waited this long and was then leaving the day before the song was to be tried out. At first I was upset, but Randy said, "Hey, it might be a good idea if he goes—he'll stay out of our way for a while." Agreed.

We were all nervous about the reaction. I sat out front and by God if the dread Turk, Ahmet Ertegun himself, was not on hand, seated not three feet from me, on an aisle. The matinee was packed, mainly women, and although the song and their little dance steps were a bit shaky, it was obviously appreciated by the audience, who gave them an immediate standing ovation.

Backstage, we all congratulated them on getting through it, although they knew it was messy and had to be cleaned up. They were pleased. Ahmet barely spoke to me. "Hello . . . Yes, the show's much better now. . . . Goodbye." What a charmer. I found out he was in California not necessarily to see the show but to attend Swifty Lazar's annual Academy Award party.

On March 25 we rehearsed the song again. After the first runthrough, Carol in a very pleasant way asked, "Annie-Joe, when we go over it again, could you please play the glissandos? It throws us when you play them at night but not in rehearsals."

Annie-Joe looked her smack in the face and said, "I'm sorry, but I don't play glissandos at rehearsals." She held up her hands and added, "My skin is too sensitive."

Annie-Joe was out of sorts in general. Later, when she didn't come in with the ladies on the end of the song, Mary turned to her and said, "Come on, Annie-Joe, sing along with us."

"No," Annie-Joe said, "my voice is too much stronger than yours, I'll drown you out."

"Come on," Mary urged, "sing with us."

A sullen "I don't know, I'll see how I feel."

After rehearsal Mary called a meeting in her dressing room with Bob Regester, Carol, Charles, Susan (her girl Friday), Randy, and me. "I've heard that Annie-Joe is complaining she's not being paid enough," Mary said. "But something has to be done about her attitude, it's just terrible." Bob said she was getting a raise, and we all pitched in with what we thought might be bothering her, but it was all guesswork.

Seated with Jerry at the Hungry Tiger before the performance, I saw Bob come in the front door and head for our table. "Oh, Christ!" he said.

"What's the good news?" I asked.

"Kevin's in an uproar."

"I thought he was in New York."

"He is—he's in an uproar there. He found out a couple of new lines were going in and he's furious; he's got Randy on the phone, and he's making him go over the entire script to find out if you've been sneaking in new lines without his knowing about it."

"Oh, shit," I said. "Will Kevin ever stop inciting to riot?"

Bob added, "And of course I told you our last week here is going to be a killer, didn't I?"

"Yes, Bob, you did. Did I tell *you* I'm going back to New York day after tomorrow? I am. We've only a week or so left, and I can't take this kind of demeaning bullshit from Kevin. All the changes have worked; the lines we've added are getting laughs. Please, I've had enough."

Two new lines, *two*, had gone in, to great response, but Randy had been hauled on the carpet for allowing me to put in anything without the Great Ziegfeld's approval.

Goodbye, Los Angeles. It seemed as if I'd spent twelve years of purgatory there. As I got on the plane a few days hence, I made a general confession: "If You never make me come to Los Angeles again—I promise to burn all my sex toys!"

APPROACHING THE FRISCO QUAKE

How good to be home in my own bed, with no play in the same town to fret over except *A Chorus Line,* over which one needn't bleed.

There was a bit of other bleeding to do, after all, however. Elliot Lefkowitz, Esther, and I were informed that the last week in Los Angeles was not a good one financially, and of course the producers asked me to waive my royalties. Since they were losing money that week, I felt obliged to comply. A week or so after I'd agreed, we received another communication, saying, in effect, "Listen, the two weeks before were not all that good, either; how about taking a slice in royalties for them, too?"

This did not seem entirely kosher. Apparently once we'd agreed to the one week someone had said, "Well, let's see if we can't get them to cough up some loot for the two weeks before." Esther said they felt embarrassed to ask me but they were asking nevertheless. I thought this was cheeky; if they were facing financial difficulties, they should have said so at the time, instead of waiting for me to waive the last week, then go back and cry wolf retroactively.

(A minor side note. To wave goodbye is spelled "wave," but to waive royalties is spelled "waive." Why is that? Because when you "waive royalties" you're really waving goodbye to them.)

I spoke with Kevin on the phone several times after I got home; he was having second thoughts about the new beginning I'd written, which had not yet been put in in its entirety; perhaps we would be able to try it soon. On another front, he'd had a nasty meeting with the dread Turk, who, because of the slump in business at the end of the L.A. run, was threatening to close the show again. I told Kevin how rude I felt Ahmet was, to which Kevin replied, "He's a very busy man, he has a lot on his mind, he doesn't mean to be."

I think the real reason would be: He hates your guts because you haven't handed him *My Fair Lady*.

Of course, I kept pushing for us to get an American director who would be on the scene. Kevin dropped word that Clifford might join us in San Francisco; Jerry asked how long he'd be there if he did come. "As long as we need him," Kevin said, but then reminded us that every trip of Clifford's cost the production at least five thousand dollars when you added up round trip to England, hotel accommodations, and per diem. "Oh, for a peppy young American director," I said.

"Well, we're going to try to find someone," Kevin promised. "And, you know, Mike Nichols and Ahmet are good friends, and Ahmet's going to get Mike to come and see the show."

"When?"

"He's got the flu now. As soon as he's better."

Kevin said he didn't think we'd get hurt in New Orleans, where the play was about to open for ten days, or in San Antonio, but our six weeks in San Francisco, no longer known for being the smashing theatre town it once was, could kill us off. I'd been told that by Tom Davis, Doug Baker, Bob Regester, their lawyer, Alan Wasser, my lawyer, and my agent, so by this time I was seriously beginning to worry mightily about the Great San Francisco Earthquake, in which the city is left standing but the play falls into the bay and is swept out to sea.

Just before I flew to the Mardi Gras City, I got a call from Charles saying New Orleans was so looking forward to the play. Then he put on Carol, who asked, "Darling, you know in the second act when Gary comes in and I start to speak to him and then I don't finish my line but I turn to Mary and she finishes it?"

"Yes," I said, not believing my ears.

"Well, Jimmy, why don't I finish the line myself?"

"Well, Carol . . ." and I explained it to her as if the subject had never ever been touched on before.

"Oh, I see," she said. "Thank you, dear—can't wait to see you."

I flew to New Orleans for the official opening on a Wednesday, in early April. The theatre, the Saenger, is a barn and too big, but the show played well, and opening night was a benefit for the Actors Fund of America. Nedda Harrigan, wife of Josh Logan, flew down, and there was a large party afterward at which Nedda presented awards to Mary and Carol. I sat next to Zev Bufman, the Florida theatre impresario and Broadway producer. I'd known and liked Zev for years. He was extremely excited about the play and said he'd love to book it into his Florida theatres: Orlando, St. Petersburg, Miami, Fort Lauderdale, and Palm Beach. This was good news; everyone was cheered by Zev's enthusiasm.

After a few days in New Orleans, I returned to New York. Kevin wanted another strategy meeting, which I suggested be held at Esther's office, because she has her head screwed on. We all agreed that the play is basically what it is now. Kevin waffled about Clifford—now he's coming, now he isn't. Esther asked, if he did come to San Francisco, what would he do? Well, Kevin talked about building up Mary's character more, saying we know so much more about Sylvia. This was true, because so much of Mary's dialogue had to be cut. One couldn't imagine getting her to put dialogue back in, not at this point, when she's just really starting to play it. Kevin finally agreed to let me put in the balloons at the beginning of Act I, the in-and-out-of-doors scene where Annie-Joe and Carol keep missing each other and Annie-Joe finally gets a frying pan and, thinking there's a burglar in the apartment, almost bops Carol over the head.

Went over the figures later that afternoon with Elliot about what we faced in San Francisco. As of April 14—and we don't start playing there until the 23rd—their subscription list has brought in $650,000 and they have sold $90,000, which gives us a total of $740,000. Our weekly break-even (or "nut") is $175,000 with full royalties; with waived (or without) royalties it's $150,000. This means we must take in another $160,000 to get out alive without royalties. In other words, we need $900,000 to get out without royalties, and about $1 million to get out with full royalties. These figures came from Doug Baker, who now is not all that worried about our six weeks there.

Around this time, the producers asked if I would not take my royalty weekly but instead lump all the weeks together and take it for the aggregate number of weeks—after the engagement was concluded, according to profit or loss. I am happy to be a member of The Dramatists Guild Council—a body of people elected within the Guild to represent playwrights and their basic contracts with producers. I called David LeVine, executive director of The Dramatists Guild, to ask his advice. He said sometimes it might be better to take the total number of weeks, instead of taking or waiving royalty for each separate week, explaining that you might have one losing week and then more than make up for it in the ensuing week or weeks, thereby putting you in line for full royalties for the engagement. Every playwright would do well to join The Dramatists Guild for sound advice and protection.

I sent the original rewritten first scene to Randy Buck so he could rehearse Annie-Joe and Carol and put it in in San Antonio. Charles Lowe, my almost daily caller, phoned to say the opening night in San Antonio was a smash, the audience was the best ever, Mary was perking along, the reviews were an improvement, and business was terrific. Randy phoned several days later to say the new beginning had gone in and played very well. Carol and Charles called soon after to say how pleased they were with it; Charles repeated the audience reaction was the best ever and said we might gross $230,000, which would be extremely healthy. About this time, Charles wondered why the ladies were not seeing much of their percentage. I told Charles I doubted it was anything more mysterious than the producer's having spent money unwisely: sets had to be repainted, furniture re-covered, costumes changed, the arrangement for the song prepared, untold man-hours of rehearsal pianist.

Charles was all for finding other producers to take over the show. We agreed things would come to a head in San Francisco. Someone would have to be named creative honcho; either Clifford would have to come back and dig in for good, or we'd have to find another director. It was difficult to imagine us going on like this.

SAN FRANCISCO

Tuesday, April 22, 1986

A dear friend of mine met my plane and drove me into San Francisco.

Now, dear reader, you must take my word for this: I am not a heavy doper, but I do occasionally smoke pot. I smoked on the way in from the airport, and since I had not had any in a long time I was soon blitzed. Some people can smoke and go about their daily business with no apparent hitches. I can only laugh, cry out for ice cream, and eventually go to sleep. I have no compulsion to cook, drive, appear in public—I can barely change the cassette or turn over a record. I do get chatty at times and usually lose my point halfway through a story. Are you listening, Carol?

I checked into the Majestic Hotel, an old, restored, beautifully decorated establishment that used to be a famous brothel and is now one of those small exclusive hotels with a fine restaurant, Café Majestic, actually run by the former San Francisco critic Stanley Eichelbaum. I had a living room, a bedroom with a huge canopied bed, and a large bathroom. Perfect. My friend said, "You look tired and tense."

"I am."

"Take off your clothes and let me give you a massage."

"How can you give a massage?" I asked. "I can barely move."

"Don't worry, I can."

She soon threw me onto the living-room floor and gave me one of the best massages of my life. She then put me to bed, went to see the first act of a play, and brought me back a hamburger with everything on it. Service deluxe. I felt so relaxed, so happy to be alive, that I even forgot why I was in San Francisco. But not for long.

My first phone call was from Charles. "Have you heard our fucking producer's latest? He took Gary out shopping, bought him a completely new outfit for the first scene at the most expensive men's shop in the city, cost a couple of thousand dollars. He's insane, The Shopper—no wonder they're worried about money, the way he throws it around."

We had a benefit the next evening, Wednesday, a matinee and evening Thursday, and then our official opening Friday night. The Curran Theatre, one of the best, is perfect for a play such as ours. The benefit audience, as opposed to most, was extremely good. I don't know what happened in the second act, but Annie-Joe seemed to wander through the lines or spit them out with great disdain.

The benefit was for the Boys Choir of San Francisco; after the show a large dinner dance was held at the Saint Francis Hotel, to which we were all invited. Everyone in the company was asking: What happened to Annie-Joe? It was normal for people connected with the show to notice her behavior, but that evening many "civilians" who'd been in the audience, when commenting on the play, asked, "What was wrong with the actress who played the maid?"

One man and his wife who had nothing whatsoever to do with the theatre told me how much they enjoyed the play, after which the man actually said, "I never noticed an actress to be as angry as that gal that played the maid." "Yes," his wife added, "and she even showed it when they all took their curtain calls. She looked like she wanted to hit someone."

The next matinee was showdown at OK Corral. For the entire first act, Annie-Joe absolutely raced through her part, as if she were going to miss the last plane out of Casablanca. Mary could barely keep up with her; in fact, at times she was out of breath. Carol had that wild look in her eyes, as if to say: What in God's name is wrong with the woman?

Kevin was there, and in the intermission we hurried backstage. Carol was standing by Mary's dressing-room door; the two ladies were clutching each other's hands. When Carol saw me she said, "What's wrong with her? She's gone crazy. Look—Mary's in tears."

Mary *was* in tears, and Carol was not far behind. After Mary calmed down somewhat she said, "What's wrong, is she sick or something, should we get a doctor?"

"No," Carol snapped, "but somebody, for God's sake, go out and buy her a big box of chocolates—or something."

"I'm going to talk to her," I said.

"No, I will," Kevin said.

"I'll talk to her first; you can talk to her after."

I raced up the stairs and into her dressing room, where she sat at her makeup table as if nothing had happened at all. "Annie-Joe, what in Christ's name were you doing?"

"When?" she asked, feigning innocence.

"In the first act, that's when."

"Nothing."

"Don't give me that crap, you know what I'm talking about. You threw the whole play right down the toilet. Now, what the fuck's going on with you?"

"I'm just looking for my character, I'm trying to find my character."

"After all this time! You *know* your character and you know how to play it and you're not doing it, you're screwing up the whole play.

"You just come downstairs and you'll find two ladies, two stars, in tears over what you did." I also told her about the comments I'd heard the night before. Kevin was waiting outside in the hall. "Now, I'm going down to try to calm Carol and Mary, but before you go on for the second act—and you'd better give your regular *good* performance or there'll be hell to pay—I want you to stop by Mary's room and see what kind of panic you've thrown her into."

I left, and Kevin went in. The rest of the cast were being extremely quiet and not all that much in evidence. I did stop by Gary's dressing room, and he simply shook his head. I went down to Mary's; Carol was still there. Mary was worried about going on in the second act; when Annie-Joe took to the speedway, it was difficult to keep up with her. Randy Buck kept saying, "She's talented when she wants to be, but. . . ."

They held the curtain an extra ten minutes; after a while I heard Annie-Joe coming down the stairs; she headed right for the stage and I shouted out, "Annie-Joe, look over here and see what you've done to these two. Look at them! Does this make you happy?"

She glanced our way, muttered something, then walked onto the stage as I called out, "And you better do the second act the way you usually do it. Do you hear me?"

Grumble, grumble.

The second-act curtain finally went up, and she gave her usual good, peppy, humorous performance. (I don't know why she'd put us through this; if it was an attempt to goose the producers into a raise or extra expenses, I hoped it wouldn't work!)

That evening, the night before our opening, she gave an excellent performance. Esther arrived from New York, Tony Fantozzi came up from Los Angeles, and we all got dandied up for the opening night, to which I was taking my good friend Jane Montgomery. The new opening scene with the balloons was working well; all we had to worry about was another surprise from Annie-Joe. I'd bought a bottle of Stoli vodka and left it in her dressing room with a note that read, "Dear Annie-Joe, if you give the same performance as last night, you can keep this. If not—*I'm* drinking it! Love, Jim. P.S. Happy San Francisco opening!" Good Lord, I thought, now it's come to bribing actors in order to get a decent performance. Next thing she'll want a Toyota.

The opening-night audience in San Francisco was dressy and extremely responsive for the first act, which really flew. We were all happy; Esther commented on how much better the show was than when she'd seen it in Los Angeles.

Then came the second act and one of those theatrical mysteries took place. The second act, which almost always had more laughs, more poignant moments, more pace than the first act, simply lay there. None of us could blame it on any of the performances. The entire cast played it exactly the way they always had. Even Gary's last scene, which always brings down the house, got nothing like the response it usually received. It was a total mystery. Of course, anyone who'd not seen the play before might not have been able to tell, because there was a standing ovation at the curtain call, extended applause, but those in the know felt the failure of the second act to ignite.

The day after our opening was top meeting day. First Bob Regester, Kevin, Esther, and I met for a late breakfast in the hotel restaurant. After a general discussion, we decided it would be best if I retired to my room upstairs while Esther and Tony had a top-level talk with Kevin about our future.

I thought it would take an hour or so, but it was five-thirty—over three hours later—when Esther called for me to come down. I'd read an entire book by then. Kevin had just left, and Esther and Tony looked bushed and somewhat defeated. They had talked tough in my behalf, but Kevin was adamant about freezing the show just the way it is now. Not a word to be changed, cut, or added. There's nothing I can do about it, which is frustrating. He would not let me come in as director. There was the usual tease: Oh, Ahmet's going to get Mike Nichols, etc. He has now become our Little Caesar, and he's got the balls to bluff it through. Esther and Tony are a pair to go up against, but even they could not dent Kevin's skull.

Esther had friends to see, Tony was off to visit Carol and Charles, and I went to the theatre around half-hour to see the cast and make nice. By the time Tony met me for dinner, he'd had his share of happy hour and was fuzzily amusing in the colorful language he used to describe Kevin. He said Carol and Charles wanted him out and added that Kevin himself said he and Ahmet would be bought out if Tony, or anyone else, could find a buyer. I asked Tony please to spread the word and see if he could come up with someone. Criminal record, no problem.

One afternoon, as I was coming out from backstage, Tom Davis, Mary's man Friday, drove up in a car and said in a loud voice as I hit the sidewalk: "This play will never make any money as long as you keep getting your eight percent." Having just waived royalties and negotiated the San Francisco deal so that if they lost money I would waive again, I found this to be totally inappropriate and also none of his business.

I'd been hearing rumors that Mary and Larry Hagman were grumbling about my royalties, and Tom Davis had obviously taken it on as a Holy Crusade, so on Sunday morning I dropped off a note for Mary at her hotel. It read:

> Dear Mary,
>
> Just a brief note. There seems to be a lot of talk going around about my royalties. So you and Larry understand, I came down from my contracted ten percent to eight percent when you wished to do only seven performances a week instead of the usual eight.
>
> In addition to this I either waived or deferred royalties for the last three weeks of the Los Angeles run and I have also agreed not to take anything in San Francisco until we have passed our operating costs.
>
> I believe I have been entirely fair and hope this will set to rest all this talk of unreasonable pay for the author.
>
> Love,
> Jim

Sunday evening Charles and Carol had invited us to join them to see Gregory Hines at the Fairmont Hotel showroom. Gary was also there. I had smoked, and I took this opportunity to tell Carol that she'd never seen me under the influence until now, so she should watch carefully. Carol, this evening, looked absolutely lovely. She had the barest amount of makeup on, and I couldn't help wondering why she didn't realize how grotesque her heavy stage makeup made her look—especially to those sitting up front. I rambled on, lost my point a couple of times, said to Carol, "See what I mean . . . ?" She only smiled in return. Then I told her that pot also makes one candid upon occasion, which led to: "Carol, you look absolutely gorgeous tonight without all that awful makeup you wear."

"What awful makeup?" she asked.

"That clown makeup you wear in the play, all that rouge and the line across your nose, the dark shadowing here and there. It's grotesque. You look so lovely without it."

Now was played out a scene that I have never fathomed.

"You mean there's something wrong with my stage makeup?"

"Yes, of course. Everyone's told you that, but you keep on wearing it."

"Everyone?" she asked, eyes wide in amazement. "No one's ever mentioned it to me. Ever!" she emphasized.

I was thrown for a moment; had Carol been smoking, too? Everyone had mentioned her makeup. I'd heard tons of people comment on it in front of her: our director, producers, friends of hers, fans of hers, agents of hers; critics had written about it. Almost everyone had complained that it was too much, and now she was saying again, turning to Charles, "I've never heard that before in my life. Have you, Charles?" Charles sort of sidestepped the issue and said, "Gregory Hines should be coming on very soon."

Carol looked straight at me and said, "If you thought there was something wrong with my stage makeup, why didn't you ever say anything until now?"

"I have told you."

"Well, that's strange, I don't remember anyone ever mentioning that before."

Then I remembered that one day at rehearsal Carol herself had said something about how much Mary hated her makeup, but I thought better of making a federal case of it now. I looked at Gary; Gary looked back at me as if we were in the Land of Oz and the Wizard was trying to bollix us completely. Jane simply sat there grinning, as Carol went on about not understanding why no one had ever mentioned this before. And I thought, Well, I'm losing my mind.

On the way home that evening, we stopped to pick up the San Francisco *Chronicle* and other papers. Gerald Nachman said the show had improved since he'd seen it in Los Angeles but he was still not strewing roses in my path. The other reviews were mixed, but some from surrounding cities were very heartening.

The next morning I bumped into Kevin and Ann in the lobby; he placed a hand on my shoulder, said "Cheer up, Jim," as if the governor had just refused to grant a stay of execution, and walked off on his way to a business meeting with Doug Baker. I knew my percentage was in danger; rumors had reached me that there were serious talks in the offing about renegotiating my contract again.

Wednesday, April 30, 1986

Kevin and Ann have gone back to New York, and I was preparing to go home to Key West. I told Randy I wanted to say a formal farewell to the cast before I departed. Kevin had phoned Randy and asked if anyone—whom could he be referring to?—had called rehearsal. No, Randy said, everything was fine, but he did mention offhandedly that I was leaving and planned to say goodbye to the company onstage after the matinee. Kevin fell into a fit and told Randy I was not to be allowed to speak to the company as a whole. I would be allowed to go around separately and say goodbye to them in their dressing rooms.

When Randy relayed this edict to me, major shit hit a fan the size of Montana. I could not believe his paranoid stupidity. This was unheard of, not allowing the author to speak to his cast, thank them for all their good work, wish them a happy engagement in San Francisco, and see you later.

I almost ripped the phone out of the wall calling Esther in New York. She could not believe this latest pronouncement from our own Mike Todd, said she'd track him down and I should wait right there. She called about a half-hour later. Esther had read him the riot act and called him a few choice names; he'd backed down and eventually said, yes, I could say goodbye to the company.

Thank you, oh, master! That did it with me. I was livid. I watched part of the matinee; full house, lots of blue-haired ladies having a really good time. I asked Nigel, a very nice fellow who ran the box office, to have a drink toward the end of the matinee. Nigel said our take now was between $970,000 and $980,000. This was only our first week, and he predicted we'd break a million by the weekend. This means we will get out of San Francisco with full royalties and make money besides.

After the matinee Randy called the company onstage and I

made a short goodbye speech—I'd never intended anything else—saying they all knew Kevin wanted the show frozen for a few weeks; therefore, if there was nothing for me to do, I'd be going home to Key West. I thanked them for all the time, effort, and energy they'd put in rehearsing and making changes, told them I loved them all, said there was work I'd still like to do but that would come later. I'd be looking forward to seeing them toward the end of the San Francisco engagement, or in one of the other cities soon after.

I spoke to Esther again before I left. She'd been getting calls about renegotiating my contract. Because of this latest gaffe of Kevin's, I told her I didn't feel like renegotiating the price of a box of Kleenex.

MUDDLES AND MIDDLES

Key West, not the sanest city in the world, seemed like a rest home now that I was away from the play. I kept up contact with the company, mainly through Randy and Naomi, with whom I was becoming closer and closer. And Charles and Carol, who phoned often with news of the World of Legends. Charles reported that business was building constantly and San Francisco audiences were extremely responsive. This was good news.

We had discussed with Mary the possibility of her trying to get through the first act without the ear bug; she'd been doing the show for some five months, not counting rehearsals. She promised to try when they left San Francisco. Perhaps in their next city, San Diego.

In the meantime Doug Baker (acting for the producers) was trying to regenotiate my contract with Esther and Elliot. They made a ridiculously low offer as far as percentages were concerned, and figures and threats were flying back and forth. Also around this time, our weekly break-even suddenly jumped from $175,000 to something around $186,000. When questions about the difference were posed, the response came back that the lower figure had been a mistake. A costly mistake, one might say. Toward the end of May and the San Francisco engagement, Charles phoned to say we had grossed $246,904 that week, a house record for a straight play doing seven performances a week. He also reported Annie-Joe was again causing trouble, being rude to Mary and Carol, and the ladies both wanted the piano arrangement put on tape so they would not have to put up with her moods. Charles also said Mary was talking about getting two follow spots for the song; this would cost a fortune, not only the weekly rental but adding two men to the crew who would only work for three minutes, tops, at the end of the show. Artistically, it seemed a bit odd for two stars reminiscing about a number they'd sung in a movie to start it off a capella and suddenly wind up with two follow spots blasting at them in the living room of an apartment. But reality had not bothered us much so far.

Word reached me that Kevin's relationship with Mary was disintegrating and that he was going to San Francisco for the last few performances there. Mary phoned around this time to say the show was going beautifully; she sounded pleased and happy, and when I said, "I hear Kevin's coming out there," her only reply was, "Yes, that's what I heard." Warning!

The next call was from Randy, who said, "I suppose you know the Great Ziegfeld is out here. He, Mary, Carol, and Charles are all going to have dinner." Followed up by a call from Charles: "The Shopper's here. He went into Mary's dressing room, and when he left, Mary came out saying, 'We're going to get checks' " (meaning percentage-of-profit checks, besides their salaries). Charles laughed and said, "He's a fucking liar; there are no checks going out, we know that, Carol knows that. Christ, Mary wouldn't know a check if one hit her!" I don't know why, but that made me howl with laughter. He promised to let me know what transpired at dinner, adding: "He better not pull any changes on Carol. He's been treating her like a fucking chorus girl from day one. One more trick from him and I'll have Carol in the hospital so fast he won't know where she went!"

The next day Randy phoned to say the big dinner had been canceled. When I asked why he said, "Both ladies decided there wasn't all that much to talk about with him."

And so it went. They closed in San Francisco to sellout crowds. Word of mouth was obviously the reason the show had gained business each successive week of its run; it was definitely a crowd pleaser, if not a critic pleaser.

The San Diego engagement followed, one week only, but from all reports the audience was eating it up. About this time Kevin had a talk with Esther and spoke about "the play going on to a new plateau." I asked what that meant and Esther said, "Beats me, I don't know what he's talking about most of the time anyway."

Renegotiating talks continued; I tried to use my bargaining power to achieve some sort of artistic control; I would gladly give up money if I could continue to work on the play. Kevin was adamant that the play remain frozen, so on June 10 I told both Elliot and Esther that, as long as I had no say in what went on and there was no director tending to the store, I wanted my name removed from the play altogether. "Let Kevin do what he wants with it, but take my name off!"

I'd recently had three dreams within a week's time in which I killed Kevin. Once I strangled him, the second time I ran over him with my car—and then backed over him to make sure I'd done the job right—and the third time I pushed him off a very high cliff onto one of your rockier, more heavily surfed coastlines.

Although the dreams obviously afforded me some form of cathartic relief, if not outrageous joy, even I realized they were unhealthy. About then I also happened to be talking to a friend in Boston who is well acquainted with certain underworld figures, and I inquired—just for the hell of it, of course—about the fee "to disappear someone," which is the language they use. I was told that if the person was highly identifiable, that is, famous, it was twenty-five thousand. "If the person is just a pain in the ass and don't mean dick, ten thousand should do it."

"Good, I can spare ten thousand—let me think about it."

I had fantasies of calling a meeting of the company and saying, "Look, if we all chip in and collect a mere ten thousand bucks we can have eternal peace." I figured Charles and Carol would jump in the pool for about eight thousand themselves.

Speaking of the devil, that evening I received a phone call from Kevin, the first in a long time. We had a civil conversation.

"Jim, I hear you want your name taken off the play."

"You heard right."

Pause. "It's a shame our relationship has disintegrated to this point," he said.

"My feeling, too."

"We should do something about it," he suggested.

"Kevin, it's impossible. You've treated me shabbily, you cut my balls off in San Francisco. I really think you ought to have thirty years' experience in this business and then come back and deal with me in a professional manner."

"I think I have," Kevin replied.

"I don't, and there's the problem." I reminded him of his edict to Randy, in which I was not permitted to say goodbye to the company.

"That was a misunderstanding," Kevin said. "I was told you'd called a meeting."

"What kind of a meeting would I call—a mutiny, for Christ's sake?"

We got into a long talk about semantics. After a while I told Kevin about the talk with my friend regarding a hit man. We both laughed at this. I thought it better to tell him, so that I wouldn't go ahead and in a rash moment head for the bank, withdraw ten thousand, put it in a brown paper bag, and . . . At least now he could jot something down on paper: "In case of my sudden death—James Kirkwood blah-blah-blah."

"Jim, we've come such a long way with this show, we've been through hell, I know, first with Mary's learning thing, and . . . But the show was playing beautifully in San Francisco. They're in Phoenix now. Why don't we meet in Sacramento the following week, see the show, and talk about what we might do, changes we might make, and see if we can't work together?"

I said I would think about coming to Sacramento. What happened that week in Phoenix clinched it.

A MIRACLE IN PHOENIX

Thursday, June 12, 1986

A call from an excited Naomi in Phoenix. "Jimmy, did you hear what happened?"

"No—what now?" I ventured.

"Oh, it's so thrilling. Yesterday we opened here on a Wednesday matinee, and toward the end of the first act, Mary started receiving taxicab dispatch calls in her ear."

"Whaaaat?"

"Yes, the frequencies got all mixed up and she was getting calls to send out *taxis!*"

"You mean like 'Will cab 302 go to John Gardner's Tennis Camp in Scottsdale and pick up Mr. and Mrs. so-and-so'?" I asked.

"Exactly!" Naomi said. "Steve Shull and the crew did everything they could to try to change or fix the frequencies, but nothing worked, so they just had to take the goddamn thing out of her ear in the intermission."

"You don't mean—"

"Yes. And you won't believe it, Mary got through the whole second act with hardly a hitch."

"My God—a miracle!"

"Not only that, she's so ecstatic, she says she's never going to put the bug back in again, never. In fact, Mary's out on stage now rehearsing the first act to see how solid she really is."

Naomi and I talked about what a break this was. "It makes a big difference. Randy thinks she's much better, too, because now she's actually listening to the other actors." Naomi added, "Which seems to be a natural prerequisite for acting."

That evening I put in calls to Gary, Randy, and Mary. Gary said, "Oh, Jim, it was thrilling, it was like opening night. Oh, and listen, when Carol and Mary were walking down the hall after the performance Mary said, "Oh, I'm so happy I can't tell you!" Carol replied. "Yes, well, I'm twice as happy as you are!"

When I talked to Mary, she indeed sounded like Peter Pan. "Oh, Jimmy, I can't tell you the freedom. I feel like I'm flying now!"

"And you really got taxi-dispatch calls?"

"Yes—imagine!"

"Did you answer any of them?" I asked.

"Stop it, silly. Oh, and I also heard boat whistles."

"Boat whistles—in Phoenix? Those must be some boats!"

"I don't care what anyone says, I heard taxi calls and boat whistles. Oh, Jimmy, I wish you'd been here. I can't tell you how I feel. What a relief! It's so great, for my own sake and for everyone else's, of course." Beat, beat. "But," she added, "mainly for mine!" She went on: "And I'm never going to put it back, never. You know, that darned thing hurt my ear, my ear's been sore for six months. But now that I know it, promise you won't make any changes—I couldn't take that."

You're damned if you do, damned if you don't.

Kevin called later on. The miracle in Phoenix seemed to augur a major change; he even spoke about the possibility of doing the play in London for five months and coming to New York in the fall, if Mary was up for it. We agreed to meet in Sacramento.

THE WEEK THAT WAS

I'd never thought of Sacramento as the Heavenly City. It's hot, humid, and not the most sophisticated garden spot in the world, but Sacramento was the week that was for us. I will always remember Sacramento. Like the swallows come back to Capistrano, I will return to Sacramento one day in my dotage to meditate upon that one gorgeous lovely *peaceful* week.

Mary was high as a kite without the ear bug. She seemed to have dropped ten years, maybe fifteen. She was all sunshine and smiles, and I don't know if this translates across the footlights, but the audiences in Sacramento were sensational. Not only did we do excellent business, but the laughter and applause, the excited talk of approval during intermission, the ovations they got at the end were incredibly heartening.

Carol was equally happy. "Do you know the relief to be on the stage with Mary and not have to wonder if the pause she's taking is for timing or if she's waiting for Keith to throw her a line?"

The entire company stayed at the one motel that had a good restaurant, a comfortable bar, and a pool. Not to get overly sentimental, but we were really one big happy family that week. There was a member of the family missing: Tom Davis, who'd been so concerned with my percentage, was nowhere to be seen. When I inquired, Randy said he'd been sent back east after San Francisco and had never appeared again. Mary made no mention of him, and

Susan Grushkin stepped up to a position of more authority.

Kevin and I got along, too. There were plans to keep the show running and—surprise!—even talk of letting me work on it. Finally, I thought, this play, after approximately six months, has settled down. Now to polish it.

It was decided that, because the next three weeks were single playing weeks—one each in Portland, Seattle, and San Antonio—we would wait to rehearse and put in any changes during the Boston engagement, which was for three weeks. This would give us a breather instead of packing and moving on to a new city at the end of each week.

I left Sacramento content, happy, in tune with the world—and myself, for a change. As they say in mystery stories, little did they know they were headed for the Gorgon, The Three-Headed Monster, and the most horrifying times of their lives!

ACT III

BACK IN THE RED AGAIN

I returned to New York full of hope. I suppose in those of us with a creative bent hope is a necessity. We must have it to face the overwhelming odds against the happiness of a successful work.

The next day, Wednesday, June 25, I was kvelling over the phone with Elliot Lefkowitz about the article in *Variety*, which follows, noting our successful and, more than that, happy week in Sacramento. The show was opening this evening in Portland.

This pleased us both, and Elliot ended the conversation with "Jim, maybe this means the whole thing's settling down and you won't be going through this constant hell anymore."

No sooner had I hung up the phone than it rang again. It was Kevin. "Hello, Jim—we're in one helluva mess in Portland." I held my breath as he went on: "The promoters of the theatre there—a married couple, I think—they've been bringing in shows for thirty years or so. Anyhow, seems they've been having some bad times

Road Down; 'Legends' Sets Record; Denver 'Cats' 600G; 'Tango' 467G

Attendance on the road was down last week. Total receipts for 18 shows was 11.9% below the previous week's level. The Broadway-bound "Legends," starring Mary Martin and Carol Channing, drew $288,619 of a possible $323,962 for seven performances, to set an all-time record for a straight play at the Sacramento Community Center in its single stanza there.

SACRAMENTO

Legends (P-TR), Sacramento Community Center ($20-$22.50; 2,450; $323,962) (6/16-22) (Mary Martin, Carol Channing).

PW, $199,269 (7p), Civic Center, Phoenix.

Last (single) wk, $288,619 (7p). House record.

lately. They took our entire advance—around $140,000, I'm told—paid off some bills, declared bankruptcy, and disappeared."

"Oh my God! So . . . ?"

"Doug Baker's already on a plane out there to see what he can do, but it looks bad." Kevin went on to say he didn't see any way we'd get the money back; the Portland engagement would be a benefit; the people who'd bought ahead had paid their hard-earned money, and we had to honor their tickets and perform.

Portland put us in the red. And that was only the beginning.

Trish Garland had gone up to choreograph a simple little soft shoe to go with the end of the song; she phoned to say Mary couldn't learn it. I begged Trish to drill her until she got it, but Trish was not optimistic.

I spoke on the phone with Cheryl Crawford. Dear Cheryl had not been kept up to date by anyone and wondered what was going on. I filled her in and asked if she could please join us in Boston for some really professional producing help. She still hadn't been feeling well, but said she'd try. Within two weeks, however, Cheryl was paralyzed in New York Hospital.

Kevin began phoning soon about rewrites; he went on about the opening scene with Annie-Joe and Carol, which I thought had been settled. He talked in circles, and I could no longer register his exact point of view. He also kept insisting we cut Mary's mastectomy speech; he had "a thing" about it, even though almost all the professional people who'd come to see the show commented especially on how well Mary performed that section and how touchingly real it was. I was against cutting it and said so. Things got extremely dicey again between us. Soon it was as if Sacramento had been a dream—a delightful one, but ephemeral.

Friday, July 11, 1986

Around seven in the evening received a conference call from Bob and Kevin. Unfortunately I took it. Kevin started off saying again what a long way we'd come with the play, but then he turned vituperative. "Jim, you're undermining the morale and the play by calling Mary and Carol and getting them to form a united front in the crying need for a director."

"Kevin, I haven't made any specific calls about that, but I have spoken to them about it, and they certainly realize we need one."

"But we have one!" Kevin shouted.

"Who?"

"Clifford."

"No," I said, "I mean one who will be *with us and working on the play in a creative way!* Not a director we haven't seen since the middle of Los Angeles. I like Clifford but he's never here!"

"Jim, let me tell you something. I've done everything in my power to keep the show open."

"I know that and I appreciate it."

"Well, then, don't you realize we've flown in people from all over the world to help!"

I couldn't believe he was actually saying this. "Who?" I asked, hoping perhaps I'd blacked out somewhere along the way and had missed something or someone.

"Clifford," was his reply.

"Clifford! Clifford came in as the original director, and every-one knew he was from England. What do you mean, flying people in from all over the world? What a ridiculous statement to make."

Bob tried to inject a few words acknowledging that this had been a bit hyperbolic, but Kevin was on a run. "Let me tell you something—no one could direct the show until Mary learned her lines, and then we'd have a director come in."

"Well," I said, "she's learned them now, thank God, and now it's time, if you want to protect your investment, to have a director come in."

"We have a director!"

"Who?" I asked again.

"Clifford!" he shouted at me. Right about now I thought Kevin was trying to gaslight me; his next few sentences cinched it. "And Ahmet's doing everything he can," Kevin said.

"What???"

"He is. He's going to have Jerry Robbins—who hated the play, by the way—come up to Boston."

"That'll be a big help!"

"And he's still trying to get Mike Nichols. But right now we have Clifford, and he'll come to Boston, and let me tell you some-thing—no one else thinks we need another director. No one."

When I gave him a list of people—Randy, Carol, Mary, Gary, Jerry, Annie-Joe, Bobby Fryer, Alan Wasser, Esther, Elliot, Jim, our stage manager, and on and on—Kevin actually replied, "Oh, they're just telling you what you want to hear."

Finally I began to yell. "You're talking like a man with a paper asshole; you make no sense whatsoever. I cannot get through to you, and half the time I don't know what the fuck you're talking about. I hate to hang up on you, but I'm afraid the time's approaching. If you want to discuss anything, call Esther or Elliot, but I've got to go now to preserve what's left of my sanity."

Click.

Bob called later on to express his dismay at Kevin's behavior and delusions. I asked Bob why Kevin was allowed to go on this way, and Bob said he had more financial control over the play. Also, Bob had not been feeling well much of the time, describing what he had as "the longest case of flu in recorded history." He promised to help more. Especially with regard to a director and making our three weeks in Boston as productive as possible.

I went ahead doing work on my own. A week or so before it was time to go to Boston, Esther called, having talked to Kevin, who promised both Mike Nichols and Jerry Robbins would be coming up. I told her what Kevin had said about Jerry Robbins and Esther asked, "Then what would he go up for?" I had no idea.

In the meantime, for the good of the production and the backers, I had agreed to a sizable cut in royalties. The following plan somehow evolved. We would all meet in Boston, see how the show was playing, try to agree on further changes, which I would then make. Clifford was in fact coming over from England, and he'd insert the new work, cuts, or whatever. This seemed like the same old dreary game to me, but . . .

A funny thing happened on the way to Boston. A musical by Joe Stein, *Rags*, starring Teresa Stratas and featuring Larry Kert, was trying out at the Shubert right before us. They got mixed reviews but word of mouth was good, business was building, and they wanted to extend their engagement at the Shubert in order to bring in a new director and continue work on the show. Our booking was definite, and there was no way to alter the schedule, so they had to move out and on to New York.

Someone connected with our show who went up to Boston to do advance work—it might have been Chris Holman, who did PR for the Giffords—phoned and said some joker in the *Rags* company had taken their poster and ours and made a combined one that read:

MARY MARTIN AND CAROL CHANNING
IN
HAGS

This poster was hanging backstage at the Shubert. I told him, for God's sake, to get it out of there, before the ladies got off the plane. That's all they'd need to greet them. As it turned out, we needed no outside interference to stir things up.

IT HAPPENED IN BOSTON

Opening night in Boston, I sat on the side of the mezzanine, which unfortunately left me with a good view of those sitting in the orchestra. It's difficult not to watch various people equipped with pen and paper. Elliot Norton, critic emeritus of the *HeraldAmerican* and, of course, now not reviewing, appeared to be enjoying the play; he smiled, laughed, and nodded in approval. The current working critics were scowling when they weren't scribbling so furiously they could not possibly be watching what was going on onstage.

On the other hand, I had a flock of dear cousins who were simply having a good time; I could look down on a beaming Nick, Lila, Linda, Fred, Geoff, and John. The opening-night audience was the usual seven points cooler and eighteen points more judgmental than a regular group. But the performance was a good one. Drinks and cousins and cousins and drinks after.

Thursday, July 24, 1986

The usual mixed notices, the main one even edging a bit into a money review. Breakfast with my favorite cousins, then a noon meeting at the Copley Plaza with Kevin and Bob, who seems rather flushed and does not look well. Kevin began with a speech. "This is our last shot, the work we can do here and in the other Eastern cities. We all have to sink or swim together, no time for fighting, nothing but work." I hoped this would turn out to be true. Kevin suggested a new scene at the beginning of Act II which would find Gary in a subway station, now on his way to meet the ladies. He had his first scene and his last, and this would keep his character alive. He might be juggling three phones as he talks to his backers, tries to contact the ladies and also check on his current Off-Broadway hit, *Craps*.

I was not averse to investigating this possibility at all. It would help the play plotwise. The other huge plus was this: Gary is a joy to write for, talented, inventive, always optimistic, and ready to give it his best shot.

We also spoke about a final scene, after the song. This would take place in the apartment, after the opening night; the ladies would both be reading their own rave reviews. Gary, their triumphant producer, would read his, and finally Annie-Joe, dressed in a smart business suit, would enter, briefcase in hand, now being their manager and fending off movie offers coming in from Paul Newman and Robert Redford, playing them off against each other. It could be fun, and would certainly add dimension to the play. It would also be an "up" ending; the audience would be assured the ladies had made a successful comeback.

It was a good lunch, but we'd had so many rapprochements before, only to have them later disintegrate into near-nuclear conflicts, that one tended to tread on hopes made of eggshells. We walked to the Shubert, where a matinee was taking place, and spoke to Randy of our plans. It was suggested we meet with Mary and Carol after the curtain and get their reactions to the proposed new work.

After the matinee we all trooped into Mary's dressing room. Carol, Charles, Kevin, Bob, Randy, and me. Once settled, I waited for one of our producers to speak, and when silence reigned I launched into a speech about an added scene for Gary and a new ending for the play after the musical number. After I finished explaining in detail, Carol looked somewhat surprised, Mary looked weary, but they agreed to go along. I borrowed part of Kevin's speech to me earlier to end by saying, "We must all stick together during this final round and work hard to pull it off." The meeting ended with Kevin saying Clifford was coming back—a slight frown from Carol—that Mike Nichols would be coming up to see the play, that we should all pull together and make this into a smash hit.

Kisses and good wishes from the ladies, and we left. Kevin complimented me on the meeting and we all said goodbye. I was shuttling back to New York and my trusty word processor to work on the rewrites. Again.

The next few days I put in hot, heavy, and long hours. Jim Piazza joined me, to monitor the work and my spirits. He's a joyful spirit to have around. And not all that silent when it comes to good suggestions. By Monday afternoon both new scenes were in good enough shape to zap-mail them off to Kevin. I also sent a copy to Jerry Paonessa in California; he was coming to Boston to be my backup system—helper, support, referee, in case we needed one—for all the extra work such changes would require. Reactions were good.

Wednesday, July 30, 1986

Checked into the Copley Plaza, then went down for a meeting in the open-lobby coffee shop. Present were Clifford, Bob, Randy, Doug, Jerry. When we began talking about the last scene, Clifford said, "Well, then, in other words, Mary—is she Leatrice or Sylvia?"

"Leatrice," I said, glancing at Jerry, whose eyebrows made a quick trip to his hairline.

Clifford had arrived the day before and had seen the play that night. Apparently the show had gone exceedingly well, and again Clifford said he didn't quite understand what all the screaming was about regarding changes. He was very up about the play.

Kevin outlined the plan. We would call Gary at one the next day and go over the subway scene; at two-thirty the ladies would arrive. Kevin and Randy would apprise them of the work we were setting out to do, then read over the new material and give them a few cuts to make room and time for the added scenes.

Had to rush back to the hotel for a meeting with Dave Richards, critic on the Washington *Post*, who'd flown up to do a feature interview that would run the Sunday before we opened there. Interview went well. Dave had reviewed several of my novels, had liked them; the publishers had even used a quote or two from him in advertising. He is an attractive man with a straightforward style, looks you right in the eye and asks penetrating questions. He was acquainted with the entire history of the play, Mary's problems, the reviews, the feuds, etc.—and he assured me critics went to the theatre wanting to like a play, that there was no cabal against authors. It's always tricky talking to critics, because you are aware so much of wanting them to like you, wanting them to understand the problems of putting on a play, but unable to come out and say certain things. You don't want to be wooing them, but, in effect, that's what you're doing, and anyone who says he isn't, is a dirty, rotten liar.

When he asked what I did for relaxation, I said tennis came first on the list. He said he was currently taking lessons.

"Good," I said, "I'd like to play you while we're in Washington."

"When?" he asked. "Before or after my review comes out?"

"Well, I'll tell you one thing, if it's after, I'll do my best to whip your ass and really humiliate you on the tennis court!"

When I went back to the theatre, I learned Annie-Joe had simply not shown up for the matinee. No one knew where she was, so her understudy, Gwen Shepherd, went on for her. The matinee was sold out, very good house. Gwen got through it without a hitch.

The story with Annie-Joe turned out to be not nice. That night, when asked by Kevin what happened, she said she'd told Randy she had a doctor's appointment and would not be at the matinee. Confronted with this, Randy denied her ever telling him anything. Confronted with *that*, Annie-Joe said, "Oh, I *meant* to tell you; I guess I forgot." Unforgivable behavior for anyone in the theatre.

That evening Jerry and I worked in the basement of the theatre, trimming Gary's subway scene and making a few minor alterations in the new final scene. Now the public-address system was on, so we could hear the audience's reaction, which this evening happened to be outrageous. Waves of laughter roared over the system just as I'd be saying, "Yeah, we can cut that" or "Maybe this line could be a bit stronger." Every so often Gary, whose dressing room was nearby, would glance in at us laboring away, the sound system blasting all the time. At one point he stood in the doorway as I said, "Yes, I think I can fix that . . . !" just as a huge laugh and then applause were heard over the sound system. Gary laughed, shook his head, and, pointing to us slaving away, called out, "What's wrong with this picture?"

We all laughed. I was tired, the work was grueling, but at least, so far, most of us were all in agreement. Except I did not agree at all about cutting Mary's mastectomy speech. After the show a bunch of us gathered at the Copley bar for a nightcap. I lifted my glass and said to Jerry, "To tomorrow!"

"To tomorrow," we all said.

Tomorrow should never have come.

TOMORROW CAME

Thursday, July 31, 1986

The day formally began with a luncheon some few blocks from our theatre. The official staff was there: Kevin, Bob, Randy, Clifford, Jerry, the author. Clifford had seen the show the night before, which he said played smashingly, and ventured the opinion to Kevin that some of the cuts we'd planned needn't be implemented if the show continued to be played at last night's pace.

Kevin waved a hand and attempted to brush this attitude aside. Things turned immediately dicey when Clifford raised his voice and said, "No, Kevin, listen to what I'm saying. I'm the director and I'm telling you my considered opinion."

Jerry and I looked at each other, hoping this attitude would permeate the day's rehearsal, that Clifford would assert himself. No matter what, Clifford understands the workings of the theatre and its inhabitants much more than Kevin.

We then went over the schedule. Unfortunately, Kevin had the entire thing upside down. First, we should present the cast with the new material, get their approval and enthusiasm for doing the work, then go over the minor cuts and leave the major one, Kevin's insistence on cutting the mastectomy speech, until last or perhaps—because I was certain Mary would not approve—wait until another day.

Kevin said no, we had to give the changes to them all at once. I asked why. "Because that's the way it should be done," he said. Jerry agreed with me; I think the others did as well, but this is where Kevin fails to listen and barges ahead like Tammany Hall with his own bullish party line.

He and Randy would meet with the ladies in Mary's dressing room and brief them; then we'd present the new work, followed by the cuts. Why Clifford wasn't going to be in on that little meeting I didn't know. Or myself, for that matter. Again I pleaded for Kevin to take it easy on the mastectomy speech: "We need Mary and Carol in their best moods, and—"

"No, it will be fine, don't worry, I can handle Mary," Kevin assured us.

After lunch Clifford and I made our way to the Shubert. I knew our relationship had been damaged and felt, as long as we were going to give it one last go, we should at least be friendly. As we walked, Clifford ended up saying, "You know, Jimmy, I think this is going to be a much rougher day than anyone imagines."

Gary arrived on time and read through the subway scene. We all laughed, and I could imagine it working extremely well; it was almost a standup comedian's dream encased in a play. The third phone call is a wrong number: a suicide-hotline call, and Gary becomes caught up in keeping this poor wretch from killing himself, while dealing with his own Off-Broadway show and pretending to be lunching at Sardi's with Carol and Mary while talking to his major backer, whose wife wants to speak to the stars. At the end, just as the sound of a subway car roars into the station, he has to pretend to be Carol as he shouts, "You'll have to speak up, Esther, here comes the dessert cart."

We were all delighted with Gary's approach and feeling good about the piece itself. Soon it was time for the ladies to arrive. Mary appeared in an ankle-length orange dress, black and gold boots, a black hat with wimple underneath. Carol sneaked in a mite late, all in black: pants, shirt, jacket, hat, the works. I caught her coming in across stage right, and for an instant, in the dim lights we are allowed for rehearsal, she looked like a burglar.

We all said hellos, then Randy and Kevin took them into Mary's dressing room for a twenty-minute talk, briefing them and—as I thought—telling Mary of Kevin's desire to cut his unfavorite speech. It did seem odd that the director, who had flown all the way from England, and the author, who hadn't, were sitting out in the orchestra twiddling their thumbs and making small talk.

When they emerged, Carol and Mary came out onstage and sat side by side on the sofa. Gary then read through the subway scene for them, indicating the three phones and pantomiming the confusion of dealing with all of them at once. They laughed gently several times, but didn't seem to get the full humor or the reason for it. At the end, when Gary says to the backer's wife, "Hello, Esther . . . this is Sylvia Glenn. [This is followed by Carol's stage laugh "Ah-hah-hah"; then, as the subway roars in:] You'll have to speak up, Esther. Here comes the dessert cart!"—he did more of an imitation of the real Carol Channing instead of Carol's stage voice as Sylvia.

We all laughed, but Carol's eyes bulged as she looked at Gary. "What was that?" she asked.

"What?" Gary asked in return.

"What was that supposed to be at the end?"

Gary gulped and said, "You."

"Me?" she said, then in a deadly serious tone, "That didn't sound like me at all! Isn't it funny, whenever anyone imitates me it doesn't sound anything like me!" She turned to Mary. "What do you think, Mary?"

Mary didn't say much of anything, except she thought it might have been a bit long. Poor Gary was left standing there with serious egg on his face, not his fault. And Carol adored him—both ladies did. Actually, I had thought he was going to imitate her deep Sylvia Glenn stage voice whenever she answers the phone in the play, which is more like Bankhead.

Then it was time to read the end scene for them, which takes place after opening night. I decided to read Carol's part, not wanting to nail Gary by having him go through *that* again, and Gary read Mary's part. Annie-Joe and Eric had arrived to read with us. Someone suggested Mary and Carol sit in the orchestra so they could get a better perspective. They got up and headed for the steps, and held hands as they descended into the theatre proper; Gary whispered to me, "Uh-oh, watch out, they're holding hands, we're in trouble."

They sat steely-eyed in the front row, and I don't remember them laughing once, not even at the reviews Sylvia and Leatrice read, which were outrageously complimentary and quite funny— we all thought.

When we finished the scene, there was a silence; finally Mary said, "I don't know what I think . . . I really don't."

Carol piped up with approximately the same line. "Well, I don't either, I don't know." Then, after a pause, "What is the purpose of it?"

I explained it was to round out the play, give us more of a plot, more of a time span and a legitimate ending. "I think it will satisfy the audience more; they've been rooting for you, and now they'll know you've pulled off successful comebacks."

There was much stewing and hemming and hawing and talk of how well the show was playing now with the two of them singing and ending up in an embrace. It was finally agreed the new scene could be shortened somewhat and be tried. If it worked—fine. If it didn't—we'd just take it out.

That finished—not really shooting one hundred percent—the ladies were asked to come back onstage for the cuts and other business. They again held hands as they climbed the steps. I stayed out in the orchestra, as did Jerry, Kevin, and a few others, while Clifford and Randy got their scripts and went up onstage with the ladies, who once more sat side by side on the sofa.

Mary and Carol opened their scripts as they were given cuts in the first act. Carol accepted several in the first scene without complaint, and both she and Mary took a cut that eliminated a few lines of dialogue right after Eric's strip routine.

I was sitting in about the fifth row of the orchestra, jotting down on a yellow legal pad what had gone on before, when they suddenly approached the middle of the second act. Kevin sat behind me, Jerry off to the right. Clifford was perched on the coffee table right in front of them. Randy sat in a chair off to the side. They started to give the cut for the mastectomy scene by the page. "All right," Clifford said, "cut from page two-twenty-one to two-twenty-three."

Sound of pages turning. Then both ladies said "What?" at the same time. The page cut was repeated. A moment of stunned silence, after which Carol said, "You mean you're cutting Mary's mastectomy scene?"

"Yes."

"Oh, my God," Carol said, "you're cutting the heart out of her character."

I'd thought they'd been told about this in the dressing room. My blood ran cold as I realized it was a no-go. Or, as we say in the business, a deal breaker.

Mary had seemed a bit confused as she turned her pages, but when she realized this was, in fact, what was intended, she said in a deadly quiet voice, "No, no. I won't cut it, there is no way I will do that. No." When Clifford went on to explain, she let him get out only a few words before she said in a firmer voice, "No, I will not touch it, there is no way I will do that. I do it well, it means a lot to me and to my character, and I will not lose it."

Kevin tapped me on the shoulder and mumbled he was waiting until the right moment, then he would add his clout. I quickly whispered for him to leave it alone, which, I suppose, soon propelled him to go bounding up onstage and start babbling to Mary, "Mary, let me tell you something, we've gotten a lot of feedback, and some of the critics have said—"

Carol cried out, "Oh, for God's sake, if you're going to please the critics, cut the brownies, cut the stripper, cut the whole damned play. Really!" I was proud of her, and she wasn't finished: "Don't you know that in a comedy or a farce, if the audience doesn't love the characters, they won't laugh at them?"

Kevin, crashing about the china shop, kept pressing his case as I sat there wincing and praying reason would at last strike him mute. Reason did nothing to stop him, but Mary did. At last she overrode him in a firm no-nonsense voice: "Kevin, I will not cut the speech, ever. Now, let's not talk about it anymore, because it will affect everything we've established together."

I'd have thought that one heavily armed sentence would have done it, but Kevin still squeezed out one more: "Mary, let me tell you something—"

Mary slapped her script shut and gave the final edict in an emotional but extremely cool voice. The emotion was held in rein behind the coolness of the tone, but it was there. As she spoke, I looked around at the theatre and I could feel icicles forming, hanging from the boxes, the chandelier.

"I don't need to work. I don't ever have to work again. I wanted to quit in Dallas, but I stuck with it and I worked on and on and now I know it and I like doing that speech, it means a lot to me." She paused. "Now I don't think I'll even be able to do it tonight. Or ever again, for that matter."

I actually felt a chill and shivered. I glanced over at Jerry. He looked frozen, too, as Mary continued: "I don't know, I don't know. This is a very rare moment in my professional career. Not only is the speech ruined for me, but also the play is ruined for me. I will go on, but I will not play London, and I will not come to New York. I'll fulfill my contract, and then you can get someone else and cut anything you want."

Mary stood up, sighed, looked out over the almost empty and

extremely frigid theatre, and said, "I don't think I've ever had a moment like this before in my entire career. It's very sad, and I don't think I will ever forget it."

With that she walked offstage, carrying her script and as much dignity as any one woman could muster. It was now below zero. Carol busied herself gathering her things together, muttering, "How could they even think of cutting that speech of all things!," and then she, too, left.

There was silence in the theatre for a long time. The theatre itself felt dead, like the shell of a building that had once contained life but was now derelict.

I'd felt like applauding Mary's speech. Now I felt like a coward for not having spoken up early on to shut Kevin the hell up. I also felt like crying. I knew that what had happened would eventually affect the entire life of this production. Jerry and I walked up the steps onstage and we all stood around, as if the wake had just ended but no one knew how to say goodbye. Soon little huddles of people were standing in corners of the theatre. We concluded that a major gaffe had been made, and Kevin admitted he'd done it. There was nothing to do but disperse.

I had promised Jerry a good Boston lobster, and although my appetite had been cut down, we went to the Legal Seafood for dinner, where we raked over the day's coals. Jerry summed it up when he said, "Kevin has the brain of a goldfish; talking to him is like talking to an ice cube."

We both admired Mary more than ever. Carol, too, for that matter. I still felt soiled. Although I know Mary and Carol knew I was against the cut, I should have stood up tall and thrown my cards on the table. But I was so caught up as spectator to this onstage accident, I could not come to life myself.

Back at the theatre before the evening performance, I knocked on Mary's dressing-room door. No reply. Knocked three more times—nothing. Susan came down the hall. She said Mary had left word that no one was to talk to her; she wanted no visitors before or after the performance. I asked Susan to give Mary a message for me. "Tell her I was proud of her for speaking up." I went to Carol's dressing room. She was still highly agitated. "How could anyone think of cutting that speech! It's just terrible." She was banging her hands around on her dressing-room table. "My God, how will I ever get my makeup on? I'll never get ready for the performance."

I went downstairs to the basement, to join a confab in Randy's office. Oddly enough, Kevin was in a jolly mood, laughing about the afternoon while still admitting his mistake, making jokes and obscene references to Charles, who every so often passed by or came in for coffee. Kevin was like a high-school kid who'd gotten in big trouble and tried to turn it into a shrug-off joke. It was around this time that I named him The Terminator. Randy then informed us that both Carol and Mary had issued an edict: there would be no changes, no additions, no cuts; nothing would be done before Washington, if then. Kevin again said he'd made a major blunder (and certainly one he'd been advised against), but this was old news. We sat for most of the first act trying to sort out the alternatives.

It was agreed I could shorten the epilogue, although the chance of getting that in appeared to have flown over the horizon. I could trim the subway scene a bit and work on it with Gary. Clifford said Gary was extremely demoralized by Carol's attitude at the end of his reading; he felt Gary would probably not want to chance working on it.

The public-address system had been on but turned down; however, the reaction to the play this evening was incredibly positive. Huge laughs, breaking into applause now and then. After intermission Jerry and I stood in the back of the theatre. I wanted to see how Mary would get through the mastectomy speech. She did it beautifully, of course, as usual, with perhaps a tiny dash more of poignancy. The rest of the act played like gang-busters; Gary's final scene with the ladies got huge laughs, and as Jerry and I walked backstage during the curtain calls, we heard cheering and stomping and bravos. We stood to the side of the stage, near Jim Bernardi, who was calling the curtain, and looked out at the spectacle of the cast receiving these wild acknowledgments of pleasure. The entire cast was very much aware of the day's happenings, and as the curtain came down for a fourth and fifth time, still to bravos and cheering, Don Howard, our cop, held his hand up to the audience and said, "That's all right, we can fix it!"

I heard him, and so did Gary, who almost fell down with

laughter. Gary immediately passed it on to Mary and Carol as Don repeated what he'd said, and they laughed as well. As Susan led Mary from the stage to her dressing room, I called out, "Mary, you did the speech beautifully." No reply. Carol huffed, "I'm surprised she could do it at all!" I called out again, in a stronger voice, "Mary, you did the speech beautifully, as usual!"

Mary turned and gave me a very nice and very cool "Thank you very much."

FALLOUT

The edict that there would be no more changes left us all sitting around with our fingers in our ears. Jerry and I walked around the city; he bought presents for his kids; we had lunch; then I went back to the hotel for a lie-down and figure-out; I also made a few phone calls, informing Esther and Elliot of The Terminator's latest coup.

In the evening we went to the theatre, to see if we were still playing there. Check in with Randy. Both ladies' dressing-room doors were closed, but he said they seemed to be in fair spirits. Clifford had already fled our shores and gone back to England. That had been an unproductive trip if ever there was one—an expensive five thousand or so to add to our production costs. Jerry flew to California the next day, and I returned to East Hampton.

Weeks before, I'd asked a dear and extremely talented friend of mine, Arthur Laurents (author of the books of *Gypsy* and *West Side Story*, screenwriter of *The Snakepit*, *The Way We Were*, and *The Turning Point*, and director of *La Cage aux Folles* and the revival of *Mame* with Angela Lansbury, and these are only some of his credits), if he'd see the show and give me his opinion. Arthur called to say he and a dear friend of his and mine, Tom Hatcher, were thinking of trooping up to Boston for a few days. I said I'd gladly take them to dinner and to see *Legends!* It was agreed we'd meet in Boston for dinner Tuesday, August 5, and catch the Wednesday matinee the next day.

Wednesday, August 6, 1986

Backstage met the new understudy for Eric, a very nice fellow named Vincent Cole. Poked my head in to see Carol and tell her Arthur Laurents was here for the matinee. "Oh, good," she said, "they finally got someone to come up here that knows something!" I told her Arthur was coming as a friend of mine, to give me his opinion. I didn't tell Mary, because she doesn't like to know who's out front. I went to meet Arthur and Tom in the crowded lobby. Sold-out matinee, tons of ladies on the loose.

As Tom, Arthur, and I took our seats, my armpits dampened. Arthur is not only extremely bright, he is *extremely* candid. And I was ready for both barrels. But it was a good show, the audience was responsive, and I could tell after a few minutes that Arthur and Tom were getting a kick out of it, smiling, laughing, not sitting there silent and bored. This helped me relax. In the intermission Arthur said, almost a trace of surprise in his voice, "It's fun, it's a romp!" He gave me a suggestion about making the stripper more integral to the plot, and we went back for the second act with a thousand or so happy ladies. The second act played extremely well, even the dread vacuum-cleaner scene; Gary lit into his final bit with all his might, and Arthur thought he was extraordinary. Terrific curtain calls, standing ovation, etc. On our way backstage, Arthur said he was quite taken with Mary. "She's honest and very truthful; I think she's very good."

I took Arthur and Tom back through the connecting door and nabbed the ladies in the hallway. Arthur took Carol's hand and told her she was terrific and very funny just as I was introducing or reintroducing him to Mary. He told them both how much he'd enjoyed the play. Carol disappeared immediately, having agreed to speak to a group of ladies who'd attended the matinee. She often did this as an added incentive for theatre-party groups. They'd remain after the theatre was cleared of other patrons, and Carol would come out onstage and speak to them, graciously answer questions, and sign autographs. Arthur spent a few minutes speaking with Mary, praising her performance, and also congratulating Gary. Then we left, while Carol was still entertaining her group.

Over dinner Arthur told me exactly what he thought. His criticism, I felt, was totally candid and constructive. When he spoke of the performances, he went on about Mary and what a truthful actress he felt she was (especially in the mastectomy scene, which he thought she performed beautifully). He thought Carol was very funny and had managed to get away from Lorelei Lee and Dolly but felt she played out front too much and also milked the laughs, letting a laugh peak and fall and then waiting for the next laugh. "I feel she goes from laugh to laugh, instead of playing the intent of the play, but I like her, she's funny; she could use some direction." He felt Annie-Joe was a bit mean-spirited. I asked Arthur if I could relay his opinion to Carol; I knew she'd want to know. He said, "Of course." We had an easy flight back to New York; it had been a good day.

Thursday, August 7, 1986

Sure enough, Charles and Carol called early in the morning to hear Arthur's comments. Carol first said something about "he avoided me." I told her he hadn't, he'd had to get right back to New York, and we'd had no idea she had to speak to a group after the matinee.

"Well, what did he say?"

"Do you want me to be completely candid?"

"Of course," Carol said.

"All right. He really enjoyed the play; he felt the chemistry between you and Mary is excellent; he thought you were very funny, was delighted you were playing it sort of mean and tough and in the brown wig; but he did feel you play out front a bit too much and tend to go from laugh to laugh, instead of playing the intent of the play."

"Umm," Carol said, "and what does that mean?"

"Well, you know, he felt sometimes you deliver a laugh line— and deliver it well, mind you—but then you wait for the laugh to peak and fall before going on like bam-bam-bam with the delivery. Playing out front is . . . Well, just playing out front, like when you talk to the crucifix, you know, we've talked about that."

I could tell Carol was not all that pleased, and I waited for sarcasm or frontal attack, but we had a pleasant talk and I did keep praising her—and not falsely. I was happy when the conversation ended. Except—

Friday, August 8, 1986

Charles called at eight-forty-five in the morning and got right to the point. "We want a written apology from Arthur Laurents to Carol Channing!"

"What—Charles?"

"That's right. He was rude to her, he ignored her, and his comments . . ." And on and on he went.

I immediately tried to put an end to this inquisition. "Charles, please don't dump this on me. I told Carol how much Arthur liked her, she asked for all his comments, and—"

But Charles was in an uproar. Arthur was rude, insulting, how dare he, etc. I begged him not to go on and asked if he'd like me to call Carol later when she was awake and re-explain Arthur's comments to her. Yes, he would. I begged off with a heartfelt sigh.

Twenty minutes later Carol herself called. She had obviously been brooding over Arthur's comments, letting them simmer and then boil over. "He was rude to me!"

"He wasn't, Carol. I was there when he greeted you and told you how terrific you were and how funny."

"Yes, but he went right to Mary and he sneered at me!" I told her she was mistaken, but she'd have none of it. "Playing from laugh to laugh—that's the worst thing that could ever be said to an actress, and playing out front!" (As if she'd never been spoken to about that; both Clifford and I had begged her at times not to.) Then she waxed sarcastic with me: "Maybe you're the one that goes from laugh to laugh. Did you ever think about *that?* But everything Mary did was perfect, I suppose. Right?"

"Carol," I implored, "don't do this to our relationship. We've had a good—"

No win, as she went on: "Did you see *La Cage?* Did you like *that* direction? Did you like the casting?" And on and on, until finally she just began garbling her words and eventually hung up.

Charles and Carol! They cannot cease forming ranks, attacking, regrouping, fomenting, exploding, backing off, and starting all over again. I decided I wouldn't go to Washington on the Monday of our opening; I'd had enough of walking into a hornet's nest.

Carol did phone the next day, a brief sarcastic call to say, "I played all of my comedy lines upstage last night and ruined the whole play!" I checked with Randy and he said it was a terrific show.

Please!

A few days later, early Sunday morning, Charles phoned. "Hi, Jimmy, there's good news and bad news."

"Give me the bad."

"Randy tells me they've hired a new understudy for Annie-Joe without the ladies' approval. It's in their contract, and, goddamnit, the two of them will walk out two weeks before the end of the Florida engagement and, not only that, tell Kevin to stop breaking their fucking contracts!"

I'd reached a point where I had to say, "Charles, I can no longer be a go-between. If you want to tell Kevin something, please . . . *you* tell him. I'm bushed."

The good news, according to Charles, was that we'd grossed $244,000 the week before and it would be better, almost capacity, this week. It was as if the Arthur Laurents incident had never occurred as Charles went on to say the show was playing well, Larry Hagman was coming to Washington, and if he was pleased he'd want his mother to stay in it as long as possible. He was entirely friendly, and said they were looking forward to seeing me in Washington. I did not say I was planning not to attend.

Kevin phoned later that same day and I gave him Charles' message. "He's crazy," Kevin said. "The ladies don't have understudy approval in their contracts. Jim, you're coming to Washington for the opening, aren't you?"

"I don't think so."

"I wish you would. I'm having lunch with Mary on Thursday to try to make everything up and go on with plans to work on the play. And we can work on Gary's scene and get that ready to put in in Philadelphia."

"Really?" I asked, biting at the carrot. I finally agreed to come for opening night but not the previews. The big word had been, of course, that Ron and Nancy, old friends of Mary's, would be seeing the show in Washington, and this would give us a giant boost and national publicity.

The day was crammed with phone calls. Gary called to fill me in on what had happened at the Saturday matinee. In the brownie scene, when the ladies feel the effects of the hashish, Mary, in the play itself, had a line she couldn't finish, but on

Saturday she really went up and foomfed and fuddled around, and the more she did it the more the audience laughed and the more she fluffed, until she got a huge laugh and then a hand. Gary said the scene, which he was in, went wild. But Carol apparently disapproved, because as she was leading Mary on for the curtain calls she said, directly to her, "That was the most tasteless thing I've ever seen. Why, that was something only Ethel Merman would have done!"

As if this weren't enough: Gary reported that they'd both agreed to address several hundred matinee ladies who'd come from out of town, in the lobby, after the show. Mary and Carol came out, were hoisted up on chairs so they could be seen; during this interview Carol put what Mary had done in the matinee up to a vote, saying, "Toward the end of the play, remember when Mary flubbed her lines and then went on and on—did you like that? Or did you think it was—"

Before she could finish, the ladies all called out, yes, they'd loved it, and applauded. Gary was hysterical, saying, "Imagine, two of the biggest stars in the theatre, and one of them is putting the other's performance to a public vote in front of the audience!"

There was one scary phone call. Lou Miano, an old friend of mine, one of the backers of the play and a former employer of Bob Regester when Bob worked in advertising, called to say Bob was not feeling well at all; they were trying to get him into the hospital and thought he might have pneumonia. In this day and age the wrong kind of pneumonia can mean The Plague. My heart was heavy, and I said prayers that it was *just* pneumonia. Thinking back to the long sieges of flu Bob had been experiencing did nothing to lighten my mood.

A friend of mine phoned and read me Dave Richards' interview with me in the Washington *Post*. It was very long and quite good, except he described me as looking like "an older version of a scrubbed Canadian Mountie out of the chorus of *Rose Marie.*" Very funny, if it's not you he's describing.

Before I went to Washington, I wanted to be certain something would come of the trip. I spoke to Naomi, who thought the order to build the subway set was already in the works. It would not be able to go in in Washington, but if it were rehearsed and ready it could be put in for the Philadelphia opening. Word was our advance sales in Washington were fifty thousand dollars more than they'd been in Boston.

Wednesday, August 13, 1986

Hopped the Metroliner for the capital, checked into the Washington Hotel. Randy and Chris Holman both said the preview the night before had been excellent. I asked Randy if the Reagans, Mary's great friends, were coming to the opening.

Here's the word on that little caper. Nancy, only a month or so before this, had gone Major Public over Say No to Drugs. Some wag said Nancy had been advised she better come up with a big issue soon, or else she was going to get picked over for doing too much shopping and spending too much money on red dresses. At any rate, the campaign was in its first weeks, big publicity—the President and Cabinet members were having their urine tested as an example. (Like they were really going to come up with cocaine traces in Ronnie's specimen?) Apparently, before Mr. and Mrs. President see a show, advance men are sent ahead to check it out to see if there's anything objectionable.

The word was: a couple of checkers had caught the show in Boston and reported the two leading ladies by mistake get their mittens on some hashish brownies that belong to the maid, turn a bit goofy, and actually end up *laughing* about it. *Verboten!* Nancy and Ron could not attend a play in which Mary Martin, of all people, gets swacked out on drugs. So they were not only not coming to the opening night—so long, Ruffles and Flourishes!—they were not coming, period. Instead Mary was going to have breakfast at the White House.

The coincidence of the war on dope fit right in with the timing of this play since word one. If we had played Washington two months before there would have been no problem about the Reagans' seeing the play.

Washington opening night was seven o'clock; very snazzy crowd. As I was going in, Dick Coe grabbed my arm and said, "Jim, the play is terrific now, it's just fine, don't do a thing to it, just let them play it." That meant a lot coming from him; on the other hand, more "timing"—Richard Coe was no longer reviewing for the *Post*. Doug Baker was there with his kids, and Kevin had brought his two lovely young daughters, Mary and Emily.

The first act played very well; the audience, especially for an opening night, was very responsive. Afterward there was a huge reception in the Helen Hayes lounge of the theatre. Lots of politicians there; it was fascinating to watch them wangle their way into the camera's lens, either TV or still photographer. They're experts and could give movie stars lessons. Spoke to Roger Mudd, who is very nice and has hands about the size of hams; he said he liked the show. At one point a woman I didn't even know tapped me on the shoulder and said, "Look, there's———!"

"Who's that?" I asked.

"That's the one that fucked President Kennedy all the time," she snapped, as if I were retarded. "And there," she sighed, "is Hubert Humphrey's sister, such a dear, sweet thing." The combination of the two broke me up.

The stars made a stunning entrance, Mary in a lovely white gown and Carol in a red one with a halter. At one point, as the photographers were shooting her, Carol asked, "Have I got this thing on backwards?" It was a bash. Big news: Washington loves gossip. They love to tell who's doing it with whom, and they don't seem to care much—why?

Thursday, August 14, 1986

Reading the Washington *Post* curdled my breakfast. Dave Richards hated the play. Oh, Richard Coe, where are you when we need you? It was, I thought, a vicious review. His headline was "WHAT BECOMES A LEGEND LEAST" and he took off from there. I was surprised, because he'd liked a lot of my other work and the way I spoke about the kind of ladies I knew when I was a kid in Hollywood. Despite his review, the box-office man told me later that day we'd rapped thirty-one thousand dollars, which was excellent.

Kevin's big meeting with Mary was to take place at two-thirty, appropriately enough at The Watergate, where she was staying. Larry and Maj were to be there also. Kevin had copies of some of the changes and cuts we never managed to implement in Boston because of the big blowup, which he was taking to the meeting in the event that work was going to continue. Randy and I were to meet Kevin in the lobby at three-thirty to get the final word from the mountain. We cooled our heels there for two hours. Finally Randy decided to call up. Kevin got on the phone, said the meeting was just ending, he'd be down soon.

He arrived shortly, a grin on his face, with his two daughters, who, someone suggested, had probably been brought along as bait to help win Mary's affection back. At any rate, an enormous stretch limo hauled us to a restaurant for dinner. Kevin said it took a while for the atmosphere to clear, and at first it was merely socializing, but then they got down to business and the meeting actually went very well. Larry had read over the material and given his stamp of approval to most of it. We'd proceed as if nothing had happened. Kevin was happy and grinning, so Randy and I picked up on his mood, although I was beginning to feel more and more like a typist than the author. Also, tomorrow in New York was a big day for us. Annie-Joe had finally given her notice, and we were holding auditions for her replacement.

I was going back to the theatre and taking a late train; the last thing I said to Kevin as he got into his limo for the airport was "I'll see you at auditions tomorrow at ten-thirty at the Minskoff."

"Yes," he said, "let's hope we get lucky."

Having gotten this far—where would you place *your* bets?

FINAL MISTAKES

Friday, August 15, 1986

Reported to the Minskoff studios at ten-thirty, joined for coffee and chatter with Vinnie Liff, Andy Zerman, and Tara Jayne Rubin, from Johnson-Liff, our casting people. There had been talk of trying to find a black lady who would not be playing what people thought of as an old-fashioned stereotypical maid—that is, not a zaftig lady of some weight.

This was fine with me. The main prerequisites for the part were humor, sass, warmth, and a sense of herself with these two overpowering legends. Because, in the end, Aretha is the catalyst who talks some sense into them and finally gets them to agree to do the play together.

We were seeing perhaps twelve women today. They began backing up as we waited for the ever-late Kevin. We called; no response at any numbers. Eventually, we had to begin without him. It was a good day, some excellent actresses—most of them carrying a bit of weight, though. And then along came Loretta Devine, one of the original *Dreamgirls*, who had just won a Tony for her costarring role in Bobby Fosse's *Big Deal*. Beautiful, young, great figure, and she read warm, funny, energetic, caring. We were all wildly enthusiastic. I was mad about her; I took her aside to explain we were trying to get away from the way the part was being played now, and she fit the bill exactly. She understood what I meant and was anxious to do it.

We wanted to make her an offer immediately, but we couldn't do it without any of the producing team's approval. Bob was in Lenox Hill; Cheryl was in New York Hospital and unable to speak; Kevin could not be located; and I had no communication at all with Ahmet. I told Miss Devine we wanted her and we'd be in touch very soon.

I left the readings extremely excited and went to Lenox Hill to see Bob. I waited in the hall for a long time while a doctor and a nurse were busily whipping in and out of his room. Finally I was asked to put on gloves and a mask—I'd been through this before and shuddered—and allowed in. The minute I saw Bob, I had to hold back tears. He looked absolutely awful, watery bloodshot eyes, feverish, face so red he looked as if he'd had a bad sunburn, hands trembling, voice unsteady.

He'd just been given the bad news, not an hour or so before I got there. He'd been sleeping, and when he awakened, the doctor was standing by his bed and said, "I'm afraid I have some bad news. You have pneumocistic pneumonia. . . ."

"You mean . . . ?" Bob asked.

"AIDS." The doctor nodded and soon left, leaving Bob with every sort of unanswered question in the books. Is this a death sentence, is there any hope, what should I do?

What do you say to someone who has just been told this? You say, "Of course you can lick it, they're working on all sorts of cures and drugs, and . . . so much is a positive mental state."

But the words have a hollow ring. Bob was being, to his credit, extremely brave. He went on to say he was sorry he wouldn't be of much help anymore, apologized for not being able to block Kevin in some of his more reckless moves. I mentioned that Kevin had not shown for the audition and told him of Loretta Devine and how she'd captured our hearts. He was glad to hear this. After a while a dear friend of his from England, Mary North Clow, arrived. I stayed for two hours or so. As soon as I left the room, tears rolled down my cheeks and my vision blurred.

The first word about Kevin's no-show was that he hadn't known; I shot that excuse down by repeating to Doug Baker our discussion of the night before in Washington. Then the story was changed to: he'd forgotten. Later it was: he'd been so emotionally drained from his meeting with Mary and Larry that he didn't have the energy. There was never an apology. I urged him to sign Loretta; Kevin, of course, wanted to hear her read. All of this took time. Kevin finally arranged for Loretta to audition for him five days later; I was not present, having already given my whole-hearted approval. Our casting people said she read very well but not quite as well as the first time, because she was rushed: she had another reading immediately afterward for a new play at the Public Theatre, *The Colored Museum,* and had to hurry to change clothes and be on time for it. Kevin liked her but was not completely captivated.

Kevin waffled. I could not understand this; he'd been the one who was adamant about trying to get away from an older, heavier woman for the part. I explained to Kevin that Loretta Devine was considered a star of sorts and we'd better not stall too long in offering her the part. Although she'd read twice, Kevin decided to send her down to Washington to see the Saturday matinee on August 23. Why he did this, none of us could figure out. I begged him not to, saying she'd be seeing the part played the opposite of the way we were now planning to have it done. What good could that possibly do? But he was insistent, so days later he had Loretta Devine take the train to Washington, sit through the matinee, and speak to Randy after. Randy was impressed with her; I don't believe she even met the ladies. Kevin still would not sign her. He procrastinated, finally asking her to read a third time, on Wednesday, August 27.

Wednesday, August 27, 1986

The reading was scheduled for four o'clock at Actor's Equity. Early in the day Vinnie Liff called to say Loretta Devine had been offered a lead in the play at the Public and had decided to take it. The reading was off. I was dejected and furious with Kevin.

Later on I received another call. There was a ray of hope. Her agent had asked for "first refusal" if the play moved to Broadway—meaning that an actor or actress who does a play Off-Broadway must be offered the part if the show moves uptown—and Esther, whom I called, said Joe Papp doesn't give that to anyone, not even Meryl Streep. It's simply not a policy of the Public Theatre. Esther thought this might augur well for us. The ray of hope rekindled when another call advised me that Loretta Devine would indeed read for us at four o'clock.

I'd asked everyone to show, so we would not put this lovely actress through any more hell than had already been inflicted on her. Ed Gifford, Doug Baker, Vinnie Liff, Andy Zerman, and—late as usual—Kevin. Loretta Devine, looking adorable in a long knitted sweater, a skirt, and flat shoes, read beautifully. She was everything she'd been the first day I heard her.

When she finished, I walked her out, told her I was sure she had it. I was so happy and apologized to her for having had to read three times and troop to Washington. She was most gracious. When I walked back in the room there was Kevin, all puffed up: "She's terrific, she'll be sensational, she'll really help the play, too." He turned to the casting people and said, "We should make her an offer immediately."

He'd taken three weeks and put everyone through hell, but now—yes, get her. I wanted to staple his tongue to his feet, but I was delighted the ordeal was over.

Until the next day, when Doug Baker phoned and said, "Jim, I'm afraid I have some bad news." My heart hit the floor as he went on to say, "Loretta Devine's decided to take the play at the Public."

Toward the end of August, just before the move from Washington to Philadelphia, I got a report from Randy that Carol was once again correcting Mary on stage. According to Randy, Mary swore she'd leave in January and said she would never think of coming to New York "with that woman." Cheery news like this helps keep the spirits up when one is away from them.

We were actually putting Gary's subway scene in for the Philadelphia opening, so I went down to rehearse Gary and see how the scene played. Charles Lowe talked me into staying at the same place as he and Carol, the Warwick, a very nice hotel, but they were redoing the kitchen or some such thing and there was no room service. I phoned Charles the first morning to yap about this and suggested he take me to breakfast to make up for it.

"I can't, Carol's on her way out right now to do an interview. Well," he added, "someone has to sell your goddamn jams and jellies. Why do you think your play's grossing more than any other straight play in the country?"

I liked the jams-and-jellies line. Then he launched into another tirade against Kevin. I skipped breakfast and went to the Forrest Theatre (where I had played years before with Sylvia Sidney in *Joan of Lorraine* when I was treading the boards) to see the subway set. It looked splendid, entirely different from any other piece of scenery we had, with a good solid phone bank containing three of the shiny instruments. There was a mockup of the set in the basement, so Randy, Gary, and I could rehearse there while the stagehands—swarms of them—were working getting the actual set on and off. Gary is extremely funny in the scene, and it's a devil, has to move like wildfire.

Wednesday, September 3, 1986

Went to the theatre early for tech rehearsals of the subway scene, sound and lights and moving it on and off, and for Gary to be able to work onstage. Many stagehands standing around; that's where much *dinero* goes, and in the meantime the producers are holding back my pay for certain weeks in Boston and Washington.

We geared up for our first Philly performance, a matinee. Gary was raring to go. Kevin missed the train from New York and arrived during the matinee, which was attended by extreme geriatric cases. The oldest audience we've had by far. We were all waiting eagerly for Gary's scene. It played well, although to not nearly the response we'd hoped for, but, then, the audience was not all that lively.

Still, we all felt it would be a good addition. Kevin was a bit hangdog with me; he must have gotten his letter (I'd fired off a scolding epistle about the gross mishandling of Loretta Devine). Charles was also in an uproar about the sound: "Carol won't open tonight if the sound's not fixed!" etc.

Opening-night curtain: seven-thirty. A packed house and a good response. Gary's subway scene played very well, but it does somewhat diminish what used to be the second-act opening, in which the ladies are found sitting in a state of disarray after their fight, being questioned by the cop. Gary's final scene, with the ladies, played even better, however. You gain some, you lose some. The ladies are getting sloppy in some places, the end of Act I in particular; they are simply snatching wigs off at random and have lost the precision of various beats which lead to the curtain. No director.

There was a tacky little opening-night party at a restaurant across the street; Mary came in her all-orange outfit, Carol in her silver top and huge hat. Mary skipped her last line to the cop before he exits, and I reminded her as we spoke about the performance. The cop's gotten the ladies' backs up, and they both insult him when he leaves, Mary's last crack being "And when your next child is born and people ask if it's a boy or a girl, I hope you have to hesitate about an hour before answering." She's always delivered it well, and it's always gotten a good laugh.

Tonight she totally surprised me when she said, "Oh, I didn't forget, I'm just not saying that line anymore." I asked why. "Because the audience practically boos me when I say it."

"Mary, you've been saying that line for months now, and it always gets a great response."

"Well, I don't want to say it anymore. The audience hates it. I'm saying I hope his wife gives birth to a child with two heads."

"No, no, you're not," I said.

"Well, that's what everybody thinks. What does it mean, then?"

"It doesn't mean a two-headed child, I never thought of that. It's deliberately ambiguous, but if you have to nail it down, it means he would have to take a long time to decide whether it's a boy or a girl."

Then, very sweetly, she said, "Well, whatever it means, I'm not going to say it anymore. You can write another line or else I'll just skip it and let my last line to him be the one before that."

At least Gary was in a good mood, because his subway scene played very well.

Other minor rewrites went into the show in Philadelphia. I had to submit copies to Kevin for his approval and accompanied them with a little note saying how delighted I was "to turn in my homework to the principal." All of this was going on as they were withholding monies due me, supposedly because of the cost of putting in the subway set and other production problems. I'd also heard rumors that Mary was asking for another choreographer to restage the song, and still talking about having two follow spots added for the ending. This would cost thousands and thousands of dollars for rental of the spotlights and the hiring of two extra men to work them—and for only the last three minutes or so of the play.

Esther and Elliot were having meetings with Doug and Kevin, attempting to settle our financial problems, and on September 9 I wrote the following letter to Elliot.

September 9, 1986

Dear Elliot,

    This is a note I think you should read to Kevin and Doug, expressing some of my concerns about the production.

    Since my creative wings were clipped in San Francisco, we have not had a director, except for a few unfortunate days in Boston when Clifford came over, to not much avail I'm afraid. Consequently we have no creative director with the show. Randy is terrific, but he can only do so much with the ladies. He will attest to that himself. They tend to take notes from him when they feel like it and then do exactly as they wish. They are badly in need of an outsider to come in and shake them up. Anybody who has been in the business knows this is the only way to pull a show together.

    I think the changes we've made in the script have been for the better. However, I do believe, at this point, the performances are disintegrating. Carol is getting way too broad and slow; Mary, now that she has learned her lines and is enjoying getting laughs, is stretching her shtick beyond all decent levels. The end of Act 1 is extremely messy.

My fear is that the production will get sloppier and sloppier unless someone comes in to keep a tight rein on it. I think, if I had been allowed earlier on, I could have helped in this area. But I have been, more or less, made impotent. It's too late for me to suddenly come in and start cracking the whip, which is what is needed.

Outside of the regrettable handling and loss of Loretta Devine, which is causing us all angst and a drain on our time what with added auditions and trips to Philly, etc., these remarks are not set down in anger.

They merely express my considered concern. If Kevin's relationship with Mary is, in fact, mended and if he can prevail upon Larry to advise her to play New York, I'm sure the production could recoup and even make money. But lately she's been dropping somewhat more than hints about leaving when her contract is up. In that case, what do we do? Replace her—with whom? Or close? It seems a shame to let a show that we know is an audience pleaser simply fall apart because there's no leader. As I've said before, I appreciate Kevin's efforts to keep it going, but I don't believe in personally subsidizing an effort that has been made difficult at almost every turn in the road. I have written and rewritten and made myself totally available since last December and I am feeling the wear and tear now.

Yours,
Jim

Wednesday, September 10, 1986

Trained to Philly, got to the theatre by two-ten. Gary's new scene is playing very well. Kevin was to meet with Mary after the matinee, then it was changed to six-thirty, so I checked into the hotel, cleaned up, and came back to the theatre at eight for a dinner meeting with Randy and Kevin. As we walked across the street from the theatre, Kevin appeared tight-faced, too; I took it their meeting had not gone well.

Once in the restaurant, however, Kevin indicated all was fine and Mary has agreed to continue working on the play. (By this time I don't actually know if this is good news or not.) But, Kevin added, she is not all that happy with Carol, who at last Sunday's matinee was apparently displeased with Mary's position during one scene and grabbed her by the shoulders and shook her. Mary once again indicated she would not put up with this much longer.

Kevin said they were approaching the choreographer Peter Gennaro to come in and work on the musical number. "Listen," I said, "he's terrific, but I know he's expensive, and it's only three minutes tops, and the audience is eating it up the way it is, for Christ's sake!"

Kevin looked at me. "How are you?" he asked.

"Depressed."

"About what—the play?"

"You guessed. . . ."

"No, no," Kevin said, "we're making great headway."

"We are?"

"Jim, you know we are. And Ahmet's leaning on Mike—"

"—Nichols to come and see it," I finished for him.

"Yes, in Chicago."

"Why Chicago?" I asked. "He should see it now, the sooner the better."

"No, let's get it in as good shape as possible before he comes."

"No, Kevin, we can go on and on saying that. The reason to get him in the first place is for him to help us, not to present a dazzling finished work to him. We need help!" (I suddenly wished I'd gone along with Mike's original idea of doing it with Harvey Fierstein and Betty Bloolips; it could not have turned out any crazier than the way it was now, and Mike Nichols could have dealt with them/it/Kevin.)

Walking back to the theatre, Kevin suddenly started talking about recasting Leatrice and getting Debbie Reynolds or Elizabeth Taylor. He'd just indicated a half-hour earlier Mary would renew her contract, and now this talk of recasting. Very confusing.

My favorite hassling-onstage moment occurred during one matinee, while I was sitting out front with friends. Toward the end of the second act, when the doorbell rings, announcing the arrival of Martin Klemmer (Gary), Mary is suddenly shy of facing him and eventually says, as she crosses toward the bedroom, "I'm going to hide under the bed."

Carol says, "Oh, stop it, you've been doing that for years."

This afternoon there was a small laugh before Mary's line, and although I heard her say it and so did the audience, Carol didn't hear it clearly enough and called out, "Say the line."

Mary stopped walking, turned, and asked, "What line?"

Carol said, "The line where you say what you're going to do."

I could not believe this was going on, but go on it did, as Mary replied, "I just said it."

Carol snapped, "I didn't hear it, say it again."

Mary looked her right in the eye and announced in a loud, clear voice, "No!"

"All right," said Carol, "I'll say it for you. You were going to say you were going to hide under the bed, weren't you?"

"I already said it," Mary said.

I looked at the audience, mostly matinee ladies, who were turning their heads from one legend to the other as if they were watching a tennis match. I wondered what they thought: Is this part of the play, or are they doing it for real? My friends leaned over and said, "What was that all about?"

"Beats the hell out of me," I replied. And it did. What a pair!

Barbara Sohmers, who had valiantly been standing by for both Carol and Mary these many months, gave her notice and wrote me a lovely note, saying she had to get back to acting and obviously she was never going on for either lady unless one of them was struck by a train.

At one performance Annie-Joe loused up a laugh in the second act and Carol called out in a loud voice, "Thanks a lot, you sure killed that one!" Dear Mary chimed in with her own "Yeah!" Now perhaps they're both going to gang up on her. Sheila Ellis, our new understudy for Annie-Joe, read with Mary after a matinee as a possible replacement to play the part. She read very well, but I gathered Mary was not all that enthusiastic, because she immediately began complimenting Sheila on her sweater. I like Sheila; she's a good actress. Randy later reported Mary thought she was good but perhaps a little too sweet. That's a matter of direction and shading, of course.

On one of my many trips back and forth to Philadelphia I bumped into George Yaneff, a principal investor through Bob Regester's group, which had put up three hundred thousand dollars for the play. He said he'd talked to the people who own the St. James Theatre and they would like us to play there in New York. He said the doctors had told Bob he had two years to live at the most. This was a shocker to hear. He added that Bob was going to appeal to Mary to come into town with the play because he was broke and sick. We both agreed this was definitely *not* the way to go about it! It should be done through Larry, with the idea that the play would pay off completely with a limited twelve- or fourteen-week run on Broadway. We all felt it was a good show for the theatre-party people, and certainly Mary and Carol together on Broadway in this dull season would stir up interest, even if the play was considered vulgar by certain critics. I told George, who is a nice, decent fellow, that he should exert more influence with the production, be more forceful, especially now that Bob wasn't able to be on hand.

Toward the end of the Philadelphia run I had a long interview with Richard Christiansen of the Chicago *Tribune* for a Sunday piece prior to opening there. A few days later Doug Baker called to say Glenna Syse, critic on the Chicago *Sun-Times*, had just printed an article headlined "MARY MARTIN, CAROL CHANNING SHOULD STASH THE HASH." It started out with a memo to playwright James Kirkwood (of course): "Could I persuade you to remove a scene from your new comedy *Legends!* before it arrives here on October 8 at the Shubert Theatre?" And went on about how touched she was when she'd seen Nancy and Ron on television making a plea to Say No to Drugs.

I happened to be at Elliot's office. He was furious that a critic would ask an author to rewrite a play two weeks before bringing it to his or her town. "My God," I said, "there are all sorts of unpleasant things in life, and they're reflected in our plays and novels. What would she want Steve Sondheim to do in *Sweeney Todd?* Cut out the rather brutal murders, have the barber only *nick* his customers whilst shaving, change the meat pies to tuna and let them give everyone a headache or the trots? That would be an amusing finale!"

I put in a phone call to her. (I'd met Glenna and even been to cocktail parties with her after functions.) She was quite righteous and not lacking in attitude. I tried to explain to her as calmly as possible that her suggestion would mean restructuring the entire second act, which would mean closing down, going back into rehearsals, and . . . However, she stuck to her guns, going on about Nancy and Ron. She said, "Well, couldn't there be some other—"

I explained I didn't want to make the ladies *alcoholics*, because that would preclude their doing a play together for any length of time. I also tried to explain that hash, a distillation of marijuana, was the mildest form of drug one could come upon. It certainly wasn't coke, crack, heroin, or morphine.

She was obviously hooked on our President and First Lady, and we ended the conversation as civilly as we could, although I wanted to shout, "Oh, why don't *you* rewrite the play? You figure it out and see how it flies! *You* give Mary an entirely new second act to learn!"

Can hardly wait to hit Chicago.

CAREFUL...!

Because we hadn't settled the replacement for Annie-Joe, we had readings for that part in New York toward the end of the Philadelphia run. We could not agree on a lady, but we did find a good dancer, Garry Q. Lewis, to come in as understudy for Vince Cole, who would now step up into Eric's part. We also found a new lady to stand by for Mary and Carol, a good actress named Natalie Ross. Our casting people suggested Kevin and I fly to California to see actresses there for the part of Aretha. We planned to do that at the end of our Cleveland week, which preceded the Chicago engagement.

I graduated from Elyria High School in Elyria, Ohio, where I lived with my Aunt Peg and Uncle Leonard because of the extreme poverty each of my parents was experiencing at the time, so it was almost hometown boy makes mediocre when we played Cleveland, Elyria being only twenty miles away, and Cousins Lila, Nick, Chris, and Barbara still in residence there. So I joined the company again in Cleveland.

Peter Gennaro, a talented and extremely nice choreographer, was on hand with his assistant, Dee Dee Erickson. We exchanged greetings during intermission opening night, which went extremely well, and I wished him good luck teaching the ladies a new routine. He asked if I would please come to rehearsal on the morrow. I think he saw me wince, but I said I'd be on hand.

Thursday, October 2, 1986

A good money review in the paper. Said it was fluff but good fluff. Whipped off to the rehearsal hall in the morning, where John Klingberg was playing the piano for Peter and Dee, who were working on the routine before showing it to the ladies. There was again word that we might put in the new ending that had been shipwrecked in Boston; I read Peter the scene so he'd know where the song was coming from.

Watched Peter and Dee dance—so stylish, great flair, but the routine seems a bit complicated and overly suave for Carol and Mary. It should be a number that can be fouled up without wrecking the overall effect—in the event they don't get it down one-hundred-percent cold.

This night was Elyria night. The Arts Council, together with the YMCA and the Elyria *Chronicle Telegram,* sponsored a couple of hundred people who roared in on buses from Elyria to see the play and throw a party for me at Sweetwaters restaurant after. The theatre was packed, but they'd given all the Elyrians seats in the rear of the orchestra. I was embarrassed that so many dear old friends were consigned to the rear of the Palace, a very large theatre. However, the audience was extremely responsive, and this was gratifying, especially with hometowners present.

The ladies were not all that wild about going to the party, but I asked them as a favor to attend, knowing the Elyrians would be glad to see me but they'd *really* be glad to have Mary and Carol at the party. Unfortunately, they were *too* happy to have them, and crushed in on them at a corner table, taking pictures and getting autographs, until I could tell both were feeling the heat. Charles looked at me as if I'd planned this assault. I tried to forestall an avalanche, but the crowd kept pressing forward, and finally the ladies made a rather speedy exit, plowing their way out, as Charles threw a few sharp curses at me: "You and your god-damn friends! Well, that's the last time we're ever . . ."

When they'd gone, we had a more relaxed time. Sheila Ellis sang, and very well; so did Don Howard; everybody pitched in to put some fun into what turned into a very late evening.

Friday, October 3, 1986

Up early, dead-tired, drove in the rain to the airport for the flight to California. Slept fitfully most of the way. Jerry Paonessa picked me up, whipped me to Jamie Herlihy's where I was staying; then we zapped over to the rehearsal studios at the Shubert Theatre in Century City for readings.

I was delighted to see Bob Regester there, looking so much better than when I'd seen him in the hospital. He'd put on weight and appeared to be doing well. Kevin and Ann were there, but unfortunately only two women showed up that day. One of them never took her eyes from the script, never looked up once while reading two long scenes. The other was Roxy Rokker, who had been on "The Jeffersons" for many years, playing more or less a straight part. She's attractive, young, graceful, and elected to read the scenes in a lovely lilting Jamaican accent. Roxy is an excellent actress but not a downright comedienne. We were all impressed by her but felt she was not necessarily right for the part of Aretha. We held out hope for the next day.

Saturday, October 4, 1986

Finagled Jim Herlihy into driving me to the Shubert and staying for the readings; any time I can spend with my best friend and guru is gravy. Again we saw only two women. Mabel King, who was in *The Wiz*, gave a dandy reading. Big, expressive eyes, energetic and funny. And Virginia Capers.

Virginia was a presence, a large elegant woman in a red silk patterned dress with a string of pearls tied around her neck. The casting people had told me she was not going to read, but was coming in for a meeting only. She has extremely refined speech, star attitude, and was anxious to fill us in on the year she'd won the Tony Award for her performance in *Raisin,* thus snatching it away from Carol in *Lorelei.*

When she saw us exchange glances she waved a hand and said, "Oh, but we're very good friends." (I'd want to check that out with Carol.) We talked on and on, and finally someone had to broach the subject, so I said, "The Johnson-Liff people said you didn't want to read."

She looked at me and laughed gaily. "Oh, now, why would you want me to read? I mean, the part's sassy and full of p and v, just like me!"

If she were really full of piss and vinegar, I think we'd have gotten more than the initials. I spoke up. "Oh, come on, we'll just have an easy read right here, just one scene. We came all the way out to California. Come on."

Virginia Capers, who *was* wonderful in *Raisin,* finally gave in, opened her envelope, and took out her script with a sigh. She read one scene quite well, fondling her pearls. I somehow couldn't picture her playing maid to Carol and Mary without a bit of trouble. I just sniffed it. We thanked her for being so gracious and she left.

As soon as she closed the door, Kevin and Bob raved about her. "Oh, she'll really change the play, she'll—"

"She sure will," I said. "It would be rather like having Ethel Barrymore play a maid to Joan Crawford." Jim agreed with me, and fortunately, after some investigation, they found out Virginia Capers was on a new series and wouldn't know if it was being picked up until the end of October.

We'd come all the way from California to hear four ladies read. Not what I'd hoped for. The only plus connected with this trip was seeing Bob Regester looking well. Before we enplaned for Chicago, Kevin put in a plug for Roxy Rokker, who was lovely, but seemed not totally right for us.

My dear friends Kecky Kirschenbaum and Arthur Beckenstein, who was staying with her for a few days, picked me up in Chicago and took me to the Palmer House, only a block away from the Shubert Theatre. Kecky was throwing a party for me the day before we opened, at Suzie Wong's restaurant, and had also arranged for Mayor Harold Washington to designate "James Kirkwood Day" in Chicago. (Hasn't Chicago been through enough riots?)

Tuesday, October 7, 1986

Kecky called early, worried that Mary and Carol wouldn't attend the party after their Cleveland experience. I promised they'd be on display.

Checked out the Shubert Theatre in the morning. Good to see people standing in line; it's a great theatre to play; you can smell the past in it. Someone brought me a copy of the Chicago *Sun-Times* with the following article. I could imagine throngs of perplexed Chicagoans when they heard, saw, or read that bit of hot news.

CHICAGO SUN-TIMES　　　　　　　　　　　**TUESDAY, OCTOBER 7, 1986**

It's James Kirkwood(?) Day

Pulitzer-winning playwright here for 'Legends' opening

James Kirkwood
Threatens to walk the streets

I f you see a handsome, bearded and slightly mad-looking man roaming Chicago's streets today wearing a sandwich board, it's only James Kirkwood.

"One side will say, 'This Is James Kirkwood Day in Chicago,'" he threatens with a wink. "And the other side will say, 'I'm James Kirkwood!'"

Indeed, it *is* James Kirkwood Day by proclamation of Mayor Washington. If the name doesn't ring a bell, you need only know that the Pulitzer Prize- and Tony award-winning Kirkwood is author of "Legends," which will open at the Shubert Theater tomorrow night starring Mary

Martin and Carol Channing.

And don't forget "A Chorus Line"—"which has made me financially secure enough to do what I want," he marvels. And "There Must Be a Pony," though Kirkwood admits he was less

than thrilled with the ABC-TV version that aired Sunday night starring Elizabeth Taylor and Robert Wagner.

There are others, of course. He credits his second career as a writer—he began as an actor, like his father of the same name—with "keeping me halfway sane."

"I'm forever surprised that I'm allowed out in public. I really ought to be in a rubber room."

His bizarre childhood featured his silent-film-star mother Lila Lee, on whose life "There Must Be a Pony" was based. He's now working on a novel, *I Teach Flying*, about his "charming, crazy, leonine" father. -

Kirkwood says he loves Chicago, despite the fact that his dear old dad was arrested here in the '30s for performing in the then-banned "Tobacco Road."

"As long as *I* don't get arrested," he philosophizes with a grin, "I think I'm doing pretty well."

Just to make certain Carol would show after Charles' anger in Cleveland, I went by to escort them to the party. Charles was in a good mood, except when he got onto the subject of Kevin. At one point, just before we left, he said, "I love our producer, always wanting to change a Pulitzer Prize–winner's words, when he couldn't write 'fuck' on a shit-house wall!"

"Charles," Carol giggled, in half-admonishment.

"Well, he couldn't!" Charles has a way with a colorful phrase.

Kecky had pulled out all stops for the party. Suzie Wong's was decorated up to its eggrolls. Streamers, posters, balloons, with the logo of the play—lots of Chicago friends, tons to eat and drink, plus a favorite of mine, Bobby Cook, who not only plays a mean piano but can stand at the keyboard and tap dance upon a section of hardwood floor at the same time. Carol was in white with a huge white hat; Mary was done up in black with an enormous black hat. I think the ladies are coordinating now; if not onstage, at least socially.

The mayor's representative presented me with a plaque and read a proclamation, "Whereby . . ." etc. Mary and Carol both sang and Bobby tap-danced and played. But the highlight of the party came when Arthur Beckenstein, an excellent graphic artist, presented me with a large picture he'd had made up, featuring me with a blonde wig superimposed and eyes enlarged as Carol and, doctored, standing next to myself in the same photograph as Mary in a brown wig. The original had been a photograph of Mary and Carol taken for the souvenir program. It was hilarious; Arthur had also made it into a front book-jacket cover with other pictures inside. Mary somehow thought it had been made up for her, snatched it from me, and took it home. (It was weeks before I could get Susan to snitch it back for me.)

The party was a success. The pressure of that is over; now the real pressure begins, unless I've been totally fooled until this point.

Wednesday, October 8, 1986

Bumped into Trish and Vince Cole; Trish is in town to rehearse Vince's strip routine and pissed that Peter Gennaro's coming in to redo Mary and Carol's last number, but most of all, she said, "because of the way Kevin mishandled it." A nonmusical farce comedy, and suddenly we have two choreographers in attendance. How strange! (But, then, what's the name of this play?)

A geriatric matinee to warm them up for the opening. One problem with the Shubert: there's no longer a stage door, so you have to come in through the front lobby doors, and as I tried to get past the matinee crush to go backstage, a lady flailed at me with her cane, crying out, "Watch out, young man, I have a lot of broken bones here."

"Sorry," I replied, "I have a broken head."

Then I got the news that Cheryl Crawford had died the day before. I went to see Mary, who'd just been told and was way down, naturally. Dear Cheryl had nothing but sickness and accidents this last year. At least she's finished with suffering and pain and the humiliation of illness. Oh, to have had her as producer when she was in top form! Cheryl Crawford—there was a legend.

Randy said there was talk of Roxy Rokker being brought to Chicago for the ladies' approval. I'd thought we were going to continue our search in New York after the Chicago opening. I did not think the ladies would go for Roxy, far too pretty and distinguished-looking for the part.

Opening-night crowd was good. Packed house and responsive; I watched the first act but then was summoned to Kevin's suite, along with Randy. Kevin had skipped opening night in favor of the playoff games leading to the World Series; he'd attended enough openings, as had we all. The purpose of the meeting was to tranquilize me into letting him go ahead with Roxy. I heard a lot of "Let me tell you something"'s and the financial pressures and how he wasn't making a penny and the giant steps we'd made since Boston and the inducements/promises that we could probably put in the famous new ending, which was now lying on yellowed paper, and how much the new musical number would mean to the show—*if* we went ahead, and we'd go ahead *if* we went ahead with Roxy. He assured me he could handle the ladies on this score. This sudden campaign for Roxy was as surprising as it was forceful. Kevin made it clear he was not interested in continuing with the play without her.

The reviews in Chicago were not valentines. But the audiences were good and I like the city, its energy and drive. Spent most of the next day bringing a script up to date for the Argentinian production of *Legends!*, which is to be called *Chispas! (Sparks!)* there, because "legends" doesn't translate to mean what it means here.

Friday, October 10, 1986

In the afternoon Peter Gennaro planned to show a final version of the end number to the ladies. I watched with Randy while Peter and Dee Dee polished it. It's very stylish but still a bit complicated; even Peter was having trouble getting through it without a hitch. Carol and Mary arrived and sat next to each other in the orchestra. Before they went through the number, Peter said, "Now, you have to understand, I make mistakes."

To our surprise Carol said, "Oh, then you should be playing *Mary's* part!"

Even more surprising was Mary, who finally chirped, "Oh, shut up!"

As Peter passed me to get up onstage he whispered, "Wish me luck!"

Carol heard him and said, "You'll need it, you know, because we may not like it!"

I wondered if it was going to be that kind of afternoon, but—surprise again—they *did* like it, and although they were not due to rehearse this day, Carol said, "Oh, come on, why don't we start in right now!"

Off came their shoes and excess finery, and they worked for two solid hours.

I retreated to New York for a few days and was finally summoned back to Chicago—Kevin had indeed arranged for Roxy Rokker to come in and "meet the ladies."

Thursday, October 16, 1986

Sheila Ellis approached me first at the theatre, and asked if I was going to be in Chicago Saturday. She was going on for Annie-Joe. I wondered how this had come about, and Randy explained. Months ago Annie-Joe had told Kevin that October 18 her grandmother would be one hundred years old, and Annie-Joe was going to her birthday party. She'd mentioned she was going only to Sheila, not even to Randy. Someone, I believe it was Alex Holt, had overheard her talking on the phone, making plane reservations. If it hadn't been for that, no one would have known. Randy also explained that Kevin had arranged for Carol and Mary to meet Roxy at Mary's hotel suite the next day, so the meeting would be tilted toward warm and informal—to avoid the rigidity of a cold audition in the theatre.

Went to say hello to Charles and Carol, who immediately began agitating against Roxy. Too pretty, not really a comedienne, and on and on. Mary soon arrived, and plans had changed. Mary said she didn't get up until noon, and since she had to be at the theatre to rehearse with Peter Gennaro at two, we wouldn't meet at her suite but at the theatre. Both ladies asked what was all this about Roxy *not* reading. I said she'd read for us without a problem, and I didn't think there'd be any objection now. I could tell a Maginot Line was being formed, especially when Mary turned to me and said, "You *will* be here when Sheila goes on Saturday, won't you?"

I said yes. Wouldn't these two events have to overlap, as it were? Damn Annie-Joe and poor Roxy Rokker, I thought. Roxy due in this evening, but not in time to catch the performance.

Friday, October 17, 1986

Roxy Rokker arrived at the theatre right after Sheila Ellis finished rehearsing, around twelve-thirty. Tall, beautiful, gracious, and stunningly dressed in a lovely sweater over a perfectly tailored brown dress that flared out at the bottom, she sat and spoke with us until Mary and Susan arrived. They hugged and kissed and joined in the conversation until Charles and Carol showed. More warm greetings. Then we *all* chatted some more, sitting in the orchestra of the theatre, not on the stage. After a while conversation ebbed and Kevin, sitting behind, said, "Jimmy, what about reading a scene?"

I turned to Roxy. "Would you mind?"

"No, no, of course not," she said, taking out her script. "Shall we do it right here?"

The ladies both piped up and said no, it would be better on the stage. I suggested a scene with Leatrice, but Carol quickly said, "What about the opening scene with me? That comes first."

So the two of them, followed by me, went up the stairs onto the stage. Since Roxy had rehearsed using a Jamaican accent, I suggested that perhaps she should do it that way first and then once without it. Roxy sat on the sofa, but Carol took her position for an entrance and insisted upon going through the scene just as she did during a performance, although Roxy, not having seen the play, had no idea of the moves. This was unfair and confusing to Roxy, although Carol tried to make it as easy as possible. They read through the scene twice; the second time Roxy dropped the accent.

By then I'd returned to the orchestra to watch, and when they finished Carol looked right down at me and said, "Now, the truth is, she'd make a perfect Sylvia, wouldn't she? She'd be just perfect!"

"Oh, Carol—" I started.

"No, no, she'd be perfect." She turned to Roxy. "You'd be a wonderful Sylvia." Roxy was left standing there while Carol addressed Mary. "Mary, you'll have trouble reading with her, she's so beautiful! And look at that sweater. Mary will want that sweater."

Roxy took the sweater off, and then Carol went on about what a gorgeous dress she had on. It took a while for her to quiet down, vacate the stage, and let Mary have her turn.

Once up there, Mary said to Roxy, who'd perched on the sofa by this time, "You can stay right there, it's just a reading." I breathed a sigh of relief, until Mary went to the foyer, from which she made her entrance and began walking through the scene exactly as she did in performance. It was impossible to remain seated while Mary roamed the stage, so Roxy was forced to stand and attempt to keep up with her. After a while Mary even stopped her: "No, no, you don't say that until I get down to the piano." (How I hoped Roxy would say, "Oh, yes, I almost forgot!") Again it turned into a semi-staged reading. They went through the scene twice. Then Kevin suggested a scene with the three of them, in which Aretha discovers they've gotten into the brownies. That was terrific, with Mary and Carol up there together, going through their paces, and poor Roxy not having any idea of where the hell they were from moment to moment. She got through it very well, but it had to be difficult keeping up with them and concentrating upon giving a performance as well.

When they finished, complimentary words were dropped. I hugged Roxy, thanked her for going through the reading with such good humor. Kevin had ordered cold cuts, salads, desserts, and coffee, which were then served offstage right. We all helped ourselves and chattered away. Carol got out her thermoses and dove into some bluefish; she and Charles stayed together off near the lightboard. Mary mixed more and spoke with Roxy, who had to catch a three o'clock plane back to the coast. There were more chirpings from Carol about how "marvelous Roxy would be as Sylvia!" When it was time for Roxy to leave for the airport, there was bussing of cheeks all around and thanks for coming, except for Carol, who held up a hand: "No, no, I smell of bluefish. Good-bye, dear."

Roxy left, and within a minute or so came dashing back. "I left my script," she said, taking an envelope from the lightboard. Then, giving a perfect reading, she waved it and added, "I'll take it, probably just as a keepsake—if nothing else."

After she left, there was a big flurry of "Of course, no one's going to make a decision until Sheila goes on tomorrow." We all agreed. It was obvious both ladies wanted Sheila to take over. The atmosphere was tense, with Kevin and Charles and Carol never speaking directly to one another. Soon Mary and Carol began rehearsing with Peter. I went back to the hotel. Amen for this experience.

That night, when Kecky and I approached the theatre, a rat the size of a small cat scooted out of the alley and crossed the street. Kecky screamed, and when I told Kevin, whom we bumped into right after, he said, "That wasn't a rat, that was Charles Lowe going out for a bite." People—please!

Saturday, October 18, 1986

Kecky and I went backstage before the matinee to wish Sheila well. We sat in a box and watched the entire show. Sheila was very good, certainly better in spirit than Annie-Joe. Charles sat beneath us in the third row, howling at every one of her lines and even applauding now and then to make his point, and Carol and Mary's. At intermission I went back to compliment Sheila for getting through it so well, and Carol and Mary were all over me with praise for how good she was and wasn't it incredible, etc.?

Sheila was even better in the second act. The ladies were in an uproar—a bit of overkill afterward—as if the Second Coming had just taken place onstage. I agreed to put in my two cents for

Sheila, and then Kecky took me to the plane for New York.

Each time I left the company now, I felt as if I were hotfooting it out of Transylvania just before darkness fell.

PING-PONG

Back in New York, I kept in touch with the company by phone. Dark clouds, smoke signals, and the beating of drums were upon us again. The ladies did not want to play with Roxy Rokker. Her talent was not in dispute; they simply felt it was a matter of miscasting. I thought so, too.

Kevin phoned me on Sunday, October 19, his voice locked in a dead-flat level I'd never heard before: "I just had a long talk with Ahmet and I don't want to go on with Carol. I can't have her and Charles running the show. I want Roxy Rokker in and that's it. I'm going to the line with this. I won't have it any other way—either that or we close." I gave him my opinion: if he insisted on this change, Mary and Carol would then have a common cause to unite against, and that cause would undoubtedly be named Kevin. He didn't care, he was the producer, and he was going to enlist Mary's aid. I warned him about pushing her to the wall as he had in Boston. He stood firm. The Boston experience had apparently taught him nothing about diplomacy.

Now, I must score myself for being a—what, coward? Or simply abdicating because of extreme battle fatigue and letting Kevin strong-arm it out by himself against them. I should have joined them actively and, as author, said, "No, you will not put Roxy in. I have casting approval, and if you do, don't you worry about closing the show—*I'll* do it." And if he wished to close it, I should have realized he couldn't before the end of the Florida engagement, which was when Carol's and Mary's contracts were up anyhow. He'd signed contracts with Zev Bufman, and there was no way they could not have been honored. I should be horsewhipped in public for not doing this. I wasn't positive the change would hurt the play, but I had a hunch. It probably is that vestigial trace of hope lodged in the back of the mind; Kevin, despite being my nemesis, had kept the play open so far; perhaps he would go on and on, regardless of the countless gaffes—perhaps that's just the kind of freak this play is and will always be.

A few days later I spoke to Randy in Chicago. He had an odd tale to tell. Kevin had told me he was flying in for yet another meeting with Mary. After the matinee he told Randy everything was fine, he was going ahead with Roxy Rokker, and they were also going to put in the new (??) ending. He hadn't actually had a meeting with Mary, but with her new representative, Jules Powers. Kevin left, flying back to New York. That evening, when Randy went to Mary's dressing room to ask when she wanted to rehearse the new (??) ending, Mary was astonished. Randy reported Mary didn't know anything about it, was not going to change anything except for putting in the Gennaro song and dance. She also said Kevin was free to change anything he wanted after she left in January. Kevin had brought the curtain down again.

So, as Esther Sherman said when I reported this, "Kevin's going to win the battle but lose the war."

When next I talked to Kevin, he said, "I have a hunch Mary's going to leave after Florida." I should think so. When I spoke to Doug Baker, he was expecting a letter from Jules Powers that would explain Mary's choices. Kevin had not mentioned a letter. When I spoke to Doug a day or so later, Kevin had just come in the office with the letter but he, Doug, did not know what it said yet. He'd call me when he found out. When he phoned back, Kevin had already left, not wanting to talk to me, I'm sure, because he knows the reason Mary is leaving is Kevin. Doug read me only parts of the letter, which were definitely chilly and stated in no uncertain terms that she would fulfill her contract and then it was bye-bye, Peter Pan. I had an idea there was much in the letter that Doug did not read me. I sniffed deviousness.

About this time there was a feature article in the New York *Post* about the fate of *Legends!*, ending up with the story about me writing a book on my year with the show and adding: "Kirkwood's book will surely include the story of how Charles Lowe, Channing's imposing husband-manager, was once asked if he ever had sex with his wife. 'Only when it's good for her career,' he replied."

Esther phoned, saying the article with the anecdote about Charles read as if it could have come from me (it hadn't). She suggested I phone Charles and let him know I'd had nothing to do with it. I did, and Charles believed me, even laughing at the story. He went on to say Mary had invited them to dinner the night before and let them read the letter Jules Powers had sent Kevin. From it, Charles deduced Kevin had made several proposals to Mary in order to keep her. Number one: he would gladly replace Carol with Carol Burnett or Shirley MacLaine (lined up and panting to read for Kevin!); he would also get another author to come in and write a new ending for the play! Charles suggested I get a copy of the letter. He also wanted me to call Larry Hagman.

The next day Liz Smith took the *Post* to task in the lead item of her column.

★★★★
I DO HOPE that Pulitzer Prize winner James Kirkwood doesn't have included in his coming book "Diary of a Mad Playwright" the anecdote about Carol Channing and Charles Lowe as it appeared yesterday in another column. That version had Lowe, as his wife's business manager, being asked if he ever had sex with his wife. He answered: "Only when it's good for her career!"

That hoary chestnut and apocryphal funny tale has been making the rounds for years and nobody enjoys it more than Carol and Charles. But let's get the joke right. Someone reportedly asked the super-dedicated, highly loyal Lowe: "Charles, do you ever sleep with Carol?" Lowe, by more correct reports, pretended to be startled and answered, "Why? Would it be good for her career??!!"

★★★★

In the meantime, the play had moved on from Chicago to St. Louis and Atlanta, before launching into the Zev Bufman circuit in Florida. Without me, I might add. I received almost a daily phone call from Charles, eventually—as time approached for

Roxy Rokker to join them for rehearsal—to the effect that "Now that Mary's leaving, Carol will, of course, say she wouldn't think of doing the show without Mary."

I said, "That doesn't make sense. Mary's the one who's choosing to leave, so why wouldn't Carol continue? If Mary were *fired,* then I could see Carol issuing that statement, but not when it's Mary's choice."

All I got was double-talk and something about "William Morris might be taking a full page ad out in *Variety* saying how much the show has grossed, and of course it's not going to pay back, and there could be a big scandal!"

By this time, column items almost every day reported Mary leaving, with intimations of feuds and strife in the company. Also by this time, a full orchestration of the last number had been recorded, the follow spots and their operators ordered, thus bumping up the weekly nut by several thousand dollars.

Randy phoned when the number finally went in at the end of the St. Louis run: "It was rough. The ladies haven't quite nailed down Peter's routine. Also, the audience doesn't really know what the hell to make of it at first—I mean, a full orchestration and follow spots suddenly appearing in Sylvia's apartment. Takes them a while to catch on to it."

I had to laugh—all this money and time and effort, and the phuquing thing probably isn't going to work at all.

Soon came days that turned into weeks of dizzying Ping-Pong. One day Jeff Johnson of Johnson-Liff phoned to tell me Kevin had sent a script to Lena Horne. Madness. The next day Kevin phoned to say he and Ahmet would gladly be bought out. A few days later Dorothy Loudon's name came up as a replacement for Mary, and Kevin called, full of enthusiasm, asking me to arrange a meeting. (Dorothy and I had worked at Le Ruban Bleu together when I was part of the comedy team of Kirkwood and Goodman.)

Dorothy read the script and, of course, wanted to play Sylvia. She reread it, and I explained that some of Leatrice's part had been cut and I'd gladly reinstate that material for her. A meeting was arranged between Kevin, Dorothy, and me at Dorothy's. Dorothy was now intrigued with the part of Leatrice, although she mentioned she'd first taken to Sylvia. "Play Sylvia, then,"

Kevin said. "Carol won't be with us anyhow; we'll get someone else to go with you!" Kevin was enchanted by her, I could tell, and soon Dorothy had switched to Sylvia. When Kevin left the room to go to the john, Dorothy whispered to me, "Do you think he likes me, do you think he really wants me to play it?" "Yes," I told her. "Oh, good!" she said. By the time the meeting was over, we'd practically opened and come into New York with a new play and a hit on our hands.

The next day word came that Dorothy had changed her mind. "No, no," I cried, "not this, not now, not after last night." Further word came that her agent, Lionel Larner, didn't want her to replace Carol Channing. Dorothy had replaced her recently in *Jerry's Girls,* and he didn't want Dorothy to be known as Carol Channing's replacement.

Scripts were sent off to Alexis Smith, the ever-mentioned Debbie Reynolds, Elaine Stritch, Raquel Welch, Elizabeth Taylor, etc., etc. Randy phoned from Atlanta the day after Roxy arrived. After all the shtuss, Carol greeted her with open arms, crying out, "Oh, we love you, it's so good to have you with us, we've been waiting for you!" (I would beware this last sentence.)

Apparently there is a restaurant connected to the theatre in Atlanta, because Kevin and Charles were having a shoutdown there, moderated by Doug Baker, who admonished them, "Shh ... you better keep it down." To which Charles retorted, "Oh, they don't know who we are." "No," said Doug, "but you keep shouting 'Carol Channing this' and 'Mary Martin that'—people can figure it out after a while."

I'd written a letter to Larry Hagman saying I thought it was a shame that, after getting through all the difficulties, Mary would not play New York for a limited engagement, reminding him that she could settle into an apartment for three or four months and not endure the packing and unpacking and traveling, all the tech rehearsals, different theatres with different acoustics, etc.

He responded with a gracious and funny note, saying his mother had worked very hard to get a solid footing on the show and after a year was just plain bushed. He reiterated his fondness for the play and overpraised me as "the funniest writer in America," saying he hoped we'd work together on a project someday, ending with, "Call me when you get back here to reality and let's get shit-faced."

While scripts and plans were changing as fast as phone calls could be made to advise me about who was offering what to whom and which way the winds were blowing at any one moment, I decided to write Mary and Carol a frank letter and let them know exactly how I felt. So I shot off a copy of the following to each of them.

November 16, 1986

Dear Mary and Carol and Carol and Mary,

It's about time the writer was heard from, don't you think?

This is not a plea, I'm not down on what's left of my bloody knees groveling. I sold my tin cup, I'm not begging. This is just a plain statement of fact. And I will try not to make it boring.

Believe me I've worked with a lot of people in the theatre, all the way from Spanky McFarland to Tallulah Bankhead to Sylvia Sidney, Myrna Loy, Martha Raye, Elaine Stritch and all of the Lane Sisters, Priscilla, Rosemary—but you probably don't even remember them.

Yes, and a lot more. And all I have to say is: I've known some dummies in my life but you are two of the dumbest white women I've ever encountered. Talented and dear and both a bit crazy in your own very different special ways, but dumb as cat-shit.

Why—you may well ask. The answer is simple: here you've been breaking your kishkas, to say nothing of your balls, whipping this play and your performances together over one helluva long, torturous, painstaking year. I know it's not been easy. It hasn't been easy for me either. I have an ulcer the size of Wrigley Field and my blood pressure went way over the counter that clocks the speed of the Concorde—we're talking past the speed of sound. That's one helluva blood pressure count. The doctor can't even get the sleeve to stay on my arm anymore. But enough of me.

You two! So now you have this contemporary comedy

that is tickling the pisshkas out of the audience. You two hear it and feel it every night. Immediate standing ovations. Audiences love it. Lately, even the critics are liking it. So—now what happens?

Well, Mary's tired and doesn't want to come to New York and Carol wouldn't think of doing the play without Mary. Again, remember this, I'm not begging, I'm not even asking. I'm stating a plain logical fact. Everybody I talk to in the theatrical community here—and that's a lot of people—is saying: "What the (excuse the F-word, Mary, but that's what they say) fuck is the matter with you/them/it/the producers?" Why do they say this: BECAUSE this is the one season you'd clean up in New York. There is nothing to see. People come to town and there's ME AND MY GAL and a couple of others—A COUPLE—coming in and that's it. Empty theatres up the kazoo and people dying to be entertained. I'm now beginning to get requests for house seats for A Chorus Line *AGAIN after twelve years! There is nothing new to see in this town. Do you possibly think you would* not *entertain people in New York, that the audiences in Boston, Chicago, Cleveland, Philadelphia, Washington etc. etc. got it all wrong and the audiences in New York would react differently? Not possible. Everyone knows it, feels it and absolutely cannot understand it.*

So what if some of the critics jump on the playwright. No one ever gives a flying hoot in hell about him anyway. I don't even. I'm up for it—only because I know they wouldn't dump on you two. That would be like defecating on the crossed flags of Britain and *the United States in front of the White House with the Supreme Court looking on. "Mary and Carol having a good time on stage and giving the audience one helluva show" is what it would be.*

I am on the Council of the Dramatists Guild. At our meeting last Tuesday just a few people you might have heard of in the theatre: Garson Kanin, Robert Anderson, Marsha Norman, Mary Rodgers, Arthur Laurents, Terrence McNally, Peter Stone, Joseph Stein, Betty Comden, Adolph Green, Gretchen Cryer, Ruth Goetz, John Guare, John Kander, etc. etc. Just a few—all said, "What???— you're not coming into New York! That's unbelievable, why, what's the matter?" I just said, "Please, I can't talk about it." "But, but, but—" they went on. I wanted to say you're both nuts, but I refrained.

You see, if I may make an analogy: it's like two chefs have been laboring over this huge banquet for a year, getting everything ready, making the hors d'oeuvres, the Beef Wellington, the endive salad, the dressing, the cake, setting the table, writing out the invites, and then when everything is perfect: i.e. the new musical number's in, the follow spots are in place, all the guests are standing up shouting, yes, let's go!—then taking the whole banquet and flushing it down the toilet. "Oops, sorry, we decided not to go through with it. We've worked so hard, we're bushed and we've decided not to have the party after all. We don't want to enjoy the fruits of our labor, and you're not going to either. Everybody go home!"

And you can't flush it back up, you know. It doesn't work that way. Once it's down the tube, it's gone.

And, yes, I know there are all sorts of MAJOR problems. Mary's foot hurts and Carol said this and Kevin did that and Charles told Kevin to blah, blah, blah and the chairs aren't spiked right, the sound was down in the first scene, and so and so doesn't like whoseywhatsit. BUT THE AUDIENCE DOESN'T GIVE A FLYING F-WORD ABOUT THAT. THEY LOVE THE EVENING IN THE THEATRE THAT YOU TWO PROVIDE AND THEY WOULD EAT IT UP FOR A LIMITED ENGAGEMENT IN NEW YORK AND SO WOULD THE THEATRE PARTY PEOPLE. YOU'D HAVE A SOLD OUT TWELVE WEEK RUN AND END IN A BLAST OF GLORY AND THE SHOW WOULD EVEN PAY BACK BECAUSE THE BREAK-EVEN IS SO MUCH LOWER IN NEW YORK.

And you wouldn't have to be packing and moving and traveling and airplaning it. You'd just go to Sardi's or "21" and have people swarm all over you and tell you what a good time they had watching you perform. But apparently that isn't important. Mary can go back to Rancho Mirage and get in the pool and Carol can do HELLO, DOLLY! in Fargo, North Dakota. Let's throw this new orig-

inal entertainment we've been slaving over right out the window.

And, sweethearts, this isn't sour grapes. It's just logical goddam sense, the way it seems to me and a whole lot of other people in the theatre, including Liz Smith and Richard Barr, President of the League of New York Theatres and on and on and on.

Holy Cow, we've already got some biggies set to replace you two. I could drop a few names like Jane Withers and Donna Reed and Patsy Ruth Miller and Yvonne de Carlo, but I don't want to play those games.

I love you both in a perverse way. When I think of what it all started as just about a year ago and how far it's come—yeah, I suppose it's right to dump it all now. What the hell—why overdo a good thing?

And when you look at the theatre history books, you'll always have a juicy chapter: Why didn't Mary and Carol come to New York in LEGENDS!? The answer will remain a mystery. Except in your hearts. Certainly not in mine.

Love,
Jim

P.S. And if you think I don't appreciate what you've both been through in this last year, you're even crazier than I thought!

cc: to almost everyone involved.

About this time *Legends!* was opening in Florida at Zev Bufman's theatre in Orlando, slipping into the final booked engagements. Charlie Cinnamon, Zev's very able and funny PR man, called to say the advance in Orlando alone was excellent and he was certain we'd do terrific business at all the theatres. He said Zev wanted to talk to me; Zev said he loved the show and claimed opening night in Orlando was a ten-year high for audience reaction to any show he'd played there. He was highly enthusiastic and went on to describe sitting next to Mary at the opening-night party. "I sense a duality about her."

"How do you mean?" I asked.

"Well, one minute she'd be talking about going back to Rancho Mirage, and a few minutes later she'd say how she ought to continue working, now that she's into it. I think she could be turned around."

I explained her relationship with Kevin and the problems inherent there; he seemed to know about this. I asked if Zev couldn't become involved with the production, even take it over, since he seemed so high on it. Zev explained he was going public with his corporation in Florida and was prevented for one year from bringing anything to Broadway. But he would try to persuade Mary and do whatever he could as a friend to the production. Our conversation left me with a ray of hope. Don't ask for what.

Regarding my letter, I got no response from Mary, ever. But Charles phoned to say he and Carol thought it was one of the funniest letters they'd ever received, adding as he roared with laughter, "You son of a bitch, how did you know Carol always wanted to play Fargo, North Dakota?" He went on laughing as I told him I'd always had a hunch and then felt compelled to add, "I didn't mean the letter to be all *that* funny." From his tone I did not detect a positive bent for defection on their part.

Before Thanksgiving I retreated to my house in Key West; it was so peaceful being home and in the sun, able to swim and play tennis every day, but I was just a bit too close to *Legends!*, which was playing right across the Gulf of Mexico in St. Petersburg. I could feel the vibrations. I'd heard reports that Clifford was journeying from London "to put Roxy in the show." I had long since, for reasons of mental and physical health, decided that, as far as St. Petersburg and most of the Florida engagement was concerned, they should—in the words of the late Samuel Goldwyn—"count me out!"

I kept in touch, mainly through Randy and also, from time to time, Gary, both of whom I trusted for a more or less unbiased report.

According to Randy, Clifford arrived in time for rehearsal the day Roxy was going in. Roxy knew every line, every move, as Randy conducted the rehearsal and Clifford sat in the back of the theatre. I asked Randy why Clifford didn't take over; Randy said, "Well, he doesn't really know the play, he's been away for so many months." True. Apparently everyone was pleased, or acted pleased, with the rehearsal, and when it was finished there was a dinner break. After dinner, back at the theatre, Roxy received a dozen red roses from Carol and Charles. (As in *Medea*, I imagined this gift bursting into flame when the box was opened!)

Then came the performance. Randy and Gary both indicated Roxy's performance was not as solid as it had been in rehearsal, but, then, it takes time to become accustomed to audience reaction, to time the laughs, to find the moments. Also, the audiences in St. Petersburg are mostly *extremely* retired and not nearly as perky as the usual group.

Apparently, during intermission, Charles stormed out to the box office and began screaming at the man in charge, "They're ruining the play, this is a disaster." After the curtain fell, Randy and Clifford were summoned into Mary's dressing room, where Charles, Carol, and Mary announced they would not go on with Roxy again. They wanted Sheila to take over immediately. Charles then tracked down Zev Bufman, who was on vacation in Colorado, and vowed they would not continue with Roxy, that if they opened with her in Miami it would be disastrous, they'd get terrible reviews (such a change!), and on and on.

When I asked if The Terminator had been in on this scene, Randy said, "Kevin appeared for the last ten minutes of rehearsal, then in the evening saw about the first ten minutes of the show and left."

Terrific. Randy asked if Carol and Charles knew where I was. I said no; he suggested I keep it that way. "Jimmy, you're well out of this one. Don't answer your phone, whatever you do."

That evening—or morning, rather—my phone in Key West rang about twenty times, about 2:00 A.M., but I took Randy's advice and didn't pick up. "Ring away, ring your bells off," I muttered. I was finally growing a self-protective layer of plastic over my skin.

I was anxious—amend to read "curious"—about what would happen to provide backstage entertainment before the Saturday matinee, so I phoned Randy at half-hour. (All the time I kept phoning Kevin and Clifford but got no answer.) According to Randy, he'd given Roxy a few notes, and she was standing by prepared to go on. What an awful thing for her to go through!

I phoned again later and the curtain had risen and Roxy had gone on. Everyone was waiting with bated breath for whatever might be a-hatching next. Although the last time I phoned Clifford he'd checked out and I didn't receive his official report until much later, I will print his letter now, for *his* account of what took place. It says a lot, not only about Mary and Carol, but about Clifford and Kevin.

2/43 Onslow Square, London, SW7 December 19th, 1986

My Dear Jimmy,

My news from St. Petersburg is obviously out of date in that you've been to Miami, I imagine. However you may welcome the odd note or two (for your book)!

It wasn't a very pleasant trip (it also rained all *the time). I presented myself at the theatre for Annie-Joe's last perf., and was summoned to meet the ladies who said—*

Roxie Roker is a great lady—wonderful person—absolutely wrong for the part—we want the understudy to play the rest of the tour—and why did that silly producer get rid of A-J?

I listened—as one does—and said I could make no comment since I hadn't seen RR in action. Nor presumably had they since she had only rehearsed with the u/s group. I suggested that we had best do the rehearsal the following afternoon with RR as planned, and then we could pow-wow again. I also promised to pass on their remarks to Kevin, which I duly did but not that day since K. wasn't there. Anyway, that was Thanksgiving Day.

The next day's run thru' (if one can call it that) was excellent. Randy had been a bit laid-back in describing Roxie's work. It transpired she really knew the play backwards, was grace personified in her attitude to the ladies, and we had a really good rehearsal. Carol said that she thought RR was immaculate! (and I don't think it was meant as a crack!). KE turned up during the run-thru but didn't say anything to the ladies. I then had dinner with him and Randy when I did retail the previous day's chats. It seemed as if the storm clouds had gone way tho' I suspected they hadn't. I was, alas, right. The evening show went quite well. RR a little nervous, but much appreciated by the audience. You certainly wouldn't have guessed she was playing it for the first time.

Curtain down. Another summons. This time Charles was there (but K. had disappeared so I got the blast all alone). In essence—

CAROL: She's a very nice lady and I'm sure a good
             classic actress—but she knows nothing about
             comedy.
MARY: And she's too pretty.
CAROL/MARY/CHARLES: So we don't want RR. We want
             the US.

I crept from the room promising once again to tell K. this which I did when I finally traced him in the early hours. Charles by this time had also got Buff whateverhisname off the Colorado ski slopes to say they wouldn't be playing the rest of Florida unless RR was fired forthwith. And Buff of course spoke with K.

Saturday 29th. To the matinee. Arrived after curtain up and was relieved to know it had *gone up and with Roxie still doing her stuff. K. got Charles out of his centre front row seat, and we had a showdown in Alec's office (with Alec present non-speaking). Contractually, as I understand it, Charles hadn't a leg to stand on, and Mary apparently had written to K. accepting Roxie weeks before.*

So Charles, after shouting a bit, said:

We will, of course, abide by the decision of the Artistic Director (sic).

To which I could only say that it seemed to the Artistic Director that from every point of view it would be best to continue with Roxie in the part.

Charles presumably conveyed that message very promptly. Mary sent a reply (I don't know by whom) to Kevin saying that she would stick by the contract and that she never wanted to SEE OR SPEAK to him again. I rather felt I was in the dog-house too, and tho' I lurked about the theatre that evening and all the Sunday matinee I was unable to say farewell.

It was all pretty silly. I hope that by now Mary and K. have made up (Carol too) and that I am forgiven on the grounds that British foreign artistic directors don't know any better!

As for the show which you must have seen subsequently, I thought Gary was sensational in his new scene, that Mary was as ever (tho' quicker) and that Carol remained Carol (but very very slow and ponderous). Randy has obviously done a wonderful job keeping things together. I saw your 'Open letter' which made me chortle, but I guess Mary is weary, and the show will finish January 18th. But then again maybe it won't. Either way I hope we get some money out of Florida (and earlier dates). I seem to have received the merest trickle. And told K. so. But I just don't understand how contracts work in the USA. Except it seems they don't!

By the way, I also said to K. that if (1) you were going to do some rewriting, and (2) two new ladies rehearsed the rewritten script, then I thought it better that a new director was found. I think this sensible and proper, and I feel sure you would agree.

Don't suppose I'll be in NY before the Fall—when Jacobi hopefully plays BREAKING THE CODE. Otherwise, I hope for a quiet year.

Fondest love, Cliff
(and from Josiane and the princesses)

P.S. Don't bother to reply unless you have some startling revelation which you just have to pass on.

P.P.S. What rotten news about Bob R.

P.P.P.S. I'm too late for Xmas wishes I expect. Have a sensational 1987!

Charlie Cinnamon asked me to attend a press conference for Mary and Carol at the Jockey Club in Miami preparatory to their opening in that city. Although by this time I was luxuriating in my separation from the production, I felt obliged to help. From there I had to go to New York on business before returning to Key West.

December 2, 1986

My friend Beth Sarvi picked me up at the Miami airport and we drove to the Jockey Club, where an entire battery of TV, film, print people was on hand; you'd have thought we were at the front of some new global outbreak. Swarms of people with cameras, mikes, and cassette recorders. Zev arrived before the ladies and said he'd not had a relaxing Thanksgiving because of the fuss over Roxy. Many phone calls, and strong ones, from Mary, which he found unusual.

Lights, cameras, action as Carol and Mary arrived together. I wondered how the ladies were feeling about me; I knew how I felt about them, and when they made a much-photographed entrance I ran up in front of them, got down on my knees, and groveled. "Oh, my ladies, my precious ladies!" I cried, making as if to kiss their feet. The reporters didn't know what the hell I was doing; the ladies merely laughed and said to get up. Both seemed warm as we were seated at a long dais along with Zev, who sat next to Mary, then Carol and me.

Carol truly knows how to plug a play. When the questions began from reporters, she was asked which role was her favorite. "Sylvia Glenn," she said, without hesitation. "I love the character, and we get such laughs, it's so rewarding. And you have to remember that we don't make up the lines, they were written by our author, James Kirkwood, right here."

Mary is not so adept. She reverts to the party line: she's seventy-three, didn't want to do the play in the first place, her son made her, how tired she is. She went on about all the trouble she had getting back into action on the stage, saying, "You have to keep at something or you get out of shape, just like golf or tennis." I took this opportunity to ask her in public, "Mary, when you get back to Rancho Mirage and you relax and have a vacation—after a while how do you think you'll feel at night when eight o'clock rolls around? Will you miss it at all?"

She evaded a direct answer by repeating, "You have to keep at it." And then the questioners were on to other matters. The joint interview lasted maybe twenty minutes; then we all broke up into separate groups as reporters interviewed Mary, Carol, and me individually.

I didn't get a chance to speak to them alone, because Carol

was off to a department store for another promotional gimmick. Charles did grab me before he left. "Jimmy, you've got to come to the tech here and speak to Roxy. Get her to speak up, punch out some of those comedy lines."

"Charles, I won't be there. I have to go to New York today."

"Well, something has to be done. Carol feels like she's acting with Katharine Cornell, for Christ's sake!"

I signaled Beth to get the car and drive me to the airport as Charles vowed Carol wouldn't go on with the play. This little taste reaffirmed my feeling that I was indeed in the process of separating myself from the group.

In December the games of Ping-Pong continued. There were calls from George Yaneff about Olivia de Havilland and Joan Fontaine. I phoned Super Agent Milton Goldman, who said they would *never* work together. There was talk of Jane Powell, continued rumors that Alexis Smith was interested. At one point Kevin called and said, "What about Rita Moreno?" "What about Chita Rivera?" I countered. "We'll get the two of them, that'll be fun." And on it went, until it was becoming outright dizzy, like a merry-go-round none of us could jump from.

The juiciest bit of casting came when Alan Wasser, who'd general-managed *Sugar Babies,* said he'd had a conversation with Ann Miller, who'd seen the play in Los Angeles and told him she'd like to do the play with Carol. According to Alan, she'd said, "The only thing wrong was Mary. I know the character of Leatrice should be sweet, but only up to a point. What you need up on that stage is two cunts, and with me and Carol you'd have a couple."

Alan and I roared with laughter; he gave me Ann's number and suggested I phone her. She was most enthusiastic and candid. "Honey, when I saw that play opening night in L.A. my feet were just itching to jump up on that stage. You know, Mary's terrific and God only knows she's a legend, but I don't think she knew all her lines and, you know, after you get to a certain age, well, let's put it this way—you start skipping beats."

We spoke for fifteen minutes or so, and she was genuinely interested in replacing Mary, saying toward the end of our conversation, "I love Carol. We worked together once on a 'Love Boat' and got along just fine. Now, I know she's not all *that* easy to work with. Carol swallowed up little Mary on that stage, but I'll tell you something right now—Carol's not going to swallow up little Annie."

"Atta girl," I said.

"Now, if I play Leatrice, you gotta write me a few more bitchy lines, because I can say 'em!"

I told her I thought there was still a whole batch of them lying around from the original script. She certainly sounded full of p and v. We ended the conversation saying we'd be in close touch. Now, *I* could see Carol Channing and Ann Miller trashing each other up on the stage and having a high old time of it. The play would become truly what it had become . . . whatever that was.

To feel them out about this, I put in a call to Carol and Charles. No answer; I left a message. Charles finally phoned back. "Sorry, Jim, but we just got back from the hospital! Last night Carol tripped over the cord in the vacuum-cleaner scene and fractured her wrist. They just put it in a cast and . . ."

I asked to speak to Carol, who, when I inquired about her accident, how she was, and how long she'd be out, said, "Oh, I'm going on tonight."

"But—"

"Oh, don't worry about that, dear. Just write me some funny lines to explain why I have my wrist in a cast and my arm in a sling. We're meeting before the performance to change some of the blocking, but I'm fine, I won't miss a show, don't worry."

She was not at all interested in talking about how she felt or the accident, only wanted to make sure the lines explaining it would be funny. I promised to call back with a choice of lines and then said, "You really are a gem. I wish you'd continue with the play."

"Yes, but *not with Kevin Eggers!*" Then Carol went off on a wild tirade about something entirely new to me, saying Kevin had threatened blackmail. "Blackmail!" I exclaimed. Yes, she insisted, he'd threatened to give pictures of Carol and Mary to the *National Enquirer,* along with pictures of Annie-Joe and Roxy. "He's going to claim we're anti-black and only want to work with stereotypical blacks."

I said I found this hard to believe, but she was worked up. I got her off course by suddenly mentioning Ann Miller. That stopped her. "Ann Miller?" she asked.

"Yes," I said.

"Umm, well, who else are you considering?" she asked.

I said there were a few other ladies but did not get specific. Carol and Charles were on separate phones, and they both jumped on Kevin again until I calmed them down by reminding Carol how good she was and that if she really felt this was one of the best parts she'd ever had, she should consider not deep-sixing it. Charles finally said, "Carol, we really should think about it, for Jimmy and the play."

We ended up friendly and warm and once again there was hope of continuing. How could I so easily get sucked back into caring, after over a solid year of such insane, damaging games? I'll tell you. It's like a parent with a retarded child. You might realize the baby is incurable; still, it's yours, you've spawned it, given it birth, given it all the care you possibly could, and you simply don't want to see it die. You want it to live. Call it pride, call it stupidity, call it masochistic, there's a point at which—after you've gone way beyond the line of all sanity and reason—it seems that if you stick it out that one extra ridiculous mile a miracle might possibly occur. As in *A Day in the Death of Joe Egg*, the child might just jump out of the wheelchair and start tap-dancing. Anything—but give up. So many of us have been taught: Don't be a quitter. Yes, I know all about "cutting one's losses," but it's as difficult to do in this gamble called theatre as it is at the crap tables in Vegas.

Apparently *no one* connected to this sinking ship could actually man the lifeboats. Instead we kept trying to rearrange the deck furniture. A few days later Bob Regester phoned from Fort Lauderdale; despite his health, he'd flown in from L.A. for the opening and felt it had gone very well, good performance, good reaction. He'd had a talk with Mary, who said she was simply worn out, tired, can't wait to get back to Rancho Mirage. Bob suggested taking a vacation, resting for six weeks, but he could not stir her to make plans at this time. Bob said, "Jimmy, I did everything but say, 'I've got AIDS, I'm broke, and I'm dying. Please don't close the play.'" This unspoken plea gave me shivers. He'd also talked to Carol and Charles, who said they liked Ann Miller but were not all that anxious to work with her as Leatrice. Charles keeps saying, "Get Julie Andrews."

Shortly after, Kevin called to say he would raise Carol's salary by five thousand a week and hire Alice Ghostly to play the maid, thus *really* changing the character. This had been touched on once or twice. Alice is a an old friend of mine and very close to Gary; she's extremely talented and funny, but it would entail a heavy rewrite. Still . . .

My business in New York was concluded and I returned to my home in Key West. Even on Christmas Eve there were calls, last-minute, of course, for saving the show, all sorts of schemes, ideas, fantasies of who could keep it going and how. I was not able to "really get it up" for much of this. I felt bone-weary and a bit scraped out inside. At least we were at the point where we would soon know the fate of the baby for sure. There were no more bookings after Palm Beach. The Palm Beach Story would tell all.

THE PALM BEACH STORY

Tuesday, January 6, 1987

Gary picked me up at the airport in Palm Beach, one of the most cloistered spots in the world. This town or city—no, state of being—is so much what it is: the perfect setting for a movie musical with Franchot Tone and Fred Astaire both snapping at Grace Kelly's hand, called "Who Gets the Heiress?" A gorgeous, lush spot that brings on claustrophobia of the rich and also tends to stir up the communist in me, where there's barely a socialist to be found way down deep, panting for breath to sustain its very existence.

"Pissed off because you weren't born rich?" Gary asked.

"Of course. Even though my parents *were* movie stars," I quickly added.

Visited the Royal Poinciana Playhouse—would the theatre be called anything else in Palm Beach? I'd forgotten what a jewel the Playhouse is, right on the waterway, immaculately done, all crimson and crystal and glitter, with great sight lines and immaculately comfortable backstage conditions. (I had played there years earlier in a production of *Brigadoon* with Eddie Villella; opening night was such a social event we onstage were blinded by the bejeweled women and dapper men as they drifted in and were interviewed in the lobby, whose doors were constantly opened for latecomers, constituting the majority of the audience. They finally stopped arriving, waving to each other, chatting, and being photographed around intermission. Just in time to return to the lobby and *really* check out who was with whom and what whom was wearing. The company was appalled; we all agreed that as actors we'd never felt so neglected in our lives; we actually started playing to one another, not only as characters but as audience as well. Other nights and audiences were normal—all things being relative.)

Went backstage and posted clippings, reviews, which were excellent, and newspaper ads for *Chispas! (Legends!),* which had opened in Argentina. I thought the cast would get a kick out of reading the coverage and seeing pictures of their South American counterparts. But then Natalie Ross walked by and said, "My God, they look so young and beautiful." Someone else made a crack, wondering how Mary and Carol would react to seeing pictures of Nora Carpena and Thelma Biral, who were both in their forties and had gotten rave reviews and many comments on their boundless energy and physical prowess. I left them up.

Mary soon came by in one of her long red outfits—skirt, jacket, boots, wimple—looking sumptuous. She glanced at the board, and I explained what I'd just put up. "Oh, yes . . ." she said, barely glancing at the clippings before walking down the hall with me after her. As we got to her dressing room, Mary made the mistake of saying, "Oh, Jimmy, the audiences have been loving the show!"

Knee-jerk reaction from the bedraggled author, who immediately switched to automatic pilot: "Then you should say to hell with it and bring it to Broadway."

"Darling, you're not seventy-three," she said, eyes narrowing, barely suppressing a sigh that I was still going on.

"No," I said, "but I feel like it. At seventy-three *you* should come to New York for three months, take a lovely apartment, do the show, see your friends, have supper at '21,' bar the producers from backstage, and thumb your nose at everyone but the audience."

Why couldn't I stop? If I had known why, I would have.

I could tell it was a no-go and didn't waste a full performance, but saved a portion for dear Carol and Charles, whose dressing room I invaded next.

Carol was sitting at her dressing table in that soiled white terrycloth robe I was beginning to love, putting on her clown makeup, which was enough to paint a wall with. Charles was reading *Variety* and said, "I'll tell you a secret, if you promise not to tell. William Morris is going to take out a full-page ad, congratulating Mary and Carol and you for touring a year and grossing ten million dollars, and those are the only names that are going to be mentioned. Now, don't you tell a soul."

He'd already told me this, and I wondered why the big secret at this stage of the game. With some of my performance with Mary left choked up in me, I said to Carol, "You know, it's just occurred to me recently that, if you give up this part you claim to love so much and the show closes, Kevin will have won."

"What?" Carol snapped. "Because he didn't want me to begin with!"

"No, no . . . but in some perverse way The Terminator will have stopped both of us from going on with it."

Charles muttered something about "checking with Lee Stevens at William Morris to see what TV engagements we have."

I had the temerity to bring up Ann Miller. Carol, who had just finished slashing that red streak across her nose, laughed and said, "Oh, I like Ann, but really—she's a joke."

I barely held off an instant of anger and cracking "Turn around and check your mirror, sweetheart!"

Randy called five minutes for the tech rehearsal and I went out into the theatre. The company was present, and I gave Roxy a hug and told her I hoped the goings-on hadn't been too rough. She looked at me in a lovely, knowing way and said, "Oh, no . . ." as if to say: I've been around, I can take care of myself.

Mary and Carol rehearsed the last number, which I had not seen performed yet. The full orchestration coming out of nowhere, along with the hot spotlight shafts, tickled me. The number itself was messy. As they stopped and started, trying to pull it together, I thought of two lines they could say just as the music begins and the spots come blasting on. Mary: "Why, it seems just like yesterday." Carol: "It *is* yesterday!"—to let the audience know it's in their imagination. I relayed the lines; Carol giggled, and Mary went on complaining about her bunions.

Opening night. More limos and Rolls and Mercedes than you could count, more glitter and spangles and flashbulbs and elegance, genuine and false, and a few billion real bucks. Pleased to see opening nights have changed—somewhat. Although it took forever, the curtain didn't go up until almost everyone was seated. Not only that, the opening-night audience was unusually attentive and warm in its reaction.

Roxy is a lovely, ingratiating, truthful actress but she is not a down-and-dirty comedienne, and the lack of punched-out comedy lines hurts the play, especially in the first act.

Spoke to Zev and Charlie in intermission; both are very happy with the engagement. Gary's telephone scene played beautifully at the beginning of Act II, and his last scene with Carol and Mary flew. Their song and dance at the end got the beginnings of applause three different times, although I couldn't quite understand why. It is extremely slipshod; Carol fairly yanks Mary from one spot to another. Major response at curtain calls. Backstage afterward was like opening night at the Met in miniature. Bumped into Greg Sherwood Dodge, whom I hadn't seen since the old days when we palled around with showgirl Temple Texas.

Then it was off to the opening-night party to end all opening-night parties, given by Celia Lipton Farris, an extremely wealthy and attractive Palm Beach socialite, at her mansion on El Dorado Road. Swarms of parking attendants roaring off with the cars of the four hundred guests. First we entered the grand living room and, by God, there was a reception line made up of Celia and her stunning daughters, then outside to the dance floor and tables set up over the swimming pool and spreading out from it into the gardens, all covered by a huge colorful tent complete with chandeliers. Throngs of elegantly gotten-up guests snatching at hors d'oeuvres, champagne popping in counterpoint to an orchestra playing show tunes, and soon the entrance music for the stars, who arrived coordinated, Mary in a black evening gown with sleeves and Carol in a white halter gown with no sleeves and low-cut back.

High spirits abounded; everyone said how much they enjoyed the play; most everyone got drunk. At first Carol was at the table next to me. As the dancers hit the floor, it had a spring to it, and the chandelier above that table bobbed away merrily and looked as if it might pull a *Phantom of the Opera*. Charles kept a wary eye on it and soon moved their seats.

Celia Farris had been a performer in England years before

and I believe had understudied Mary in a show there. After we'd all been stuffed with food and sated by drink, she took to the microphone set up in front of the band and voiced a lovely long tribute to Mary and a somewhat shorter lovely one to Carol.

As Mrs. Farris moved on to other announcements, I noticed both our ladies had gotten up and gone inside the house, which was just as well, because after a while Celia Lipton Farris said how marvelous it was of Mary to continue touring around the country, "and she's practically eighty." All of us with the show glanced quickly around to see if Mary had heard that one, but she was nowhere in sight. Which is the way it should have been.

Later on I bumped into Kevin and Ann, who I don't believe had attended the show. "Well, Jim," he said—I suddenly realized that people with whom I've tangled never call me "Jimmy"—"we had quite a good year out of it, didn't we?"

"A *good* year?"

"Oh, come on," he said, patting my shoulder.

A good year, I thought. *Good?* No director, a star who couldn't remember her name, one producer dead, another down with AIDS, robbed in Portland, all manner of feuds, a stack of dreadful reviews. "Yes," I finally said, "a really great year. One more like this and I quit."

I decided then and there to hotfoot it out of Palm Beach the next morning. Once more I escaped to Key West.

Of course I'd planned to attend the closing. One has to be there at the end, just as one has to attend the funeral of a dear friend to realize he or she is actually gone—not just hiding out. Then word reached me that Ahmet Ertegun was actually flying Mike Nichols down to catch the show Thursday, January 15, prior to our closing performance that Sunday. It seemed a bit late for help at this point, but I flew up from Key West to be on hand for the long-awaited, if belated, event.

Thursday, January 15, 1987

When I arrived backstage at the theatre, the question was asked: Is Mike Nichols really coming? "He hasn't so far," I reminded people, "but, who knows, it would fit our history if he did catch us just as the trucks are gathering to pack the set away." Randy said Roxy had been out the last two performances, because of the death of an uncle. Gary said the show had flown. I went to stand outside the theatre; actually, I had other friends who were coming this night, but I was also curious to see if Ahmet was arriving. The smell of closing was in the air, and suddenly those who realized they'd probably never catch Mary Martin and Carol Channing on the same stage together again were frenzied in their attempts to get tickets.

For me, a Felliniesque aura surrounded the last few gasps of *Legends!* There was a circus atmosphere about the theatre, the audience. I could almost hear persistent background music hammering away. After all this time, instead of winding down, the entire experience seemed about to explode up and out and away into the stratosphere of gauzy memory.

I'd been handed several phone messages that had been taken at the box office and jotted down on little yellow slips of paper. As I stood out front reading them, a very well dressed lady snatched them out of my hand, saying, "How much do you want?"

"Please, those aren't tickets," I said, reaching out for them.

She quickly put her hands behind her back. "What do you want? I know my friend paid a hundred dollars . . ." she said, a gleam in her eye.

"Honestly, those are phone messages, really they are."

A look of deep disappointment crossed her face. She brought them out in front of her, looked at the little slips, said, "Oh . . . ," thrust them back in my hands, turned, and went after other quarry without a "sorry" or anything.

Another lady and two men approached me within a few minutes and asked if I had tickets to sell. I must have looked like a scalper, so I moved away from the front of the theatre just as a huge limousine pulled up along the drive ahead of me. The chauffeur hurried around to open the door and out popped Ahmet, Mike Nichols, and Kevin Eggers. They headed up the path leading to the stage door.

By the time I went backstage, they were standing in the hall outside Randy's office. Mike was very cordial in his greeting, which forced Ahmet to put on—certainly not a "happy face" but at least one with the semblance of pleasantry. Kevin seemed anxious.

Mike and I moved a step aside. "Where was your Christmas

card? It wasn't Christmas without your card this year," Mike said. "We always look forward to it."

"I wasn't up to it this year," I told him. "I really hate Christmas anyhow. But this year—well, it's been some year, I'll tell you."

"I can imagine."

"And then some," I added. "Actually, remember my card the year before, with Mary and Carol, the three of us?"

"Yes."

"Well, this year I had an idea to use the same card, only to grease-pencil an X across each of their faces." Mike laughed. "But even that was too much effort, so I skipped it."

I watched part of the first act, which is very different with Roxy, especially in the first scene. The audience are attentive, but they don't get rolling until Carol hits them later on, when she and Mary dive into their relationship.

I was backstage at intermission when I saw Mike and Ahmet walk toward Randy's office at the opposite end of the long hallway. They looked fairly grim; Mike only gave me a wan long-distance smile and a nod.

I went out for a drink and later came in to watch part of the second act, which was playing much, much better than the first. Thank God. Gary's scene went like wildfire. After the show, the second I got backstage, Charles grabbed my arm.

"Why is Mike Nichols coming to see it at this late date?"

"I don't know. Ahmet brought him."

"But why now, what's going on?" By this time Charles had hauled me into Carol's room and shut the door; Carol sat at her table looking agitated. "Why is Mike Nichols here now?" she asked.

A knock on the door interrupted her, and Randy stuck his head in. "Mike Nichols would like to see Carol."

Carol frowned and said, "Do I have to go down to *her* dressing room?"

"No, he's right here," Randy said, stepping aside as Mike walked into the room.

Mike congratulated her for giving such a good performance, and then Carol said something about "Remember when you didn't think I was Jewish enough for *Dolly* but Barbra Streisand was?"

This flew over my head as Mike grinned, they exchanged a few other words, and he left. I started after him, but Charles grabbed my arm again and once more demanded to know what was going on. I assured him I didn't know, that Ahmet had been threatening to bring Mike Nichols to look at the show and he finally had—that was all I knew. I finally managed to get out of the room.

Mike had gone down the hall to Mary's room, but Jack Paar had come to see the show and was inside with her, so Mike had to wait twenty minutes or so. In the meantime we spoke.

"The second act really flies," Mike said, reinforcing my opinion of the way the show had played tonight.

"Yes," I said, "but the first act used to take precedence some nights."

"How is that?" he asked.

I explained the change in approach to the part of Aretha as best I could without saying anything damaging about Roxy. And we spoke more of the show. Of course, what one wants to say is "Well, Mike, what do you think? Do you have any interest in resuscitating this? Are you going to step in?" But—what?—ethics, not wanting to put someone on the spot before there's been a chance to think and evaluate—prevents that.

Mike praised Gary's performance highly. I thought it best not to be around when Mike spoke to Mary; I didn't want to inhibit whatever candid remarks they might want to make. I excused myself and went to Gary's dressing room to pass on Mike's compliment. By the time I left, Mary was standing in her doorway talking to Mike, and I could hear the familiar "It took me so long, but you have to keep at it or you forget," etc.

I finally walked down the hall—I had to pass them to leave—and quickly kissed Mary on the cheek, saying, "Good show." Mike shook my hand and said, "Congratulations." I didn't ask, "For what—closing at last?"

The next day I found out they'd gotten into their corporate jet and headed back to New York that night. The word was they were going to have a meeting.

Saturday, January 17, 1987

The show was closing the following day, after the Sunday matinee. I arrived backstage a good hour ahead of time. I was going to schmooze with Gary and Vince and the cast in general; there wasn't much time left. When a show closes, people disappear quickly, so it's best to get formal goodbyes and thank-yous on the record early.

The door to Carol's dressing room was open, so I walked in. She was alone, putting on her makeup, and when she saw me she started to say, "Well, Jimmy, it's hard to believe—"

The little kid in me made me say, "Well, just remember— you're the one who's closing the show."

That did it. I suppose the time had come anyhow. The tension had been layered underneath the last week. She turned on me in a rage. "What?" she shouted.

"Carol, I—"

"How dare you speak to me like that, how *dare* you come into my dressing room before the show and upset me! I've never heard of anything so unprofessional in all my life!"

"Oh, Carol, stop it—"

"I will not, I don't know if I can go on!"

"Carol—"

"I'm leaving the show because *Mary's* leaving."

"That's displaced loyalty; that doesn't make any sense at all if you love the part."

"And don't tell me you don't admit no one wanted me in this show but Mary."

"Everyone wants you in it now."

"Aha! And then you come in and say something like that to me, something so unprofessional."

I was vaguely aware of Charles' presence behind me as I said, "Unprofessional? You want to talk *unprofessional?* I can give you about a dozen unprofessional things, if you want to get into that!"

But she was up and screaming for the stage manager, so I quickly left and walked down the hall to Randy, who'd heard the shouting, just as Charles, the enraged husband-manager, came after me, clutching at me and demanding, "Unprofessional? Unprofessional? I want you to name just one of them!"

"Charles, let's not—"

"Go ahead." He shook me. "Name just one of them."

"All right," I shouted. "What about all the times Carol's

corrected Mary onstage in front of the audience? You call that professional?"

His answer (in retrospect it's funny): "Mary has never once complained to us."

"Of course not, she came to *me!* And then I had to go to Carol and—"

Charles ranted and raved and clutched at me. "Carol won't be able to go on for the matinee because of you!"

"Oh, Charles, let's cut the shit! You know I didn't mean to upset her, you know that, now let's cut this out!"

Suddenly Charles took off again on the ad William Morris was going to run in *Variety.* I couldn't imagine how that figured in with this current argument; it was a total *non sequitur.* Randy began trying to break this up, and we both wound down; I was suddenly aware that the backstage area had become deadly silent. Obviously everyone was getting an earful. Also, in the well over a year we'd all been together, this was the first public battle I'd been involved in.

When I walked past Carol's dressing room, her door was closed. I knocked to apologize for upsetting her, but there was no reply. I was not happy with my behavior; I should not have given in to the pressure; I should have maintained my cool. I was ashamed of myself. I suppose the end of the show triggered the exorcist in me.

In the evening, although I wasn't seeing the show, I stopped by the theatre and apologized to Carol before half-hour, saying I hadn't meant to upset her. She accepted the apology with a certain cool, and I gathered damage had been done.

Sunday, January 18, 1987—Closing Day

Went backstage before the final matinee performance—something strange about closing on a matinee. It should happen at night. Daylight makes it too . . . bald. Huge white trucks were already parked in the side driveway by the theatre. To me they looked like hearses. Spoke briefly to Carol and Charles; we were all on our best behavior. Although there was activity—people were packing, saying preshow goodbyes, exchanging addresses, checking who was actually flying out of Palm Beach immediately—there was beneath it a numbness that this was our last performance, our last gasp, after all this time.

Out front the circus atmosphere prevailed. The audience was packed into the theatre; extra chairs had been set around. There was a manic festivity at this closing performance that somehow equaled that of an opening night.

The show, of course, played like a son of a gun, with a thumping subtext to so many of the lines pertaining to the business and loving it or missing it or hating it. Almost every line carried double its usual weight. I was near tears at times. I had brought my flash camera, and at the curtain calls, which were raucous, with the standing ovation and shouts of "Bravo!," I ran forward up the aisle and snapped away as the furor continued and the entire crew was called out onto the stage for applause: Randy Buck, Jim Bernardi, Bob Saltzman, who could always make me laugh—the whole bunch of them. I kept on snapping and flashing.

Soon a huge cake was wheeled out, and along came Zev and Vilma Bufman, joining hands with Carol and Mary, and no one, to my embarrassment, even acknowledged this author with his flash camera standing right by the lip of the stage.

The audience was on its feet now, cheering and stomping, and suddenly I took a fit and hoisted myself up on the stage—where I was belatedly greeted—and quickly embraced Carol and Mary, applauded the cast, then turned front and held my hands up for silence. It took a while for the audience to calm down, but when they did I said, "Hello, I'm the author of this play, and—" I'd figured I'd better let them know who this strange creature was who came lurching up from their midst onto the stage. There was immediate applause, but I cut it off, saying, "I know a lot of you came here today thinking you were seeing the last performance of *Legends!*, but I have good news."

This silenced the entire place, except for an intake of breath. I glanced at the cast, who all looked as if a Martian had landed onstage, before going on in as close to one breath as possible: "However, there has been a reprieve. Dear Mary Martin has decided to continue with the show. We're taking six weeks off for vacation; then Mary and Carol and the company go back into rehearsal for our Broadway opening at the St. James Theatre in New York in April. Isn't that wonderful?" I turned and applauded Carol and Mary, who stood there with—shall I say—benumbed expressions upon their faces as the audience broke into wild cheering, whistling, and applause. Soon Mary had stepped forward and was swatting my shoulder with an open hand, shouting, "Stop it, stop that!"

And I did. Before long the cake was rolled off, to more applause, and the curtain came down for good on our little charade.

There was a gaggle of people around the cake; some laughed at me, others looked as if I'd taken total leave of my senses. Pictures were taken of Mary and Carol and Zev. Mary wielded a huge knife, and I tried to get a picture of her cutting my throat, but she wouldn't pose for it. I felt as if I'd had a shot of adrenaline. I jammed a huge piece of cake in my mouth, then promptly walked down the hall to the men's room and threw it up!

I skulked away from the crowd, which was still around the cake. Strolled outside by the water, took a few deep breaths, and stood on the patio. When I came back I quickly agreed to join Gary and Vince Cole and a close friend of Gary's, Paul, at his apartment for a drink.

I never said a formal goodbye to Mary or Carol. There was too much to say in one way, and yet, in another, not enough. I'd said my goodbyes to the rest of the company prior to the show.

I followed Gary in my car to the little bungalows most of the cast had occupied during the run there. They were quaint by Palm Beach standards—near the sea and very, well, rustic. Vince was near tears. Gary was operating on the surface as always, but underneath was a layer of deep shock that we had really put the lid on this little baby and closed it.

Soon Vince had said goodbye and left for the airport, and there was nothing to do but have a few more drinks. Later we drove to a rib place on the mainland of Palm Beach, where we gorged ourselves and, of course, rehashed many Golden Moments in the Theatre.

Driving back to get my car, we came off the bridge, and there to our right were garish outside lights illuminating the huge white trucks that absolutely glistened as they were loaded up with hunks of scenery, a rack of costumes, and cartons of props. We pulled the car around in back and got out. We stood there in silence and watched as the entrails of our show were hauled out the loading door and dragged across the drive to the vans.

Gary and I looked at each other and shook our heads at this

eerie sight. After a while, although the night was warm, even balmy, I felt the small blips of chills in my stomach, the kind you feel at the beginning of a bad case of the flu.

Only this wasn't the beginning, but the end. And it wasn't the flu. I don't know what I'd call it. But whatever it was, I'd most certainly had a full-blown case of it. And now it was over.

Nurse—oh, nurse!

EPILOGUE

It's been a year and a half since the show closed. I have not spoken to or seen Mary, Carol, or Charles since. I sent them Christmas cards this year, and I received one from Carol and Charles, but no word from Mary.

I spoke with Bob Regester often in California. His health was up and down, but he was optimistic and had plans to enter a film-and-theatrical venture with his good friend Vanessa Redgrave. Then, in the middle of October 1987, I received a call from Lou Miano saying Bob had taken a sudden turn for the worse and been rushed to the hospital in California, where he had died. I felt a strong mix of sadness and rage that his last venture had to be such a tortuous one.

Kenn Duncan, our official photographer, also died of AIDS, not long after he'd taken our pictures in Dallas. Ed Gifford said he thought it might have been his last professional job.

In April 1987 I was invited to Buenos Aires for the opening there of *Chispas! (Legends!)*. It was an exhilarating trip—the Pope had descended upon B.A. at the same time, but not for the same purpose, and opening night was thrilling. To see the show in a totally different production and in another language was exotic. During its engagement in Mar del Plata, *Chispas!* had already won the equivalent of our Tony Award for best comedy of the year, the Estrella de Mar (Star of the Sea Award). The reviews were excellent, as were the performances of Thelma Biral and Nora Carpena, whose age and approach to their roles made them entirely different from their American counterparts. I spent a memorable week, doing press, radio, and TV interviews and visiting old friends I'd made when *Postdata: Tu Gato Ha Muerto! (P.S. Your Cat Is Dead!)* had played there several years before.

In the summer of 1987 I turned down a proposal to make a TV pilot for a series based on *Legends!* The "deal" was not all that good, and I thought perhaps I'd put in my time in hell with this property. I have also thus far not done any writing for television, but the word is definitely out: it can make you rich and crazy. I may not be rich enough, but I would not think it advisable to take on another load of crazy.

Two months ago, on the way from someplace to my home in Key West, I stopped off in Kansas City to see Ruth Warrick starring in a three-act version of *Legends!* in its first dinner-theatre incarnation, at Tiffany's Attic. Ruth, just as Carol had done, had taken a nasty spill onstage during a blackout and had fractured her shoulder and injured her wrist. Despite this, she'd only missed a week or so, and was playing the show with her shoulder and wrist in a sling and partial cast. They were doing SRO business and Ruth and the company were top-notch. A local actress, Dodie Brown, played Sylvia, and she was excellent.

I have not seen Kevin, but Randy Buck was stage-managing a Brazilian revue, *Oba Oba*, which opened to some good notices but was short of money in the late winter of 1988. Randy phoned Kevin, who came to see a Sunday matinee, and on Monday he (one presumes in concert with Ahmet) bought the show, lock, stock, and barrel, and was then in full control. Randy invited me to see *Oba Oba*, and the show, though an old-fashioned revue, was a delight. The women were some of the most gorgeous I have seen; the men were muscular and handsome; and the entire company was completely ingratiating and radiated the joy of performing throughout. It was an evening of pure entertainment. I learned the Giffords had been brought in to publicize the show, and called them offering whatever help I could give. I wrote Liz Smith a note, urging her to see it. They deserved a run, but unfortunately the show closed after a few weeks of slim business.

On Friday, May 27, 1988, I got a warm phone call from Michael Gifford in East Hampton, where we both have summer houses. She invited me to lunch on Sunday at one o'clock, and I looked forward to seeing her and Ed, to catch up on whatever theatrical gossip we might exchange. I was also certain they, being very close to Kevin, were curious about this book. The next afternoon the phone rang and a stunned voice asked, "Jim Kirkwood?" "Yes," I replied. "This is Ed Gifford." "Oh, hi, Ed, I'm seeing you tomorrow." "I don't think I'll see you for lunch tomorrow, Jimmy," he said. "Michael is dead!"

I sat there mute as Ed went on to say she'd been on her way to pick him up at the East Hampton Airport and had been found dead in her car by the side of the road. Ed asked me to phone a mutual friend who was also coming to lunch and call him off. He was able to speak no more, and burst into tears. Later I learned Michael had suffered a heart attack. She was only fifty-three and appeared to be in excellent shape and health before this tragedy struck.

Gary Beach is currently playing the part of Thenardier in *Les Misérables* in Los Angeles, and I hear he's excellent.

Legends!, which was capitalized at approximately $1 million, never fully paid back its investors. If we had played eight performances a week at a lo-ball figure of $25,000 per each eighth performance, that would have added up to $1.3 million, which would easily have brought us into profit.

I thought relating the story of this freakish theatrical hegira would be a catharsis. It was, at times, but mostly it was reliving it—tramping through the forest of angst all over again, tripping over broken limbs of disappointment, being switched in the face by branches of anger, and becoming lost in the wonder of why and how it happened the way it did. I have dragged my way through many heavy days while poring over hundreds of pages of journal, going over notes, clippings, etc. The more distance separates me from the experience, the more it all seems utterly ridiculous.

Mary has been keeping a high profile of late. She has been seen on the Tony Award show, the "Phil Donahue" show for the reopening of the Rainbow Room, and the "Today" show, has appeared in a tribute to Cole Porter at Town Hall in which she sang "My Heart Belongs to Daddy," and the word around town is that she is seriously scouting about for a new musical to appear in. I was astonished to hear this, but I certainly wish her success in the event she takes the plunge. Timber! No matter what, she is a legend and a trouper, and one can only award her the Theatrical Purple Heart and the Croix de Théâtre for what she went through with *Legends!*

I think back on Carol and Charles with affectionate incredulity. I know of no couple who live, breathe, eat, and sleep theatre as they do. They are totally dedicated to Carol's career. There are times when I miss them all, when I fervently wish we'd had clear sailing and barged into New York for a limited engagement. I look back upon the entire experience with loving horror. Wanting to entertain people, which is all the pack of us wanted to do, should not entail such torture. We know the theatre is not glamorous, but really—!

The play has been optioned for several foreign-language productions, and currently meetings are going on again in London regarding a possible production of *Legends!* there.

You don't suppose I'd be crazy enough to . . . ?

September 1988

P.S. I promise not to keep in touch!